Gin: a spirit that derives its predominant flavour from Juniper Berries, has its origins in the Middles Ages. It evolved from use in herbal medicine to a commercial product in the spirits industry. The first Gin Craze in the UK started in 1695 when unlicensed gin production was allowed by the British Government - resulting in over 15,000 Gin Shops springing up across the country. It's enjoying a huge new resurgence now with a wide variety of delicious Craft Gins being made in many exciting flavours.

Gin And It: is a classic cocktail, made with Vermouth. IT, is also a euphemism ;-)

How to make a Gin And It

1.5 Shots Dry Gin
1.5 Shots Vermouth
1 Dash Angostura Orange Bitters
A twist of Lemon Peel

Stir all the ingredients with ice and strain over a cocktail glass filled with ice. Run the lemon peel round the rim of the glass and garnish with it.

Cheers!! And enjoy reading...

Gin And It

Elaine Sturgess

First published January 2017

978-0-9957210-3-6/ Gin And It / Softcover Edition

Published by Raise A Laugh Publishing. Designed and set in Garamond font. For more information visit www.raisealaugh.com or email: happy@raisealaugh.com

For Maria
Love always

Chapter 1

"No licking." She was gentle but firm, maintaining her determination to keep control despite the temptation to give in. She gazed down into Stan's big brown eyes, his tongue hanging eagerly from his mouth. She flicked an eyebrow in wry amusement.

"Just quickly? It won't take long?" A cheeky smile spread across his handsome face.

"No…" She couldn't help but be amused at his saucy insistence, despite his knowing that she had certain restrictions. "Anyway, there isn't enough time."

He looked up at her, his eyebrows, now furrowed, rising pleadingly. "Please?"

She became firmer. "Stan, no. You can't do it now. I've got people waiting."

He extended his tongue out further, dropping his head down, determined to get his way.

"Stan!" She gestured behind him and Stan turned his head, still at the ready, to see four sets of eyes trained on him. He quickly retracted his tongue and straightened up.

"I'm sorry Stan, you'll have to lick them somewhere else. You know the rules. When people stop and lick here, they get in the way and it causes a queue." Theresa tapped the sign tucked by the weighing scales, clearly stating 'NO LICKING'.

Stan shuffled his envelopes together, mumbling to himself as Theresa motioned the next person forward to the post office counter.

"Morning Tony, sorry for the delay." She flicked her eyes at Stan in mock despair, "he's a habitual offender. How can I help?"

"Ten first class stamps please Theresa. Any news on the planning permission?"

"Oh don't ask Tony, it's a nightmare." She lowered her face closer to the glass panel and whispered, "they're a bunch of tossers," before standing back again. "It's been six months since I put in the applications and they're still wrangling about it."

Tony shrugged sympathetically. "I see Virginia's in the club?"

"Yep… Graham finally persuaded her it was the right thing to do."

"She's a bit cheeky that one." Tony winked at her, his tongue in his cheek.

Theresa laughed. "Yeah, not a bad catch."

"Ok, well, see you Sunday then." Tony headed towards the bakery section as Mrs Jenkins shuffled painfully up to the counter.

"Bunions again?" Theresa shouted.

"No dear, plenty of vegetables at the moment. Just the pension please."

Theresa smiled and pushed a pen through for Mrs Jenkins to use. Glancing up she saw a new face in the queue. Since they didn't get much passing trade in the village, it was likely to be one of the new residents that she'd been told about. Curious, Theresa appraised the newcomer as she stared down at her feet. Slim, casually but neatly dressed in jeans and a cable knit sweater. She was wearing a cap, which made it difficult to assess age, but she speculated that she was probably in her late twenties or early thirties. She had enough hair showing to confirm she was a redhead. The woman looked up and Theresa smiled brightly before returning her attention to her current customer.

"That's it Mrs Jenkins, just put the date in here for me." She tapped the gap in the document. She glanced up again as Mrs Jenkins completed her paperwork, noticing that the woman seemed determined to keep her gaze to the floor and wondered if she was shy. As she completed Mrs Jenkins transaction and watched her shuffle off, she beckoned the woman forward. "Hello. How can I help?"

"Hi. Um… just a book of first class stamps please."

Theresa took a book of stamps from a drawer and pushed them under the glass, "are you just visiting Hetherington?" she asked casually.

"Just moved in actually. To St Valentines in Main Road."

"Ah yes. Where old Thomas used to live. He died in the pantry."

"Did he?" A faint look of concern passed across the newcomer's face.

"Yes. Sad loss. Lovely old chap. But he had a good innings. He was one of our oldest residents. Knew everyone and everything about the village. Keeled over as he was feeding his cocks."

"He kept cocks in the pantry?" The look of concern was replaced by one of distaste.

"Yep. Kept them indoors away from the hens. That's two pounds eighty please. I'm Theresa by the way."

"I'm Rachel. We didn't know. About exactly where Thomas..." she struggled for the appropriate words, "...passed away. We bought it from his daughter. Grace."

"Who's we?" Theresa handed over the woman's change and looked enquiringly and directly into her eyes.

"Me... and my partner." A pause filled the air and Theresa watched with interest as Rachel started to blush. Her discomfort was intriguing. Theresa gave an encouraging nod for her to continue, but to no avail.

"Right. I must go." Rachel pocketed her change and went to turn away.

Theresa quickly held up a finger to stop her. "Hang on. Just a minute." She ducked down below the counter, reappearing with a bottle. It contained a clear liquid and had a distinctive green label and lid. "Here, take this. Please. It's complimentary for all residents in the village. Our way of saying welcome." She released the catch on the glass partition and opened the window, holding it out to Rachel and winking. "It's the local gin. It's made in the brewery here, very special recipe."

"That's kind, but I don't really..."

"Drink gin?" Theresa interrupted with a knowing look and smiled broadly. "You will this one. It's unique. The secret ingredient is the natural spring water that flows under the village. Haven't met anyone yet that doesn't absolutely love it, gin drinker or no." Theresa pushed the bottle nearer to her encouragingly.

A tad reluctantly, Rachel took it. "Cheers. Thanks." She lifted it in salute and then turned to leave.

Theresa raised her eyebrow contemplatively as she watched the hurried departure of their new resident before turning her attention to her next customer, Mrs Jackson, who had already launched into a complaint. The postman had been delivering 'filthy, disgusting post' in brown envelopes to Mr Jackson—which he swore to her he hadn't ordered. She listened patiently and promised to look into the matter,

3

grateful that Mrs Jackson was her last customer of the day. After pulling down the blinds, she locked up the Post Office counter and went to see her husband Roy, who was gazing distractedly out of the store's front window. He felt her presence and turned towards her.

"So. What's she like?" Roy spoke slowly. But then Roy always spoke slowly. He was the kind of man people always made that comment about; 'it's the quiet ones you've got to watch.'

"Seems a bit shy. Her name's Rachel."

Roy raised his eyebrows. An extreme gesture for him. "She caught your attention then?" He gave a lazy smile as he started cashing up the till.

"She seemed nice enough. Still not right though. That house should have gone to the Taylors. This hasn't happened for nearly ten years."

Roy did not respond. Theresa stared at him but he kept his concentration on totting up the coppers. She knew him well enough to know that it wasn't worth pursuing an answer. His silence would be either disinterest or disagreement with her opinion, there was no way of knowing which. Irritated, she changed the subject, "who's coming on Sunday?"

"The Master, The Dragon, Jodhpurs, Black Lace, The Major, Floosy."

"No Jumper?" Theresa sounded surprised at the absence of a regular from their weekly events.

"Not this week."

"Do you know why?"

"Nope."

Theresa crossed her arms, momentarily disconcerted. "Hm. Odd. Ok. Do we need anything?"

"Might need a new riding crop."

"I meant refreshments." Theresa tapped her top lip with her finger, still perturbed that one of their regulars was going to be absent. She felt a strange sense of foreboding and couldn't quite work out why. Perhaps she was just feeling off kilter because of the arrival of the strangers in the village. The implications of the change disturbed her.

"I sorted food and drink out yesterday." Roy pulled the string on the cash bag and let out a heavy sigh. "Another slow day in Paradise." He referenced the lack of trade that they'd experienced recently in the store, but to Theresa, a temporary downturn in grocery sales was a minor issue.

"It'll come round again." She said it dismissively. Taking the cash bag from his hand, she ushered him out, pre-occupied with her thoughts about the new resident she'd met earlier and frustrated by Roy's careless reaction. He knew as well as she did that there would be repercussions.

Rachel stood by the doorjamb in the kitchen, staring into the pantry. She sniffed hard, trying to catch a whiff of anything that might seem off. She couldn't get the image out of her head of an old geezer in mucky dungarees lying dead on the floor with his cocks crapping on him. "Do you think bird shit easy to get rid of? Does it leave germs?" she called out to Frankie, whose back was turned to her, head stuck in a kitchen cupboard.

"What on earth are you talking about?" Frankie's muffled voice was confused.

"The woman at the post office said that Thomas kept his cocks in here." She hesitated, maybe she shouldn't mention the fact that he'd died in there, it was disturbing her, no need to share it with Frankie. "We should really give it a good scrub out."

"I'm sure it got thoroughly cleaned Rachel. There's no way there's still bird shit in there." Frankie was chuckling.

Rachel drew her eyes away from the pantry and was pleasantly distracted by the sight of Frankie's bum sticking out of the cupboard. It was irresistible and she crept over and squeezed a good chunk of flesh between her fingers.

"Ow!" Frankie's head thudded against the top of the cabinet.

"Oh shit, sorry." Rachel was laughing. "Couldn't help it. Nice ass!"

Frankie shuffled backwards and stood up. "Rub it better."

"Your ass?"

"My head!" They both laughed as Rachel massaged the top of Frankie's head and pulled it down towards her to kiss it better. Then, turning, they stood with arms across each other's backs as they stared out of the kitchen window at the garden. They fell silent for a few moments. Rachel sighed.

"Happy?" Frankie asked.

"Mmmm. Beautiful isn't it?"

"She lived in a house, a very nice house in the country..." Frankie sang cheerfully. It made Rachel feel like she wanted to enjoy the evening; the unpacking could wait.

"Bugger the cleaning, let's go for a drink."

Frankie kissed her gently on the lips and Rachel, for the millionth time, felt her heart melt. "A drink sounds great, but I'm a bit tired darling, can we just hang out here?"

"Of course!" The possibility of more kissing won her over instantly, "we'll still have a drink though. I'll get a takeaway so you can test the local bitter. Apparently, the pubs and the brewery all do four-pint jugs you can bring home."

"Cool. So hit me with the lowdown on the drinking holes of Hetherington."

Rachel repeated what she'd been told on a visit to the local pub. The Royal Oak was supposed to be good for food. The Gate was your typical village Inn. The Greedy Pig was good all-round and The Old Trout was a bit youth and a bit rebel.

"I wonder what a bit youth and a bit rebel actually means in a village like this. Under forty's wearing leather trousers?" Rachel speculated wryly.

"Oh, now I wouldn't be too sure it's that mild. You know what they say about village life and all the secret goings on." Frankie winked playfully. "I like the sound of The Greedy Pig for troughin'."

"Apparently, there's one called the Moody Cow as well, in Lower Stoughton. We'll have to take your mother there."

"Oh ha ha ha," Frankie gave Rachel a playful slap. "So, a few pints of best?"

"Sounds good to me. Oh... wait..." Rachel remembered the free bottle of booze she'd been given earlier and reached into the pantry to pull it out. She held it towards Frankie, "unless you want some gin?"

Frankie's face immediately screwed up. "Since when might I like

6

gin?"

Rachel laughed at the horrified expression and described how she'd been offered the gin for free at the post office. She turned the bottle towards Frankie, pointing at it and raising an eyebrow. All it said was 'For Good Time Girls and Boys'. She tapped the label, "honestly, I tried to decline, but the woman was insistent and I felt rude saying no. And as you can see from this, it has promise."

Frankie laughed, "yeah right. Like a bit of clever branding is going to change my taste buds. Even free gin doesn't get past these lips."

Rachel continued, undeterred by Frankie's cynicism, "well apparently they make it in the village from the natural spring water. It's supposed to be delicious and unlike any other gin."

"It would have to be *not* gin for me to drink it," said Frankie firmly.

Rachel accepted defeat. "Ok, I'll try it myself on one of my dark and lonely nights without you." She winked and put it back on the shelf.

"Oh yeah? Well just be sure there aren't any good time girls with you."

"Ha ha. That's a game from my past. And anyway, we're in the middle of nowhere, I probably wouldn't be able to find one if I tried." Rachel grinned lasciviously and pecked Frankie on the cheek before grabbing her coat and heading for the door. "Won't be long. Missing you already!" she called back as she stepped out into the cool evening air.

As she wandered along the narrow lane that was the main road through the village, she took in the beauty of the thatched cottages with their quaint wooden doors and wisteria covered walls, thinking that she still couldn't believe how they'd found the place. They'd been visiting the nearby town of Badbury and had popped into an estate agent on a whim after looking at the chocolate box cottages in the window. All of them had offers on them—but by chance, the agent had just taken instructions on a property in Hetherington. The agent had mentioned that she couldn't remember them having handled a property there before, but knew it to be a stunning village off the beaten track. They'd gone to look at it there and then—and fallen in love with both the house and the village. They offered at the asking price and within six weeks they'd exchanged. Their flat in London had been easy to sell—and now here they were in the country. It was like a whirlwind romance. She sighed as she passed the pretty church and its surrounding graveyard, dotted with angled ancient headstones, heavy with moss. At that moment, in the soft light of the evening, with the only sound coming from the light breeze ruffling through the hedgerows and trees and with not a soul in sight, it seemed perfect. As if it was all just meant to be.

Pleasantly relaxed and giggly from their beer, Frankie pulled Rachel up the narrow staircase that led to the top floor conversion of the cottage.

"Stop it, I'll trip over!" Rachel stumbled on the bottom step and laughed at Frankie's keenness to get to the bedroom.

"Ok, I'll let go. But only because it's too narrow." A feigned look of desperation made Rachel laugh.

"It's only eight stairs. You can survive."

"Barely." Frankie quipped.

Rachel made her way to the top, tripping over the top step too and laughing at herself. "That's bloody strong beer."

"Tell me about it. Now get yourself in the bathroom."

Frankie pointed toward the far end of the eves conversion from where they stood at the top of the stairs. This third floor of the house had been one of the real selling points for them and had strongly influenced their decision to buy the place. A large double bedroom in the centre, with the original cross beams either side, so low that they forced them to duck their heads when they passed under, quaint and cosy and full of light from the dormer windows. Then there was a study room on one side and a shower room on the other.

Frankie followed Rachel as she went in and they stood at the sink and brushed their teeth, staring at each other in the mirror. When they'd finished Frankie grabbed Rachel's hand and led her into the bedroom, laying down beside her and gazing into her eyes. "What are you thinking? You're miles away."

"Sorry I was thinking about the pub earlier. Do you think we'll fit in here?" she asked pulling the duvet back and covering them both.

Frankie reached over, stretching an arm across Rachel's belly, yawning as the beer started to have its soporific effect, "I'm sure we'll be fine."

"Yeah, but do you think we'll get any hassle? In small places, everybody wants to know your business."

"Well, if it's a problem, just don't get too friendly with people. You said you chatted to a bloke at the bar. What was he like?"

"I asked him if he was a local and he said no, he'd only been in the village twenty-four years. I thought flippin' 'eck, we've got no chance then!"

Frankie laughed.

Rachel thought back to the peacefulness of her earlier walk to the pub. She'd had such a lovely feeling of belonging, but the atmosphere in the bar had felt less welcoming. "Do you think we made the right decision?"

"Of course!" Frankie was positive. "Come here." Frankie pulled Rachel in and pressed against her body. "It'll be fine. We'll just keep ourselves to ourselves. Anyway, you worry too much. Just be happy. Sod 'em if they don't like it."

"I know, I'm sorry. I am happy and I love this place. I've always wanted to live in the country. In a beautiful beamed cottage."

"Exactly. Dream come true." Frankie kissed the top of her head. They both sighed simultaneously—and then laughed.

"I keep doing that."

"Me too."

"Must be bliss then."

Rachel felt more relaxed again. There were a million reasons she loved Frankie, making her feel so safe was just one of them. She started to chuckle.

"What are you laughing at?"

"I just remembered something else about the Post Office today. It's tiny. They had all these signs up telling you what you could and couldn't do. There was one that said 'NO LICKING'," she laughed harder as Frankie snorted.

"No licking?"

"Yeah, they meant for people not to hang around the counter licking their stamps because they take up all the space and make it crowded." Rachel paused, "the woman behind the counter, I mentioned her earlier, Theresa, she was having a right go at this bloke who was trying to sneak in a quick lick. I had to stare at the floor I was laughing so hard."

"So he got a tongue lashing for licking? Sounds like it could be fun here." Frankie turned towards her, "talking of licking..."

Rachel bit down on her bottom lip, "mmmm you must have read my mind..."

Chapter 2

The toastmaster, a short grey-haired man in his sixties, stood to the side of a heavy wooden podium which was draped with red cloth, holding his gavel aloft and looking around the room to make sure everyone was accounted for. There was little space between him and his audience, who stood in front of their respective metal chairs, squashed shoulder to shoulder, looking up at him, elevated as he was by his Cuban heels and a small wooden milking stool. An air of anxiety hovered over them. Satisfied he had their attention, he began proceedings.

"Call to the Order of the Sloe!" The toastmaster slammed the gavel down and the room fell silent. "Salute all those that honour The Club!"

It was hardly necessary for him to bellow, thought Theresa, from where she stood in the front row. They were in a room hardly big enough to swing a cat and none of them were hard of hearing. Still, she went along with it all as usual and raised her middle finger in the customary salute. Then she stepped forward the half a pace that the room allowed and turned to give the agenda.

"There are three main issues for discussion on this, the night of the Pre-Hunt Forum. Firstly St. Valentines, secondly the Abstainers, thirdly the Hunt Schedule." She folded the paper and turned around again, squishing herself back between her neighbouring attendees. "I call upon The Master, He Who Shall Be Obeyed."

The Master made his entrance from where he had been hiding behind a wine coloured velvet drape in the corner of the room and sidled along behind the podium before taking the toastmaster's place on the stool. He readjusted his horned Viking hat before motioning the audience to be seated. Placing his ringed notepad on the podium to his side, he turned to address them. "The Club is concerned about the issue of St. Valentines and wishes to raise with the Maddox family the sale of the property to outsiders. As you are all aware, the Maddox family were Abstainers, but had entered into the Club Rights of Transfer Agreement and had been paid the appropriate compensation. Though the property was designated to Doctor Taylor, Grace Maddox placed the property on the open market and it was sold before we were able to prevent her from doing so. We must now enforce the contract and impose the penalty. All in favour?" The overwhelming majority of the room raised their hands.

"Carried." The Master made a note on his pad and moved on. "Do we have any information about the new residents of St Valentines as yet?"

"One of them came into the Post Office today—a woman called Rachel," offered Theresa, going on to describe Rachel in appearance.

"Anyone else?" The Master cast his eyes around the room, but no-one responded. "Ok. Let's get Ivor in there. And if that doesn't work, tell Jane to pop round." He nodded at Theresa to make a note accordingly. "Moving on to The Abstainers. Paul Mason of Beany Way has been overheard discussing some objections he has. I understand it's not The Hunt itself he has a problem with, but The Chase. His wife has apparently been approached inadvertently even though she's no longer on the list. He's quite upset about it and I don't want him breaking ranks. Theresa—will you have a word?"

Theresa sighed. "Who approached her?"

The Master cleared his throat. It said it all

"Oh, don't tell me. Doug the Digger. He's a menace. No, he's worse, he's out of control."

"Here here!" Two or three members piped up their approval for her comment.

"I'll agree to talk to Paul if you'll motion a First Refusal for Digger?" ventured Theresa.

The Master hesitated, "seconder?"

"Seconded!" a voice responded quickly from the back of the room.

"Fair enough. Motion tabled. I'll discuss it with him before Sunday."

Theresa nodded, satisfied with the outcome.

"Now. On to Sunday's Schedule. This week's club meeting will be at The Banks's. For anyone unaware, they're at Tweedledums Cottage in Break Street. It's scheduled for three. The code is 'Red Rum'. That's about it, unless anyone else has any other business?" The Master scanned the room once more and getting no response, he closed proceedings.

"Adjourned."

The assembled group raised their middle fingers once more and then left the room in silence.

Rachel stood before the Victorian bookshelf in the front room and wiped the shelves with a damp tea cloth, ready to unpack the books that still sat in boxes on the floor around her. As she reached down to open the first carton, she heard the tinkling chime of the brass door bell and smiled at its charming sound.

"I'll get it!" she called to Frankie, wiping her hands on the tea towel as she strode to the door and opened it. A huge man filled the frame of the small entrance to the cottage and thrust his hand towards her.

"Hello, I'm Ivor, I deliver wood to all the houses in the village."

"Hello!" Rachel threw the towel over her shoulder before reaching out for a handshake. Folding her slender hand in his giant palm, he shook it and simultaneously stepped up into the room. She stumbled backwards, surprised by his audacity.

"Don't mind if I come in do, you?"

"No. No. Well, we're in a bit of a pickle. Sorry, we've only been here six days." Rachel wondered why she was apologising to a lummox who had just barged into her home.

"I know. 'tis ok." Ivor's amiable eyes darted around the room. "On your own are you?" He craned his neck towards the kitchen door.

"No." Rachel was becoming a little concerned. "Look, um I don't mean to be rude, but we've got an awful lot to sort out. Can I take a card or something and let you know if we need your services?"

"Just ask for Ivor," he said as he picked up a picture frame and turned it round. "Your husband is it?" He pointed at the photo.

"My brother. Don't you have a telephone number?" She took the frame from his hand.

"Yes. But everyone always knows where I am. Just ask." Ivor thrust his giant hands into the pockets of his dungarees and regarded her. "Big open fireplace this. Stove gets very hot. Need to put a guard up if you've got children."

"Thanks for that. I'll bear it in mind. And I'll get in touch." Rachel tried to close off the conversation and headed towards the door, but he seemed determined to hang around.

"Might need your chimney swept, will I take a look?"

He pointed at the wood burner, just visible behind a stack of boxes, and made steps towards the inglenook.

"No. Really, it's fine. It's blocked at the moment with all this stuff. It's too difficult to get to it. Honestly, I'll call you when we're ready."

He nodded slowly and a silence fell between them. He looked at her, frowning, like he was studying her. She felt herself colouring up.

"Lived in the country before have you?"

"No."

"Has your husband?"

Rachel regarded him, unsure what to say. "Um, I'm not married." Was he trying to find out whether she lived on her own for some sinister reason?

"Right right. Expect it's a bit strange then?"

"What is?"

"Being in the country."

"Not really. Not yet anyway, it's like living in a town, but quieter. And with trees." She tried to be light hearted and laughed, but he remained expressionless "...and cows," she added to fill the silence. He still stared at her blankly. She felt her heart beating faster and the onset of panic. Then he finally spoke.

"We have our ways." He nodded at her and winked.

"Like?"

He paused. "Gas."

"Gas?"

"Yeah. Gas tanks. Don't have them in the towns." He pointed towards the back of the house and she realised he meant the four cylinders that supplied fuel to the house—there was no mains supply in the village.

"No. That's true. Gas tanks do seem to be a country thing."

"And the Hunt."

"Oh..." Rachel's interest was piqued at the thought of a

14

traditional hunt, "is there a local one? With hounds and all?"

"Oh yes. Yes, there's a local hunt alright. And we got some bloody good hounds. Deep sniffers. Ain't no foxy lady as can escape them in undergrowth. That be the truth."

"Lady fox? Is that what you mean? A female fox?" Rachel felt another pang of discomfort. Hadn't fox hunting been banned?

"Lady Fox. Foxy lady. All the same to a hound."

"Of course." Rachel tried to dismiss her concern. "Well, I'd be interested to see that. Is there anything coming up?"

"Always. Always something coming up here." He crossed his huge arms across his chest and she couldn't help but look at his massive thighs as he spread his feet out and rocked back on his heels.

"You have to be invited. If you wanna see it."

Aware of where her eyes were focused, she looked up, horrified that he might have got the wrong impression.

"See what?"

"The hunt."

"Right. Private then?" She nodded, waiting for him to explain further. But he just stared at her, rocking back and forth a little. She pushed on, "so is there a contact? For the hunt? I'd love to go."

"It'll come. Anyway, must be off." Ivor turned quickly on his heel and strode towards the door, opening it and stepping through as quickly and purposefully as he had when he arrived.

"Ok, I'll be in touch. About the wood…" she called after him as he disappeared through the doorway.

"Right you are, me duck." He shouted back, already half way up the street.Rachel stared at the empty doorway, a little dumbstruck.

"Jesus. What was all that about?" Frankie appeared at the bottom of the stairs.

Rachel shook her head, bemused. She barely knew how to answer Frankie's question. "Well, I suppose he was just trying to sell me logs. Bloody strange way of going about it though. Nosy bugger. I was starting to get really uncomfortable."

"Yeah, sounded well odd from what I could hear. But then I suppose village folk have different ways. He was probably just trying to be friendly. Anyway, I need a hand putting the beds together on the first floor." Frankie grabbed her hand, "come on, forget it. Let's just get on."

Rachel smiled, happy at the prospect of building their nest, but her mind was still on the conversation she had just had and she felt a lingering sense of concern as she followed Frankie up the stairs.

Chapter 3

The sun streamed through the window as the alarm went off. Despite the early hour, there was no need for it, Rachel had been awake for some time. Frankie stirred beside her as she leant over and turned off the bell, then groaned and stretched.

"Come on Frankie baby, time for you to go out and earn some bread."

"Mmmm. This is the bit I don't like about living in the sticks." Frankie rolled out of the side of the bed and headed towards the shower room, shuffling in a new pair of cow slippers.

"I'll make some coffee," Rachel volunteered as she slipped her feet into her pigs.

"Well, there's not really any need for you to get up at this ungodly hour."

"No. But I feel bad, so I will."

The choice to move to the country had one major drawback. Frankie worked in London, so it meant staying in town five days a week. At least until they decided whether a change of job was in order. Leaving at six on a Monday morning and getting back around eight on Friday evening, with maybe a mid-week visit if it looked feasible, was the most likely scenario. The idea was for Rachel to stay in the village and concentrate on her writing. It didn't feel like much fun right now though.

"Do you want a bagel?"

"Yeah, that sounds good. Just butter."

Rachel heard the shower start as she made her way downstairs. They'd both taken the week off to move in, now it was time to start the work routine. Rachel knew she would have to practice self-discipline. She'd started her novel a couple of months previously, writing in her spare time as she kept up her full-time position at the advertising agency. But this was now a fresh start. She'd resigned her position to write full-time. But she wasn't going to cut herself any slack just because she was working from home. As she drew back the downstairs curtains, she was already mapping out her day, when her thoughts were interrupted by a shadowy figure hurrying past. Somebody else was making an early start. Unable to resist a bit of a nosey, she craned her head round to see who it was. Rachel giggled as she recognised Theresa in a frightful floral summer dress teamed with an unlikely pair of muddy wellies. She watched as Theresa crossed the road and headed for the pathway that led into the fields behind the houses opposite. Rachel shook her head; she'd have to get used to the odd behaviours of village folk. Like getting up at the crack of dawn to flounce through the fields in a frilly dress. She shrugged and went into the kitchen to fix Frankie's breakfast.

By the time she'd dropped Frankie off at the station and returned from Badbury, it was six-forty-five and Rachel was eager to get started. Though the house was still relatively disorganised, she'd taken care to set up her work unit and PC. Tucked into the corner of what would be the dining room, her desk faced French doors that led out into the pretty, well-planted cottage style garden. It felt so right and she found she was inspired. It generally took her time to get going and she'd often type and retype several times before she got into the flow. But this morning it had all come right away. Time passed quickly and before she knew it, her watch showed noon and she was feeling peckish. Time to pop down to the village shop and see what they had in the way of sandwiches. It was just a short distance into the centre of the village and she'd determined that she would make a habit of walking, but given that she needed to sort out her road tax, she let herself off the hook and jumped into the car. Driving slowly, she found herself smiling happily as she enjoyed the pretty cottages. She felt as if she might never tire of seeing their beautiful stone walls and tiny wooden framed windows. Then, as she reached the brow of the incline that led up to the church, something odd happened. A man walking in the opposite direction stopped in his tracks and waved. Rachel slowed and peered through the window, wondering if she knew him. He seemed to be dressed like a farmer. And he was oldish. Probably in his eighties. She was absolutely sure she didn't know him, but she tentatively gave him a quick wave back. Then, smiling broadly, the man slowly raised his right hand and flipped her the finger! Rachel recoiled. She shook her head; probably just some mad old bugger, she thought as she sped up. But somehow her mind couldn't just leave it there. Maybe it was because she was an incomer? An invader. Or had he mistaken her for someone else? And why was he smiling? These perturbed thoughts were still tumbling through her head as she walked into the store and she barely acknowledged the chap behind the counter as he wished her good morning. Still ruminating she picked up a paper, her mood now felt much darker and she could feel the onset of paranoia. She checked herself and mentally admonished her reactive way of reading so much into such a minor incident. She resolved to put it to the back of her mind and enjoy exploring the store. Moving on, she spotted a chiller cabinet with a variety of freshly made sandwiches, but by now intrigued by the warren like layout, decided to explore a little further. Her disturbed thoughts waned as she enjoyed the tardis like journey of discovery through the shop's interconnected little rooms. The next contained fresh and pre-packed bread, sweets, biscuits, cakes. The kind of cakes your Mum used to make. Coffee and walnut, date and banana. Further on, she found tinned and packet foods then another chiller cabinet and frozen food section followed by fresh fruit and veg and even a flower display. Just about everything you could need. She wondered fleetingly at the village's ability to sustain two shops when most rural communities couldn't even support one these days. Deciding on some fresh bread and a pack of ham, she took these and a newspaper to the counter.

"That's Edna's bloomer."

"I beg your pardon?"

"That loaf. It's Edna's bloomer." The man behind the till offered an apologetic smile.

"Right. I'll put it back then?" Puzzled, Rachel returned to the bread shelf and swapped the bloomer for a sandwich tin loaf and went back to the counter.

"Donna's." He looked her in the eye.

"This is Donna's?" she asked, exasperated. "Are any of the loaves not spoken for?"

"No." He paused, "you can put your name down for one tomorrow though."

"No, that's ok." Rachel went back and replaced the second loaf and opted instead for a sandwich. She approached the counter. He raised his eyebrows.

"Don't tell me, it's Bert's," she said wryly.

"Noooo… no. That's not it," he lifted his hand to his head and rubbed his forehead as, relieved, she put the sandwich on the counter.

"Bert has a Ginster's beef and onion pie. That's Nora's."

Rachel laughed, "you're kidding me, right?"

He stared at her blankly. Then smiled. "Yes, I'm kidding you. Sort of. Nora does usually buy a ham sandwich, but we don't hold it for her. And not everything in the shop has a name on it."

"Thank goodness for that. You really had me worried there."

"We're not completely barking. The fresh loaves are cooked to order because we have too much wasted if we just push them out willy nilly. If you want some just give us half a day's notice." He handed her a card, "number's on there. I'm Ian." He stretched his hand over the counter and she shook it.

"Rachel."

Ian rang up the items and she handed over her cash, deciding to raise the issue of the flipping finger. "Ian, um, I don't know how to say this…" she pulled at her earlobe awkwardly as she regarded him.

"It's not a toupee!" he said, placing his hand on his head.

"What?"

"It's not a toupee! I know it looks like it, but I had a bubble perm and it went a bit wrong. I can't do anything about it."

She glanced at the top of his head; she could see the problem. He had a mass of tightly curled, thin, graying hair sort of perched on top of it. She let out a burst of laughter, "no! Sorry, no I wasn't going to… that's not it."

Ian went beetroot. "Ah well, gets it out of the way." He let out a sigh.

"I was going to ask…" she was giggling now, "I was going to ask you…" she clutched her side, "I was going to ask you… about this old bloke…" she doubled over, tears in her eyes, "…who gave me… the finger," she couldn't hold back now and was laughing uncontrollably. Ian's face fell and she realised she was offending him. She collected herself, "sorry, you gave me the giggles. I honestly hadn't even noticed."

She felt herself blushing.

"That's alright. That's good then. Must be calming down if you didn't notice. Girl in the hair place told me the bubbles would fall out like." He patted it again. "That's old Michael that gave you... waved at you. Don't worry he does it to everybody."

"Really?" Oh dear." She took a tissue from her pocket and wiped the laughter tears from her eyes. "That's a bit unfortunate."

"He's been doing it for years. Just ignore him," said Ian lightly, though he looked concerned.

Rachel, calmer now, picked up her purchases. "Well, I feel better now. I thought it was because we're new here."

"No. No. Nothin' doin'. That's just old Michael for you."

"Thanks, Ian, I really appreciate that. And it's lovely to meet you."

"You're welcome, me duck. You take care now."

Ian winked at her and waved as she walked out of the door, waiting until she had crossed the threshold before picking up the phone.

Rachel, smiling now at Ian and his bubble perm, decided to walk from the village store to the Post Office, which was literally around the corner and then just a couple of hundred yards up the road. As she approached it, she thought again of how remarkable it was for such a small village to sustain two shops. Though the post office had nowhere near the breadth and depth of variety of the main store, it still had a considerable amount of groceries packed into its limited shelf space. The bell on the door rang as she went in and she immediately made eye contact with Theresa, straight ahead of her behind the counter, phone in hand. The property was so small that you could hear every word from one end to the other.

"...coming in. I'll give you a ring later." Theresa ended the call and gave Rachel her attention.

"Good morning... Rachel, isn't it?"

"Uh huh. Good morning Theresa. Nice walk earlier?"

"Walk?"

"Yes, I saw you first thing this morning just as I was

opening the curtains. Heading off over to the fields for a walk."

"Goodness you were up early."

"Yep. Up with the lark." Rachel paused for an answer to her question and reddened slightly as Theresa's even stare confirmed that she wasn't going to get one. She decided to dispense with the chat. "Do you do road tax?"

"We do everything here. Everything we can squeeze in." Theresa smiled and rubbed her hands together.

"Great." Rachel handed over the documents and flicked absently through some cards on a unit by the counter as Theresa sorted out the disc. She read another one of the trade mark hand written notices, tucked into one of the trays: 'Don't Bend The Cards. For The Club Collection, Ask'.

"What's the Club Collection?" she enquired, spinning the stand round. She glanced up when the silence made her think Theresa may have disappeared and she might be talking to herself. But she was there, studiously writing out the disc. She must surely have heard her? She decided to let it drop.

"There we go. Paying by cheque?" Theresa pushed a piece of paper towards her showing the total due. "Have you got kids? It's Child Benefit today, in case you forgot."

"No kids."

"Can I help you with anything else?"

"No, other than a bit of help with my gas supplies. Do you know a reliable local supplier?"

"I certainly do. We try to keep it all in the village. Support local businesses, you know?"

"Sure, that makes sense to me."

Theresa scribbled a name and number down. "There's a monthly village magazine as well…. hang on a second." Theresa scrabbled round in a drawer, "… there you go, last month's."

"That's great, thanks."

"Did you try the gin?"

"Oh… er, no, not yet."

"Really?"

Theresa's face fell, immediately making Rachel feel ungrateful and guilty. "Sorry. We will soon."

"You should. It's good. I'll tell you what, you can have a chance to try it this weekend. We're having a barbecue Saturday afternoon. Just a little get together. We live just up behind you in Huntsman's Lane and your neighbours will be there, so it'll give you a chance to get to know a few people. How about it?"

"Sure. Sounds great. Thanks." Rachel collected up her papers, internally cursing herself for not giving herself the space to decide if she actually wanted to go. And then jumped as she heard a shout behind her.

"No!"

Rachel span round to see what was causing the commotion coming from the front of the store.

"Damien, out!" a gruff voice ordered.

Rachel stepped to one side to look down the aisle. She saw someone bending over, a man, she thought, in what looked like a black frock coat, obviously trying to grab a hold of something that was struggling to avoid his grip.

"Damien!"

A nose poked through under his arm—and then a pair of horns. It looked like a goat. She caught sight of a heavily bearded face as the man turned to grab the horns.

"Sorry Roy," he puffed as he struggled to pull the animal towards the door, "must have slipped free."

"No problem, vicar, at least he didn't get in the cabbages this time," Roy looked across and winked at Rachel.

"The vicar has a pet goat?" Rachel turned back round to Theresa.

"Three."

"Called Damien?"

"No, only one's called Damien. Then there's Lucifer and Satan." Theresa's eyebrows lifted wryly.

"He's got a good sense of humour then, the vicar?"

"You might say that. So, Saturday at three?"

"Three, yes," Rachel confirmed dsitractedly, still bemused by the vicar and his pets.

"Good. How many should we expect?"

"Just me and Frankie." Rachel turned her attention back to

Theresa, " so should I bring anything, apart from a bottle?"

"No. You two and a bottle will be just perfect." Theresa smiled at her, "we'll make sure eveything else is there for you to start enjoying some village-style fun."

Chapter 4

The branding iron sizzled as he touched the surface of the water and its white-hot surface became shrouded in steam. Leaving it immersed, Trevor's aim was to cool it down to a level that the skin could withstand, but still leave the unmistakable mark of The Club.

"Bring her over," he gestured impatiently to his assistant; timing was everything. Nathan straddled Mrs Blair and held her steady, presenting her rump to Trevor.

"Hold hard," he said as he placed the steaming iron against her flank. Nathan kept a firm grip on her as she tried to buck and push away from him.

"That'll do it!" Trevor arced the metal rod back over to the coals and wiped the sweat from his brow.

"How many more Nathan?"

"Just The Little Devil and Patsy. Then you're wanted in the top barn." Nathan flicked his head towards the run-down shed at the end of the yard.

"Uh huh. Bad business that," grumbled Trevor. "'it has not been heard of since 1971 when that fool Brendan took it upon himself to hand over his home to the outsider from Gloucester." Trevor shook his head, "it was my father that did the deed then and it wasn't somethin' he could easily forget."

Nathan grabbed The Little Devil by the horns and swung his right leg over his back. "This one spawned by the Vicar then?"

"Aye, teamed Damien up with Mrs Blair over there, nigh on a year ago. Good little cheese maker now." Trevor took the branding iron to The Little Devil's rump and then pushed him on his way. "Now then, last but not least our little Patsy. Treat her careful Nathan, she's my little pet this one."

Nathan stroked the nervous animal as she waited her turn.

"There my little beauty," Trevor spoke softly as he prepared the iron, "that's my girl," he muttered with fondness, keeping her calm as he marked her skin and then slapped her rump as she bleated and headed off for the pens. "I'll leave you to sort them out now, Nathan, duty calls."

Trevor rolled the iron in the coals a final time and then wrapped a thick rag round the handle as he marched off towards the top barn.

"Your father would be turning in his grave, Grace Maddox." The Master towered over the slight woman tied to the chair in front of him. She shook her head violently as the gag tightened round her face.

"Stop struggling, you stupid woman, you're making it worse. Now you listen to me," he lowered his face until he was within an inch of hers, "you know the rules, you know the penalty. We've kept ourselves to ourselves for over ten years. That property was destined for Doctor Taylor. You knew what your duty was and you willfully disobeyed."

Grace's head shook yet more violently, trying to escape the Master's excruciatingly bad breath, a mixture of onions and beer.

"You'll be given your chance to answer the charge and offer mitigation, but as we stand now, you will be branded traitor, so help me you will." The Master stood up and back as Grace's head stilled and her eyes bulged. The Master span round in the direction of her stare and saw the advancing Trevor, branding iron in hand. "How long do we have Trevor?" he called out.

"It'll be good for another five minutes Master."

"Right. Lady of Gordon's, hand me the clamps." The Master addressed a figure dressed in a full-length white gown, who stepped forward holding a red satin pillow before her. On it were two shiny silver clasps. Grace squirmed and rocked on the chair.

"Be still!" the Master roared as he grasped the lapels of Grace's blouse and ripped it apart. She started to whimper as he deftly snapped the clasp of her front-loading bra to bare her breasts.

"Lady of London, swabs!" Now a figure dressed all in bottle green stood forward and bathed Grace's bared breasts with cotton wool and alcohol. After she had retreated, the Master took the two metal clamps from the pillow and stood before Grace.

"In the name of The Club, I use these clamps to serve as a great lesson. So shall these clamps cause our subject Grace to clench her jaw, to teach her to keep her mouth shut in future and to understand in full the need to retain the secrets of The Club even in times when to do so should create great pain. In her suffering let her be forgiven."

Grace wriggled for all she was worth but was unable to prevent the Master applying the clamps to each of her nipples.

"Time, Lady of London." The woman in green set the stopwatch in her hand.

Grace wept and squirmed more, trying to dislodge the clamps against her arm as the three shrouded figures looked on.

"Ten seconds!"

The Master spoke again. "Prepare the tonic!" he ordered and the Lady of Gordon picked up a bottle from behind Grace's chair.

"Five seconds! Four, three two, one. Release her!" The Lady of London shouted and pointed dramatically at Grace, swishing her long velvet dress like a flamenco dancer and toppling the Master off balance as the material caught in his spurs.

"Alright, alright, don't make a meal of it," he said, glaring at her crossly for trying to steal his thunder. He swatted at her hand and pushed her away before readjusting his viking hat and re-establishing his authority by pulling himself up to his full height and sticking his chest out. He turned his attention back to Grace.

"Let us be merciful." He stepped forward and removed the clamps as the Lady of Gordon poured the tonic on Grace's chest.

"Now Grace, you will have your say in mitigation. But I warn you, unless you are able to offer significant reason for your actions, you will be branded." He stooped and removed the gag from Grace's mouth.

"You bastard!" she spat at him. "I only sold it outside because Taylor tried to rip me off. I couldn't afford to take her offer." Her eyes were wild with anger.

"Money can be no excuse. You shall be branded." He clicked his fingers and motioned Trevor forward. "Your name shall forever be shamed."

Trevor moved in with the branding iron, it's twisted metallic formation of G&I, still glowing red with intense heat.

"Nooooooooo…" Grace cried out, weeping as Trevor plunged the branding iron onto the great beam of the barn and held it there.

"See you there Grace Maddox," said the Master, pointing at the steaming beam, "your name shall be etched beneath that brand and shall for all eternity be disgraced."

Trevor removed the branding iron, leaving The Club mark G&I on the great beam. Seven other names had already been shamed, Grace Maddox was to be the eighth.

"Never again shall a Gin and It pass your lips under the auspices of The Club." He lowered his face to hers once more, "breathe a word of this and the consequences will be dire." He said it menacingly. Then, he straightened, turned on his Cuban heel and strode from the barn.

"Grace, would you like ice?" asked the Lady of London.

Chapter 5

It was Thursday and Rachel still couldn't sleep beyond five-thirty. As the sun rose, it streamed light into the loft room, for which they had not yet purchased any curtains. Added to that, the birds were twittering at what seemed like decibel level. And she missed Frankie. Feeling weary, she rose and went downstairs to make coffee. She trudged to the front window, steaming mug in hand and pulled back the curtains to see the shadowy figure of Theresa sweeping by once more. Rachel craned round to see her march towards the fields, her cotton dress swishing against the green wellies. Rachel's curiosity was peaked—it just 'felt' like there was something odd about Theresa's morning jaunts—it just didn't ring right. Taken by an impulse, she decided to follow. Placing her mug on the hall table, she quickly grabbed a raincoat from the coat hook and pulled it over her pyjamas, shoved her feet into her wellies, grabbed the keys and headed out the door.

The fresh air flooded her nostrils with the scent of magnolia as she climbed the steps to the leafy walled pathway that led across to the fields. It was a 'glad to be alive' day. Reaching the end, she caught her breath as the path opened out onto a stunning view over a vast dewy meadow. Stream water tumbled over its stony bed making a muted tinkling sound as it wound its way across the field, which was punctuated with little dense copses of trees. Taken with it all, Rachel started to run across the meadow, leaping like a lamb. It was like she'd caught a sudden dose of spring madness, brought on by an injection of English countryside. No wonder Theresa headed out here each morning. It now made perfect sense, it was glorious! She giggled gleefully and floated her arms out dreamily to embrace the morning air—until reality was returned to her by a cow pat. It was a relatively fresh one, she could tell by the smell and the way the soft, warm center squelched and splashed up onto her boots and coat. She looked down at the greeny-brown globs that clung to her. "Shit!" She glanced around in search of a stick to scrape it off with, but found none nearby and decided to make her way down to a clump of trees by the stream. Picking her way carefully now, she thought she caught the sound of laughter. Or was it the water? Rachel stood stock-still; no it was laughter, coming from somewhere in the copse. Was it Theresa? Now, convinced the laughter must be from the postmistress, she was caught in two minds; head back before she got caught, or carry on and take a peek at whatever was going on. Her stick hunt now forgotten, she was unable to resist her curiosity and, rationalizing that she had a legitimate reason for being there, she took the option to investigate. Stealthily, she crossed the open part of the field and reached the edge of the copse. Masked by the impressive trunk of a tree, she held her breath and listened. For several seconds there was silence and then she heard a sort of high-pitched whinny. Then more giggling. Then bleating. Then it fell silent again. She decided to get closer. She peeked out and seeing it was clear, dashed to the next tree. Again, she glanced round to check and then ran on. This time, standing with her back against a sturdy trunk, she heard a rustling sound. Her pulse started racing and she began to feel distinctly uncomfortable. Perhaps this had been unwise. The rustling sound came closer. Rachel took a deep breath and held it, her heart thumping in her ears.

"Hello!"

Rachel nearly jumped out of her skin. It was Theresa.

"Are you alright?"

"Yes." Rachel breathed heavily, "you made me jump."

"Sorry." Theresa regarded her with a vaguely amused expression, which alerted her to how she must appear. She was in her pyjamas and a raincoat with wellies on, splattered with cow dung, back pressed against a tree trunk, arms rigidly by her side and a look of sheer panic on her face. Not exactly normal.

"Yes... looking for the cat. Sonic. Escaped." Rachel laughed nervously and tried to relax herself, "I, er, thought I spotted him in the bush over there and um, decided to hide behind this tree. See if I could creep up on him."

"Oh, what a pain! Do you want some help?"

"Oh no, you're alright. Could take hours. You know what cats are like."

"What does he look like?"

"Who?"

"Sonic." A smirk appeared fleetingly on Theresa's face.

"He's a Ginger Tom."

"Well at least he'll stand out a bit." Theresa peered past Rachel at the bush, "though I still think you'll have your work cut out. Can't see anything in there now. Are you sure you don't want help?"

"Positive. You get on. I'll be fine. I've got all day if I need it."

"Alright, if you're sure. See you later then." Rachel watched, relief spreading through her as Theresa set off over the field towards the school. She let out a huge sigh and bent over to ease the slightly sick feeling in her stomach.

"Morning!"

"Oh my God!" Rachel clutched at her chest as the sick feeling now leapt up into her throat. She looked up to see who had crept up behind her. "Vicar! Oh! I'm so sorry." She was mortified by what she'd said.

"It's alright. I've heard worse." He transferred the three leads that tethered his goats to his left hand and held his right out to her. "Brian Falstaff."

"Rachel Stretton." She felt the squish at the same time as he did and looked down at their joined palms. "Oh dear. I'm so sorry," she pulled her hand away and wiped it on her mac. She was suddenly aware that she smelled.

He laughed as he took a tissue from his pocket. "Not to worry. A memorable introduction," he said as he wiped away the cow poo, "well, welcome to Hetherington. We have an interesting flock here. Will we see you on Sunday?"

Rachel felt her eyeballs dart quickly from left to right as she paused, searching in vain for an excuse. "Yes. Absolutely." She smiled politely, the memory of her mother chasing her round the house to make her go to Sunday school flooding her head for an instant.

"Excellent! Well, must be on my way. Goats to feed." He motioned at his three pets as they strained on their leads, "see you Sunday then."

"Indeed. Yes. Bye for now," she gave him a nervous little wave and watched him walk off, wondering how she'd sodding well let herself agree to go somewhere she'd fought so hard to avoid for most of her life.

31

Rachel jumped as the door bell jangled. She'd just settled to her writing, so was mildly irritated by the interruption. Turning, she momentarily thought of ignoring it, but then rose and marched to the front door. Opening it, she was greeted by the smiling face of a handsome, fit looking man with some light stubble, who was standing casually with his hand against the door jamb.

"Hey! I'm Ben, I live across the road."

"Oh, hi!" Rachel, glad she had bothered to answer the door, felt an immediate warmth and held out her hand, "I'm Rachel."

"I've just made a coffee. Fancy a cup?" He indicated to his front door just across the way.

"Yeah, why not, that's really nice of you. Give me two ticks and I'll be over."

"Cool. See you in a minute."

Five minutes later Rachel was standing in his kitchen, looking back at her house opposite. "Crikey you can see into our windows!"

He winked at her, "yep, though I only use my binoculars late at night."

She laughed out loud and felt him regarding her. She was surprised at how relaxed she was in his company despite the already intimate nature of the conversation.

"Kidding. Milk? Sugar?" he asked as he pushed the plunger down into the cafetiere.

"Neither thanks, just black."

"That'll help."

"Help what?"

"Help me remember. I have so many women over here, sometimes it's difficult to get the drinks right."

"Oh." She didn't know what to say.

"Kidding. Don't look so shocked. I'm a handsome man." He pointed over to a kitchen work top where a solid looking cake sat on a wooden cutting board. "I've been baking. Want some of my fruit 'n nut? It's bloody delicious."

"Yeah, why not." She was amused by his confidence. There

was not an ounce of ego in a statement that might have sounded like pure bragging from someone else. She relaxed and sat down at his little kitchen table, thinking that she really liked him already. She looked around the room as he sliced into the sponge and put it on a plate for her. His kitchen was lighter than theirs, more spacious. And neat.

"So how's it going? You settling in alright?"

"Yeah it's good, we're doing well. My other half works in London, so that's a bit tough, but other than that we're doing ok."

"I've seen you both about. You're the ugly one," he quipped, winking at her again.

"Thanks!" she laughed. "Good job I'm not suffering from low self-esteem."

"Bloody right if you're going to live in this village. Good cake right?"

"Very good cake." she said as she took another forkful.

"I like baking. It's manly."

She laughed again, enjoying herself, "yeah, incredibly manly, all that puff pastry and soft sponge."

He nodded, "women love it."

"I bet they do. So how long have you lived here?"

"Got to be, let me see, twelve years now. Seen a few people come and go. At least you're prettier than Old Thomas."

"Cheers, that makes me feel better."

"Him and his cocks."

"Yes, I've heard about that. Bizarre. But then there seems to be a few odd characters around here."

"Oh yeah. You just wait. To be honest, I don't get that involved in what goes on. I like the pubs. Me and my mates have a laugh at the locals, but other than that I keep to myself. Well, myself and all my women." He sipped at his coffee and regarded her. "Thing to remember here is that you can take it all with a pinch of salt." He watched her frown. "You'll find out. Just take it easy, incomers are rare, it takes time to settle in. What do you do?"

"I'm a writer."

"Of?"

"I'm writing a novel."

"Woo. I'm impressed. What's it about?"

Rachel explained that she was writing a semi-biographical story about her Grandmother, who had been born into a grand colonial family in India and then found herself in service, a grinding life in Victorian London after her family returned to England and fell on hard times.

"Bloody hell. That's a bit clever."

She blushed. Compliments made her embarrassed. She opted not to acknowledge it.

"How about you?"

"Chimney sweep."

She giggled.

"Eh, what's so funny?" By his tone, she knew he wasn't offended.

"I don't know, it's just, it made me think of Oliver Twist."

"Nothing wrong with that. Everyone likes a bit of Oom-Pah-Pah. I do weddings as well. Lucky, innit, to have a chimney sweep at your wedding?"

"Guess so. I'm sorry though, I just can't imagine you carrying a chimney brush." She laughed harder.

"I'll have you know I look spectacular in my overalls. And I happen to like the fact that so many women ask me to unclog their pipes."

"I bet you do!" She looked at her watch, suddenly conscious that she needed to be working, "well much as I'm loving your confessions of a chimney sweep, I've gotta go." She put her coffee cup down.

"Oh go on, fuck off then."

She looked up at him. He was grinning broadly.

"Kidding!"

She laughed again and got up from her seat, stretching lazily, aware again of how comfortable she felt with him. "Thanks for the fruit and nut. And the coffee."

"Your turn next," he said as he opened the door. "I like pecan pie and Costa Rican. Just so you know."

Chapter 6

"I'm not going to Church, I can tell you that much."

It was Friday evening and they were sitting out on the patio with chilled wine, Rachel recounting the events of the week.

"I know. I can't believe I agreed to go. Suppose I was so mortified at what I said to the vicar, that I had to make amends. God, what must I have looked like?"

"Yeah, but more to the point, what were the vicar and the postmistress doing in the copse with the lead piping?"

"Don't be blasphemous. He's a vicar."

"Oh, hoh, don't let that fool you. Doesn't mean a thing these days."

"Oh stop it. I'm sure there was nothing going on. They were both just out for a walk."

"Yeah, yeah."

"It's a bit strange though. Keeping goats. I thought they were linked to the devil?"

"Yeah, I've got some vague idea there's an association there. But at the end of the day, a goat's a goat. Why not have them as a pet? We *are* in the country."

"Suppose so." Rachel paused, thinking about the Vicar's extraordinariness, not just the clothing and his choice of pet, but his disheveled casualness. "He's very hairy."

Frankie huffed, "and?"

"I don't know. Just doesn't feel right for a vicar to have a great big beard and lots of hair."

"Why?"

"I don't know." She shrugged, not able to put her discomfort into more words. So she changed the subject. "And I met the bloke opposite. Ben. He's nice. Cheeky chappy, he invited me over for coffee."

"Oh cool. Good to get to know the neighbours."

"Yeah, I liked him. He's a chimney sweep."

Frankie laughed. "Do those still exist?"

"Well yeah, I mean look at how many real fires there are here."

"You know what, I hadn't even thought of it. True dat. Filthy job though.'"

"Indeed. Anyway. Tell me about your week."

"Not much to tell really. Same old, same old. Nowhere near as exciting as yours."

"How was Sally?"

"Good. On form." Frankie was lodging with an ex-girlfriend. It wasn't something Rachel had particularly wanted, but she'd known them both long enough to know deep down that there was no chance of a spark re-igniting. Probably. "Not that I saw much of her. She was out and about most nights. She's got a new lover she's being very secretive about."

Rachel nodded, pleased. "Did you go out at all?"

"Only with clients. Saw Rob from CityBank on Wednesday— he sends his best. But I worked late most evenings. The markets are really jumpy and it's tough to tie up deals at the moment. I've been putting in some extra effort to line up new clients. Don't want to jeopardize the bonus."

"I really missed you," Rachel leant her chin on her palm and gazed at Frankie.

"I know. Me too. Let's get this next bonus and then we'll see. I might become a farmer!"

"Ooh aaarrr, 'n oi'll be the milk maid."

"Does that mean getting your jugs out first thing in the morning?"

"Only for the cows."

"Can I be a cow?"

"You certainly can."

"Or maybe a bull?"

"Oh yeah, you're full of that."

"Ouch!" Frankie breathed in deeply, eyes closed. "I have to say, it's fantastic to come back here. It's so peaceful."

"Mmmmm. I keep pinching myself."

"Actually, I meant to say to you, I nearly got lost coming back tonight."

"Oh?"

"Yeah, it's weird." Frankie recounted how she had driven back and missed her usual turning to get into the village. She'd driven a circular route around the main road, but hadn't found any signposts. Not a single pointer in the direction of Hetherington.

"That's bizarre. Maybe they've been knocked down, or taken down or something. Mind you, shouldn't complain, it's probably the reason it's so quiet here."

"Mmmm." Frankie sighed, "so, when's this barbecue then?"

"Tomorrow at three."

"Big do?"

"Don't think so."

"OK. Well, I guess it's time we exposed ourselves. Should be interesting."

Rachel smiled and raised her eyebrows, "but who for…?"

Sunday afternoon turned out to be the perfect weather for a garden gathering. Theresa watched Roy as he fussed round his barbecue and glanced at her watch. She was getting anxious, she knew the pressure was going to rise for her over the incomers. She needed to get the ball rolling on integrating them and this was the ideal opportunity to start the process. But they were late and she was beginning to think they might not turn up. She and Roy were on the patio at the top of the garden, their guests standing chatting at the far end of the long sloping stretch of grass. Theresa heard the gate latch close to her left and looked over. Relieved, she touched Roy on the arm. He was hunched over the steaming coals, concentrating on the job at hand.

"They've just come in the gate. This could be interesting."

"Alright, alright, I'm trying to turn my bangers." He shrugged her off irritated and carried on with his cooking.

Theresa turned her attention to their new guests as Rachel walked up to her, holding out two bottles of wine.

"Hi, Theresa!" She smiled brightly and handed the bottles over before turning to introduce her partner. "This is Frankie. Frankie, Theresa." Rachel watched as Theresa put the bottles down on the grass and took Frankie's hand. She seemed confused. Rachel speculated that she had probably already pictured her other half as a man. Fair enough she thought. She smiled warmly and proudly put her hand on Frankie's shoulder.

"Hi, Frankie. Good to meet you." Theresa tapped Roy on the back and he turned round. As he took them in, his face was a picture.

"Well, I'll be... you're a woman!" His craggy features changed quickly from surprise to what looked suspiciously like pleasure.

"Er, yes, last time I looked anyway."

"Sorry, sorry, forgetting my manners." Roy flicked a glance at Theresa, whose face was frozen. "Nice to meet you. I'm Roy." He wiped his hand on his butcher's apron and held it out.

"Good to meet you too Roy. Great looking sausages." She nodded at the barbecue.

"Oh yes, local ones," he couldn't seem to take his eyes off her. "All local stuff this." He waved his tongs towards the grill, finally dragging his gaze away as Theresa dug him in the back.

"Drink?" She looked at Frankie, "got some cracking gin cocktails...?"

"Sounds good, but I think I'll have a beer if you've got it?"

"Ok. Rachel? Want to try a cocktail? Your chance to try the gin?"

"I think I'll have some of that white wine, Theresa." She pointed at the bottles lying in the grass, "thanks."

"No problem, I'll be back in a tick." Theresa grabbed the bottles and turned back to her husband, "Roy, can you make some introductions?"

Roy, who would normally hate to make some introductions, responded with enthusiasm, "certainly will." He placed the tongs down and happily placed an arm across the shoulders of each of the women. "Let's find you some new playmates," he said as he marched them off down the garden. A long narrow strip of grass sloped down towards a pond, where a small group of people were enjoying their drinks in the afternoon sun. "Everybody," he announced as they reached them, "let me introduce you to your new neighbours."

The group turned in unison and both Frankie and Rachel wished simultaneously that they'd had a camera. A couple of sharp intakes of breath and some very broad grins regarded them.

"Frankie and Rachel. Our new friends at St. Valentines Cottage. Left to right, we have Doug, Sue, David, Angela, Graham, Ida, Roger and Lisa." They all acknowledged them cheerily. "Well," Roy squeezed the two of them tightly then removed his arms, "I'll leave you to it," he said with a wink and then headed back for his barbecue.

An awkward moment of silence was broken by Theresa as she arrived with their drinks - and the conversations started up again. "So, Frankie, what is it you do?"

"I'm a bond trader. I work in the city." Theresa nodded, holding Frankie's eyes. Rachel watched her closely; she seemed to be fascinated by her.

"Sounds lucrative," Theresa commented.

"Can be. Hard work and stressful too though."

"Is that what made you move to the country?"

"Kind of. Yes, I suppose so."

Theresa suddenly laughed loudly. Frankie and Rachel shared a glance.

"Sorry. I was just about to ask if you had children..." Theresa stopped abruptly and went red.

"Well that is possible," said Frankie, a might testily, "but we don't."

"I'm so embarrassed," said Theresa as she covered her mouth with her hand, "I'm so sorry."

"Don't be," Rachel touched Theresa's arm in a gesture or reassurance, "it's not a problem. Really. We're not offended. Are we Frankie?" She nodded at her to capitulate.

"No. Not at all," Frankie's tone softened. Another awkward silence followed. "Good beer," Frankie raised her glass.

"Yes. Have you been down to the brewery?" Theresa was grateful for the change of subject.

"Is there one in the village?"

"Yes! Crikey. I thought you'd know. Yes, we have our own brewery. Built on a spring. That's what gives the beer its distinction. And the gin. They make the gin too. I gave a bottle to Rachel? Doug over there works at the brewery."

Theresa pointed over to what looked like Neanderthal man. Frankie was mesmerized.

"Blimey."

"It's not that unusual, lots of people from the village work at the brewery."

Doug caught their glance and walked over. Theresa introduced him as Frankie took in the glory of his extreme hairiness. His beard bushed out over his cheeks and grew down to his chest. His head hair could only be described as wild. He'd sort of brushed it back from his forehead, but it was so dense and wiry that it still had a manic look about it. He offered a huge grimy hand to Frankie.

"Pleased to meet you," he had a deep country accent and a voice like gravel. It sounded like phonetic grunting.

"Likewise," Frankie offered her hand, slightly concerned about it being mangled, but he took it in a surprisingly gentle grip. He did the same with Rachel. Frankie noticed that Theresa was staring hard at Doug. He winked cheekily at her and she raised her eyebrows in a 'don't you dare' kind of way.

"So you girls just moved in then?" He turned to Frankie, eyes twinkling.

"Yep."

"In The Club yet?"

"Doug!" Theresa reprimanded him

"What do you mean?" asked Frankie, bemused.

"Nothing, he's being an ass," said Theresa crossly, "Doug, go and help Roy with the Barbie."

"Aw, come on Theresa, I can't cook."

"Well you can bloody learn then can't you, you old bugger. Now... off!"

Though Theresa was smiling, it struck Frankie that there was more than a hint of irritation in her voice.

"Sorry about that," Theresa turned back to them as he ambled off.

"What did he mean? Was he asking if I'm pregnant?"

"No... no."

"So what did he mean by 'In The Club?'"

40

"Oh, it's an in-joke. He was… er… making reference to the last woman who came to the village. She er, got pregnant by a local very soon after moving in. Anyway, come and meet his wife, Angela."

Frankie and Rachel swapped another bemused glance as Theresa beckoned to a striking woman with blonde hair tied back in a ponytail. As she approached, Frankie got a drift of a conversation elsewhere amongst the group.

"They're a couple of what?" the woman called Ida was saying.

"You know, they make their own arrangements," bald headed Roger winked madly at Ida, then stopped as he caught Frankie's eye. He coughed loudly. Ida turned and smiled charmingly.

She turned her attention back to Angela, who was a handsome and striking woman. She greeted them in a booming posh voice.

"Hello, guys! Welcome to the village! Jolly nice day for a barbie and jolly nice company," Angela patted Theresa on the shoulder, "you can always count on the old tart for a good do."

Theresa rolled her eyes.

"Oops, let one slip. That's our nickname for her at The Club. They call me The Floosy." Theresa rolled her eyes again at Angela, who seemed to take whatever the hint was. "Actually do excuse me. I've lost Fred again. Must see if I can track him down."

"I'll give you a hand," said Theresa, "you guys alright on your own?"

"No problem," said Rachel, "catch you later." Rachel raised her hands and shoulders and looked at Frankie, mouthing silently "The Club?"

Just as Frankie was about to respond, a strikingly attractive woman, slight and with a boyish short-cropped hairstyle approached. Frankie raised her eyebrows towards Rachel, who smirked knowingly.

"Hi, I'm Lisa," she introduced herself with a handshake, "so, are you settling in alright?"

Rachel glanced at Frankie and spoke for them both, "fine, yes. Though we haven't got out much yet. We're still finding our way. And it's easier for me than Frankie because I'm here all the time, she's been away all week, working."

"Oh really, what do you do?" asked Lisa, turning to her.

"Bond trader in the city. Very dull. How about you?"

"I'm a prostitute."

Frankie choked and spluttered, a mouthful of beer spraying embarrassingly out through her nostrils.

"Oops!" Lisa calmly wiped a few drops from her t-shirt. "Sorry, a bit blunt. Most people know around here, so I'm not used to it being a shock."

"No. Really, I shouldn't have, um..." she was lost for words, "please don't be sorry." Frankie mopped at her face with a tissue.

"Can I get you another drink?" offered Lisa.

"Oh, you're a star. That'd be great" said Frankie, grateful for the space. She watched as Lisa walked off, waiting until she was out of earshot.

"Shit! Talk about awkward," she rubbed at the beer stains, "and I thought our guilty secret was shocking. Fuck. I'm not sure I just heard that right. She did say it didn't she?"

Rachel realised her mouth was hanging open as she watched Lisa stride off to get the beer. She snapped it shut, but the stunned look remained on her features as she turned to Frankie, "I can't quite believe it, but yes, she did. She absolultley did. Um, do you think if we pinch ourselves, we'll land back in reality?" asked Rachel, "I do feel a bit like we're in lala land."

"Smile and be happy, we're being watched," Frankie had caught the little group at the barbecue staring at them, "and don't turn round."

"That was too weird. Maybe we're being tested," said Rachel mysteriously, "to see how shockable we are."

"Why?

"Don't know. Maybe there's secrets."

"The hooker's on her way back. Change the subject."

"I hope it's clear tomorrow, I fancy a walk." Rachel tried hard to control her voice as Lisa approached holding a pint of beer for Frankie.

"Mmmm, as long as it's not too early... ah, thanks, Lisa," Frankie turned to her and took the glass from her extended hand.

"My pleasure. Sorry about before." Lisa said it brightly, as if it really was no issue at all.

"Listen, forget it, it's no problem."

"Anyway, I thought I'd just explain. "

"Oh no need," said Rachel quickly, but Lisa pressed on.

"There are two of us in the village. You might as well get the lowdown now that I've spilled the beans, so to speak. There's me and Sue over there," they looked over to where a tall, slim brunette aged probably early forties, was standing, "one of us does the locals and the other does the incomers. I handle the incomers. There's much more demand from locals than incomers, obviously. I'm sort of a part-timer," she said it very matter-of-factly.

"Obviously," echoed Rachel, feeling a bit spaced out, but hoping she didn't look it.

"We live next door to each other in Park Lane, up over the back of the village. You'll have to come round for a drink one evening. I'm sure it sounds odd. It's..." Lisa suddenly dropped her head and shuffled her feet, almost as if she had heard her own words and realised the impact it might have.

"No... no," Rachel shook her head reassuringly, "it's fine really. And yes, of course, we'd love to come round. That would be... super," she smiled graciously as Frankie disguised another splutter by momentarily turning away.

"Good, well let me give you my card," Lisa fished around in her backpack and pulled out a neat yellow business card and handed it to Frankie, who took it and stuffed it quickly into her back pocket.

"Thanks. We'll give you a call."

"I'll look forward to it. Now, you'll have to excuse me, I have to leave, got work to do. But I hope you have a fun evening." She squeezed Frankie's hand and then turned to the group at the pond, "see you all later!" She waved to everyone and then headed towards the gate.

Frankie and Rachel stared at each other, stunned into silence.

"This is surreal." Frankie shook her head in wonder.

"Grub's up!" Roy called down from the barbecue area.

"Think they're cooking sacrificial lamb or something?"

"Behave!" Rachel pinched her bottom as they made their way up the garden, "but I can't say I feel very comfortable. Let's eat quickly and make our excuses."

"Yeah. Let's get out of here before it gets weird."

Frankie leant and struck a match and lit the candles she'd placed either side of the wood burner in the inglenook fireplace, then stood back and watched the flickering flames reaching into the air. She turned from where she was kneeling and shook her head at Rachel as she lay back on the sofa, a glass of wine in her hand. "That was just unbelievable. You know it serves me right. I really thought the biggest shock of the afternoon would be you and me."

"Pah, we're old hat. There's no shock value in being a dyke anymore. Not in the country anyway." Rachel raised her glass in salute, "cheers to us being the normal ones."

"I'm almost lost for words. Can you believe Lisa just coming out with the fact that she's a prostitute? Unbelievable..." Frankie picked up her beer and raised it back.

"Yeah. What the fuck? And she's so young. And... hot!" Rachel held her hand out, palm up, in a gesture of disbelief.

"Oh yeah? Hot eh?" Frankie nodded at Rachel, mockingly.

"Don't make out you didn't think so too," Rachel raised a single eyebrow and Frankie smiled.

"Ok. Well, I guess it's pretty undeniable." Frankie tried to raise an eyebrow back and, as usual, failed. "Sooooo, do you think she was making a pass at you?"

"Of course not... and anyway, she gave her card to *you*." Rachel raised her left eyebrow repeatedly this time in a more suggestive way.

"Yeah, while looking at *you*," Frankie crawled over and dug her in the ribs gently, "mmm... and I love it when you do that." She touched Rachel's raised eyebrow and kissed her. "God, wait 'til I tell them at work about this."

"Don't be cruel."

"What? They're never gonna meet her are they? Can't do any harm."

"You're sure about that are you?"

Frankie stuck her lip out. "Oh alright, I won't then. For now anyway."

"Did you catch all the looks and stares between Roy and Theresa and the rest of them?"

"Well, I probably didn't catch all of them, there were far too many. But yeah, I get what you mean. D'you think there's something going on?"

"Definitely." Rachel nodded, "and Roy couldn't keep his eyes off you," she nodded at Frankie knowingly and winked.

"Oh puh..lease!" Frankie rolled her eyes, "that's all I need."

"No. Don't be hasty. Man in his prime. Could probably show you a thing or two."

"Yeah... why is that?"

"Ah, the age old question. Why do all men think all we need is a good screw to sort us out?"

"That's the one. No matter how many times I ask it, I just can't figure it out."

"Theresa couldn't keep her eyes off you either."

"No. More weirdness," Frankie acknowledged. "She made me feel very uncomfortable." Frankie frowned, "there was something... I don't know, familiar about her. Like I'd met her before?"

"Well, maybe you have," she elbowed her with a grin, "one of those drunken educational one-nighter's with older women in your youth maybe?"

Frankie huffed. "Not." She paused, scanning her memory, "no, I don't know. Probably just looks like someone." She waved her hand dismissively, "anyway, I'm pooped. And I don't want to think about it anymore. Just bloody hope we've run into the odd set in the village. It's a big enough place, hopefully we'll find the normal folks soon." Frankie sank into the sofa at the other end and grabbed the remote. She patted the seat between her legs, "what are you doing all the way over there? Come and lie on me bumpkin. Let's country veg."

Chapter 7

"Oh, Rachel!" Frankie groaned.

"Sssshhh.. go back to sleep."

Frankie raised her head off the pillow and squinted at the clock, "for God's sake, it's nine o'clock on a Sunday morning, what are you doing?" She watched Rachel as she went through the wardrobe in search of something to wear.

"Going to church."

"Church? Are you mad?"

"No. Go back to sleep." Rachel took out a shirt and looked at it contemplatively.

"You haven't been to church since you were seven. And you don't have an itchy suit to wear. Come back to bed," Frankie pouted and held her arms out.

"No. I promised the vicar."

"Oh, for heaven's sake, he's not going to remember that! You were in a field, he didn't know what else to say." Frankie pushed the bedding off her body to reveal her nakedness and rolled on her side towards Rachel.

"I don't care, I'll feel guilty if I don't go. And that's not going to work," she leant over the bed and ran her finger lightly down Frankie's body, "however gorgeously tempting it might be."

"Oh here we go, you can take the girl out of the Catholic school, but you can't take the Catholic school out of the girl."

"Whatever. You won't change my mind. But I'll get the newspapers on the way back." She kissed Frankie's forehead, "and then we'll read them in bed. Or... not." She grinned and bent down to suck Frankie's bottom lip into her mouth.

"Aaaghh you can't do that!" Frankie hung her arms round Rachel's neck and tugged her down.

"Oh yes I can. Go back to sleep. And dreeeeaam about me." She kissed her forefinger and placed it on Frankie's lips, pushing her down again.

"Be quick?" Frankie pleaded.

"Quick as I can. See you later."

"Bye. I'm dreaming already…" Frankie said lazily as she rolled over and snuggled back under the duvet.

Rachel crept down the stairs and took a last check that she was presentable. Any occasion where a skirt was needed was both exceptional and uncomfortable as far as she was concerned, so it had better be a good sermon. Satisfied that she was acceptably attired, she stepped out and started walking up towards the church. As the bells rang out and the sun shone, she actually felt very good and she was pleased with her commitment. She strolled along the lane thinking that actually this was kind of a good way to integrate; to show some respect for the local church and its flock. Yes. A good, responsible way to show a sense of community. "Well done you," she thought as she took in the prettiness of the stone cottages again, so beautifully kept. But then, as she wandered further, she started to feel as if there was something that didn't feel quite right —what was it though? She looked around. Back down the street behind her and then up ahead. And it suddenly struck her that there didn't seem to be anybody else making their way to the center of the village. Slightly perturbed, she strode on past the library and then the graveyard. Odd— there didn't seem to be anybody up by the church itself either. The bells still rang out, but the place looked deserted. Rachel walked up the path to the door. Not only was the church not open, but the door was bolted and barred with a heavy wooden plank. She shook the handle, but it was firmly shut. She turned and looked both ways along the street again. Not a single person in sight. Shading her eyes, she looked up towards the top of the bell tower, but there was simply nothing and no-one to be seen. Approaching the notice board, she looked for any sign that might tell her she was too early, but there was nothing on it at all. Exasperated, she decided to ask at the shop.

"Morning Rachel," Ian called out as she came in. It was comforting that he'd remembered her name.

"Morning Ian." She approached the counter, "I don't suppose you know what time the service starts at the church do you?"

"The church!" Ian chuckled, "Lord love you, there hasn't been a service at the church for over fifteen years."

Rachel frowned.

47

"No, 'twas locked up years ago." Ian continued with a wry smile.

"But the vicar… ?"

"Aaah, well, strictly speaking, he's not a vicar." Ian looked uncomfortable.

"What do you mean? He's either a vicar or he's not."

"Well if you put it that way, then he's not."

"He's not?" She hadn't actually expected that confirmation.

"No. Truth is, we just call him the vicar because of the way he dresses and er…" Ian coughed, "…and all that."

"But the bells…?"

"It's a recording. Lots of people in the village like the bells, so they recorded the bell ringers back in 1984 and now they play the tapes."

"Of course. Makes perfect sense." Rachel threw her hands up in the air, "I'll just get the papers then."

"Right you are me duck." He was clearly completely oblivious to her sarcasm, "we have them there croysaints on a Sunday too, if you're partial."

She looked at him blankly, "croysaints?"

"Yes. It's a kind of French pastry. From France," he explained seriously, "I think it's made with butter. And pastry."

"You mean a croissant?" Her amusement at his pronunciation relaxed her mood.

"That'll be it," he replied, a little grumpy at her correction.

Rachel winked at him and headed into the store, where her confusion over the church returned. She felt disturbed. She couldn't get her head round this. Why had the vicar, even if he wasn't the vicar, asked her if she was going to be there on Sunday if there hadn't been a service for years? She collected the papers and a couple of 'croysaints' and turned to head back to the counter, almost knocking into Grace Maddox as she wheeled round.

"Grace!" Rachel hadn't seen her since she'd shown them round the house.

"Hello Rachel, how are you?"

"Oh, dear what an earth have you done?" Rachel looked in alarm at her domelike chest. It was either very heavy padding or a bizarre cage-like structure.

"Oh, 'tis nothing," Grace was distinctly uncomfortable under Rachel's gaze, "'tis just... um, jogger's nipples."

Rachel laughed; she couldn't help herself. Apparently relieved by her reaction, Grace laughed too.

"I know it looks very strange, but it's so painful when my clothes rub against them."

"Oh I can imagine," Rachel nodded sympathetically. "So you're still living in the village then?"

"Oh, yes. Up in Beany Way. How are you settling in?"

"Fine, getting to know our way around. Just found out about the church being closed though. Bit of a shock."

"There's a Baptist Church in Lower Stoughton," offered Grace helpfully, "otherwise it's Badbury."

"Ok, thanks for that." Rachel got the impression she wasn't going to learn anything more from Grace, "nice to see you. Steady on the the jogging now, eh?."

"Oh, I won't be jogging for a while. My nipples need a rest."

Still smiling, Rachel approached the counter, determined not to let this go.

"Ian, is there any other, I don't know... event or something else going on at the church on a Sunday?"

"Not as I'm aware."

"Mmm. Is there any event anywhere in the village on a Sunday?"

Ian fell silent.

"There is, isn't there?" she pressed him.

He nodded, relenting.

"Would the vicar be there?"

"He would."

"So what is it?"

Ian went quiet again as he contemplated his answer, "don't know as I can tell you."

"Ok. Ok. Well, when I bumped into 'the vicar' in the week, he said 'see you on Sunday' and I thought he meant in church," she explained, "so you see my predicament, the vicar's invited me somewhere and I don't know where it is," she raised her eyebrows and shrugged, "so what do I do?"

Ian contemplated again. "The Club." He ventured finally.

"The Club?"

"That's all I'm saying."

"Somebody else was talking about a club." Rachel pondered as she held Ian's eyes. Disappointingly his expression stayed steady despite the weight she put behind her stare.

"Tell you what, if I say the right club, you nod, right?"

"Fair enough."

"Ok. Residents Club?... Church Club?... Sports Club?... Film Club?... Dance Club?" Ian remained expressionless, "Bowling Club? Chess Club? Pudding Club?..." Still no response. "Let me see, what's really villagey... Oh, Hunt Club? Riding Club?" She started to feel frustrated, "oh, I don't know Ian, Farmers Club?... ah," she snapped her fingers at her inspiration, "Goats Club?" She looked at Ian hopefully, but he remained expressionless. "I give up. What is it?"

"Can't tell you, Rachel, you'll have to speak to the vicar."

Rachel sighed, "Oh alright." She picked up her papers, irritated now, and turned to leave. "Vicars and Tarts Club?" she threw back at him. There was a flicker in his eyes and his cheeks coloured slightly, but he shook his head.

"I think that was close Ian." Rachel winked cheekily at him as he smiled coyly, "but I guess that's as much as I'm going to get right? Fair enough." Rachel acknowledged his raised hands as a sign that he had given as much as he could and left the shop, mentally adding two and two to make at least five.

Chapter 8

It was the perfect sunny Sunday and the breeze against her legs helped to cool her down, but was also invigorating. The smells of freshly cut grass, crocuses and honeysuckle mingled and filled her nostrils as she rode, and her ears were filled with a sound like rushing water. She quickened her pace and flicked her riding crop against the Headmaster's flank as he whinnied softly in mild objection.

"Come on boy," she urged as she rose in the saddle and fell again, rose and fell. She flicked the riding crop again, harder this time and moved up a gear, hearing her own breath now in shorter, harder gasps. The Headmaster was panting too.

"Keep going boy," her teeth gritted in determination as she neared the finish line. "Come on, now, faster!" The Headmaster bucked and groaned beneath her, "that's my boy, that's my boy, ooooooh, yesssssss…." She dropped her head as her thighs gripped him and then relaxed.

"Bloody hell Theresa, take it easy, I've got welts all down my left thigh," the Headmaster winced and examined his injuries, "I mean, fair play to you, it was a cracking ride, but my wife's going to have kittens."

Theresa breathed in deeply and sighed, ignoring his objections; she had her own complaint to make, "you weren't really with me there," she said, pouting.

"Well, no. Maybe not as I should've been. To tell the truth, having those women around makes me nervous. We've never had to worry about people sniffing about before."

"Mmm, though the chances of them coming over here are pretty slim."

"Yeah, but all the same..." A groaning noise rose out of the bushes a few feet away.

"Shall we join them?" asked Theresa.

"You go ahead, I'm going back in."

"Chicken!" She laughed and tossed her hair back luxuriously, looking down at him through stray strands that evidenced her own abandon. She felt strong and wild. She was disappointed in his lack of response to her desire.

"Maybe, but I'm not clucking mad enough to keep taking risks out here."

Theresa pecked him on the cheek and rose to her feet. She wore riding boots and a single leather strip around her waist—and nothing else. The leather band had a series of loops and attachments and she slotted the riding crop back into place. She bent over and untied the Headmaster's ankle straps to release him from the stakes that had been driven into the ground over a decade ago. Then took off his handcuffs.

"Cheers," he said, as he sat up and took another look at the deep red streaks on his leg, "no public swimming pools for a week then," he leered up at her and she held out her hand to pull him up,

"I like to leave my mark," she said, handing him his leather chaps, "I'll catch you later." She slapped him playfully on the butt and strode off enthusiastically towards the groaning sounds. Ducking under the cascading branches of a weeping willow, she joined the other group, laying herself down lazily on the grass and watching The Floosy, who was pressed up against the tree's trunk, kissing Sue. Doug, Roy and the Master watched, but the action was clearly at its end. Theresa felt vaguely disappointed that she hadn't been there a little earlier. The five of them joined her where she lay. They were all relaxed and were silent for a while. The Floosy sighed deeply, when she spoke it sounded like she felt obligated, she was clearly very tired.

"So, How's the progress? With them..." she nodded over towards Main Street on the other side of the field, too exhausted to finich the sentence.

"I gave one of them a bottle of gin when she came in the other day, but I'm pretty sure she hasn't tried it." Theresa twisted the riding crop in her hand contemplatively.

"I vote we start a Chase."

"Digger, you always vote for a Chase."

Digger raised his eyebrows, which instantly disappeared into his hairline. He was still smarting from being given his First Refusal. He knew who was behind it and he was sure he'd eventually get even.

"Actually..." Theresa spoke slowly, "that's not such a bad suggestion."

"Even though they're lesbians?" The Floosy bellowed.

"Of course," Digger piped up, "all the better, they need a good seeing to."

"Oh, for Christ's sake Digger, grow up." Theresa scolded him.

"So what are you suggesting?" The Master propped himself up on an elbow and sucked on his corn straw.

"Well, we could set up a 'bi-polar' attack," Theresa was pleased with her brainwave.

"What's manic depression got to do with it?" asked the Master, looking confused.

Theresa tutted exasperatedly as Digger piped up,

"Oh, I gets ya," he said excitedly, "an Arthur or Martha Chase - I'd be up for that!"

"There's a revelation," Theresa rolled her eyes, "but that's the idea, yes." She tapped her lip thoughtfully, "we'll need to be really careful about it and probably have approaches coming in from a number of directions, but I think we could give it a go."

The Master nodded, "ok, so who'll be the Beagles?"

"I'll be one," she could feel Roy's eyes on her, "and I think Lisa would be a good second. As for the men, let's see..."

"I'll be first and Stan can be second... he's a good sniffer."

Theresa closed her eyes despairingly, "not this time Digger."

"But I…"

"No!" Theresa snapped, "you've already caused enough problems with Paul's wife."

Digger leapt to his feet, angrily. He stabbed his finger at Theresa. "You please yourself, but I can guarantee satisfaction an' there's not many as could say that. But 'ave it your own way an' I'll try not to say I told you so."

He glared at Theresa and then stomped off, his tackle swaying like a pendulum as he marched across the field.

Theresa shook her head. "Roy will you have a word once he's calmed down."

Roy nodded.

"Ok. Then for the men, I think David and, let me see... Gazz."

"Isn't Gazz a bit wet behind the ears, old chum?" piped up The

Floosy, distractedly. She was watching the diminishing figure that was her husband, stomping his way across the meadow.

"Uh, huh, but I think that'll be to his advantage. They're not going to be offended by him. His naivety will get him off the hook," Theresa paused, "of course the next question is which one. Has to be Rachel in my opinion."

She felt the weight of Roy's stare again. "Well, Frankie's only here weekends, so I guess Rachel is right?" he said, though he sounded reluctant.

Theresa nodded positively.

"Yeah, ok, we'll make Rachel the primary target," he kept his eyes on her as he said it.

"Hang on, what do you mean by primary?" asked Theresa anxiously.

"Just that if Frankie gets caught in the crossfire and… responds, then we can switch." Roy said lightly as he fiddled absently with his cat of nine tails.

"No. We stick to Rachel. A clear target, no messing about. We can focus better if it's just her." She stared adamantly at Roy.

Roy looked hard back at her and nodded as if he had just confirmed something in his mind.

"Will you brief?" asked the Master.

"Yes. I'll hold a meeting tomorrow evening," replied Theresa, "I'll let you know if there are any problems and what the plan of action will be."

"Good," the Master said with finality, "now that's sorted, does anyone fancy a quick one over my bonnet?"

Frankie's breathing was fast and loud, she lay back on the pillow, feeling her heart beat so rapidly she thought it might burst. "Oh my god I love it when you do that."

Rachel looked up at her with a massive grin on her face, pushing aside the papers that were strewn on the bed, "that's the only news I need today." She let out a contented sigh and rested her head against Rachel's inner thigh, listening to her breath and feeling happy.

"You need to patent your tongue. Or bottle it."

Rachel laughed, "what and pickle it in a jar at the Darwin exhibit?"

"No, alright, well just write down some instructions for posterity." Frankie sighed deeply again.

"I need coffee—and foooood." Rachel lifted herself on her elbows. "I'm going to fix us some breakfast." She held Frankie's hand in hers and kissed it.

"I love you," Frankie whispered the words as she gazed into Rachel's eyes,

"I know," Rachel grinned, "now foooood. I'm starving! I've already exercised some parts of me... AND I've been to *not* church this morning. I need fuel before I put some more miles on the clock."

Rachel stood up and stretched her naked body, loving the feel of the sunlight that streamed in.

"Hold it there," Frankie looked at her adoringly, "just while I gaze at the woman that feeds me in bed... *and* feeds me in bed. Hmmm... I'm so lucky."

"Yeah, you are. But today I'm not feeding you in bed because I need a feast. You'll have to get up." Rachel pulled on a pair of sweats and a t-shirt. "Rest. Come down in half an hour and it will all be ready." She kissed Frankie deeply, her tongue entwining hers.

"Mmmm you taste good."

"Yeah. I taste of you. And if I wasn't so hungry, I'd eat more."

Rachel drew back and headed down the two flights of stairs, feeling happy. She whistled as she reached the bottom steps and glanced towards the front door as a passing figure caught her eye. She only just glimpsed whoever it was as they dashed past; was it Doug? And she could have sworn he was wearing chaps? For a second she debated running to the front window to see if she could catch another look, but her hunger was pressing and anyway, she reasoned, he would almost certainly be out of sight by the time she got there. So instead she turned left and headed into the kitchen to gather together the ingredients for a luxury brunch. As she started to cook, after ten minutes of preparation, she felt Frankie sneak up behind her and fold her arms round her waist. Leaning back against her, Rachel sighed, "you're early. It's not ready yet."

"I know, but I couldn't stand being away from you any longer."

"Mm. I can understand that." She turned in her arms to face her and ran the tip of her tongue across Frankie's lips.

"Maybe we could have a starter?"

Rachel laughed, "you're so greedy. You already had a starter."

"Hm. Well, my palate needs refreshing before the main course." Frankie eased her hand down and slipped it inside Rachel's sweat pants, "how about yours?" Rachel responded to the pressure from Frankie's fingers and leaned back, "oh yeah, you're definitely ready for some inter course activity."

As they sat at the kitchen table an hour later, Rachel fed back the story of her morning and the strange situation with the church.

"So let me get this straight. The vicar is not a vicar, the church is not a church and there's some sort of secret club that he invited you to, but he didn't tell you where or when?" Frankie placed her coffee cup down, "and this is the best breakfast *ever*," she said as she sliced into the perfect fried egg on her plate

"You always say it's the best breakfast ever. And yes, that about sums it up. So weird."

Rachel flicked absently through The Sunday Times Style magazine as she responded to Frankie's question, "it's really bloody weird actually. There's definitely something odd going on. Do you think it's the same Club they were talking about the other day? What do you think? Some sort of strange religious sect?" Rachel looked up from her magazine, "or something satanic?"

"Oh, come on Rachel. I know it's a bit odd, but this is a little village with thatched cottages populated by middle-class families and farmers. Satanic rites are hardly likely to be on the agenda at the village hall, are they? Tell me you're not serious," Frankie chuckled.

"No, I am. I mean think about it," Rachel counted the points on her fingers as she reeled them off, "firstly, the vicar's not what he says he is. Secondly, the church is closed up in a way that suggests it's been shunned by the entire population here. Thirdly, I catch the postmistress, the so-called 'vicar' and a goat doing unspeakable things in a copse..."

"Rachel, you didn't catch them!"

"But I could have done," Rachel wagged her finger at Frankie seriously, "who knows what they were doing in those bushes. And anyway, I have a final and irrefutable piece of proof." Rachel paused for effect. "I will have—and I quote—a devilish time addressing issues that have thus far been kept secret from me." She nodded and tapped the magazine on the table in front of her, "it says so in my Shelly Von Strumpet horoscope for this week."

"Oh, you silly cow," Frankie slapped her playfully, "you actually had me going for a minute there." She picked up her pastry, "lovely croysaint," she winked at Rachel, "see what I did there? I'm picking up the local lingo already. A croysaint will never be a croissant again."

"Mmmmm... loving that sexy village accent, much more seductive than a French one." Rachel became contemplative, "I wish you didn't have to go back down there."

"Yeah, I know baby," Frankie reached over and touched her hand, "but I don't feel like I can afford not to right now."

"I know, I know." Rachel pouted, "you're not... you know." She stuck out her bottom lip like a tearful child,

"What?" Frankie shook her head bemused,

"You know... interested again?" A meek little voice.

"Oh, for Christ's sake!" Frankie threw the half eaten croissant down on her plate, "this is too much. It's not easy living *effectively* on my own down there you know."

"Okay, okay." Rachel put her hands up defensively, "don't go spacky, I'm sorry, okay?"

Frankie looked at Rachel crossly, "Just leave it out, okay? I'm not, *for the last time*, interested in Sally. She's offered to put me up, which is a very friendly thing to do under the circumstances." Frankie waved her hand between the two of them to indicate their relationship, "so let's just be grateful and stop all this nonsense."

"Yeah," Rachel looked down guiltily, "I'm sorry."

"Let's not talk about London anymore today, right? It just spoils our time together."

"That's it, I won't say another word. Let's forget all that."

A little awkward silence fell between them.

"Tell you what," Rachel piped up brightly, "let's go for a walk across the fields, get some fresh air."

"Do the country bumpkin bit you mean?"

"Yeah, let's get in touch with nature."

"Steady on now, don't get carried away."

Roy lay his head back on his arm and flicked distractedly with his free hand at the long grass that was tickling his thigh. The sunlight felt good on his body. He loved Sundays in the meadow like this. The ultimate freedom. He rubbed his chin thoughtfully and glanced over at the Master, who also was leaning against a fallen tree trunk. He appeared equally contemplative. Roy decided to broach what was on his mind; the incomers. "I think we should go for both of them."

The Master looked lazily over at him and nodded.

"You mean the incomers." The Master's immediate understanding was satisfying to Roy, he clearly had the same subject on his mind. That meant they were on the same wavelength, which gave Roy the boldness he needed to present his case.

"If we set up one of them and keep the other in the dark, we take a risk the other one gets suspicious. If what's her name... Rachel?" The Master nodded, leaning forward and listening more intently, "... if Rachel joins us, she might give on to the other one. But if the other one... Frankie?... if she's been not up for it, she'll think the other one's gone mad and cause trouble."

The Master scratched at the stubble on his chin, deep in thought. Roy watched him, patiently waiting for his point to sink in. He was pleased he'd managed to keep the Master back to address this problem. There had been no takers for his bonnet offer and gradually the members had all drifted off, back to their Sunday roasts.

"It would be better to bring them both in," the Master was pensive, but firm, "you're right."

"I knew you'd see that. Obviously there's no guarantee they'll sign up for this, but at least we'll know about both at once." He looked slyly at the Master, measuring his effectiveness by the reaction on the older man's face.

"Yes, but if the one on her own doesn't come in, we just bring in Doctor Taylor. Get her sorted."

"Ah, but that's assuming we know in time to get Taylor in. What if she slips through our fingers before we know there's a problem?" He could see he was having an impact now, so he hurried on. "I mean think about it. Say we go on Theresa's suggestion. Reel in the red-headed one, leave the other one in the dark... if she comes along, all well and good and she might lead us to the blonde. If she doesn't join, she'll influence the blonde and we'll have no chance with her either. Get it?"

"Mm," the Master then threw a probing stare at Roy, "sure this is about the situation at hand and not anything else?"

The question momentarily threw Roy off guard. "What else could it be?" Roy put his hands up innocently and held The Master's stare. He felt blood rising and fought to maintain calm.

"I mean, you know *The Rule*, Roy," the Master emphasised the two words, "it's at the heart of our ethos. 'All For One And One For All?'"

"Hey," Roy threw his hands up higher in protest, "this is Roy you're talking to here. One of the originals. I was one of the first to fire my musket on that pledge. And I've never waivered on that. Never."

"I get your point. And I agree to a certain extent. And I appreciate you bringing your concerns to me, I know that must have been difficult. But there's a plan in place and we haven't given it a chance yet. We'll leave it as it is for..." The Master stopped speaking abruptly and made a sudden jerk of his head. He looked at Roy and held his finger to his lips as he turned his ear to one side, motioning for him to duck down too. "I think I heard someone say Rachel," he whispered as a crackle sounded out from their left. The two men glanced at each other and the Master swept his hand round to the right, indicating Roy, should follow him. The two picked their way through the long grass, towards the rhododendron bushes, Roy's nine-tails swaying silently by his side. The Master looked back and signaled towards the back of the bushes as the sound of voices carried over to them. Roy nodded in agreement. They heard giggling and the swish of grass underneath—what, two pairs of feet? The men peered through the leafy bush trying for a glimpse of the unwanted visitors.

"Stop it!" Giggling again. "Someone will see us."

"Oh, what, the vicar and his goats?"

The two men shared another glance.

"No, stop it, come on..." More giggling. And then they saw Rachel, stumbling backwards and falling into the grass in a clearing, not thirty feet away. There was a double intake of breath from the two men. Frankie fell on top of Rachel, laughing hard and Roy felt his colour rise. And something else.

"You're wicked!" Rachel rolled Frankie over and knelt above her.

Roy felt a tap on his shoulder and turned to the Master, who mouthed 'over here' and pointed frantically towards a huge boulder behind them. Roy, now on hands and knees, looked back at the women, taking the weight off one hand and moving it towards his groin. He felt another tap on his shoulder, it was more insistent this time and, regretfully, Roy dropped his hand back on the grass and slowly started to move backwards as he caught a final glimpse of the redhead bending down towards the blonde's face.

"We need to get out of here," the Master hissed urgently.

"Why?" Roy whispered back.

"Because they might see us."

"So? We've a right to be out here haven't we?"

Exasperated, the Master looked Roy up and down to make his point.

"Oh. Yeah." Roy had not thought about their state of attire. Two middle-aged butt-naked men with a few leather accessories in a meadow on a Sunday afternoon. "Better make a dignified retreat," he finally whispered in agreement.

"If we back up and crawl over towards the hedge over there, we should make it."

Roy nodded and the two shifted backwards on their hands and knees, before turning and crawling away.

"Did you hear something?" Rachel's head snapped back.

"No."

Rachel rocked back on her knees, "I'm sure I heard something."

"Don't be silly, you're just paranoid." Frankie grabbed at Rachel's t-shirt.

"No, listen, it's a rustling noise."

Frankie groaned with frustration as Rachel suddenly leapt to her feet and strode over towards the rhododendron bush.

"Frankie, quick!" Rachel snapped her fingers urgently.

"What? What? I can't see anything." Frankie stared over Rachel's shoulder, seeing only grass and bushes and a fallen tree trunk in the immediate vicinity.

"No, nor can I now," Rachel paused deliberating on whether to say anything, "but I don't know, I swear..." she paused.

"You swear what?" Frankie was getting irritated.

"Well, it was only a glimpse."

"A glimpse of what for chrissake?"

"Bottoms."

Despite her annoyance at the interruption, Frankie couldn't help but laugh. At that moment she completely adored Rachel's seriousness. "What kind of bottoms? Rabbit's bottoms, squirrel's bottoms?"

"Men's bottoms."

Frankie roared, "right—and what were these bottoms doing? Were they attached to anything? Like men?"

"Oh, ha ha. Frankie, I swear I just saw two men crawling across the grass into the hedge over there." Rachel closed her eyes in recall, "yeah, yeah, definitely two bottoms." Her eyes were still tightly shut, "one of them had some sort of leather strapping on his bum."

"Oh, now you're really taking the piss. Stop it Rachel."

Frankie strode back towards the grass where they'd been laying and picked up her cap, reluctantly giving in to the fact that their moment had been stolen.

"That's mad isn't it?" Rachel glanced back towards Frankie.

"Yeah, that's mad," Frankie nodded firmly.

"You're right. It was probably a..." Rachel struggled for an alternative explanation.

"Flash of sunlight off wet grass? Hallucination? Come on, let's get back."

"Sorry darling, broke the spell didn't I?" Rachel looked forlorn.

"Never mind. There'll be plenty more chances for a roll in the hay." Frankie grabbed Rachel's hand, "and anyway, it might have stopped me here, but a roll between the sheets is still on the cards."

Chapter 9

"Mrs Blair's sick."

"I know… I know Mrs Blair's on your mind, but we have to concentrate on this. We have to make an effort to address this problem, or it'll get out of hand?" Theresa massaged Trevor's massive forearm gently in a sympathetic gesture

"It's bad timing," Trevor paused rubbing his furrowed forehead anxiously, "he's probably got his hand up her, as we speak."

"Yes, but he knows what he's doing, Trevor."

"I know that!" Trevor shrugged her off, irritatedly.

"Calm down Trevor, she's going to be fine. Donald has been a vet for over thirty years, Mrs Blair couldn't be in safer hands."

"It does my head in when this happens." Trevor paced. "It's a dodgy procedure and Mrs Blair's getting to be an old goat."

"You've got to stop thinking about it, Trevor. Look, spend a few minutes talking to me about the incomers and it'll take you mind off it."

"Bad business that, with Grace," he looked rueful.

"But you did your job. You kept the faith." Theresa grabbed his arm again and nodded at him reassuringly, "just like your father before you."

Trevor nodded. "So, what is it I can do for you?"

She came straight to the point, "we're starting a chase. For the redhead."

"Might as well. Need to know don't you?"

"Yeah," Theresa looked up at him, "but I'm worried about Roy."

Trevor shook his head, not comprehending.

"He thinks we should put out a chase on both of them, the blonde as well."

"Yeah?" Trevor responded, quite excitedly, not at all sure what the problem could be with that.

"It won't work that way. We need to focus on one and use her to get the other. It's obvious, but Roy wants to split the chase. I think he's got some weird idea I might be interested in Rachel. The redhead."

"Wait a minute. So are you chasing?"

"Yeah, but only as one of a team. There'll be me, Gazz, David and Lisa."

"Are you?"

"Am I what?"

"Interested in the redhead."

"Don't be ridiculous!" Theresa flapped her hands dismissively, "not in the way Roy thinks anyway, it's strictly business. Club business." Theresa turned away and fiddled absently with a bridle that lay across the stall door. "There's something else," she said it quietly without looking at Trevor, "I think there's something going on between him and the Master." She glanced back at Trevor to make sure she still had his attention, "they stayed out in the field on Sunday after we'd all left. When he got back, his knees were very heavily grass stained." She turned to look fully at Trevor, "and his nine-tails was in tatters."

Trevor shrugged, "All For One?"

"I know, I know, but also Rule seventeen Out In The Open?" she paused, "and he didn't say a thing."

"Well, he might not have had a chance." Trevor offered by way of explanation.

"He's always been absolutely upfront about his dealings, Trevor, He's always told me in advance. This time he's said nothing. Before or after."

Trevor shrugged again, "well, I can't see as it's a real problem. The Master's everybody's, always has been. Maybe Roy didn't see the need."

"Maybe. Anyway, we need to sort out this business with the incomers." Theresa shrugged off her concerns about Roy and the Master, at least temporarily, and moved on to the more important of the issues on her mind, "for now, the Chase will just be with Rachel. But I want you to have a word with Roy, to make sure it stays that way."

Trevor eyed her suspiciously.

"Trevor, don't look at me like that, there's nothing in it for me. It just makes better sense to leave Frankie out of it. Don't you agree?"

"Maybe." He shoved his hands in his pockets, in a gesture that indicated to Theresa he wasn't comfortable with her request. Her mind ticked. She leaned forward, her chin raised, her tongue flicking teasingly at the corner of her mouth.

"There's *nothing* in it, Trevor. I'm only interested from a club perspective," she rubbed his forearms as they remained rigidly by his sides, "I'm still a club girl, Trevor. Totally committed to the club ethos."

Trevor stared down at her, his heart beginning to race. "I have to get back to Mrs Blair. She may have been done by now."

Theresa placed her cheek against his broad chest. "I can hear your heartbeat," she looked up coyly and he struggled to maintain his implacable stare, "I can take your mind off Mrs Blair." Theresa tugged at the belt round his waist. "Speak to him, Trevor? It would be worth it."

"I might," he managed in a tight voice.

"You will," she grinned as she started to snap open the buttons of his fly.

"It was very tasty and I want another one."

Theresa looked up from her paperwork to see Mrs Bentley at the front of the store with Roy. She listened to their conversation, knowing it would progress through the usual pattern.

"Yes, but there isn't another one," Roy explained patiently as she leant dangerously close to his sausage rolls, "you know we only cook once a day Mrs Bentley and all the pecan Danishes went this morning."

She continued to scour the basket for signs of the distinctive lattice tart.

"Please Mrs Bentley, I can assure you there isn't one there." Roy came round the other side of the counter, throwing an exasperated look at Theresa as he did so, "look, come and take a peek at these treacle tarts," he encouraged.

Mrs Bentley, grumbling, followed him to the pre-packed foods. "Not fresh," she said wrinkling her nose.

"Ok. How about I promise to have you a nice fresh pecan Danish—or even two—ready for tomorrow morning?"

Mrs Bentley's nose twitched and he knew he was getting close.

"I could have them delivered, eh?" He smiled cheekily, "send our nice young Carl round to your place in the morning?"

Mrs Bentley's hand quivered on her walking stick and he knew he'd won her round.

"Make sure it's early," she sniffed condescendingly, "and very fresh."

"Oh, he's always fresh, Mrs Bentley," Roy said winking exaggeratedly.

Mrs Bentley tutted and made her way out, shaking her head. Roy watched her go, then walked over to where Theresa was totting up the Post Office takings.

"You spoken to Gazz or any of the others yet?"

Theresa looked up from her numbers.

"Not yet. Been thinking about the best way to start the chase." She went back to her work, expecting Roy to move off. He didn't. He hovered. She looked up again.

"Yes?"

"Nothing, nothing," he wrung his hands, "nothing." He turned to head back to the front of the shop and casually picked a tin up off a shelf as he wandered by, then dawdled alongside it. She watched him, aware he was disturbed and wanting to say something.

"Roy is there something wrong?" Theresa straightened up and looked at him directly.

"No nothing," he paused, "so when are you going to start the chase?"

"I just told you, I don't know. I've been thinking about how to kick it off."

Roy nodded. "Could have a go at the Barn Dance on Saturday?"

"What Barn Dance?" She was irritated now. Nothing went on in the village without Theresa's knowing.

"Grace organised it. Fundraising for the Church."

"Pah." Theresa spat scathingly, "it'll never happen."

"Don't know. It might. Decisions can be overturned."

"The council's refused permission for that proposal for fourteen years. There's no way it'll happen."

"Grace has a plan."

Theresa's eyes narrowed, "what plan?"

"Don't know. Don't know any more than that. But that's why she's organised the dance."

"Why didn't I know about it?"

"You weren't supposed to," Roy said it quietly as if it meant nothing, but he knew it was a red rag to a bull.

"What do you mean, Roy?"

"Just that Grace didn't want you interfering." Roy knew this to be an outright lie. Grace had asked him to hand on information about the event days ago.

"Why? Is she submitting different plans?"

"No, not that I'm aware of. Plan is still to turn it into a swimming pool. Still got a sauna and mini gym and a massage parlour. Even still calling it 'Doing God's Workout' as far as I can remember..." Roy stopped mid-sentence, realizing he'd given the game away.

Theresa stepped out from the Post Office counter. "How long have you known about it?" she demanded angrily, "who's been keeping it from me? Grace... or you?" she stabbed an accusatory finger at him.

"Oh alright it was me," he conceded, slamming his apricots back down on the shelf. The tin wobbled and fell off under the force. Now Theresa knew there was something going on.

"Why?" she demanded.

Roy stared evenly and then pointed at a customer who had just entered the store.

"Afternoon Mr Plimpton," Theresa flicked a look at Roy that told him she would be returning to this subject, "come to update your club pension have you?" The old man nodded, "got your stamp book?"

Alfred handed over the dog-eared book with a shaky hand. Theresa flicked open the pages and grabbed her stamp and ink pad. "Got two carried over from last month?" Theresa looked up and Alfred nodde, "been under the weather have you?"

Alfred Plimpton shook his head, "couldn't get a repeat prescription from Doctor Taylor. No pills. No visits."

Theresa nodded. "I hear Sue's got a busy book this month coming, Alfred, what with the Harvest Festival. You'll need to get your appointments in," she said as she stamped four times on a fresh page.

"Probably end up losin' 'em." Alfred shook his head.

"Well you know you can carry over for up to three months, Alfred. Yours is the stakeholder pension, so you've a right to insist

67

the appointments are kept. It's just whether you're up to six visits in a month?"

"It's all in the lap of the viagra God," said Alfred dramatically, "keepin' it up isn't down to me anymore."

Theresa laughed, "alright, well you're all stamped up, so good luck! And here's your gin quota," she handed over two of the green bottles, "can we help you with anything else?"

"Wish this stuff was still enough to do it for me," Alfred shook his head, "them viagras makes me sneeze. I'll have some Red Bull, Theresa, six-pack." Theresa nodded at Roy, who duly grabbed the pack and took it to the till. "Roy's got it, Mr Plimpton."

Alfred raised his cap and then shuffled off to pay. Theresa watched him out then picked up the phone. "Doctor Taylor please," she stared intently at Roy as she waited for her connection, "Vee? Yes, just had old Plimpton in. He seems to be managing his appointments very well. The scheme relies on only 60% take up to be as profitable as we'd like. Can you sit on his pills, so to speak?" Theresa nodded at the response, "yeah, that should do it. Thanks." Theresa ended the call and marched over to Roy to speak at him. "The Club Pension is the biggest money-spinner we've had yet. I had thirty-seven residents start the scheme in the last month alone. We're going to need a whole street of hookers by the time this lot retire. Which reminds me," she said taking a pencil from behind her ear and grabbing a paper bag to scribble on, "I must make a note to get Lisa to start interviewing for the male prostitute's job." She slotted the pencil back in place and put her hand on her hip. "Now. What's with you, Roy? I can't be doing with all this strange behaviour, so let's be having it." Roy's head dropped and he murmured something she didn't catch. "What? I can't hear you," she said impatiently.

"I feel like I'm losing you."

Theresa rolled her eyes and placed the palm of her hand on her forehead.

"Any chance I can get into your box early?"

Carl, the postman, poked his head round the door, just as Theresa was about to address Roy's problem. She looked at her watch, "oh, go on then. Three minutes early isn't likely to piss anybody off too much. Will you do the rest of the collections on time?"

"Yep, no problem, just want to make up a few minutes to pick Elsa up from school." Carl winked at Roy, "you alright, mate?"

"I'm alright Carl, I'll get your sack," Roy offered.

"Look's a bit glum?" Carl said to Theresa as Roy disappeared into the Post Office.

"Nah, he's alright." Theresa glanced back before addressing Carl again, "you still alright for Sunday?"

"Wild horses wouldn't stop me!" Carl winked and jangled the keys on his belt, "gonna shoot off now and get this post box emptied. Cheers Theresa." He whistled as he sauntered off. She turned back to the post office counter and Roy brushed past with the sack full of parcels, headed for the post van as Theresa watched him. Poor Roy, she thought as she looked on. She knew there was nowhere near a balance in their extra-marital activities. But then, wasn't that his lookout? It wasn't as if she hadn't given him plenty of freedom. He just didn't appear to be that interested. He was more of a voyeur than a participator. Give him a glossy girlie magazine and a warm beer and he was happy as Larry. It wasn't her fault she was the more adventurous. She knew his games with Grace and the Master were a factor of his unhappiness. But she also sensed there might be something deeper. Something she wasn't aware of. Usually his transparency made it easy for her to deal with his little attempts at grabbing her attention. He came back in and held his hand out to her as he approached her now.

"Let's stay in tonight?"

"Oh, Roy," she was genuinely regretful, "I promised the vicar." He dropped her hand instantly.

"You're always on a promise Theresa, but never with me."

She sighed as he stomped off.

"I'm off to see Grace," he threw the statement back at her, "at least she needs me."

Chapter 10

Rachel stood in a queue of four people, patiently waiting to get to the counter. She mused at how the tiny Post Office seemed always to be busy. The store itself was very quiet. She assumed it was because the main shop took the lion's share of the grocery trade. As she passed the time looking around her, she glanced up at the convex mirror that sat in the top corner of the room above the Post Office and caught the eye of the elderly man who stood in front of her. He turned round in her direction.

"I saw you on TV last night."

Rachel glanced behind her to check if he was talking to someone else. Seemingly not.

"What me?" she pointed at herself and looked quizzically at him.

"Yes, 'twas definitely you." He nodded enthusiastically.

"No," she smiled and shook her head, "it wasn't me. What were you watching?"

"The TV." He stated with some finality. He shifted forward in the queue and she followed.

"Well hopefully you enjoyed the show, but it wasn't me." Rachel offered a kindly expression.

"I'm not stupid. 'twas you. You dropping off your empties."

How weird, Rachel was taken aback. "Actually I was dropping off bottles last night at the bottlebank by the school."

"Yeah. See, you was on TV."

Rachel was confused, but before the she could say anything further, the old man had reached the counter and turned to speak to Theresa.

"This month's new club cards in yet?" Rachel heard him ask.

Theresa flicked a look at Rachel.

"Not yet, Nathan, expecting them any time though."

"They never been late before."

Theresa flicked another look at Rachel.

"I know Nathan, but they are this month. Tell, you what, I'll

70

give you a call. Anything else?"

"My gin. And two second class. I've got last month's tapes in the car," Nathan stated as he picked up his change and the distinctive bottle that Rachel recognised. Theresa flicked yet another look at her. She felt uncomfortable and stared down at her t-shirt, fearing an egg stain.

"Hang on to them for now Nathan, I'll call you," she said pointedly.

Nathan held a shaky finger up and directed it at Theresa, "you am behavin' strangely."

"Yes, sorry Nathan. I'm a bit on edge."

Rachel swore she was offering an eye signal to Nathan, who seemed to get the message.

"Oh ah. Now that didn't occur to me." Nathan glanced behind and then put his face closer to the grill and whispered something to Theresa, who responded in similar tones. As he turned to leave he doffed his cap at her, "you look just like her, that Patsy Plaster on Eastenders."

Thirty minutes of Eastenders flew through Rachel's head as she acknowledged his comment. "Well, I'm not her."

"No. See that now." He looked sheepish. "My mistake."

"You're alright," she said as the rewind function in her mind confirmed that Eastenders had not featured a bottle bank scene - and that 'Patsy Plaster' had not been in it either.

"Parkinsons." Theresa nodded in the direction of the exiting Nathan as Rachel stood up to the counter.

"Oh, how awful." Rachel reddened as her previously suspicious mind flooded with guilt.

"Sad," Theresa shook her head, "he used to be a security guard at the old bus depot. It was where the school now is. He often goes down there like he's off to work. Even though it's thirty years since it was pulled down."

"Poor old chap."

"Yeah. Anyway, how are you?"

"Fine! Thank you," Rachel put a small packet on the scales, "need to send that to The States, first class."

They went through the process of establishing the parcel's value and insurance requirements and Rachel added her name and address to the back of the package as they chatted.

"So, you two settled in now?"

"Yeah, you know, lots of boxes still around but we're pretty comfortable now."

"Good. You're on your own in the week aren't you?"

"Afraid so," Rachel passed the packet through and sighed.

"Suppose it gets a bit lonely doesn't it?"

"Well, it does a bit. I've got lots to keep me busy though."

"Have you met any more of your neighbours yet? There are some good sorts around you."

"Yeah, I met Ben opposite. He seems lovely."

"Oh yeah. Everybody loves Ben. He talks like he's a ladies man, but he's a softie. Anyone else?"

"Not yet. Plenty of time though."

"Look, I'm having a Love Honey party on Wednesday, just a bit of fun, do you fancy coming along for a giggle?"

"Um, what's a Love Honey Party?"

"Like Ann Summers. On steroids." Theresa laughed at Rachel's expression, "you'll catch flies like that. Come on, it's a laugh

"Er, yeah, ok, why not." She damned herself for yet again not being quick enough to think of an excuse, "thanks."

"Good," Theresa seemed genuinely delighted, "seven-thirty then."

"Cheers. Do I need to bring anything?"

"No, no. Just yourself, all we need is you."

Rachel nodded and offered a quick wave for a goodbye as an echo of Theresa's response rang like an alarm bell in her head.

Rachel stared at the flickering candle as she sat in the living room and chatted to Frankie on the phone. The room was dark, apart from the singular glow of the flame, and she felt comforted by the warmth of the light and the sound of Frankie's voice. She recounted the conversations she'd had in the Post Office, still cross that she'd gotten roped into the party and ruminating over the old man's odd reference to her on TV. Had there not been so many other little bizarre references and going's on, she probably would have dismissed it. But her mind had begun to obsess over the smallest thing.

"I really think you're being paranoid."

"Do you?"

Frankie echoed Rachel's own concerns about the way her mind was working, "well think about it, Rachel," there was an edge in Frankie's voice and Rachel began to feel aware of how ridiculous she might sound, "she says he's got Parkinsons, he used to work as a security guard—ergo security cameras and tapes—he saw you at the bottle bank because he was there too, then he went home and watched Eastenders last night. Bingo!"

Rachel nodded, suddenly feeling very silly.

Frankie continued, "so you're 'Patsy Plaster' and he saw you on TV last night in Eastenders. Right? He's just a sad old man whose mind is playing games with him."

"Of course you're right."

Rachel laughed at herself as Frankie went on, "and *your* mind is playing games with *you*. So come on. It's just being lonely that's getting to you. You're over-thinking everything. And probably distracting yourself from the job at hand."

"I know. Right again. I'm not exactly making huge progress on the novel am I?"

"No, exactly. And as for the Love Honey party, that's just an opportunity for you to buy us something... interesting."

Rachel giggled. "I'm going to surprise you."

"Too right you are. Can't wait," Frankie breathed, "Mmm, actually this is getting me going."

"Phone sex?" Rachel said breathily.

"Grrrr. Yes... but I can't."

"I can."

"Don't be so cruel, you can't do that and leave me hanging."

"Want a bet?"

"Sally's here."

"Oh."

"Yes, but that's hardly surprising given I'm living in her house is it? She just came in from work."

"Sure. Well, since I've just had the telephone equivalent of a cold shower, I might as well go." Rachel was petulant.

"Oh come on, don't be like that. It's only three days to the weekend. We'll make up for it. With a little help from your friends."

"Hmmm sounds good. Actually, the prospect of this party is getting more attractive by the minute. But moving swiftly on," she broke the electricity between them, trying to distract from her desire, "what else is happening down there?"

"I saw Mum for lunch yesterday," Frankie let the feeling drop too, "that was kind of hard work."

"Is she still upset about the move?" Rachel sensed Frankie's distress.

"Yeah. I can't work it out. She seems so adamantly against it. I don't know… I feel like there's something I'm not getting."

"Well you're moving further away, she's bound to be worried she's not going to see you enough, you just need to give her more assurance. Maybe you should invite her up for the weekend?" Rachel ventured the invitation, despite the slightly sinking feeling she always had when she had to face her 'Mother-In-Law'.

"Maybe. Soon anyway. I do get it, that she thinks I'll be around less, but, I don't know, she's just really, really anxious about it, she tried so hard to stop us buying the place, it seems so over the top. Yesterday she was asking a ton of questions about who we'd met in the village and whether village people were normal."

"Well, she probably doesn't think the village people are normal." Rachel tried to make light of it, "tell her they're not all policeman and Indians and there's no YMCA."

"Yeah," Frankie didn't respond to the humour. "Anyway, we'll have her up for the weekend at some point. Maybe she'll feel better if she can actually see the place. And perhaps if she gets a sense of how quick and easy it is to get to she'll relax a bit."

"She'll be ok. Anyway, best let you go. Can't wait for the weekend. And have I told you lately?"

"No."

"Well I do."

"I love you too babes. Can't wait to see your new toys."

Rachel could literally feel Frankie's grin at the other end of the phone.

"Best stock up on batteries. Alright, darling, speak to you tomorrow."

"Night gorgeous, sweeeet dreams."

Chapter 11

Rachel pulled back the drapes in the front room and let the sun flood in through the horribly unattractive net curtains, left up from the previous owners while they decided what to do about fitting blinds. They were so hideous she faced a daily dilemma not to give in to the impulse to just pull them down. But then the prospect of nosy neighbours looking through the windows as they passed by in the street always stopped her from doing it. She peered up at the sky, which was solid blue above the thatch of the house opposite. It's rich colour as a backdrop to the country view somehow made her feel really good. And she needed to feel really good today. As the shadowy figure of Theresa once again brushed by, momentarily shutting out the early morning light, Rachel bit her lip in contemplation. She knew she was being paranoid and that much of it was down to two things; the absence of another sane individual to talk to during the day—and Frankie was right, too much time to think. Still, there were niggles in her mind about the sequence of little events that had led to her peculiar belief that 'something strange' was afoot. She realised she didn't want this struggle going on in her head, so she was going to have to set about justifying—or blowing apart—this theory with a few discrete enquiries. She watched Theresa bounce up the steps and along the path opposite towards the meadow. Just as she had every morning now for the short time that they'd been in the village. "All perfectly normal, I'm sure," said Rachel to herself as she glanced at her watch and noted the time. She turned towards the kitchen and the hearty breakfast she felt she needed. Twenty minutes later, she scraped the last piece of fried egg onto her fork and smeared it with tomato sauce, fully enjoying the decadence of her weekday fry-up. She gazed out of the window, waiting. "Right on time…" she mumbled as the vicar descended the steps. She looked at her watch, picked up her pencil and scribbled in her notepad. "Postmistress in at five-thirty, vicar and goats out at five-fifty," she murmured as she scanned back up the column from the previous days' entries. Within a couple of minutes either side, she had made the same note on the previous three weekdays. Rachel tapped the pad absently with her pencil. Something or nothing? Did it really matter if Theresa met the vicar every day? After all, it's a free world. Who was she to question it? Maybe Roy and Theresa had an open marriage? And so what if they did? She closed the pad and took her plate into the kitchen to wash up. She stared out into the back garden at the congregating birds lining up to take a peck at the seed basket she'd hung from the magnolia tree; her hands were absently going through the motions of washing the dishes, but her mind was completely occupied with other matters. The evening loomed. She'd never actually been to an Ann Summers party, although she'd heard plenty of stories about the antics, so a Love Honey one sounded like diving in at the deep end— she'd preferred the anonymity of a shop, or even better online, if she was honest. She wondered what the atmosphere was going to be like—and whether she would have the courage to buy anything if she did take a fancy to something. It wasn't as if she was amongst friends and therefore relaxed enough to share the joke, or the secrets. Though both she and Frankie were always determined not to judge others, they knew they were often judged themselves. Maybe she could mail order it afterwards. And then there was Theresa. She just couldn't shake the nagging feeling that she had invited her with some purpose. Of course, it could just be that her secrets would be of particular fascination to the others—she was pretty much bound to be the only dyke. It would make the evening a bit more entertaining for them all, wouldn't it? Rachel's heart began to sink as she became more distressed about the prospect. "Oh sod it!" she said to the dish cloth as she threw it into the sink. Wiping her hands and feeling annoyed at her stress levels over the party, she resolved to concentrate on her fact-finding mission. She picked up her wallet and jacket, grabbed her keys and headed out of the front door. She locked it behind her and turned to walk up the street, catching sight of Ben in his kitchen opposite. Seeing her, he turned and grinned, flicking the v's at her. She laughed and flicked them back. He opened the window.

"You haven't invited me back yet. Bloody rude if you ask me."

"I can't bake!"

"Any bastard excuse not to be nice to me right?"

"Oh alright, come over in an hour." She gave way.

"Don't be too effing enthusiastic. I take milk and sugar."

"Good job I'm going to the shop then. See ya later."

He nodded and flicked the v's again.

"I met old Nathan yesterday." Rachel placed her basket on the counter.

"Oh yes?" said Ian amiably, "nice old chap Nathan." He took Rachel's loaf and wrapped it in tissue.

"Yes. Bit fixated with his TV though, isn't he?" She watched Ian's sponge wobbling like a grey jelly on top of his head as he bobbed about under the counter looking for the sellotape.

"You might say that. Watches it nigh on twenty-four hours a day. Ah, gotcha," Ian held the sello dispenser up in triumph. "He's a master of surveillance, now. Though it's all voluntary. He don't get paid for it you know."

Rachel nodded, like she understood. She struggled to think of a question that might get some more information without giving her game away, but she needn't have bothered, Ian was in full swing.

"Twenty-four cameras he's got now. And he uses six TV monitors. All supplied by Bishops." Ian pointed to the dingy little shop over the road with its rather pathetic window display consisting of a few bits of aerial equipment, a couple of dusty plastic flowers and an old fifteen-inch portable.

"Sounds a bit sophisticated for them," said Rachel laughing as she hoiked her thumb over at the shop.

"Oh don't you be fooled by the outside, my love, they're real technofoals in there." He winked at her, "did all the wiring up at the manor for the TV studio. Up to the minute stuff that is."

"Technophobes," she corrected him. He shuffled his teeth, a sign she had irritated him.

"Foals, phobes, all the same to me."

"So where are all these cameras then?" she asked, trying to pursue him while he was in flow. She watched his face as he slipped his dentures back and forth. It seemed she had blown it.

"That'll be all then? Fourteen pounds all bar a penny love." He placed his hand out and she took the notes from her pocket.

"Where does he live then, Nathan?"

Ian glanced over his glasses at the till as he concentrated on her change. "Blatchett's Farm. Up past Nolly Hill." Ian called a greeting out to a customer as they walked in the door and took Rachel's empty basket from the counter, placing it carefully underneath. She'd learnt his foibles now, his deliberately slow movements were another hint. He wasn't intending to be giving her any more today.

"Thanks, Ian." Rachel picked up her shopping and turned for the door, "oh dammit, forgot the milk," she grabbed a pint from the fridge by the door, "got Ben coming over for a coffee." She placed it on the counter

"Good old Ben. Everyone loves him," he said as he rung it up.

"Oh by the way, how long's he had Parkinsons?"

"Parkinsons?" Ian frowned, "Ben?"

"No, Nathan."

"No no, not old Nathan. Not as I know of anyways."

"Right, sorry, I must have been confused, I thought he wasn't well."

Ian shifted his teeth around with greater speed, realizing he might have fallen for a trap. Rachel felt proud of herself for getting what she needed. She could play the game too.

"Thanks again Ian," she said as she headed for the door.

Ben sat at the small breakfast counter and watched Rachel as she pushed the lid down on the cafetiere. She looked up at him.

"Why weren't you at the party on Sunday?"

"Cos I'm a miserable bastard."

She poured the coffee and pushed the jugs of milk and sugar towards him, "I know. But everybody loves you."

"What?" he had a twinkle in his eye.

"Nothing."

He let it drop, knowingly and changed the subject back to his absence. "I told you, I don't get involved. Did you have fun?"

"It was… weird."

"Yep."

"We thought we would be the shock factor."

"Well yeah, never seen two such ugly women."

"You're always so good for my ego."

"Always a pleasure. So I guess you thought it would be difficult because you're lesbians? Talking of which, you two look good naked together."

"What the fuck?" she laughed. For some reason, she wasn't offended by him.

"When you're in your bedroom. I know you stand in front of the window for me deliberately," he winked at her, a cheeky grin on his face.

"You dirty bugger. I'm going to close the curtains next time."

"Oh maaan. Shot myself in the foot."

"Seriously there are some strange characters. Are there really two prostitutes in the village? It kind of feels that maybe we were being wound up."

"To answer both your questions, yes there are. And yes there are."

"Oh My God. So what's it all about?"

He shook his head, "honestly, I don't get involved. Best to stay out of it."

"Best to stay out of what?"

He shook his head again, "have you been down to the brewery yet?"

"You're not going to give me anything are you?"

"Best to…"

"Yeah, yeah, best to stay out of it, I know. You're so frustrating."

"You should go take a look at the brewery sometime. It's interesting. But then I'm a beer man, so I suppose it would be. And then there's the gin. Are you into gin?"

"Not in a major way, but I'll have one now and again."

"Don't hold much store by it myself." He gave her a long hard look and tapped his finger on the table, "it's not all that. The gin, whatever they say. But anyway, check the brewery out, take a look at its history. And if you want to know about any of the pubs around here, I'm your man. For starters, if you take a bike ride out along Folly Way, you'll get to The Hangman's Noose after about two miles. They do great pub grub."

Rachel enjoyed the lightness of the conversation as Ben listed his favourite watering holes and their merits. It felt like a relief to chat with someone who didn't seem to be involved in intrigue or mystery and had no apparent agenda, other than to enjoy a drink and some banter with a neighbour. As he finished his coffee, she realised they'd passed a happy hour together without her feeling like she needed to analyse anything. In some ways, it threw light on the bizarreness of everyone else. He stood and took the cups out to the kitchen.

"Right gotta go and get my rods up Angela's flue. It's a hard life." He patted her on the shoulder as he passed by towards the door, "life's too short to get hung up on anything, just chill out and smell the roses." He opened the door, "and leave the light on next time you're in the bedroom." He poked his head back round before he pulled it shut, "kidding."

"Oh my God, they're crutchless!" raucous laughter filled the room next door as Theresa ushered Rachel along the hall.

"Sorry, we started without you." Theresa laughed at the noise coming from the sitting room, "can I get you a drink—loosen you up a bit? I've made a special cock…tail," Theresa winked at her as she separated the syllables with deliberation, "it's called Cock-a-doodle-do-it. With gin and egg nog and a large piece of cucumber." She grinned encouragingly.

"Hmm… probably not my thing." Rachel felt herself cringe inside, thinking it might not just be the drinks that wasn't her thing. She wondered if she would be able to cope with all the male anatomy jokes. She steeled her resolve, forced a smile and handed over her bottle of Chablis, "maybe I'll just have a glass of this."

"Of course, no problem, go on through and I'll get you a glass." She pointed towards the front room and, feeling some trepidation, Rachel pushed the door gently and poked her head round it.

"It *does* taste like chocolate!" screeched someone as Rachel clocked Lisa, her fingers covered in brown sticky gel. Rachel smiled at her—and then felt her face freeze. She'd thought it had been a women only thing.

"Hey don't mind me."

She realised she must have been staring. A young, cool looking guy was lounging back on an inflatable armchair.

"I'm just along for the ride," he grinned leerily as he put his Bud to his lips and took a healthy glug. There was something oddly familiar about him.

"You've met Gazz then." Rachel jumped as Theresa came in behind her and patted her bottom. "In you go," she said squeezing past and grabbing Rachel's hand. "Brief pause while we make introductions. Rachel, this is Gazz, my son."

Ah that explained the familiarity, she thought as the dude held his hand up in acknowledgement,

"He's been granted temporary girls night access by way of the family relationship," she explained. "You know Lisa," the sticky hand waved briefly in acknowledgement, "and our Floosy of course, then there's .. and I think you've also met… Sue." Rachel nodded at the other village prostitute, "and finally our party Mistress, Lois." Rachel smiled at the grinning face of a very large woman with a black vibrator in her hand.

"Pleased to have you," said Lois wrinkling her nose.

"Likewise," responded Rachel without thinking - and then blushed.

"Ooooh that's the spirit," screeched Lois, seizing on her inadvertant double entendre as the room broke into tittering. "Now sit you down there," she said pointing to one end of a large sofa with the now spinning vibrator.

Rachel took a large gulp of her wine and picked her way between a strap-on belt, a feather tickling stick, a blinfold, some bondage chains and various other items that littered the floor.

"Mind yourself, don't want you slipping on my double ended one," shrieked Lois as the room erupted into raucous laughter again. Rachel took another large gulp of wine and silently prayed for drunken oblivion or at least a sense of humour transplant, "made it!" she said woodenly as she sank into the sofa next to Lisa.

"Now, just to bring you up to speed," Lois flicked the switch on the vibrator and set it buzzing manically at its highest setting to applause and giggles, "we're in the 'Suck It And See' phase of the evening, just to break the ice and get everybody in the mood. We all get a little taster of one of our products." She nodded at everyone for approval and they all nodded in return. "Now let me see, Lisa's been getting her fingers into the chocco body gel, right Lisa?""

"Mmm, delicious…" Lisa offered the open jar to Rachel and gave a friendly, reassuring wink. Rachel smiled as she declined politely.

"And Floosy's got the crutchless panties on for a quick try out."

Rachel held her breath and watched in horror as the Floosy stood up before her and flipped her skirt up. Screaming with laughter, she bellowed, "don't worry old chum, trying them on over my shorts," as the flimsy fabric shot up and revealed the black and red lacy panties with their gaping gusset stretched unattractively over a pair of green lycra running shorts. Rachel knocked back the rest of the wine and held her glass towards Theresa, even though her head was already spinning. At this point she wasn't sure if it was the effects of the wine or the Floosy's potentially horrific flashing. Theresa, smiling calmly, took the glass.

"Any more for any more?" she asked. With no takers, she headed out to get Rachel another drink.

"Sue has been experimenting with a large Wiggly!" Rachel almost couldn't bare to look, "but quite frankly," Lois said in a stagey, conspiratorial way, "she's had problems controlling it!"

With which Sue launched a rubbery looking willy shaped item towards Rachel. It landed with a slap in Rachel's lap, to more raucous laughter.

"It's really just a bath-time toy," Lois explained, "it's a water-filled rubber that just slips through your hand when you try to hold it," she gave an encouraging gesture to Rachel, "go on try and hold it."

Rachel gingerly picked up the rubber cylinder and almost had a heart attack as it slipped straight out of her grip and bounced like a large floppy donger onto the floor. She couldn't help, it, she let out a giggle and felt the room spin again.

"Now here's what we have for you," Lois knelt down in front of Rachel, one hand behind her back, "you're gonna love these," she pulled her arm round and shoved something pink and fluffy under Rachel's nose. Trying hard to get them in focus, Rachel realised they were furry handcuffs.

"Urph, was expecting mush worsh." Rachel shook her head. Had she said that? She swallowed and realised her mouth felt tacky and dry and her tongue had doubled in size, "prolly need a dring," she muttered, putting her hand on the sofa's arm to try and lever herself up. But her body felt like lead and she dropped back into the seat and listened to herself giggle uncontrollably. She made an effort to open her eyes wider and saw the disturbingly large and convex face of Theresa before her.

"I'll put your wine on the table, shall I?"

"Thang you very mush," said Rachel as she felt the furry cuffs being clamped around her wrists and heard her giggle moving away into the distance.

"Get Taylor!" she heard someone say—someone who must have been in an echo chamber a very long way away. How strange she thought, just before she sank into the oblivion she had so craved.

Chapter 12

"Ease up Trevor, she's had enough."

Trevor scowled and waved Gazz off, "no way Gazz," he gasped as he cracked the whip across her backside once more, "she's... not... gonna... beat me."

Gazz gritted his teeth in sympathy as he watched Trevor buck, gripping the reigns as she struggled to retain her freedom. "She's the feistiest ever!" shouted Gazz.

"Not... one of them's..." Trevor took a sharp intake of breath as he gripped her with his thighs, hanging on grimly as she reared up once more "...got the better of me yet."

"This one might," Gazz winked exaggeratedly.

The mare was less than a year old, a golden bay with a fabulous mane and the biggest deepest brown eyes Trevor had ever seen. She was sired by a three times winner of the Cheltenham Gold Cup and she exuded the kind of wild spirit and energy of a true champion—if only she could be broken in just the right way. But he had to admit, it had been his toughest challenge and he couldn't yet feel that moment that told him she was on the edge of breaking. He glanced at Gazz's smirking face and used his anger to steel his resolve. Using every ounce of the sinewy muscle he had developed over years of strenuous hard labour, he gripped her flanks and pulled her reins toward him, getting close enough to her neck to whisper in her ear.

"You're all mine, lovely, all mine."

And there it was! He felt the last strain of resistance break and fade away as she lowered her graceful head and shook her mane in a slow, sensuous roll. Trevor rubbed her frothy sweating neck, "that's my girl," he breathed, "that's my girl, Amber." He guided her head with her reins and turned her to face Gazz, triumphantly. It was Trevor's turn to wink exaggeratedly, "always had a way with the ladies, me."

Gazz looked rueful, "so my Mother tells me." He gazed steadily at Trevor, who's face reddened for the briefest of moments before he regained his composure.

"So, how did you get on with the newcomer last night then?"

Trevor threw back.

Gazz shifted his feet uncomfortably, "not my scene, man," he said regarding his shoes as though they had sprouted wings.

"Thought you were in on the chase?" Trevor's lip curled cruelly.

"Not by choice. I was nominated. Like I said, not my scene, man." Gazz glowered.

"Retiring hurt then?" Trevor huffed and dug his heel gently into the flank of the now compliant Amber.

"Never entered the running in the first place."

"Ah, right," Trevor nodded knowingly and clicked at Amber to walk on. "Not up for breaking her in then?" He threw the words back over his shoulder, a broad smirk on his face.

The irony was not lost on Gazz, "you're too big for your own boots, Trevor. You wanna watch you don't trip over yourself coming backwards, mate."

"No worries Gazz, better to know you can fill your boots, right?" Trevor roared with laughter as Gazz stuck two fingers up behind his back.

The Master stood by the lectern in the small meeting room and watched the Club members file in, shuffling along the tightly arranged chairs and standing uncomfortably shoulder to shoulder. Theresa, the last to enter, noted that he'd opted to dispense with the grand entrance from behind the velvet curtain. It didn't bode well.

"Come on, come on," he ushered her impatiently, barely waiting for her to take her place before he started proceedings.

"Call to the order of the Sloe!" The Master practically spat the words and the gavel thumped down with unusually aggressive vigour. "Salute all those that honour the club." They all dutifully raised their middle fingers. "So shall commence this closed order meeting. Each shall honour the code of secrecy. All say aye."

"Aye!" chorused the group but with a quiet despondency that augured trouble.

"Well?" The master demanded, flicking his disapproving eyes across them. "Come on, one of you. What happened?"

Theresa paused, wishing fervently that someone else would have the balls to pipe up, but realizing the reality that they would all be waiting for her. So she got on with it. "We held a lingerie party."

"Yes, yes, I'm aware of all that." The master interrupted impatiently, "I don't want to hear about the red lace knickers, I want to know what happened with the girl."

"We cocked up."

The Master huffed, "well that's the understatement of the century. Perhaps we should 'cut to the chase'—if you can excuse the massive fucking irony of that statement!"

Theresa mused absently that the purpling hue of his nose was a sign of dangerous apoplexy. But then she felt her own anger rising and took a deep breath as he continued with his explosive rant.

"As I understand it she was given a triple dose!"

"Well if you know what happened, why are you bloody well asking?" Theresa was unable to hold back.

The Master thumped the gavel down again, his eyes like fire. He pointed the hammer viciously at Theresa, "out of order! Double sling and a Mother's Ruin."

The group gasped, but Theresa managed to hold his stare. Why couldn't she have kept her mouth shut? Her eyes narrowed and she calmed herself, "call for an appeal." She stared evenly and obstinately at the Master, determined not to accept his punishment. Her audacity paid off.

"Granted."

"Can't we all calm down?" piped up Gazz and Theresa felt a rush of pride for his bravery.

"Let's get back to the question at hand," said the Master, raising a hand in acknowledgement of the request, "we need to get down to the facts. I want to know, first," he counted the points off on his fingers, "what, *exactly* happened to the girl on that night. Second, who was responsible, Third, what the long term effects are and finally, what you're going to do about it."

Gazz stepped forward. "It's down to me and Dr Taylor, no-one else here holds any responsibility for the events on Wednesday night. It was an accident. My wiggly slipped out of my hand and I knocked

Doctor Taylor when she was administering to Rachel, that's how she overdosed her. Pure and simple."

The master's jaw ground visibly and the group remained hushed as he contemplated Gazz. "And it wasn't deliberate? You weren't trying to shirk your duties?"

"I swear not." Gazz held the master's gaze until he eventually sighed and gave in.

"Right. So what happens now?"

"Taylor's taking care of her. She'll be fine in a few days. Taylor reckons it'll still take effect, but she'll have to get over the initial sickness first. Lisa will follow up when the time is right. We'll be back on track next week." Theresa was clear and calm.

The Master tapped his fingers on the table as the room awaited his response.

"Any other business?" The group relief was almost audible at his closure of the session. "Right. Adjourned." The middle fingers offered their salute and five of the group headed for the door, Gazz letting out a huge sigh of relief and heading for the exit as quickly as his feet could carry him.

After the others had all left, Theresa remained locked in her defiant stare with the Master. "I'll quash the sentence. It was too harsh." He broke the silence.

"We can't carry on like this."

"It was a mistake. I apologise. Let's just leave it at that." The Master put out his hand to touch her, but she recoiled.

"It will happen again."

"It won't. I promise." For a few moments, the silence was broken only by their breathing, which had become heavier and resonated with the kind of hardly contained passion she knew the Master had been struggling to deny.

"You can't keep punishing me." She was determined to drive home her point.

"I know. I won't, it's just… hard." It was the moment she needed to break the cloud of tension that had gathered round them.

She raised an eyebrow. The Master let out a burst of laughter and the air seemed palpably to cool and lighten. He nodded and she took a step back.

"I'll see you on Sunday?" She turned on her heel without waiting for his answer and felt his eyes on her as she headed for the door.

"Sunday." He confirmed.

As she closed the door behind her, she slumped back against it as a mix of emotional exhaustion and relief flooded through her.

Rachel watched the water flow from the rose of the watering can, still feeling dazed and confused. She still couldn't believe it was now Friday—where had Thursday gone? She'd risen pretty much as normal, but with a massive hangover. She'd left for the shop feeling as though all she had to worry about was the bill for the rather large pile of 'toys' that now filled her bedside cabinet and the embarrassment of facing the other party goers given how drunk she'd been. But when she'd walked into the shop and picked up the paper that morning, she'd been gobsmacked to find that she'd actually lost a whole day. A whole day? She'd had some pretty bad hangovers in her time—but losing a whole day? She shook her head painfully as she tried to recall the events of the evening. She remembered arriving, the antics of the other 'product testers', the attaching of the pink handcuffs... and then nothing except a vague recollection of being delivered back at the house by Theresa and someone else. The 'someone' else seemed to have hovered over her as she lay in the bed. Dr Taylor? Was it Dr Taylor? There'd been soothing words and she recalled that she'd been giggling, but other than that there was nothing. And now she wondered just when she'd been delivered back to the house. Had it been Wednesday night? Had she spent Thursday asleep in her own bed? She breathed deeply, fighting another wave of nausea as it swept through her. She bent to put down the can, dizziness causing her to stumble into the flower bed.

"Are you alright there?"

Rachel glanced up as she tried to steady herself amongst the lilies.

"Yeah, bit dizzy," she said weakly at the oddly familiar face of Dr Taylor peering through the trellis from her neighbour's garden.

"I've just been visiting Mr Stephens," she explained, pointing back to the house, "hold on one moment and I'll come round the back."

Rachel, who was at this point incapable of objecting, nodded as she sat heavily down on a peony. She heard the back gate open, though the sound was unusually distant.

"Are you feeling nauseous?"

Rachel frowned, a moment of recognition piercing through her confusion. The distinctive clipped voice sounded like it was in an echo chamber—hadn't she heard something similar the other night? She nodded in slow motion at Dr Taylor, just before lurching forward and throwing up into the watering can.

"Let's just take your temperature." The Doctor drew a thermometer from her bag. Rachel, experiencing the strange sensation of wanting to feel mortified, but not having the energy to do so, opened her mouth to take the thermometer. She felt hot and clammy.

"Mmm. A little high," the Doctor read the gauge, "any other symptoms?" She lifted Rachel's chin gently and flicked a small torch which had appeared from nowhere, running it across Rachel's eyes. She recoiled from it and felt her head drop as Dr Taylor withdrew her hand. She was utterly drained and wanted to explain how she felt, but couldn't muster the energy to do so. She tried to speak but couldn't form even a single word. She gave up and closed her eyes.

"Let me help you up." The Doctor took her arm and Rachel struggled to her feet, feeling her legs wobble like jelly and almost collapsing once more as the Doctor guided her from the border. "We'll get you back to bed and I'll give you something for the nausea."

Propped on Taylor's arm, they made their way unsteadily into the cottage and up the stairs. The Doctor released her and rolling back onto the cool sheets of her bed was a huge relief, but Rachel felt a sudden pang of fear as she watched Dr Taylor fill a needle from a small jar. She must have sensed it.

"Don't worry, it's just for the sickness," she assured her as she rubbed the crook of Rachel's elbow with a swab, "you'll sleep for a few hours. Will there be anyone here for you later?"

Rachel nodded and thought of Frankie, but was unable to say her name.

"Excellent." The Doctor plunged the needle into her arm. "It's good you have someone here when you wake up." Rachel looked up at her, wearily disturbed by that familiar but slightly sinister smile. As the face fogged and her eyes started to close, Rachel heard her voice ask Taylor if they had met before, but didn't catch a reply before slipping into a deep slumber.

"What time is it?" Rachel was relieved to see the slightly blurred face of Frankie seated on the edge of the bed as she struggled to sit up.

"Six 'o'clock." Frankie gently pushed Rachel back into the comfort of the duvet.

"You're early." Rachel settled gratefully back onto her pillow.

"Six 'o'clock Saturday."

"What?" Rachel was horrified and tried to sit back up again, "oh God, I'm so sorry."

"Ssssh, don't worry, Dr Taylor explained," Frankie said as she pushed her down once more.

"She did?"

"Yep. Told me you were taken ill at the party."

"She did?"

"Yep. Glad to see you got your shopping in first though," Frankie winked wickedly and pointed at the bedside cabinet.

"You are?"

"I sure are. Now," Frankie rose purposefully, "I've been told you're to take these twice a day." She held up a bottle of pills.

"I am?"

"You am. So, we'll do that now." She snapped open the lid and shook two tablets out, reaching for a glass of water from the table and handing the whole lot over in a determined manner to Rachel.

"You sure?" Rachel dubiously eyed the pills, feeling a sense of trepidation.

"Sure. Why wouldn't I be? Doctor's orders."

Rachel nodded and took the pills, more from a wish not to raise further questions than anything else.

"What are they for?" she asked as she held them in her cheek.

"Nausea. For the salmonella?" Frankie frowned slightly,

confused by Rachel's apparent ignorance of her condition.

"Of course," Rachel swigged the water and swallowed, "silly me."

"Yeah. Wasn't only you apparently. Everyone that ate the chicken had it."

"Chicken?"

"The roast chicken legs?"

Rachel struggled with her clouded mind. If she'd known what had happened at the party, she would have preferred to talk her confusion through with Frankie. But something was troubling her and she opted not to say anything.

"Chicken legs. That's right."

"So listen, I want you to go back to sleep now Rach. Dr Taylor reckons you'll get over it quicker if you can sleep, ok?"

Rachel nodded and stretched her hand out to Frankie, "you be alright?"

"Oh sure, I can amuse myself," Frankie grinned wickedly, "might test drive some of your toys."

Rachel stuck her bottom lip out, "can't I watch?" She grimaced as she realised her voice had slowed again and that she suddenly felt tired to her bones.

"You're sick. I mean ill," Frankie winked, "so no, I don't want you getting too excited; might put too much of a strain on your heart. Anyway, I'm only kidding. We'll save them 'til you're better. I can find something to amuse myself." She patted Rachel's hand before rising and heading for the door, "now sleep," she instructed as she pulled it closed. Rachel waited a moment and then carefully spat out the pills she had pretended to swallow. She struggled to put them behind her pillow and then reached out for the bottle by the bed. She watched her arm as it made it's way interminably towards the jar. Pulling it back with equal effort, she peered at the label and then mustered the strength required to open the cabinet drawer and take out a pencil and paper. Drawing the bottle towards her she squinted, but couldn't make out the details, it looked as if the information had been scratched through. Exhausted, she dropped the bottle back into the drawer and let the pencil fall through her fingers to the floor. Frustrated, she tried to clear her mind; something she was struggling with. The label being tampered with added to the feeling that there was something very wrong with the events of the last few days, but her mind was so fuzzy that she was unable to figure out what it was. It had something to do with Doctor Taylor and a pair of pink handcuffs. That was right, the pink handcuffs and an injection and... Gazzzzzzz. She blinked, the longest, slowest blink she could ever remember, then her lids closed again and she sank into another deep sleep.

Chapter 13

"He's no son of mine!" the Master's face was livid as he paced the corridor.

"Well, you've never been a father to him anyway," Theresa was equally angry.

"He can't be mine. No son of mine could ever be guilty of..." the Master made a fist, almost unable to say the words, "...failure to perform," he slammed the fist into the granite of the wall.

"Oh, for Christ's sake Adrian, he's just a boy!"

"Keep your voice down," he exploded thundering towards Theresa, his hand raised threateningly. She drew back. She'd never seen him so angry.

"Nobody knows my name's Adrian. Nobody!" his lips were pulled back, baring his teeth in a nasty grimace.

"Sorry," she raised her hands defensively, "sorry. It was a slip. Sorry! Ok?"

He lowered his hand, still breathing hard, "no-one must ever find out about him. You hear? Even if it is true."

"I've never breathed a word and I never will. You made it clear at the time you didn't want anything to do with him. That's the way it stays." She cupped his bleeding and bruised fist in her hands and raised it to her lips to kiss it gently.

He stared down at her head. "I've spoken to everyone who was at the party in private session. Dr Taylor too. It's clear Gazz wasn't up for breaking Rachel into the club. I knew he was lying and I only let him off the hook because of you." The Master contemplated Theresa, "send him after the other one."

"What?" she looked up at him.

"Send him in after Frankie."

"No!" she shook her head vehemently.

"Yes. Make him show he's a man."

"No. No. Absolutely not."

"I demand it."

"Over my dead body."

"Why? Why not? I don't want my son to be known this way. It's ok to cut both ways. But... he's not is he?"

"What?"

"GAY!" He said it angrily.

"Oh for God's sake, Adrian!" she was exasperated, "what if he is? Jesus, you run the club. How can you possibly judge the boy even if he is?"

"Cutting both ways is another thing altogether. There's a manliness to it. It's testosterone overload. Being GAY? That's... it's pansy. It's..." he was shaking his head, a disgusted look on his face, "it's girly!"

"Oh for fuck's sake!" she shook her head at him, "that's pure ignorance. And why do you care at all?" she asked him pointedly, "no-one even knows he's your son. It doesn't matter. None of it matters."

"It does to me," his voice rose again as he beat his chest in anguish. "He's... *of* me. I can't bear it that he's my sporn and he's... he's... girly!"

"I don't know if he is and I don't care as long as he is happy," she was truly angry now, "and he's not girly. He's grown up never knowing his real father in a household where the pressure has been massive for him to perform. It's no wonder he's got problems. So back off!!" She watched him as he paced the room, struggling with his inner turmoil. Despite all the years that had passed and the issues that had arisen between them, she still felt love for him, but at times like this, she wondered why. Though they had agreed her marriage to Roy was for the best, he'd always been her true love. But he had never forgiven her for going ahead with the birth. He'd begged her to abort, but she'd gone ahead anyway. He'd been a rising star at the time and he hadn't wanted marriage and a family to stand in his way. She'd accepted that. But she couldn't live with the guilt, so she'd gone ahead. Her original plan had been adoption, but faced with her son and his likeness to his father, she'd been unable to part with him and had taken the tough decision to keep him. The rest remained a secret even from the Master.

"Ask him then. At least do that for me. Ask him if he'll do it. See if he'll save his pride. Do it for me, Theresa?"

She looked at him and shook her head. "No."

He dropped her hand and pointed at her, "you'll regret this," he said as he turned and left the room, slamming the door as hard as he could behind him.

"Not as much as you will," she said in the empty corridor.

Chapter 14

Roy sat in the Doctor's consulting room, a hate filled stare on his face as he regarded Taylor. Despite his own issues being the root of his problem, he blamed her for her willingness to exploit his weakness. He detested the fact that he ultimately knew she had control over him. He decided to try and deny his craving and end her control.

"That's the last time."

Doctor Taylor rocked back on her chair, "no, it's not, Roy." She had a mean smile on her face.

"I can't do that again."

"You can do anything I tell you to Roy." She waved a little vial in the air before him.

Roy licked his lips, "that's all in the past."

Doctor Taylor leaned forward, "is it Roy?" she said nastily, "is it really?" Roy grabbed for the vial.

"Aaaah." She crooked her head to one side and withdrew the little bottle, "not so fast." Roy made fists with his hands and gritted his teeth. "Yes. No. I don't want it." He hugged himself. He knew it was pointless.

Doctor Taylor rose and circled the desk to stand by his side. She placed her hand on his shoulder. "Even if you don't take it, Roy, you'd still owe me."

Roy put his face in his hands. "You can't keep doing this to me."

"Oh but I can. You've made sure of that. And though, obviously, I'm a reasonable woman and when it's time I'll let you off the hook, the truth is that my game plan just isn't finished yet and until it is, I have to carry on."

Roy closed his eyes. "There's enough there for you to retire on three times over," he wailed.

"No. No Roy. There might be enough for *you* to retire on three times over, but not for me. I have ambitions. I need more. Much more. So you see, I still need you." She shook the vial before his eyes and he groaned, "come on Roy, you know you want it. And you really might as well have it. Because as I said, take it or not from me, I'm still going to be taking from you. Understand?"

Beads of sweat broke out on his forehead and his hands began to shake. If he hadn't understood how ruthless she was before, he did now. Doctor Taylor returned to the other side of the desk and placed the vial in front of her, watching Roy as he struggled. She swiveled, admiring her tanned thighs below her short leather skirt and picking a speck of paper meticulously from the arm of the chair. She turned slowly back to Roy, who's face was becoming clammy and pale.

"Feeling a little under the weather Roy? At least you're in the right place." She took a small plastic bag from the drawer. She tugged at the outer packaging and removed the needle before picking up the vial and drawing the fluid up into it. She watched Roy's face as she flicked the needle and squirted a test into the air, "what's it to be Roy?" He sobbed and rolled up the sleeve of his shirt, turning his face away as he presented the crook of his arm.

Doctor Taylor smiled as she swabbed and inserted the needle. "There's plenty more where this came from, just you keep it coming and I can always see you right. There." She withdrew the needle and watched his face relax, smiling with self-satisfaction at her power and control.

Chapter 15

The sun glinted off the metal slide as she stared ahead, swinging gently. The breeze ruffling her hair felt good. It was a beautiful early autumn day and she appreciated the warmth on her skin as she rocked back and forth, deep in thought. Though whether deep was the right expression was questionable. Since last Wednesday's events, she had struggled to string together anything other than fragments, let alone go into any depth. She sighed heavily and scuffed the ground with her feet to bring the swing to a halt. She still couldn't piece together the events of that evening, but she did get occasional flashbacks - and what she saw in those didn't make her feel good about trying so hard to remember. Frankie had been great, getting her through the awful weekend and by Monday morning she'd begun to feel much better. But she wasn't comfortable that she hadn't told Frankie of her doubts about what had happened—and the longer she left it, the harder it was to do. And though she felt physically better, mentally and emotionally she was definitely out of sorts. She felt a kind of fog of confusion, a bizarre detachment from reality. And her emotions were all over the shop. On the verge of tears half the time and weirdly euphoric the rest. But the euphoria didn't seem to have a subject or an object. She would want to dance and found herself smiling and laughing, but couldn't figure why. When she thought about it after the euphoria had subsided, she couldn't understand why she had felt that way. The story the Doctor had told had been plausible enough. So plausible that she almost believed it herself. But try as she might, she couldn't remember eating anything—or anybody else eating anything either. In which case, why the story? Rachel rose from the swing and wondered over to the bench by the slide, sitting with her legs stretched out and her head resting on the back. Looking up at the clear blue sky, she wondered if she was being completely mad. Whether she had just got drunk and forgotten that she'd eaten the chicken and been ill. Simple as that. She felt in her pocket and pulled out the pills she'd saved. She rolled them around in her hand. She frowned. Were they different? She sat up and took a closer look. Two white pills, both round, but one slightly larger than the other. Only slightly, but enough to make her mind up. She clenched her fist around them and placed them back in her pocket, rising with greater resolve.

"Hi!"

"Oh, you made me jump." Rachel turned to see Lisa standing behind her.

"Sorry. Feeling better?"

"Yes," Rachel forced a laugh, "does the whole village know?"

"Pretty much. I had it too. And Gazz and the Floosy."

"Oh?"

"Yeah. Last time I eat roast chicken I think."

Rachel nodded, "you know it's funny, I can't remember eating anything at all."

"Well I hate to say it but you were a bit slaughtered."

"But it's so weird. I can only remember drinking one glass of wine. I can't make sense of it." She looked at Rachel quizzically.

"Well, I wasn't counting," Lisa turned her palms up and shrugged, "but it definitely wasn't just one." She chuckled, "you were sooooo funny after the first couple, I didn't care how many you would have had, it was such a laugh."

"Really?" Rachel looked mortified.

"Yes! Oh my god, you were hysterical. I haven't laughed that much in ages!"

Rachel shook her head, "Really? Me?"

"Yes. You!" Lisa started laughing harder, "I can't believe you don't remember, you were adorable!"

Rachel searched her brain frantically. Nothing. No. Thing. "Oh my god, I literally don't remember anything." She looked at Lisa searchingly as if she might see the answer through her eyes, "was I really embarrassing?" she cringed inwardly as she asked.

"No! Oh my goodness no, you stole everyone's hearts!" Lisa leant forward and touched Rachel's arm reassuringly.

Rachel reddened and couldn't control the shudder that resulted from the prickling sensation it sent through her. Lisa appeared not to notice as she continued,

"You don't remember the Madonna cones?"

"What?" Rachel recoiled, horrified, "No. What the fuck...

Madonna cones?"

Rachel burst out laughing, full on. "Yes! Lois was handing out party hats—you know the pointy clown ones?"

Rachel just stared at her blankly.

"You decided to stuff two of them up your shirt like Madonna breasts and started singing Express Yourself! Hysterical!"

Rachel put her head in her hands and bent over her knees, she felt hollow. Lisa placed her hand on her back. She shivered involuntarily.

"No need to be embarrassed, we've all done it."

Rachel sat back up, hand over mouth, shaking her head in disbelief. "No, I've never done it. I'm mortified. I'm so sorry."

"Whaaaat! Crikey woman, don't be sorry, you were amazing!" Lisa patted Rachel's shoulder, "listen, everyone loved it, you were the star of the show. And we were all messing about anyway. Really, you were awesome."

Lisa rubbed her back again and she closed her eyes. Confusion now mixed with a rush that filled her body.

"Look. Whatever. It doesn't matter. Honestly hon, you have nothing to worry about. We were all... well none of us were exactly sober. It's fine. Really."

"Ok." Rachel felt the thin, insecure sound of her voice.

Lisa lifted her chin and looked into her eyes, "it's all good." Rachel felt momentarily transfixed as Lisa penetrated through her and... into where... into her soul?" She shook her head and stood up, suddenly resolving that she need to draw back from wherever bizarre place she was in, to some semblance of reality.

"Cool. Good. Well, I'm glad it was fun. I'm sure I'll get some recall when I'm feeling better."

"I'm sure you will."

Lisa pulled a packet of Rolos from her pocket and offered them to Rachel, who declined.

"Not really up for anything rich yet."

"Not been taking the pills then?"

"What do you mean?" Rachel looked at her sharply.

"Doc Taylor prescribed me some great pills. Had me on my feet again really quickly. Surprised she didn't do the same for you."

"She did. Maybe I just didn't react as quickly." Rachel fiddled guiltily with the pills in her pocket. "I need to go." She rose and started to walk away, "I'll see you around. Ok?"

Lisa jumped up and followed, "wait! Sit with me for a while longer?" She indicated a bench. Rachel hesitated. She wanted to... but she didn't. Being with Lisa felt strange, attracted but in that odd detached way. She looked at her and registered the fact that she was a prostitute—it made the feeling even more disturbing, but somehow more compelling. Reluctantly she sat down.

"I'm glad you were at the party. I mean not for the fact of getting sick or anything, but because without you there it would have been even worse. Ugh, I'm not getting this out right. Just saying that I enjoyed your company."

"Well, I can't say I remember enough to know much about it. But thanks anyway."

"Well, looked like you were a Love Honey fan anyway, you bought enough to last a while." Lisa laughed and touched her arm again.

Rachel reddened, "yes."

They sat quietly.

"What's it like?"

"What?"

"Sorry, I don't know why I asked."

"Oh. Being a prostitute. Unemotional. Mechanical. It's a job." Lisa rested her arm along the bench behind Rachel.

Rachel gathered the information but couldn't work out how to process it. It didn't make sense to her on any level. They both fell quiet again.

"You like it here?" asked Lisa.

"Yeah." She paused, "yeah sort of."

"What does 'sort of' mean?"

"I don't know. I love the house, the village shop, the quaint ways. I just... there's something bubbling under the surface." She looked across at Lisa wondering why she'd chosen to open up with her. Lisa was nodding.

"Yeah. There are a few strange things going on here. But, there's nothing sinister really. Just some harmless fun. It's just people getting on with their lives in less than ordinary ways. You know?"

"Well, I suppose put like that..."

"Like the vicar..."

"Yes?" Rachel perked up.

"Like the vicar not being a vicar and keeping goats." Lisa glanced across, checking she'd got some interest, "though that's not strictly true either. He used to be a vicar years ago down in Emsfield. He fell in love with a married Parishioner and they had an affair. He was exposed and forced to leave the church and he kind of lost his faith." She paused. "Well, not his faith really. Just his belief in the church as we traditionally know it. So he went a bit wild. Grew lots of hair and took a liking to goats. Which isn't really that wild when you think about it, is it?" She glanced at Rachel again, then continued, "his family had always lived in Hetherington and he'd moved away in his early twenties. So when it all went pear, he moved back here and resettled."

"And what about the Church here?"

"You mean why is it closed up?"

"Yes. Bit odd for a village this size. That no-one goes to Church."

"Some of them do. Just not here. The Church has some internal structural problems. It can't be used in its current state. It's also very big. Too big to warrant spending the restoration money required given the small number of parishioners it would attract. We want to convert it to a swimming pool."

Rachel laughed, "not sure I'd want to swim in a Church. Consecrated ground and all that."

"To most of us, it's just a building. If you believe in God, you believe in an entity that can be worshipped... but worshipping can take place anywhere. You could worship in a pub—or swim in a Church. They're all just bricks and mortar at the end of the day."

As Lisa took another Rolo from her packet and popped it in her mouth, Rachel contemplated what she had just said, feeling bad that she was surprised at how profound that seemed coming from Lisa. Then admonished herself internally for judging her because of her 'profession'.

"Who else have you met along the way?"

"I'm getting to know Ben, opposite."

"Oh everyone loves Ben."

"I know—and everyone says that."

"He's a blast. And he's real, you know? He's friendly with everyone, keeps himself to himself, but always kind of there if you need him."

"Yeah. He does seem pretty normal for this place."

Lisa laughed. "Have you been to the Manor?" Rachel shook her head, "want to take a look?"

"What, now?"

"Uh huh. My parents own it." She threw her head back and laughed at Rachel's disbelieving expression and once again, Rachel felt a sense of shame.

"Come on." She jumped up and grabbed Rachel's hand, "it was built over three hundred years ago," Lisa led the way across the park as she chatted on, "my Father bought it along with the brewery. They were both ramshackle and the brewery business was on its knees. He poured every penny he had into restoration and built the brewery business back up. My father's a film director, Eddie Danforth. You know him? He used all the money he'd made in the early part of his career—a labour of love. When it was done, he went back to making movies. There's a full studio, editing suite and movie theatre in the manor."

"Of course I know him," Rachel was staggered.

"It doesn't get used much these days, but they filmed part of 'Die For A Dollar" here about six years ago."

"With Grant Law?"

"Yep."

"And Sophie Priest?"

"Now you're talking. Gorgeous," Lisa winked at her, "just your type I should think."

Rachel blushed as Lisa put her lips to her ear, "and vice versa."

Rachel felt a shiver run down her spine as she felt Lisa's breath brush her skin.

"You mean she's…"

"Absolutely!"

"Mmmm. Adds a nice new twist to watching her," Rachel giggled. And then frowned, catching herself relaxing in Lisa's company just a little too much. She thought about Frankie, an image of her sitting at her desk in the city, earphones clamped to her head and concentration etched on her face as she watched the flickering screen of figures fluctuating in live time as the markets ebbed and flowed. She flipped back to the present as Lisa spoke.

"Glad to have helped."

They reached the manor gates and Lisa punched in a code on the keypad, "my Father doesn't live here any more. He and my Mother are separated. He's in Italy right now. Filming."

"I'm sorry."

"It's ok. It was a long time ago."

They fell silent again as they trudged up the winding gravel drive.

They'd reached the grand façade of the building, the sweeping drive opening out to a magnificent circular area with a glorious fountain statue in the centre.

Lisa strode up to the massive front doors and pulled the bell. "Actually, let's go round the back," she said, grabbing Rachel's hand and skipping away to the side of the house. Rachel caught glimpses of magnificently opulent rooms in various styles as she passed by the windows. They reached the side and Lisa pushed Rachel forward as they threaded their way through the huge and varied plants. Rachel then found herself in a clearing and gasped as she looked out over the magnificently manicured lawns.

"Oops," Lisa laughed and put her arm around Rachel's shoulders, "I forgot to tell you, Mother's a nudist."

Rachel looked on as four females moved from downward dog to child pose on the wide expanse of lawn.

"Hello Mother!" shouted Lisa standing on tiptoes and waving. Rachel covered her face, expecting that she had caused embarrassment. But the shoe was placed firmly on the other foot when a slim, attractive woman with gray-tinged black hair came bounding across the lawn towards them.

"Hello, darling," she said as she crossed the last few yards, not an ounce of concern on her face. Mother and daughter kissed.

"Mother. I mean Donna, this is Rachel. She's at St Valentines."

"Ah, yes. I've heard about you. How are you settling in?"

"Good. Thanks for asking." Rachel found it difficult to maintain her gaze at eye level.

Donna turned back to her daughter, "are you working?"

"No. Not til six."

"Lovely. We'll have tea then. Can you go in and tell Peters? I want to finish this class with the girls," she waved in the direction of the three naked figures, now an interesting sight in the Lotus position.

"Sure. Come on Rachel. Let's go hassle, Peters."

They turned towards the French doors leading in from the wide patio.

"Is she English?" asked Rachel, having detected a mere hint of an accent.

"No. Well spotted. She hates it when people do that."

"Oh. Don't tell her then."

"I won't. Actually, she's an Italian Countess. Donna is short for Donnatella."

Lisa pushed open a full-length patio door and ushered Rachel into an exquisitely decorated art deco style lounge. Rachel was impressed. "It's stunning."

"Yes. My Mother's heavily into naked ladies," laughed Lisa, flinging her arm wide to take in what must have been more that twenty beautiful art deco statuettes of elegantly bare ladies, "in art and in real life."

Lisa picked up a tiny china bell and rang it enthusiastically, "tea or coffee?"

"Tea please," said Rachel as she wandered round the room admiring the various China trinkets.

"Peters!" Lisa skipped over to the door and leapt at a tall, smiling woman, who'd barely had time to get through the doorway.

"Hello. M'Lovely. What brings you here you little rascal."

"Peters! You talk to me like a child. I'm twenty-eight for goodness sake!" Lisa glanced at Rachel, her cheeks now red with embarrassment.

"You'll always be a little rascal to me."

"Anyway. Meet Rachel."

Peters greeted her and took her hand. Somehow Rachel found it hard to respond with her surname only. It felt disrespectful. She didn't like the idea of treating her as if she was servile.

"So what can I get you?"

"We'll come and get tea with you."

In the massive traditional country style kitchen, the three of them set about making tea and preparing cakes. It felt comfortable, Rachel was better able to relax. The formality of the rest of the manor house together with the over informality of Donna and her yoga class made her defensive and stiff. It was disturbing how contradictory Lisa's life seemed to be. She tried to push it to the back of her mind, even though she wanted to contemplate its peculiarity and make some kind of sense of it.

"Does Mother want tea in the conservatory?"

"Yes," nodded Peters, "with the girls."

"Informal then?" Lisa winked at Rachel again.

Peters grimaced, "leaves such terrible stains on the furniture."

Rachel felt the sense of surreal again.

"You should put some plastic covers on Peters. And watch as they stick to them. Ugh, what a horrible thought." Lisa poured water into the teapot, "that's everything. Let's take it through."

Rachel picked up a tray with the cakes and followed their lead through to a bright, airy conservatory, the sound of voices growing as they approached. She steeled herself.

"Hello ladies," said Lisa brightly as she walked in with the tea tray, "good class?"

"Wonderful darling," Donna fairly bounced over to them, a bit unwisely thought Rachel as she struggled to rest her eyes anywhere that didn't appear to embarrass anyone. But then she realised that the only person in the room likely to experience any sense of embarrassment was her. She felt Lisa's amused eyes on her.

"Rachel, let me introduce you," Donna walked over and stood uncomfortably close, her breasts brushing momentarily against Rachel's hand and making her feel hot.

"This is Debbie, otherwise known as Lady Braybourne. Oh, I should explain, we all have these little nicknames. None of us really

107

believe in the titles we own. So we opt not to use them. But I'll tell you who we all are anyway."

Rachel nodded and waved at Debbie's breasts, which were by far the most outstanding feature on a plump woman in her mid-fifties.

"Then we have Ange. Lady Rotherston" This time Rachel managed eye contact as she acknowledged a petite blond, tanned and with a shapely figure.

"Charlie, or Princess Charlotte di Toricconi," a stunning flame-haired woman, probably in her late thirties, turned and waved as she picked up a cup from the table.

"And finally, dear Daphers. Dame Daphne Peterson-Smythe." A bubbly looking brunette with a large mole just above her bikini line, gave a cheerful wave.

"So now that's all done, let's get you a cup of tea."

Rachel, who was beginning to feel bizarrely overdressed, followed Donna to the tray.

"Are you enjoying Hetherington?" Donna poured as she chatted.

"Starting to get to know the place." Rachel couldn't hide her hesitancy. She watched as a smile crept onto Donna's face.

"It's always difficult when one first enters a new community, especially such a small, closed place like this. Rural communities, in particular, do have their... peculiarities. It's harmless, but it takes time to get to know the local rituals."

Rachel nodded, looking down into the brown, clear liquid.

"Each to their own."

"Milk?"

"Please."

As Donna poured, Rachel felt a presence behind her that made her skin warm and tingly.

"I'll have to leave soon," said Lisa quietly,

"Oh darling, not yet," Donna overheard and broke what felt like an electrical connection between them, "you've only just got here."

"Got plans. I really just wanted to bring Rachel over to say hello. And I didn't realise you had a class." She turned to Rachel, "drink up, sorry it's a short visit, we'll come back another time."

"I hardly ever see you these days darling." Donna turned to

Rachel, "so what do you do Rachel?"

"I'm a writer." Rachel took a gulp of the tea, grateful for Lisa's decision to head out.

"Marvellous. And what do you write?"

"Novels... well, a novel. I'm writing my first."

"And are you single?" Donna leant forward and picked a stray hair from Rachel's shirt, just above her left nipple.

"No," Rachel's eyes dropped down to Donna's hand and she squirmed away as her body responded alarmingly to the touch of her finger, "I live with my partner, Frankie."

"Of course you do."

"That's enough of the questions Mother," Lisa took the teacup that had started to rattle slightly in her hand, "we have to go." She took Rachel's hand and started to pull her away.

"Oh darling," Donna pouted, "you always spoil my fun." She slapped her daughter lightly on the arm and then turned back to Rachel, "well it's been lovely to meet you, darling. Now listen..." she placed her tea cup on the table and turned to give her full frontal attention to Rachel. She took her hand from Lisa's, "you must come and visit. Whenever you like. It can be very lonely in a new home," she patted her hand gently as Lisa interrupted.

"Mother!" she said in a warning tone, grabbing Rachel's hand away again.

"Oh don't fuss, Lisa, I'm only opening a neighbourly door to dear Rachel."

"Not now. We're off. I'll talk to you later." She kissed her mother's cheek quickly and pulled Rachel towards the door.

"Bye Ladies," shouted Lisa back to the group of women happily sipping tea in their naked glory. Rachel waved as she allowed herself to be dragged along. Outside the house, Lisa laughed loudly.

"I'm so sorry. I don't know what possessed me. I should have checked her schedule."

"It's fine. I enjoyed it. It was an... experience."

"Liar. I've never seen anyone look so uncomfortable."

"It was a bit full on," Rachel admitted.

"Yes. Well, that's my Mother for you." Lisa looked at her watch.

"Shit it's later than I thought, we'll have to hurry," she picked up her pace and Rachel followed, feeling a sudden devastating pang of sadness. She stopped and grabbed Lisa's arm to stop her too.

"Don't go," she looked into Lisa's large brown eyes. She said it impulsively and felt as if it had come from nowhere, or somewhere outside of her control.

"What?" Lisa was puzzled, slightly irritated.

"Don't go to work," Rachel gripped her arm, "I don't want you to go to work."

Lisa shrugged free, "I have to. And I'm late." She was matter of fact.

"Look I know this sounds mad," Rachel pressed her hand against her forehead, confused herself by her sudden outburst, yet unable to stop what was coming out of her mouth, "but I don't want you to do this. Not tonight. Not ever again. Don't do it ok?"

"I'm sorry, I have to." She picked up Rachel's hand, holding her eyes and gazing deeply into them as she turned it over and ran her finger gently across her palm. Smiling fleetingly, she let it fall, her eyes returning to steel as she released Rachel's gaze, turned and walked through the gates.

Rachel looked down at her palm and felt a melting sensation as she recognised the shape that Lisa had traced on her still tingling palm; a heart.

Rachel trudged back along the main street, deep in serious thought. Just as she approached the house, she clocked Ben's head pop up in the kitchen window, he smiled and flicked the v's at her. Even in her miserable state, he made her laugh. She stuck two fingers up at him and poked her tongue out. He opened the window.

"Coffee? And I've got a lemon drizzle if you're up for it."

"Yeah, why not. Just the coffee though."

She crossed the road and he opened the door for her, "so you don't like my cakes then you ingrate?" he teased.

"No I love your cake, just not feeling great."

"Yeah you do look pretty grim," he said, standing back and

inspecting her.

"Oh, thanks." She rolled her eyes and made a half-hearted attempt to acknowledge his humour.

"Not catching is it?" he crossed his index fingers and took a step backwards.

"No. Food poisoning. I got it at Theresa's Love Honey party."

"Serves you right for being a filthy bitch then." He winked, "kidding. What did you buy?"

She blushed, "stack loads. Though I don't remember much about it."

"Well, that's no good. I need details."

"Now whose being a filthy bitch?" she held up her index finger to admonish him.

"Touché! Nice one," he said generously. He handed her the coffee.

"How's it going other than sex and sickness?" he asked wryly.

"Well, that's been pretty much it for the few days."

He winked at her. and she reddened again.

"Sickness!" she felt her colour rise again and changed the subject, "I've just been up to the manor house and met her ladyship."

"You mean the Countess."

"Yeah. Lisa took me up there."

He raised an eyebrow again.

"We're just friends! Bloody hell Ben, conversations with you are just one long string of innuendos!"

"Everyone says that."

"Yeah and everyone loves you."

"What?"

"Nothing."

She liked that they had an easy banter.

"Actually everything else aside, I like Lisa. She's pretty real." He sipped his coffee, "one of the few around here I'll have a pint with."

"Yeah, I like her too. *Like,*" she re-emphasised.

"I know, you *like* her. Be a bit careful up at the manor though. Just saying."

She nodded and sipped at her coffee as she thought about the oddness of yet another bizarre and surreal experience. This village seemed to be full of the weirdest people. Or maybe she had just been unlucky and met the oddballs all at once. Maybe there were normal people too.

"Fiver for them?"

"What?"

"Your thoughts? A fiver, cos I reckon if you bought all those toys they must be worth at least that."

"Well even if they are, they're not for sale. What do you think of Donna?"

"Bugger. I'll have to try a different tack." Ben sipped at his coffee and regarded her for a few moments, "thing is, I don't really like to talk too much about people here. I'll tell you if they're a good'en but other than that I just don't..."

"...I know you just don't get involved." She held her hand up and finished the sentence for him.

"There's too much going on and too much at stake to poke my nose in and feel comfortable."

"Like the club?"

He ignored her question, "just take it easy and do your own thing and you'll be alright."

"That says so much more than it says. And begs the question why I might need that kind of warning. I know there's something strange going on, but I can't seem to get anyone to open up about it."

"Even if there are some odd folk around here, it really doesn't matter. Just get on with your life. Chill! Take people for what they are and keep to yourself. That's my advice on life."

"Yep. As good a plan as any. Well, thanks for the coffee," she handed back her cup.

"All good, you can fuck off now." He grinned and opened the door, "kidding."

Chapter 16

"It smells a bit strong to me."

"That's because it's blue."

"And it's too big for me."

"So I'll give you less."

She hesitated, "or maybe you could just knock a bit off for me?"

Roy watched as she bent closer to a particularly heavily veined slice of the Danish Blue and sniffed deeply. She pursed her lips with an air of slight distaste, "it's definitely turning."

Roy sighed heavily, "alright, Mrs Dunbar. Let's call it two quid for cash."

Mrs Dunbar nodded, satisfied that she'd got her way. "Now. About the tomatoes," she fixed him with a disapproving stare, "they're soft."

"That's right Mrs Dunbar, perfectly ripe. Ready to eat now."

"Over-ripe's the word, better bought two days ago."

Roy, restraining himself, sighed again, "I'll knock twenty pence off."

Mrs Dunbar's already shriveled lips, drew into a sort of sphincter.

"No," Roy raised his hand and made to walk away, "that's as much as I'll do."

"Ach, you have your way, Roy. I'll take them, but you should be grateful I do," she held a cautionary finger to his face, "you need to keep us regulars."

"I know and I'm grateful to you, Mrs Dunbar," he offered through slightly gritted teeth, "and it's always a pleasure to do business with you."

She patted his hand, "I know. I know Roy and you've no worries about me coming back for more. Even though I could be round there at the 'main shop'" Mrs Dunbar emphasised the reference to their village competitors and nodded knowingly.

"I'm so glad to hear it, Mrs Dunbar." He sighed as he wrapped the produce with extra diligence, "anything else we can do for you?"

She leant closer to him and he tried hard not to pull away as the effects of fifty years or so of garlic pills wafted painfully under his nostrils.

"There's the small matter of our Graham," she glanced nervously around, "he's of age," the final two words were mouthed silently and exaggeratedly.

Roy nodded and winked reassuringly. "Has he decided who he'd like to see him through it?" Roy asked as he waved at Theresa in the post office.

"Please..." Mrs Dunbar grabbed his arm, horrified that it might attract attention, "please be discreet. He's of a delicate disposition. I don't want this to be a public initiation." Again Mrs Dunbar mouthed the final words.

"Don't you worry, Mrs Dunbar. You hold on there for a tick, I'll sort it out personally." Roy patted her hand and then headed for the post office counter, glancing back at the nervous looking Mrs Dunbar as he did so.

"Pink one," he clicked his fingers at Theresa short-temperedly.

She looked at him evenly, "what you really mean is "I'd like an initiation form please darling?"

"Mrs Dunbar's waiting!" He fixed his eyes on her icily and she sighed as she pulled out the form.

"Don't forget to get her to fill out the means testing section on the back."

"I know what I'm doing. Look after the front of the shop while I take her out back and help her fill it in." He marched away before she had a chance to respond.

Theresa stood at the front of the store, grateful for a lull in the trade as she contemplated Roy's behaviour. The stability of her relationship with Roy had been the foundation on which she was able to build the club's profile and activities. Since her enrolment as club secretary, the commercial aspects had gone from strength to strength whilst the social activities had flourished as a result of the club's new wealth. The already tight-knit community enjoyed an even greater bond and the levels of experimentation and adventurism were reaching new heights. Not two months ago she had been basking in the knowledge that she had been instrumental in stimulating a new and exciting era in the club's history. But now, it seemed that the once solid foundations were starting to crumble. She'd always been able to count on his support. But now? He was so erratic, one minute he would be positive and gung ho, the next he would be morose, despondent. And often he was evasive about what he was doing when she wasn't around. She wasn't sure about what was happening, but there was a sense of something undermining. And it was starting to make her angry. She bit her lip, then stopped herself as the door opened from the back room and Roy emerged. She sighed. He didn't look happy. He looked hot and angry, whereas Mrs Dunbar was a smiling like the cat that got the cream. "Got everything you came for Mrs Dunbar?" she couldn't resist needling Roy, who's face turned a shade darker.

"Indeed I did, Theresa. Indeed I did. And most grateful to you I am. And most grateful will be my baby boy."

Theresa nodded smilingly, thinking that baby was not a word anyone else could apply to the six foot five inch son of Elsie Dunbar. "Glad to hear it, Mrs Dunbar. And of course, we are grateful to you for you continued custom." A heavy silence filled the air as they both watched her hobble out of the door.

"I take it she wangled you through the means test?"

Roy grunted and slapped the completed pink form down on the counter.

"She's got buckets of money, that woman." Theresa picked up the form and glanced through it. "No income?" she looked up at Roy incredulously, "no income?" she laughed disparagingly. Roy turned away silently and restacked the beans with loud deliberation.

"You shouldn't have let her get away with that Roy," Theresa threw the form down in disgust, "he gets a free initiation on that basis." She waited for him to respond, but he just carried on re-stacking the tins, "this isn't a charity you know?" her voice louder, irritated by his determined silence, "did you hear me?" She placed her hand on her hips, settling to her task, "Graham Dunbar will be eighteen on Saturday. Ok. He gets an initiation into the club just like any other resident that comes of age. But it's only free if both his parents pass the means test. That is to say, neither parent can afford to pay the fees. Right?" She couldn't help herself stating the absolutely obvious and grinding Roy down with her

115

need to rub salt in his wounds.

Roy stacked.

"I know Elsie Dunbar pulls three pensions and she's got a private income from her late husband's estate. She's loaded, Roy." She tapped her foot as her voice rose.

"Don't you ever question my decisions again!"

Theresa recoiled as Roy's furious face closed in on her. He placed his finger gently but deliberately on her chest and although his touch was light, she felt like it was boring into her.

"I'm sick and tired of your fucking club!" He spat the words, firing them like bullets, "and your fucking life. 'Cos that's what it is Theresa, a FUCKING life. A FUCKING life that has fuck all to do with me!" And though he pushed her only gently, the force of his words combined with the shock of his physical assault sent her reeling and she fell back against the cigarettes with a thud, dislodging a shelf and releasing a shower of Golden Virginia around her.

"Roy?" She said quietly as she watched him storm through the store and out through the back door, slamming it behind him. She blinked disbelievingly. Then she held her head in her hands, oblivious to the figure of Dr Taylor, standing arms folded and staring down at her with a mixture of self-satisfaction and disdain.

Chapter 17

Rachel swiveled in her chair and gazed out at the clear blue sky. She looked at the phone for the hundredth time, then sighed and turned back to the blank monitor of her PC. She'd been sitting there for two hours and still hadn't turned it on. She looked back at the phone and sighed again. Deeply. She leant forward and placed her head in her hands. She felt sick. But it had nothing to do with chicken. Or any kind of food. Or any illness. Well, it was a kind of sickness... She looked at the fruit salad she'd prepared for her breakfast and pushed it away distractedly. She tapped her forehead and looked at the phone again. Impulsively, she got up and ran back to the top floor and pulled open Frankie's closet. Once more she went through every pocket, each time she found them empty, becoming more frustrated. What had Frankie done with Lisa's business card? She stood with her hands on her hips and scanned the room. She looked at the bedside cabinet. She'd been through it a dozen times, surely it couldn't be hiding in the corner recesses or between some papers she hadn't been through? Damn it, she thought, I'll try anyway. But it was to no avail. Resignedly, she trudged back down the stairs and looked at the phone. She shook her head. She really didn't want to give the game away, but damn it, she couldn't resist any longer, could she? She leant over and picked up the handset... then put it down again and turned to the window once more. It was unbearable. Sweet and intense and unbearable. And loaded with guilt. She thought of Frankie and felt shame, but it was like she couldn't hold her in her head, no matter how hard she tried. The image was quickly replaced with Lisa, in a way that was almost beyond her control. She closed her eyes and told herself to concentrate. She leant forward and pressed the on button of the PC, watching the screen as it flickered into life and told her that Microsoft was waiting to greet her. She sighed again; feeling the yearning in her stomach might never end. Rocking in her chair, she finally gained the momentum she needed and picked up the phone with more determination. She dialed. She closed her eyes as the ringing seemed to go on interminably—and then felt her heart leap sickeningly into her throat as she heard the handset being answered at the other end.

117

"Village Post Office. Theresa speaking."

Rachel fought momentarily with her instinct to hang up, but something got the better of her and she spoke, "Theresa, hi, it's Rachel." She fiddled with her mouse as she felt another rush of excitement. They exchanged pleasantries and then she got to the point, "I wondered if you might be able to help me with something, Theresa?"

"Sure. What is it?"

"Well, I ran into Lisa in the park the other day. Just. You know, just ran into her when I was..." Rachel felt like her mouth and brain had disengaged, " ...on the swings. Well not literally. Actually, I was having a think. On the swings. And she came into the park." She breathed deeply. "Anyway, I promised I'd let her have this recipe." She winced silently as she said it and felt her throat constrict.

"Uh, huh?" Theresa filled the pause with some encouragement for her to continue.

"But I forgot to get her phone number. Have you got it by any chance?" The last sentence came out in a squeak and she clenched her fist and eyes.

"Sure. Just a mo." She heard Theresa put down the receiver and felt a flood of the most incredible gratitude course through her whole body. That had been way easier than she'd anticipated. She'd half expected Theresa to offer her a lecture on confidentiality.

"Here we go. Lisa on 735499."

"Theresa, you're a star."

"I know, I've been told sooooo many times."

"Of course you have. Thanks. Really."

"Sure. Anytime. Have a great day."

"You too. Bye." Rachel hung up and then frowned as she held the phone to her cheek. What had she just done?

Rachel stood at the entrance to the park for what seemed the longest time and stared across at Lisa who was scuffing her feet on the floor as she sat on the swing. She was hidden by an overgrown laurel bush and she knew Lisa hadn't seen her. She could easily turn back. Why was she so compelled to see her? It didn't make sense. She thought about

Frankie and just as her brain told her to walk away, her feet propelled her forward. Lisa turned to greet her.

"Hi."

She's so cool. It's unbearable thought Rachel, "hi." There was a pause. She listened to her own breathing, it sounded so loud. "I hope you don't mind?"

"Of course not, I'm glad."

Rachel stood by the swing, not knowing what to do. She felt Lisa's hand brush hers briefly, sending an almost paralyzing tingling sensation up her arm and across her chest.

"I got your number from Theresa." She breathed in, feeling dizzy.

Lisa just smiled, a lazy smile as she swung gently, "would you like a coffee?" She reached over and held her hand. Rachel hesitated for just an instant, "yes. Please." She heard herself laugh nervously. She felt confusion. She seemed to be watching herself from the outside, through a mist. But then the mist cleared as quickly as it started as she became aware that she had been staring silently into Lisa's eyes, but without seeing anything, "I'm sorry, I..."

"It's ok." Lisa interrupted her as if she knew what was going on in her head. It made Rachel feel intensely vulnerable. Lisa squeezed her hand and tugged softly, "come on."

Rachel allowed herself to be pulled along, wondering how she was managing to move at all on legs made of jelly. They walked in silence, exchanging quick glances and shy smiles until they reached an alley next to the post office,

"Down here." Lisa pointed Rachel down a narrow leafy corridor. Rachel raised her eyebrows but made no attempt to resist even though she had no idea where they were going.

"My secret place." Lisa laughed at Rachel's surprised expression, "don't worry, it's nothing sinister. My Mother bought a barn conversion on the edge of the village years ago. She used to use it for secret assignations. But now she's with the Free Spirit Community, she doesn't feel the need to be secretive any more. She lives out her fantasies in public. So she lets me use the barn sometimes."

Lisa motioned towards an even narrower walkway to their right.

As they ducked below the bough of a holly tree to get through, Rachel heard herself ask about the Free Spirit Community, but the question never came out of her mouth. How odd she thought to herself as they came out into an opening and a small, beautifully converted barn with deep eves almost entirely covered in wisteria. Lisa pulled a key from her pocket and unlocked the stable style door, stepping back and taking Rachel's hand in hers once more as she pulled her through into a tiny but exquisite kitchen.

"It's lovely." Rachel said as she took in the solid oak fixtures, the bright and eclectic mix of crockery and a beautiful vase of lilies in the window.

"So are you." Lisa held Rachel's eyes. "I'm so glad you called."

Rachel's heart beat faster and she felt like her blood was rushing through her chest and up into her throat, constricting her air supply. She was aware of her own breathing again, which sounded shallow and quick.

"So am I," she managed as Lisa leaned in towards her slowly.

Rachel closed her eyes and groaned as Lisa's soft, gentle lips touched hers. Lisa pulled back and Rachel looked directly into her deep brown, smiling eyes before moving forward and engaging those wonderful warm lips once more, feeling as if she might drown in the overwhelming sensations coursing through her body. She groaned again, completely incapable of controlling her desire as Lisa slipped her hand under her jumper and caressed her skin, running her thumb over her erect nipple. Their tongues explored gently and then entwined greedily as Lisa reached round to release the clasp of Rachel's bra and then cupped her breasts and massaged them. Rachel stretched her arms up and Lisa pulled both her jumper and t-shirt over her head and tossed them carelessly behind her onto the kitchen floor. She ran her fingers sensitively down Rachel's cheek and across her parted lips before placing her index finger in her mouth and bending down to place her own lips on Rachel's now aching breast.

"Oh, God…" Rachel groaned louder and then sucked harder on Lisa's left index finger as she felt her right hand move slowly and purposefully between her legs.

"No!" Rachel grabbed Lisa's hand and pulled it away. "I'm

sorry." Lisa caught her breath and looked at her, an expression of regret on her face.

"I can't." Rachel said it quickly, determinedly, "I'm sorry." She shook her head, her mind filled with shame as she thought again of Frankie, "I don't even know what I'm doing here." She searched Lisa's eyes quizzically as if she might find the answer there. "I don't mean... I mean you're lovely, it's not you." She shook her head again and dropped Lisa's hand. "I have to go." She bolted towards the door, tears pricking her eyes and clouding her vision so that she fumbled with the door handle, desperate to get out. She finally managed to open it and charged through without glancing back. Lisa looked after her and sighed.

Chapter 18

"You were seen in the lounge." Frankie pointed her finger accusatorially, her eyes narrowing.

Rachel held her hands up, "not me." She shook her head emphatically, "absolutely not me."

"It was you." Frankie's voice rose as she became more forceful.

"Ok, I was in the lounge, so what?" Rachel feigned innocence, widening her eyes with studied care.

"So... you're guilty."

"Rubbish!" Rachel laughed, a nervous edge creeping into her voice, "total garbage."

"Come on. Admit it. You did it."

"No! No way!" Rachel shook her head again, adamantly defiant, "besides, I can say categorically that I've never touched a piece of lead piping, or a dagger, or a candlestick... and anyway how do you know it wasn't Miss Scarlet or Colonel Mustard?"

"Because I've got them..." Frankie's voice trailed away.

"Ha! Thank you." Rachel grinned broadly and checked off the two characters on her Cluedo scorecard.

"Oh, you're such a bloody cheat!" Frankie pouted.

"No, I'm not. You said it. I didn't force you."

"No, but you tricked me."

"Frankie I'm surprised at you. There you are in the middle of a male-dominated city trader room and you still haven't learnt that trickery, cheating and politics are the way to get on."

"Whatever happened to honestly working it out?" Frankie whined.

"That's the woman's way. Men learn early on that getting what you want by any means is the way to win. And if you're a man, talent won't do it. So you have to cheat!"

Frankie laughed and then threw her cards on the board petulantly, "well, I'm not playing anymore." She crossed her arms and humphed.

"Ok, so I win." Rachel grabbed the answer wallet and drew out the cards. Grinning she opened them out for Frankie to see, "there, I was right!"

"Yes. You were right. But you didn't *win*."

Rachel as she stood up and headed off towards the kitchen, "another drink?"

Frankie went back to pouting, "yes," she said moodily.

"Yes, what?" Rachel said breezily.

"Yes, I want another drink," Frankie smirked cheekily.

Rachel smiled and carried on into the kitchen. "*Yes please, darling* are the words I know you're looking for."

Taking the wine bottle from the fridge, she scowled as she recognised it was almost empty. She knew there wasn't another bottle to turn to. "Bugger," she said to herself as she scanned the shelves of the pantry. She clocked the gin bottle. "We're out of wine, do you want to try this village gin?"

"Is that all we've got?"

"Yup".

She jumped as she felt Frankie's chin rest itself on her shoulder. "Hmmm… you smell good." Frankie planted her warm lips on the side of her neck and kissed her, flicking her tongue gently against her skin.

Rachel sighed, "how about I make us a couple of gin and… gin and somethings?"

"I don't want gin and anything." Frankie folded her arms round Rachel's waist and breathed against her neck. "Or maybe I do. Maybe I want a Gin and It…" She sank her teeth gently into Rachel's shoulder, "… without the gin."

"Mmmm… ok. One gin and two Its."

Rachel unscrewed the bottle and sniffed at the contents, "oooh, it smells like some sort of fruit." She held it towards Frankie's nose. Frankie drew back at first and then cautiously sniffed at the bottle.

"Ugh. I'll just have some juice."

"Right. Back up, baby." Rachel pressed back into Frankie.

"I don't want to let go…" Frankie pouted.

"You can resume your position when I'm lying on the sofa."

"Ooh yeah, deal." Frankie kissed her neck again and let go. As she headed back into the living room, Rachel poured a healthy slug of the gin into a glass and added a splash of cranberry, then sipped at it. "Oh my god, this is delicious! Are you sure you don't want any?" she called into Frankie.

"Just cranberry for me… and HURRY UP! My arms are getting cold waiting for you!"

Rachel laughed. "Ok, ok, I'm there in two."

"Make it one!"

Rachel took the two drinks in and nestled next to Frankie on the sofa, feeling a lovely buzz wash over her, "mmm this is good. I can't believe it's gin. Weird." She set the glass down on the table, turned to Frankie and pressed her self down onto her body, before leaning in for a long slow kiss.

"You're right it does taste good…" Frankie grinned and looked up into her eyes, "well at least it tastes good on you, I think I'll have some more."

Rachel smiled lazily. "What's mine is yours baby." She leaned in again, sighing deeply as the buzz turned more into something like euphoria.

Rachel looked at Frankie as she dozed on the sofa, one arm up behind her head in a relaxed sated pose, gloriously naked. She bit her lip and closed her eyes, shaking her head at the whirl of confused thoughts in her head. She couldn't stand it. They had just made love and she had felt every moment of it, *with* love and yet here she was now, her head filled with Lisa. She looked at the clothes strewn across the floor and felt her face redden and her heartbeat begin to race. She looked at her watch. Ten-thirty. Where would Lisa be? Could she sneak out? She looked at Frankie again, an agonising churn of desire rolling through her stomach. She breathed deeply. Pull yourself together Rachel, she thought as she reached for her glass and took another drink of her gin. But even as she thought it, her body stood up to defy her. She glanced back at Frankie as she hurriedly pulled her jeans back on and slipped her sweater over her head. Grabbing her converse, she tiptoed from the room and quietly out of the back door.

"I can't stay long." Rachel rushed the words out before pressing her lips against Lisa's mouth. She felt a melting hot rush as their tongues entwined. Lisa moved her lips downwards and placed a skin-searing kiss on Rachel's neck.

"This is unbearable." Rachel's head span and she let out a moan.

Lisa placed one hand gently over her mouth to stifle the noise as she ran her tongue down between her breasts, "I know." She breathed hotly against her chest. Rachel felt her jeans being tugged down and then the rough, cold graze of the wall.

"I want you so badly it hurts." Rachel gasped as she arched her back and pushed herself against Lisa's hand,

"I know." Lisa pulled away momentarily and their eyes met and locked with longing.

Rachel felt a fleetingly intense pang of guilt as she pulled Lisa's head down against her, then gave in to the exquisitely consuming desire that replaced it and let out another deep, heavy groan.

"...and?" Theresa who'd been pacing the floor in front of Lisa, stopped and made a beckoning motion with her hand, getting her to spill the beans.

"And that's it." Lisa shrugged her shoulders, "I've got her where we need her. Full stop. End of story."

"Yes, yes, you've told us that much," Theresa was irritable, "but exactly how far have you got? Is she with us?"

Lisa paused, "Well no, not exactly. Not yet."

Theresa straightened up and shook her head knowingly, "so you haven't got her?"

Lisa sighed, "well no, not in the sense of getting her to sign up. But I'm as near as dammit. I'll get her round to it tonight."

Theresa stared at her contemplatively. "What's going on?" She asked like she knew something.

Lisa looked defiantly back at her, "there is nothing going on." She said it slowly, deliberately, "...it just takes time, right?" she was starting to show signs of anger.

Theresa leant in closer, "but we don't have time, Lisa. If you don't do it I will. Clear?"

Lisa nodded. "Clear Theresa. As usual. I *will* deal with it. Ok?"

The two women stared at each other challengingly.

"Ok. Lisa. You have until tomorrow."

Lisa stood up, then wheeled around and marched to the door, turning to give Theresa one more defiant glare as she left the room.

Theresa turned to the Master. "What do you think?"

The Master stared evenly at Theresa for a few moments and then leant forward deliberately, "I think things are breaking down," he paused for effect, "I think the situation is being mismanaged and I think you have to take responsibility for that, Theresa." His voice was flat and cold and she knew in that moment that she had lost him. She dropped her head momentarily, swallowing the tears and then stood in defiant pose.

"I'm in control, *Adrian*," she said his name deliberately, gathering confidence at his wince, "and I'm going to stay that way." She placed her index finger firmly against his chest, "don't think for one moment that you'll beat me on this. You're taking on the wrong person."

The Master brushed away her hand, "you're history, Theresa," he held her gaze for a moment and then turned and strode away.

"Have you been out?"

Frankie stretched lazily and reached out to rub Rachel's arm.

"Yeah, went to the pub for some wine. Couldn't hack any more of that gin."

She placed her hand on Frankie's thigh and smiled, feeling like she was dying inside as she looked at Frankie's adorable sleepy face, all wrinkled up and red where she'd been laying scrunched against a cushion. "Are you cold?" she kneeled up and reached over to open the chest behind the sofa, pulling out a warm blanket and laying it gently across Frankie's body.

"Mmmm... take your clothes off." Frankie pulled at her sweater and frowned at her, "you should be naked with me."

Rachel smiled at her, suddenly aware that she couldn't take her clothes off, she would smell of Lisa. She felt a gut wrenching sense of shame wash over her. "It's late darling, we should go to bed."

Frankie sighed, "I don't want to move, it's cozy. Let's sleep here." She tugged at Rachel's sweater again, "come on, I want to hold you."

"Ok baby. Just let me go and get some pillows and a sheet. I'll be back in a few minutes and we can snuggle." She stood up quickly and headed towards the stairs.

"No kiss?" Frankie pouted, "you haven't kissed me for hours and hours, maybe even days, or weeks…"

Rachel smiled at her tenderly and hoped the sadness she felt overwhelmed with didn't appear on her face. She blew a kiss over to Frankie. "I'll be back before you know it. Missing you alreadyyyyy…" she called out behind her as she bounded up the stairs. Heading to the bathroom, she stripped in double quick time and ran a sink full of water, using a flannel to wash herself and staring miserably at her cheating image in the mirror. She let out a sob as she reached for a towel to dry herself off. She stared at herself again, "what the fuck are you doing?" she took a deep breath and grabbed her tooth brush, wanting suddenly to rid herself of any trace of Lisa, "you're going mad, that's what you're doing," she said around the toothbrush as she scrubbed, "totally fucking mad."

"Rewind… There!"

Nathan, sitting in front of a TV screen with Theresa and Roy standing behind him, was fast forwarding a tape that showed two figures walking together.

Theresa studied the tape closely,

"See? In the shadow there?"

She glanced back at Roy as Nathan spoke,

"Could be…" Roy peered at the gloomy picture, "what makes you think it's them, Nathan?"

Nathan leant forward and tapped the screen. "See there, those are NikeAir2017B's. And them," he tapped again slightly to the right, "they're Birkenstocks. Now, look at this." Nathan removed the video tape and slotted in another, watching the counter as he fast forwarded and slickly focusing in on a frame in which a still of Rachel showed her footwear. He tapped the screen again. "Birkenstocks." He repeated the process, this time showing a picture of Lisa as she walked past the village store. Once more he focused on the footwear, "see? NikeAir2017Bs."

"So it was them." Theresa straightened up, "how long were they there for?"

"Don't know," Nathan shook his head, "wasn't much doin' so I switched to the Atkinson's backyard car-key party."

"Alright. Have you seen any other activity between those two?"

"Haven't looked. Want me to run through the tapes over the last couple of weeks?"

"Yes. You do that Nathan and call me with an update."

Theresa took Roy by the arm and led him his towards the door, "what do you think?"

"Looks to me like she's doing exactly as she's been asked... pulling the girl in."

"You don't think she might be in too deep?"

"I don't know what you expect, Theresa, she's not going to get a conversion overnight, it'd create too much suspicion. I think you should cut her a bit of slack."

Theresa stared silently at Roy for a moment, "I can't." she admitted finally.

"Why not?"

"The Master's putting me under pressure to finalise this situation. And Lisa's been off kilter for a while now. She feels like a risk. Remember the incident with Doug over your Extra Thick Cream?"

Roy rubbed his earlobe nervously, "well, to be fair, the cream was probably off. And as for the Mater, I think you can afford not to worry too much about him."

Theresa frowned. "What makes you say that?"

"Well, I think he's losing it a bit don't you?"

Theresa shook her head to indicate she didn't get his drift.

"He's just panicking because the newcomers might find something out and spill the beans before we get to them. But chances are they'll either come along with us, or just move out. Looks like the redhead is under Lisa's control, so that's looking promising—and if Lisa gets her hooked, the other one will either be 'encouraged' to join in—or get out. Simple as that. You should chill out a bit."

"Chill out?"

Roy jangled his keys agitatedly, "yes, Theresa, chill out."

"Are you setting me up for a fall just because you want me to be less active in the club?"

"Oh for Christ's sake Theresa. Of course not!" Roy jangled his keys again, "it's just common sense. The Master's got a bee in it and he's taking it out on you. Just chill out. Now I've nothing more to say on it, Theresa. I'm going to Grace's!" On which, he turned and headed for the door.

Theresa stood silent in his wake, wondering where Roy had picked up the expression "chill out". It sounded weird coming from him. She jumped as a deep voice came from the dark of the room jolted out of her reverie.

"You am gonna lose him, my girl," Nathan stood up from the crouching position he'd been occupying as he perused the tinned meatballs, "take my word for it, he's making other arrangements."

"What do you mean?" she asked sharply,

"No more to say on that. Just you mark my words, girl." He handed her the tin he had picked from the shelf, "and these meatballs are past their sell by date. Might be an omen, that."

Theresa watched as Nathan walked past her and out of the room. Disturbed by what he had said, she picked up the phone and dialed the number for the umpteenth time. She sighed as she held the receiver to her ear and listened as the ring tone droned on. She shook her head and looked at the phone in exasperation. She was just about to give up yet again when she heard a click.

"Hello?" Theresa could hear the sound of breathing, so she knew she was there.

"Hello. Irene are you there?" The breathing continued, Theresa pressed on, "I've been trying to get hold of you for weeks." Theresa's voice was gentle. She waited. "Look I know this is tough, but we need to talk."

"I know," the voice finally responded at the other end of the line.

"It is her right?"

"Yes," came the reluctant reply. There was a heavy sigh, "I'm sorry, I should have called. I just didn't know what to do. Or say."

"Did you try to stop her?"

"Yes, of course I did." The voice was full of hurt, "but what was I supposed to do? She's a grown woman, she has her own life. I don't know what happens on a day to day basis any more. I didn't even know where she was going until it was pretty much too late to do anything about it. And if I tried too hard then it would just have raised an alarm."

Theresa sighed, "I know. I understand. And really I guess what's done is done."

"And anyway, she has no idea. So it's really only you that it's going to be painful for. I don't think she needs to know."

She knew Irene was right. "I agree... but, well, let's say it's awkward." Theresa hesitated, finally realizing there really was little point in the conversation. It would be impossible to explain the complexities of life in the village and all the implications to someone who had no idea of its history or what was going on. "And Irene, whatever happens you know I will always appreciate you keeping me in touch with what's going on."

"She's a wonderful woman Theresa, don't make this hard for her," Irene pleaded, "she doesn't need to know."

"I get it. It will be fine. You did a great job with her. Thank you Irene. I'll always be grateful for what you did. I'm sure eveything will work out for the best. Goodbye." She hung up and stared into space, letting out a deep sigh as memories flooded back and threatened to overwhelm her. Even for Theresa, this felt worryingly like a complication too far.

Chapter 19

"I've never known such a poor turnout," the Master said abjectly as he absently flicked at a fly that had landed on his naked thigh.

"It's the incomers." Roy lay his head back on his forearm and stared up at an impossibly blue sky.

"There hasn't been single ride today. That's unheard of," the Master flicked his head in the direction of the adult size rocking horse, its leather straps dangling motionless and unused.

"Well you wouldn't want to get caught on that by a stranger would you?" huffed Roy.

The Master looked at his watch. "S'pose not. D'you think anyone else'll turn out now?"

"Nope."

The Master sat forward, elbows on his knees. "It's all falling apart Roy." He glanced round, calculating how far he might go, "time was you'd get a good couple of rides and a threesome out here on a Sunday afternoon."

"Mmmm..." Roy yawned lazily, "but it's so open here—and it's only a stone's throw from their cottage. Chances are they'll come out for a walk one afternoon and catch us at it."

That was enough for the Master, he decided to seize on the opportunity, "look, Roy, this has all been badly mismanaged." The Master thumped the grass at his side, prompting Roy to sit up abruptly.

"What do you mean?"

"I know it's difficult for you Roy, given the circumstances, but maybe... well maybe Theresa's losing her grip."

Roy stared evenly at the Master, "you might be right."

The Master's eyebrow flicked almost imperceptibly, surprised by Roy's easy willingness to accept the criticism. He recognised it as confirmation he needed to pursue his case, "it's not her fault really. I mean she's just taken on too much." Roy nodded contemplatively and The Master warmed to his subject. "We need to take the pressure off—handle some of the difficult issues for her—take a bit off her plate so to speak. Roy, I need a deputy." The Master got to the point, now feeling

131

bold and determined.

Roy's eyebrows shot up, "deputy?"

"Yes. A second in command. Someone I can rely on to move things forward with me." He regarded Roy and then thrust his hand out in his direction, "I need you, Roy. Shake on it now. You become my deputy and we'll get this place back on its feet again."

Roy looked down at the Master's hand and paused, but for the briefest of moments, before placing his in its firm grip.

"You know I'm loyal Master. You know I'll always serve you and the Club first." His eyes welled up and he swallowed hard, "even if it means, well, I can't say it, Theresa's been everything and I owe her so much. This isn't easy."

"I know, I know Roy," the Master leaned over and placed his arms around Roy and hugged him, "but you know in your heart that this is the right thing to do."

"Yeah," Roy withdrew, vaguely embarrassed that his naked state left him with the need to wipe his nose with his arm.

"So," the Master slapped his thighs and stood before Roy, reaching down to help him up, "it's done. It's a new day, a new dawn for the Club. We'll drink on it and make plans to address the issues." The Master rubbed his hands together, "now let's get this mare on the trailer, I don't think she's going to be rocking any more today."

"Business first." Dr Taylor flicked the syringe teasingly as she sat on the corner of the desk, swinging her leg lazily, staring coldly at Roy. He was vaguely fascinated by the hole in her fishnets, which appeared to be expanding before him. He blinked hard and tried to restore his vision to a semblance of normality as the need for his drug of choice started to get the better of him. He looked up into her eyes and wondered momentarily how much time had passed before she'd said anything, suddenly feeling that her question had been hanging in the air for eons.

"It's in hand, it's in hand," he said it hurriedly as if speaking faster would make up for the time delay in his response. "I've got the Master where I need him and we'll be well placed to make a move within a few weeks." He felt intense pressure behind his eyes and his lips were so dry he felt they might crack at any moment. He tried to lick them, but his mouth was devoid of moisture.

"How much money have you got out since I saw you last?"

He rubbed his temple, feeling her eyes bore into him and hating her with an intensity he couldn't hide from his voice.

"I've skimmed a few thousand off. I need to be careful until I can sort the books out to cover for it."

She looked at him calculatingly.

"So when will you have the accounts?"

"Don't push me!" He snapped at her, then instantly regretted it. She was in control, it was a mistake to rile her. He held his hand up. "Sorry. It's more difficult. She has them locked away in her personal safe, I've never had the access information. I'm working on it."

Dr Taylor cocked her head to one side, regarding him with a mixture of suspicion and disdain. She stared at the needle she had in her hand, gently putting pressure on it so that a spurt of the fluid that Roy craved flew into the air. She looked at him, that mean, teasing smile playing on her lips. He thought how he hated her and how he wanted her to tell her to shove her needle... but his addiction was stronger than his courage.

"I swear I'll get them." He opened out his palms in a gesture of honesty. Dr Taylor tapped her lower lip with her forefinger and then nodded slowly.

"I have to," he continued, "if I don't, she's going to clock what's going on. So I'm not shirking. I need to cover my back."

"Alright. Three weeks. You've got three weeks to get her out," she said as she indicated that Roy should roll up his sleeve.

Roy nodded eagerly and closed his eyes as he felt the needle pushed beneath the surface of his skin and start taking him to the place he so wanted to be.

Chapter 20

"I don't understand why you do it. You're so beautiful." Rachel propped herself up on her elbow and looked down into Lisa's eyes, running the edge of her thumb down her cheek.

Lisa drew in a deep breath, "maybe beautiful on the outside." She looked away and started to get out of the bed.

"No. Stop. Stay here with me," Rachel pleaded and reached for her arm to hold her back. Lisa sighed and lay back down, but Rachel knew instinctively that she had disconnected, that the bubble of ecstasy they had been lying in had been burst, at least for now.

"Look it's hard for me to explain. It's complicated. It's about how I was raised. A warped sense of freedom. Not with typical values. And also about being needed. Wanted. Oh I don't know, a ton of things." She looked at Rachel and shook her head, "you make me feel ridiculous. I can't bear it. All you need to know right now is that I feel differently about it. I don't know if I want to do it any more, but it's not that easy. There are things... things you don't know."

Rachel frowned, she wanted to be indignant, she wanted Lisa to be definite about not wanting to do it, not to have doubt. She bit her lip to stop herself speaking out.

"I'm not what you think I am. Don't make this more difficult." Lisa sat on the edge of the bed and stared out of the window.

"I'm sorry, I shouldn't keep talking about it." Rachel slumped back down on to her back and covered her face with her arm, tears pricked her eyes as the situation and all its implications suddenly overwhelmed her, the conflict felt insurmountable. At the same time as massive confusion flooded her about the duplicitous nature of what she was doing, she had more or less given in to whatever was compelling her to carry on this relationship with Lisa. But she didn't understand why. She did know that she now cared about Lisa, regardless of what might come of their own situation. She checked herself, determined not to cry, she knew it wouldn't help. She felt Lisa's hand, warm and comforting as she rested it on her stomach and her anguish melted under the tenderness of her touch.

"Let's not spoil the time we have together," Lisa murmured and then let her tongue trace the line of Rachel's hip bone before drawing the flesh on the inside of her thigh into her mouth and sucking it gently. Rachel groaned, aware of Lisa moving down the bed. She arched her back as Lisa lay between her thighs and she felt her soft hair on her belly and her warm wet mouth open onto her lips. Still sensitive from their earlier lovemaking, she gasped as Lisa's tongue moved in circles on her, so exquisitely softly it felt like the wings of a butterfly. "Oh my God..." Rachel arched and pushed her hips forward, the feeling was so intense, almost unbearable as Lisa brought her to the edge of climax, slipping her fingers inside her and rolling her tongue harder at the same time until she felt another massive bursting flow of ecstasy and screamed...

"Fuck!" She breathed out a long, slow breath as waves of ecstasy flowed through her.

"I did..." she saw Lisa's smiling face peer up from between her legs and laughed between deep breaths.

Rachel reached down and cupped Lisa's face with her hands, "that was unbelievable."

Lisa grinned and crawled up over Rachel's; body, entwining their legs and snuggling into Rachel's neck to plant warm wet kisses on the skin beneath her ear. Rachel wrapped her arms round Lisa's back and hugged her tight. "Oh my God I think I love you..." And as she said it she opened her eyes wide. It had come from nowhere, spontaneous and uncontrollable. She felt Lisa draw away from her neck and turned to look in her eyes, almost afraid to see what reaction she might have caused.

"I'm so..." but Lisa placed her finger on her lips to hush her and traced the line of her mouth as she looked deeply into her eyes. She smiled and leant back down to place her mouth next to Rachel's ear and whispered, "I love you too."

Rachel closed her eyes and frowned. Confusion, anxiety and guilt washing through her, making her feel sick again. When she was with Lisa, it was all consuming and she was utterly lost in her. But when she was away from her, despite the yearning she couldn't work out quite why she was feeling the way she was. She didn't want to cheat on Frankie. She didn't feel any less love for Frankie when she was with her and the guilt was almost as overwhelming as the yearning. It didn't make sense. It was uncontrollable and sometimes during the time she spent with Lisa she felt eerily lost. Like it was some kind of dream; a dream that was also a nightmare. She sighed deeply as once again she asked herself silently what the fuck she was doing. She squeezed her eyes tight shut and thought about her expression of love for Lisa. At this moment it didn't feel like love, yet when she had said it the compulsion had been automatic, like it came from somewhere she wasn't aware of. And she felt bad about that too because she knew that Lisa's love was genuine. She felt like she needed to scream.

"I'm thinking of taking a week off."

Rachel jumped as Frankie's statement took her out of her contemplation. And then she froze, her hands deep in soap suds as she stared through the kitchen window out at the back garden. She felt her heart sink. She could also feel Frankie's eyes on her back.

"That's a great idea." She hoped she sounded as bright and positive as she'd tried to be.

"Maybe next week."

Rachel bit her lip. "Fantastic!" She turned round to look at Frankie, "can you do that with such short notice?" Hoping that the answer might be no.

"Looks like it. I spoke to Joe yesterday and he seemed to think it would be ok." Frankie smiled and came towards her wrapping her arms around her. Lisa held her arms aloft, "mind my suds," she joked as she drew back.

"You've been doing the dishes for ages, come on, finish up, let's talk about what to do with our week," said Frankie as she headed for the kitchen door, "we could go away somewhere," she said glancing back with a grin

Rachel turned back to the window and plunged her hands back into the washing bowl, closing her eyes and working through her split emotions. A romantic week away with Frankie. She smiled at the memory of their last week in Thailand, a magical, passionate time. But before she knew it, the memory faded and she started wondering how

136

she could possibly live without Lisa for a whole week.

"It's the biggest cock I've ever seen," Nathan grumbled as he stood behind Theresa's shoulder with a steaming cup of coffee.

"It doesn't mean he's going to win," said Theresa a little distractedly as she peered at the footage on the TV monitor.

"But it gives him a damn good chance." Nathan tapped the screen in his usual confirming manner, "see what I mean?"

Theresa examined the shadowy figure.

"Size isn't everything. And yes, I do see." She paused and contemplated the implications. "You need to keep this confidential Nathan. I don't want anyone else knowing you've added this new camera for me, ok?"

He tapped his nose, "uhuh. Confidential." He stepped back and slurped his coffee again. "My girls are good uns, but they might be frightened off when they see it." Nathan chewed at a fingernail, still concerned by the size of his rival. Theresa smiled, his pre-occupation meant she could breathe easy about keeping the camera a secret.

"Chances are they'll be separated, the Judges aren't stupid, they know putting them all together makes it harder," she offered him some comfort.

"It's is a beauty mind, got to say it. Never seen a rooster quite like it."

"Well that's more likely to sway the Judges isn't it?" Theresa glanced back at him. "Just you focus on making your hens the best they can be on the day. The best-looking chicken last year was a hen."

Nathan nodded. "True enough. And still a good two months before show day. Cocks don't always last long do they?" Nathan winked at Theresa.

"Enough of the cock," she turned her attention back to the video, "do you know what's going on here?"

Theresa rewound the tape and watched again as Roy approached Grace's door, looking round surreptitiously as he used a key to open it and let himself in. She bit her lip. Regular enough to have a key?

Nathan sucked in his breath as the tape wound on and four

more locals arrived one at a time, all equally surreptitious and nervous.

"Come on Nathan, what's going on?" Theresa became more insistent.

Nathan stared at her, cogs turning in his head. She nodded at him, "get it out." He sighed.

"Swing Anon."

"Swing a what?" Theresa spun the chair round and gave him a puzzled look.

"Swing Anon. It is a group for them who have family members addicted to Swinging."

"Oh for Christ's sake, you're kidding me?"

"Nope."

Theresa buried her face in her hands for a moment and then looked up. Laughing, but not the kind of laugh that found something funny. She shook her head, "this is some kind of joke right?"

"Nope." Nathan thrust his hands in his dungaree pockets and rocked back on the heels of his hobnails.

Theresa rubbed her forehead. "Did Roy start this?"

Nathan nodded.

"With Grace?"

Nathan nodded again.

"How did you find out about it?"

Nathan tapped his nose.

"Come on Nathan!" she shouted and Nathan raised a warning finger at her.

"Don't you get on a high horse with me. I don't reveal my sources. If I did, I'd dry up the information and that wouldn't do no-one no good, now would it?" He leaned down and peered into her face.

"Shit!" she stood up and started pacing the room. "shit, shit, shit!"

"Language! Calm down!" His words were sharp, "I don't like to hear them words from a lady." He crossed his arms and regarded her with some distaste, "that's better," he said as her face softened, "now I been warning you, Theresa, there's mucky business going on, you take it serious now and think about all this."

Theresa nodded, "sorry, Nathan. You're right. So. Who's in on

138

it? Do you know what the plan is, where they're going with this?"

"I got a list." Nathan dug in his overalls and pulled out a sheet of paper, "been going on for a couple of weeks. On the surface looks like an innocent enough thing, if your partner's playing away and you're not, can cause a lot of grief, right? Seems like a good idea to calm 'em down with a bit of group therapeutics. But..." Nathan paused for effect, "looks like they're also trying to stir up some anti-club fever from what I hear. Seems like you be the target of that mostly."

Theresa took the list from Nathan's out-stretched hand, "ok. Got it," she patted Nathan's arm, "I'm grateful. You're a good man. Keep your ear to the ground. I'm going to have a think about your wise advice on what to do about it." Theresa took her jacket from the back of the chair and put it on. "I'm off now, let me know if you hear anything more." As she strode towards the door, she turned back to Nathan who was already back in his chair and scanning more footage on the screen.

"And don't you worry about Roy's cock, it'll be history by the time the village show comes around, you mark my words." Theresa winked back at him and drew the door closed.

Rachel wiped her hands on the towel as she walked into the living room where Frankie sat with her laptop, intent on the information on the screen. She put her hand on her shoulder and Frankie held it and kissed it briefly before carrying on her search.

"Where do you fancy?" she asked looking up at Rachel, "Paris, Venice, New York... Thailand again?" Frankie's eyes glazed a little as she obviously played the memory out in her head, "that was amazing." She let out a long, happy sigh, "mmm great beaches, great food, great people, great pool... grrreaaaat sex." She wrapped her arms round Rachel's hips, raised her top a little and kissed her belly. "Your tummy was sooooooo brown. I love your belly."

Rachel placed her hand on Frankie's hair and stroked it, so torn it was unbearable. "They all sound great..." her voice tapered off, "but you know I wonder if we should do this another time?"

"Why?" Frankie looked her quizzically, "it's a great chance to just do something spontaneous, get away for a few days and have some fun. Come on, we need a break. I'm exhausted. The moving, commuting, year end, it's been hectic. So why not?"

"I know, I'm tired too." Rachel leant over and wrapped her arms round Frankie's shoulders, "but maybe too tired to travel? You know? Maybe we could just spend a week here. We can nest; and you can explore a bit more round the village. We can just relax and enjoy each other here. Don't you think? Then we can plan something later in the year. Do it properly, make it something really special?"

Frankie leaned into Rachel's arms and sighed.

"I feel like we need to reconnect," she looked up to make direct eye contact, "things don't feel right at the moment."

"What do you mean?" Rachel tried to pull away, but Frankie held her close.

"I feel like we've... disconnected, been apart too much and lost a bit of our usual magic. I don't know... maybe it's just the pressure of the move and all the changes."

They both fell silent for a few seconds.

"Do you think it's me?" she couldn't help probing, she wanted to know if Frankie was suspicious.

"No... I don't know. Probably both of us. Guess it might be because you're settling in the village, making friends and it feels like you're making a life apart from me. I just feel a bit isolated from you." She paused. "It's not your fault," she looked up again, "but I couldn't stand to lose you."

Rachel drew in a breath. Seeing the anguish in Frankie's eyes was agony.

"Babe..." she squeezed her arms tight round Frankie's body and kissed the top of her head, guilt searing through her veins again and making her heart ache. But the thought of being away... she wrestled with herself internally for a few minutes as she held Frankie and felt her body melting into hers. And still, the compromise was the only option that made any sense, even though it felt like a warped sense. She couldn't win, on any front.

"Let's spend the week here," she said assertively, "we'll go out and get you friendly with all the people I've met. We can be together, enjoy our new home and settle you in," she cupped Frankie's cheek in the palm of her hand, "everything's going to be fine."

Frankie closed her eyes and slowly nodded, she sounded resigned when she finally spoke, "yeah, ok. Sounds like a plan. Let's do that."

"Rachel!" it was a piercing shriek, "Rachel darling, do come in, please!"

Rachel looked up across the façade of the manor house to try and locate the source of the invitation and couldn't keep her jaw from dropping when she found herself staring up at two dangling breasts, a face just visible beyond them,

"Oops," cried Lisa's mother as she scooped them up in her hands and tucked them back behind the window ledge, before craning down to smile at Rachel, "it's lovely to see you, darling… but if it's Lisa you're seeking out, I'm afraid she left about 15 minutes ago. Wait, I'll come and let you in!"

Before Rachel could object, Donna's head disappeared inside the window. Rachel let out a sigh and headed for the imposing arched wooden doors that formed the manor's main entrance.

A few moments later Donna opened the door and burst through it, "daaaarling!" she enfolded Rachel in a huge hug, her silk dressing gown billowing around her like a giant red Chinese tent, "it's delightful to see you!" She air-kissed her on both cheeks and then grabbed her hand, "come in, we'll have tea!"

Rachel was pulled through the entrance and found herself trotting alongside the strident Donna who marched her through to the sitting room with its stunning views out across the lawns.

"Peters!" Donna called loudly, "oh hell, where's my bell," she muttered as she maintained a firm hold on Rachel's arm and crisscrossed the room, "Peters!"

"Is that it?" Rachel pointed with her free hand at a golden hand-bell on a side table.

"Ah yes, splendid. Would you like to ring my bell?" she raised her eyebrows and smiled.

"Er, you do it." Rachel handed it over, blushing.

Donna took it, her eyes dancing with amusement as she rang it ferociously. Rachel took the opportunity to free herself as Donna's grip loosened with the effort of bell ringing,

"Peters!"

"I'm here Donna," said Peter's softly and they both spun round to find that she'd walked quietly into the room and was standing behind them. Rachel was impressed by her stealth. Peters smiled at her warmly.

"Hello again."

"Hi!" Rachel grinned. There was something quite engaging about Peters.

"I expect you'll be wanting tea?"

"Indeed. And something to nibble on Peters. Thank you." Donna ushered her away. "Now darling, let's sit together." And despite there being an array of various chairs and sofas. Donna led Rachel to a chaise longue and settled herself thigh to thigh beside her, holding her hand between the two of hers. Rachel glanced down and was vaguely perturbed by the sausage like clumsiness of her fingers resting with alarmingly sweaty discomfort between Donna's elegant, slender and perfectly manicured hands.

"Now, I want to find out more about you," purred Donna, "I know Lisa adores you, she seems... smitten." Donna smiled and engaged her eyes, looking searchingly into them and Rachel felt her colour rise. Though Donna's voice was soft, gentle, there was something a little dangerous and challenging about her tone. Donna expertly left silence between them and Lisa realised she was expected to answer. She gulped, embarrassingly loudly.

"Ummm, we get along really well." Rachel tried weakly to remove her hand, but it was clamped, "she's really nice. I like her."

Donna smiled charmingly and edged closer, though Rachel had thought that wasn't possible. She could feel herself sweating.

"I think you like her very much, Rachel... hmm?" Donna paused, "I mean, perhaps more than just on a friendly basis?"

"I don't know what you mean?" Rachel's heart thumped.

"I mean I think your interest in my daughter goes beyond friendship," Donna's voice dropped, like a low hum and she lowered her eyes, regarding Rachel suggestively, "I believe you are lovers, are you not?"

142

Rachel drew a deep breath as her mind raced.

"We're just friends," she managed to be firm. Another heavy silence filled the air and Donna licked her lips, then moved her face in closer to Rachel's.

"Tea!"

Rachel nearly jumped out of her skin and felt a similar reaction in Donna as Peters cheerily and loudly announced the arrival of refreshments. Relieved, Rachel took the opportunity to release her hand from Donna's momentarily relaxed grip and stood up quickly. She gave a panicked look at Peters, who had crept into the room unheard with her tea tray. She thought she caught a little nod from Peters.

"Crumpet?" Peters enquired politely of Donna, raising an eyebrow.

"Why Peters, you must have read my mind. Perfect."

Rachel watched as the two exchanged a 'look'. She felt distinctly uncomfortable.

"They're very fresh," said Peters, a bit too deliberately, "I strongly suggest you wait a while before eating them. Otherwise, you might get burnt."

Donna regarded Peters somewhat ruefully. "Thank you, Peters, I appreciate the advice." Peters nodded at Donna, "You're welcome. Shall I pour?"

"We'll be just fine, you're excused." Donna was terse.

Peters turned towards Rachel and frowned, she held the tray in one hand and with her back turned to Donna, pointed in the direction of the door, then left the room.

"Do you take, milk? Sugar?" Donna patted the seat next to her as she asked.

"Just milk please." Rachel glanced at the door, "I need the bathroom, could you tell me…"

"Oh of course darling, take a right out of the door, then it's the fourth door on the right." Donna smiled at her, "hurry back though, darling, you don't want your crumpet to get cold now do you?"

"No. Absolutely not. Can't stand cold crumpet." Rachel pointed at the door, "I'll be right back."

"Oh my God," Rachel couldn't help saying it out loud as she

closed the door behind her and started marching purposefully towards the toilet. As she approached it, Peters stepped out from an archway opposite and beckoned her over, ushering her into another room. Closing the door quietly behind her, Peters spoke softly.

"Best if you leave now, I'll give Donna an excuse, tell her you're unwell." Peters hesitated, "Donna likes to share," she looked meaningfully at Rachel, "it's a common thing in this village."

"Do you mean what I think you mean?" asked Rachel, horrified by the thought that passed through her mind.

"Probably," said Peters glancing backwards, "don't worry we won't let it happen. Come with me"

"Too bloody right it won't," said Rachel, feeling a little sick as she followed behind her. "Peters do you know where Lisa is? She's not been answering my calls and she's not been home."

Peters held a side entrance door to the building open for her and ushered her through as she replied, "her life is complicated, she has many issues to deal with," Peters chose her words carefully, "when she's stressed or needs to work things out, she hides herself away. Don't take it personally, she'll be in touch when she's ready. But just so you know, I've never seen her so happy as when she talks about you. Now go, before Donna works out her real crumpet's gone AWOL."

Rachel smiled, "thanks, Peters."

She winked and closed the door as Rachel walked rapidly down the drive to her freedom.

Chapter 21

Theresa held the photo in front of her and tapped the desk contemplatively. She nodded to herself as she flicked on the tape and watched Rachel and Lisa embrace in the barn's kitchen window. She switched to the footage of Roy and the Swing Anonners congregating at Grace's house. She tapped her lip and looked at the phone for the umpteenth time. Finally, she picked it up and dialed.

"Adrian!" She heard him tut at the other end of the phone, but ignored his exasperation, "we need to talk."

"I'm tied up right now Theresa, what is it?"

Theresa heard a whip crack in the background, "it's club business and it's urgent."

"Ow, fuck! That was a bit harsh." Adrian whimpered, as the whip cracked again.

"Sorry mate."

Theresa heard Digger in the background and rolled her eyes, "I mean it Adrian, we need to speak urgently!" She heard a sigh.

"Give me five minutes, I'll meet you by the bushes in Holly Lane. It better be important."

Adrian cut the line before Theresa could respond. She looked at it as she said, "if I go down, you're going down with me." Then she dialed again.

Theresa peered out through the Leylandii that lined Holly Lane and waited for the Master. She watched as his distinctive silhouette marched down the driveway. Stepping out as he approached, she waved to ctah his attention, but he appeared not to see her. She realised he was wearing some sort of hood that was impairing his vision. She stepped out further and waved both arms over her head. Catching sight of her finally, he quickened his pace, but appeared to get confused about the direction again and he veered to the left, tripped over the flogger that dangled from his belt.

"Shit!" He picked himself up and grabbed the flailing strands of leather, tying them in a knot as he finally finding his way to her. "Bastard thing. I knew I should have ordered the regular length. Marjory said she'd shorten it. Can't frigging rely on anyone, I'll have to do it myself." he grumbled. His voice was muffled by his headgear and Theresa had to strain to hear him.

"Take that thing off," she demanded, pointing at his head.

"I can't. It's too tight and my hairs are caught in it." The Master peered at her through the narrow slits of his gimp mask, "bloody Marjory again. She can't be bothered to shorten my flogger, but she can shrink this sure enough. She put it in the tumble dryer with my underwear." He groaned and rubbed his left buttock, "christ, I must have welts all over my ass," he tried to take a look at his bum, but the mask prevented him, "Digger doesn't have a light touch with that whip."

"For Christ's sake, I can barely hear you." Theresa tugged at the hood to try and get the zippable mouth piece in line with his lips, pulling at it from where it was just beneath his nostrils.

"Ouch! Fuck it, that hurt!" He pinched his nostrils together to ease the pain as she noticed a nose hair sticking out through the zip.

"Sorry," she said grimacing at his distress as she tried to drag it down just a little further.

"Leave it, woman, I can't bloody see you now!" The slits had now dropped below his eyes and he swiped blindly at Theresa's hand to ward her off, readjusting the mask to get her back in his sights.

"What do you want, I need to get back," he said, the leather muffling his obvious aggression, "Floosy's tied to the bed and she's got to be on duty in the fish and chip van in half an hour."

"Digger will let her out."

"No he bloody won't, he'll stop her going, reckons the smell of oil and beer batter puts him off his stroke and she comes back reeking of it. Takes two days of showering to get rid of it apparently."

"Okay well, this won't take long." Theresa ducked down to be able to see into his eyes, "I think there's something being planned by Roy and Grace that you should know about. I've been reliably informed that they've set up a Swing Anon club."

"A swing a what?"

"Swing Anon. It's for people whose friends and relatives are addicted to swinging."

"What? Are you kidding? Roy?" The Master let out a muffled laugh, "don't be ridiculous. Would be more like a swing a thon..." the Master stopped abruptly, processing what she had said.

Theresa narrowed her eyes and peered into his mask. She paused for a second, holding his slitted eyes with hers, "no, it's ludicrous," he concluded, "there's no way. It's beyond comprehension that Roy would be involved with that."

"Well, that aside... I know it seems hypocritical beyond belief on the surface, but actually, the purpose is to bring you down."

Instant anger caused the Master's neck and chest to turn a deep hue of red and Theresa watched as the mask stretched to its maximum extent, expanding like a black balloon as his blood pressure rose, until it looked like it was about to explode.

"Get this bloody thing off me!" The Master clawed at his smoothly domed head, panting in his anxiety to free himself.

"Turn round and keep still." Theresa examined the mask as the Master turned his back towards her, his leather chaps scraping against her legs as he wriggled, starting to gasp for air. "Keep still!!" she tugged at the zip at the nape of his neck.

"Owww, God damn it, Tess, that's my hair." He swatted blindly at her like she was a fly and rubbed at his neck. Memories flooded back at him calling her Tess and she couldn't stop herself from smiling as she pulled his hands away.

"I remember the last time you called me that," she said as she tugged more carefully at his zipper to pull it up towards his scalp, "we were on the switchbacks in Blackpool. It was our last weekend away together."

"Never mind that!" he interrupted, bursting her bubble of happiness as he finally released the mask, pulling it back over a flushed and sweating face, "what do you mean that Roy and Grace want to bring me down?"

Theresa's romantic memories were crushed as she regarded the Master's crease marked cheeks and watery eyes.

"They're plotting to take over the club. The first move is to cause some form of mutiny amongst the abstainers. They're claiming that you

147

are responsible for pressuring people to participate when they don't want to." Theresa regarded the Master with interest as he seethed.

"How do you know this?" He jabbed his forefinger at her as he demanded an explanation.

"Someone alerted me to it. Someone who has the best interests of the club at heart."

"Who?" he demanded.

"I can't say." She crossed her arms defensively, "but a reliable and loyal source."

The Master, momentarily distracted by his pain, grabbed his buttock again and moaned, "you haven't got any savlon have you?"

Theresa reached into her handbag, "Germolene." She handed him a tube. "It's antiseptic. I always keep it on hand."

"Yeah, I remember." He grinned at her briefly as he massaged the ointment into his burning buttock, the relief bringing him back to the point of their meeting, "this could all be bollocks as far as I can see. How do you know it's true? Might just be a rumour."

"Nope. It's true. The group meets every Wednesday night at nine pm at Grace's place. You can check it out for yourself." Theresa watched him as he took it in.

"I've got to go," he said abruptly, handing back the tube of cream, "we need to speak again. I want to know what's going on here. And I warn you, Theresa, you better not be playing games with me." He grabbed his mask from her hand and turned away, his Cuban heels echoing in the darkness as he headed back through the night, the moonlight reflecting on his bare cheeks.

Theresa smiled as she regarded his retreating form. "Oh, this is no game, Adrian. This is deadly serious."

"They reckon it was Porkchop's boyfriend."

Roy listened as two elderly villagers, Elsie and Edna exchanged gossip in the surgery waiting room.

"Porkchop was cheating on him every Thursday in the butcher's back room," Elsie nodded at Edna knowingly. She noticed Roy out of the corner of her eye watching them and waved in his direction. He nodded and smiled back, turning away as she lowered her voice.

"Out where he hangs his rabbits?" Elsie asked, screwing her nose up in disgust.

Edna looked at her blankly, "well, I don't know what he was hanging in there do I? Could have been rabbits, who knows?" she tutted, "anyway, she never told her boyfriend they were at it."

"Oh, so he didn't know?" Edna was shocked.

"No. Against club rules. Apparently, she was wanting to leave him, so she kept it quiet."

"She's never been shy about it before."

"No, I know, but apparently this was different. Anyway, he found out and followed Porkchop there last week. He waited til the Back in Ten Minutes sign went up on the door and then broke in." Elsie's voiced dropped further and she ran her tongue along her cheek, Edna craned forward to hear her, "gave him what for in the meatballs," she nodded at Edna, "if you get my drift." Edna drew in her breath, "gave him a taste of his own chopper."

"Oooh, I say. That's a bit below the belt."

Elsie nodded, "then he wrecked the place. Porkchop wanted to call the police, but apparently, Terry stopped her. Didn't want anyone to find out about all the goings on."

Roy smiled to himself as he listened. There was no place to hide in this village when it came to affairs.

"Roy Jones!"

He jumped at the sound of his name. Picking up his backpack, he responded to Dr Taylor's call into the reception area of the surgery and headed down the corridor to her office. She smiled charmingly at him and held the door open as the receptionist passed by, "good morning Mr Jones and what can I do for you today?" She ushered him in and as the door closed her demeanor changed, "have you got it?" she demanded.

"Yes, but you'll need to copy it now and give it back." Roy pulled out a sheath of papers but withdrew them when she tried to grab them.

"That's not easy, I have appointments stacked back to back." She regarded him intently.

"I don't care. Theresa's only going to be gone for an hour or so, if she comes back and finds this stuff missing she's going to know there's

149

something going on. And if I get found out, you will too. So it's your choice." He looked at her confrontationally. Her eyes narrowed as she started to say something—and then clearly thought better of it. She gave a single nod and held her hand out. Roy passed her the accounts.

"I'll be back in a few minutes."

Roy watched the door close behind her and sprang into action, jamming the patient chair against it and quickly scanning the room. He sat in front of the PC monitor, feeling his heart race and sweat break out on his brow, He scanned the file structure on the left hand side until his eyes fell on a folder titled Patient Records. He went to grab the mouse and then hesitated. He put his hand in his pocket and took out some coins. He carefully placed four of them on each side of the mouse and then lifted it carefully out, feeling satisfied that he would be able to replace it exactly as it had been when Dr. Taylor left the room. He didn't want to disturb anything she might notice. He clicked open the folder and then found a subfolder for patients beginning with the letter J, Then further down found Jones. He opened the patient file and scanned quickly through it on screen. Exactly as he thought, it was just what he needed to know. He glanced quickly at the door again and then checked the printer on the desk for paper. Standing up he crept over to the door and listened. Satisfied there was no-one approaching he went back to the monitor and clicked print, thanking his lucky stars that the printer was so silent as it pushed out the page he needed. He closed the file on screen and closed the folder structure back up, carefully replaced the mouse back in its original position and then turned his attention to the Doctor's desk. Opening the drawers systematically, he scanned the contents, carefully moving items to see fully to the back. "Bingo," he said softly to himself as he found a stack of phials tucked behind a pencil tray. He took the doctor's nameplate and placed it above the drawer, stood back and took a photograph that clearly identified the location as Dr Taylor's office and then took a close up. He debated taking one of the precious phials as beads of sweat broke out on his forehead, but he clenched his teeth and forced himself to resist, knowing instinctively that she would be aware of just how much was in the drawer. Gently closing it, he put the camera back in his pocket, grabbed the chair from its place blocking the door and sat down heavily, moments before it opened and Dr Taylor strode through, dropping his files back in his lap as she passed him by. She sat in her own chair and swiveled round to face him. She frowned.

"Are you alright? You're sweating."

Mind racing on how to cover up the signs of his anxiety, Roy looked at her pleadingly. She nodded.

"Well, you've been a good boy." She opened the drawer he had just moments before been in, and withdrew one of the phials, grabbing a needle and plunging it in. "Roll up your sleeve, quickly," she instructed as Roy smiled at the irony of her rewarding him for his efforts.

A few moments later, he strode from her consulting room, the usual flood of euphoria mixed with confusion at what he had discovered. He felt both high and low at the same time. The distortion made him completely oblivious to his surroundings and he didn't notice Rachel standing by the reception area.

Rachel frowned, she had hoped not to run into anyone at the Doctor's surgery and was distressed to have looked Roy straight in the eye as he emerged from the corridor leading to the consulting rooms— but he had looked straight through her as if she were not there. He looked a bit spaced out she thought. She turned back to the empty reception area waiting patiently for someone to attend to her. Eventually, a bespectacled woman appeared and glanced at her.

"I..." Rachel started, but the woman held up her index finger irritatedly and peered angrily at her over her bifocals as she sat down at her screen. Rachel got the message - and waited. The woman sighed as she looked up things on the screen and tapped away at the keyboard. Eventually, she turned to Rachel and peered at her again over glasses.

"Yes?" She was more than abrupt. Rachel reddened, feeling as if she was being a complete imposition and had no right to be there.

"Er... I wanted to request a repeat prescription?" she said weakly.

"Name?" The woman clicked her fingers and then turned to the keyboard, fingers hovering over the keys as she waited for Rachel to speak.

"Rachel," she said anxiously.

The woman stared at her again. Feeling stupid and now starting to sweat, Rachel continued,

"Stretton." she said quickly.

The woman sighed exasperatedly and looked at her, "spell it."

"S.T.R.E.T.T.O.N."

The woman scanned the screen.

"You're not here. That makes a repeat prescription non-sensical." Another hard stare.

"But I..."

"It's alright Daphne."Rachel turned to see the face of Dr Taylor smiling at her, "I'll deal with this."

"She's not in the system," said Daphne pointedly.

"I know Daphne, it's fine. I'll deal with it from here." The Doctor was firm, which was obviously what Daphne needed. The supercilious receptionist nodded compliantly. Dr Taylor indicated to Rachel with her hand, "follow me, we'll register you in my office."

Rachel trotted along behind her feeling hot, bothered and somehow subservient. This wasn't what she'd had in mind. Her plan was just to get a repeat prescription in the hope she could identify the drugs Dr Taylor had given her. As she crept along behind Taylor, she was practicing the story she needed to tell when the reached her office, as well as processing her surprise at just how short Taylor's tight black skirt was and how straight she'd managed to keep the seams in her stockings. Taylor opened the door to her office and ushered Rachel through.

"Please. Have a seat," she indicated a chair at the side of her desk and shimmied her skirt down before sitting in her own chair and swiveling to face Rachel. She slowly crossed her long, slim legs and smoothed her skirt with her palms, before breathing in deeply and addressing Rachel with a seductive smile, "now. What can I do for you?"

Rachel could now add disconcerted and a little scared to her list of uncomfortable feelings.

"Um. Well, I've been feeling a little sick again. And so um... I thought maybe I should get a repeat prescription." Doctor Taylor regarded her coolly, swaying a little in her chair, but didn't respond. Rachel mumbled on, cursing her feeling of inadequecy, "...and I didn't want to bother you... so um... I thought I'd just..."

"Ok." Doctor Taylor stood and smoothed down her skirt again. "Hop up here for me?"

She indicted the examining bed.

"Well, I don't..." Rachel started

"Please..." Taylor said it quiely but firmly.

Rachel propped herself onto the edge of the bed

"Lay back?" Rachel obeyed. "Lift your sweater." Taylor smiled down at her. Rachel lifted her jumper and smiled back weakly.

"Have you been vomiting?" Rachel sort of tilted her head to one side as her mind raced, "not really," were the only words that emerged from the confusion.

"Not really... is that yes or no?"

"No." Rachel was sheepish. She felt her face go hot and wondered just how red it must be right at this moment.

"Diarrhoea?"

"A bit." She felt like she was sunk and completely transparent.

Dr Taylor pressed her stomach in several places.

"Pain here?" She shook her head, "or here?" she shook her head again. "Lift your sweater a little higher." Rachel looked fearfully into Dr Taylor's eyes as she lifted her jumper up to uncover her chest.

"Relax." Taylor took the stethoscope from around her neck and pressed it to Rachel's' chest on both sides, momentarily looking deep into her eyes. Rachel felt like she had just been penetrated. She felt herself breaking into a full-on sweat.

"Ok. Please sit down again." Tyalor walked back behind her desk and indicated to the patient chair. Rachel pulled down her sweater and walked obediently back to the plastic seat.

"I don't think it's anything to worry about." Taylor crossed her legs again, luxuriously, swiveling a little back and forth and regarding Rachel with a self-possessed smile, "just the usual symptoms that sometimes hang around after a bout of food poisoning. No need for any medication, it will subside, but if you're still experiencing the same problems in a couple of weeks come back and see me." She tapped a couple of items into her computer screen. "I treated you on an emergency basis before. I should have registered you at the time. My apologies. You and your... partner?" Rachel blushed again as the Doctor said the word partner; it was like she was purring it. She looked down, embarrassed, as Taylor continued, "...should both officially register with the surgery.

Pick up a couple of forms on your way out."

Rachel nodded and stood, still looking down and catching sight of the Doctor's stockinged legs as she did so, which she had now uncrossed.

"Thanks," she said as she turned to leave.

"You're quite welcome."

She rushed to the door and in her anxiety fumbled with the door handle. As she struggled, a bare arm crossed her right shoulder and the tanned, elegant hand of Doctor Taylor covered hers and helped her grasp the handle and turn it, "here," she whispered close to her ear, "let me show you."

Taylor pulled the door open for her as Rachel drew in a deep breath. As she inhaled, the familiar smell of Dolce and Gabanna's Pour Femme filled her nostrils. She stumbled into the corridor and headed for the exit, acutely aware of the perspiration popping on her forehead. As she exited the main door and the cool air hit her, she stopped momentarily to catch her breath. "Fuck," she thought to herself, "don't mess with Dr Taylor, Rachel."

Back in the consulting room, the exact same thought was passing through the mind of Dr Taylor.

Frankie was replacing the phone in its cradle as Rachel walked through the door to the living room,

"Who was that?"

"Hmmm?" Frankie was clearly distracted. "Oh, no-one, wrong number."

Rachel frowned, a little alarm bell ringing in her head as her immediate reaction was to wonder if it had been Lisa trying to get hold of her. She raised her hand and looked at her mobile, but there were still no messages.

"Oh, right, well," she was lost for words, feeling another wave of guilt at her distraction with Lisa. She jammed her hands into her jeans pockets and shrugged her shoulders. Frankie seemed not to notice her discomfort and turned away.

"I'm going out for a while, I need some fresh air." She glanced back at Rachel, "where have you been?"

"Oh, went for a walk, explored the fields behind the manor house. You were asleep, I thought I'd let you lie in."

Frankie nodded, subdued.

"Sorry, I thought you would want to lounge around as it's your week off, you're not upset, are you? I often go out for a walk during the day…" Rachel paused, aware she was rambling. Frankie smiled wanly.

"No. It's fine." She grabbed her jacket off the back of a dining room chair and picked up her keys. "I'll probably be a couple of hours. Really need to stretch my legs out—and I want to get a good look round the village."

Rachel momentarily considered offering her company but was more compelled by her need to try and track down Lisa.

"Ok. That'll be fun for you." She cringed inwardly, they were talking like acquaintances, not lovers, she tried to retrieve it, "let's go out to eat tonight, hey?" But Frankie's distraction remained and her reply was off-hand,

"Yeah, let's do that. See ya later."

As she watched Frankie walk out of the door, she glanced down at her phone again. Still no messages. She bit her lip as tears of frustration pricked her eyes. "Where are you…" she whispered. She paced the living room for a few minutes, trying to work out her best course of action. She wanted to go and look for Lisa, but there was now the added complication of running into Frankie. She thought quickly and then grabbed a recipe book from the shelves, she didn't really fancy going out to eat anyway, so if she cooked something special, it would be a good excuse to stay in. She scanned through for something simple and easy to cook, but that would need something from the village shop. She tapped the page, salmon with cream and chive sauce. She went to the fridge freezer and removed two pieces of salmon to defrost, and they had cream, but she knew for sure no chives. Perfect. She grabbed her keys and headed for the front door, glancing either way down the street to make sure Frankie was no longer in sight - and then headed out in the direction of the barn. She walked quickly, anxious not to be seen, head down and hands thrust deep into her pockets. She turned down the narrow lane, relieved to be off the main drag and largely out of sight. She continued on, starting to get excited as she neared Lisa's hide-away, but as she got closer and pulled back a honeysuckle branch, affording her a good open view of the barn, her heart sank. There were no lights on and it had that air of emptiness. She knew already her trip was in vain, but she proceeded and knocked on the stable door anyway. No answer. She tried again. Nothing. She pressed the palm of her hand against the wood of the door as if she might feel a heartbeat and whispered again. "Where are you?" She felt pain in her chest, "please tell me," she pleaded as if the door might reveal Lisa's secret. She pressed her forehead to the wood and sighed. She contemplated heading back to the manor but couldn't face a chance meeting with Donna again - and she felt instinctively like Lisa would have been there earlier if at all. She felt exasperated. Wearily she turned away from the door and headed, slowly back down the lane, her mind mulling over where else she could try. She shook her head as she came out to the main street and suddenly remembered she needed to pop into the shop. She crossed the road and went in the door, to a cheery greeting from a now shaven Ian.

"Hello me duck." He instinctively rubbed his hand across his number one haircut, with its rather interesting speckling of bald patches in it.

"Nice buzz Ian," she winked at him.

He blushed and put his hand over it again. "Best decision I ever made." He winked back, "Elsie can't leave it alone!" He raised his thinning eyebrows twice.

Rachel laughed. "Sometimes our worst times lead directly to the best of times. I'm so pleased for you."

"Thanks me duck, much appreciated." His blush deepened, "and what can we do for you this lovely evening?"

"Do you have any chives?"

She watched as Ian allowed his dentures to slip out and then suck them back in. She knew by now that meant he was thinking hard. He did a sort of chewing motion as he settled his teeth back into place and then spoke.

"There are some dance videos in the Blockbuster section in the back room, past the flowers and the secret parlour." He pointed to a doorway in the middle of the store, "through there."

156

She didn't know what to question first. "The secret parlour?"

"Oh, no, not for you that's for club... that's for... it's the bosses... customers don't..." He was so flustered that sweat started to bead on his patchy scalp. He drew a handkerchief from his pocket and wiped his head.

"It's alright Ian, I know better than to pursue these things now, I know you won't give in about 'the club'," she rolled her eyes and made inverted commas with her fingers. "Anyway, what do you mean dance videos?"

"You know." Ian swiveled his hips and curled his lip, which made her laugh out loud.

"No!" she laughed again, "chives. Chives, you know, herbs."

"Oh herbs, herbs, oh yes, now I see. Well, not much that fancy, just a bit of parsley out there with the veg. Try the dried stuff me duck, probably the best we can do. With the groceries."

Rachel started off into the shop and then hesitated. Turning back to Ian, she plucked up the courage to ask him, "I invited some friends round to dinner and Lisa was one of them, but I can't get hold of her to confirm. You haven't seen her in the last couple of days have you?"

"No, me duck, she don't come in here that often. Has her stuff all delivered by them fancy supermarkets, you know?"

"Yeah. Well, I just went down and knocked on her door, but couldn't get an answer."

"At the barn?"

"Yeah, the barn."

"No, well, rumour is that Donna's decided to sell the barn. Don't know what that means for Lisa."

"Really?" Rachel was perturbed.

"You alright?" Ian asked as she stood motionless in the middle of the store.

"Yes. Yes." She came out of her reverie. "Thanks, Ian. I'll check out the dried herbs."

"That's enough chive talking." He winked at her, clearly pleased with himself.

Rachel smiled thinly, no longer in the mood to appreciate his humour. She headed for the grocery section and thought about her next move. After grabbing what she needed, she headed back to the till.

"Is Lisa in the Club?" she tried to be nonchalant as Ian rang up her purchases. He put her items in her bag.

"Five pounds exactly." After taking money, he leaned on his elbows and looked at her. "I can tell you got a good soul me duck," he said gently, rolling his dentures around as he regarded her. He slotted them back into place in his jaw and straightened himself up, "there's funny business in this village sometimes. It ain't bad like some folk would have believe, mostly it's just folk exploring things that some don't believe in. No harm in it for the most part, but can cause trouble if you're not, well, if you're not inclined to it. Can't say more me duck, but best if maybe you don't pay no mind. Just let it be." He winked at her kindly.

She hesitated, part of her wanted to pursue what Ian meant by all that, but the greater part of her was consumed by thoughts of Lisa and so she opted to let it go, "hmmm. Ok, Ian, for now, I'll just let it be. You need to practice that chive move of yours."

He rubbed his patchy scalp again. "Got better moves to practice first," he winked again and Rachel used every ounce of restraint not to grimace.

"Gotcha!" She put her thumb up and turned quickly on her heel. That was not a visual she wanted to pursue. Feeling frustrated, she stood outside the shop and battled with her conflicting thoughts about her next move. She knew the best thing to do was turn left and head back to the house, but half of her wanted to turn right and go to the post office. Her instincts told her that Theresa was dangerous, that whatever was going on in the village and whatever had happened to her at the party, Theresa was central to it. But she also knew that Theresa pretty much knew everything that was going on. If anyone knew what was happening with Lisa, it was Theresa. She breathed deeply—and turned right. Walking quickly, she passed The Master's Arms and snaked to the left along the main road, the Post Office was now directly ahead of her, not one hundred yards away. She stopped. No. This was too risky. She turned on her heel and walked back round the corner and headed back past the pub. She stopped again. No, she needed to know. She span on her heel once more and, sighing at her indecision, she retraced her steps yet again—and then halted once more, this time stopped in her tracks by the sight of Frankie emerging from the Post Office,

"Shit!" She backed up, peering round the wall of the pub to see what Frankie was doing, ready to hot foot it back to the house if needs be. She watched as Frankie came out of the door and walked uncharacteristically slowly a few steps to the edge of the building. Then she put her arm up on the wall, as if she were steadying herself, turned, and leant against the brickwork, before bending forward and covering her face with both hands. Rachel felt her whole body shrink with shame as she watched Frankie's anguish. Her body shook and Rachel knew she was sobbing. She watched as she drew herself up and wiped the back of her hand across her eyes. Composing herself, she looked both ways, clearly trying to establish if anyone could see her. She dug into her pockets, probably looking for a tissue. Rachel knew instantly that she wouldn't find one, she never had one with her unless she, Rachel, had made sure she'd put one in her pocket for her. She realised with heart-rending guilt that she hadn't taken care of Frankie like that for weeks. Rachel's mind was a whirr of confusion and intense guilt again. What was Frankie so upset about? It must be something to do with Theresa. Did Theresa know about her and Lisa? That must be it. Oh, fuck! She breathed out, she felt sick and her head span. Did she really want to lose Frankie? It was like a massive hammer hitting her on the head and waking her up. What the fuck was she doing? She watched as Frankie wiped her arm across her nose. Aww - and her heart melted, she knew Frankie so hated it when she cried and her nose ran like that. Like a child with nothing to wipe it on. At that moment, she just wanted to run to her and fold her in her arms and tell her it would be alright. She shook her head. But it wouldn't be alright would it? Because it was her fault because she was cheating. Rachel put her hand to her mouth, leaned over and retched. Oh my god. I'm cheating! She swallowed, the bitter taste of bile. She held her hand to her stomach which had suddenly knotted so tight that she could barely move. She watched horrified as she saw Frankie heading directly towards her. She turned quickly. Her face twisted at the pain in her abdomen as she dashed back towards the shop and ran in through the door and past Ian's bemused face. She held

159

a hand up to him in acknowledgement and just managed to say "milk" as she rushed past the window and into the bowels of the store.

"Hello!"

Frankie looked up from where she was sitting on a stool at the bar of the pub, drawing her gaze away from the content of her glass with some reluctance. She had been deep in thought and felt she needed the contemplative solitude to sort through the troubled thoughts on her mind. Being distracted by idle chit-chat with a stranger was the last thing she really wanted. Nevertheless, she responded to the bespectacled, strong looking woman, who was holding out her hand.

"Frankie isn't it?"

"Yes."

"Pleased to meet you, my name's Jennifer Peters, I'm the housekeeper up at the manor."

"Oh. The manor. Right. Well, pleased to meet you too." She shook the outstretched hand and turned her attention back to her beer. But her new acquaintance was not about to leave her in peace.

"Mind if I join you?" It was not really a question, she had already pulled up a barstool next to hers.

"No. Sure. Be my guest."

"Another pint?"

Frankie looked at her glass, "no, I'm good thanks."

"Ok, my usual please Alan." Jennifer put a thumb up to the barman, who nodded and started pulling a pint of beer.

"So how are you settling in?"

Frankie nodded. Not being in the mood for pleasantries made it hard to disguise her feelings, she responded in a despondent tone, "it's... good. Interesting."

Peters laughed gently, "interesting. Yes, it's an interesting village. Quirky."

"Quirky's one word. I'm certainly finding it an eye-opening experience."

"Care to elaborate?"

"Maybe not. How long have you been at the manor?" she

160

deflected the conversation.

"More years than I care to remember. A long time. So I know the village, it's history and it's idiosyncrasies pretty well. I don't spend much time down here these days, plenty to keep me busy, but I enjoy a quiet pint or two in here every now and then. Do you like the local beer?"

"Yeah, it's good. Not that I've tried too much of it. Yet..."

Peters felt the 'yet' hang in the air.

"That sounded a bit like there might not be a yet. Not sure about village life?"

"It's all good." Frankie shut the conversation down.

"What about the gin? Have you tried that?"

Frankie started to feel irritated, this woman didn't seem to get the hint that she didn't want to talk.

"No. not my tipple." She was blunt. Another attempt at closing down. To no avail.

"So. What do you do for a living Frankie?" Peters, sensing the impending close out, tried to lighten the conversation.

"I'm a trader in the city. FinancialiInstruments."

"Ok. Specifically?"

"Specifically Asset Swaps."

"Ah. House of Cards... bit of a juggler then, are you?"

Frankie couldn't help but be a little impressed.

"Hm. People don't usually know what Asset Swaps are. I generally say Bonds to keep it simple."

"My brother was a trader."

"Oh yeah? Who was he with?"

"Rothschilds."

"Really? Hm, I spent a couple of years with them. I'm with a company called Peel Webble now."

Peters nodded. "You happy there?"

Frankie sighed, "it's ok. A stressful job And a hard commute."

"I know. Takes its toll. Early mornings and late nights socialising. And it's mentally exhausting. My brother was pretty much burnt out by his mid-thirties. Luckily he had enough to retire to a gentler life in the country by then."

161

"Yeah, that's a good plan. I aimed to leave soon and spend more time up here."

"Aimed?" Peters said curiously, "past tense?"

Frankie corrected herself, "aim."

"Oh good. You haven't given up on us yet then?"

Frankie picked up her beer and downed the last quarter of the glass quickly; the prying was getting too close for comfort, "who knows what tomorrow holds." She set the glass down and rose from her stool, "got to go. Nice to meet you."

"Good to meet you too," Peters raised her glass, "hopefully we can have another pint some time?"

Frankie nodded, "sure, some other time. Bye."

"Bye Frankie." Peters looked hard into Frankie's eyes, "you take care now."

Frankie felt momentarily disconcerted, like an invasion had just occurred. She tilted her head, pondering a comment, but instead just nodded and turned to leave.

Peters watched her go, turned back to the bar, put her money on the counter and rose to leave too, "thanks, Alan," she said waving.

"You don't want that?' he asked pointing at her three-quarters full pint glass.

"Got to get back to the manor. Just remembered something I have to do."

Chapter 22

Lisa sat with her Mother in the conservatory. They were silent. Lisa knew not to break her Mother's concentration as she sat in a light meditative state, her head moving almost imperceptibly in a complimentary rhythm with the movements of the Yoga group she was watching on the lawn. She'd explained to Lisa years ago that it was vicarious yoga. It had taken those same years for Lisa to understand vicarious meant lazy. She was not unhappy with the silence, it was a relief for her not to have to talk with Donna, it excused her from the mental vigilance required to make sure she didn't say the wrong thing. Instead, she was able to bask in the light that streamed through the glass surrounds and warmed her as she let her mind drift off to dreams of lovely things. In her childhood that had often meant the illusion of the freedom to play with friends she did not have. Today it was the illusion of playing with Rachel.

"Your Father's coming home at the weekend." Her Mother broke the beautiful thread playing out in her head and set in motion the conflicting feelings that instantly arose at any mention of her father. "He'll only be here overnight on Saturday." Donna spoke without breaking her rhythm as she continued to stare through the glass at the twenty or so naked women in Warrior Two pose, "what a vision. Though it's getting chilly now. You can tell by their lack of poise. It's like cow tipping, you can flip them off balance with the merest touch at this time of year."

"Will I see him?" asked Lisa, ignoring her Mother's contemplative appreciation of the yoga group.

"No. He's got some movie seminar in the US coming up and he needs some of the old material he has stored in the vaults. He'll collect it and be gone. I'll be expected to dine with him, but he's not asked to see you. It's wretched timing, I had a party planned."

"Is he seeing anyone else?"

"No." Donna sighed, "it's ironic that he set so much in motion is this village all those years ago and now he's wiped his hands of it. He's so self-righteous now, it's like he's erased his whole past from the history books."

"So he's not meeting with Theresa?"

"No, darling. As I said, he's moved on. Now he's holier than thou and twice as nice." Donna regarded her daughter, "are you asking about Theresa for a reason?"

"No," said Lisa, a little too defiantly.

Silence filled the air.

"She was here earlier. Your girlfriend." Donna said it disparagingly and dismissively, challenging her daughter to respond. Lisa's expression remained steadfast.

"That's not going to work, Mother."

Donna nodded and cocked her head to one side, "but you are in love with her aren't you?" It was a gentle invitation to open up... and Lisa fell straight into the trap.

"Yes."

"I knew it!" Donna let out an exasperated sigh and her tone became more aggressive, "it's a waste of your time. Forget her and move on. It will never work. Love never does."

Lisa shook her head, "it's too late Mother, I'm already in. And I'm giving up the club. I can't do it anymore."

Donna turned away and stared out of the window, deliberately ignoring her daughter's comment. "Down Dog." She watched the group on the lawn, where twenty or so bare bottoms reached for the sky in the fresh afternoon air.

"Do you have to keep up a running commentary?"

"Yes. It exasperates me that you don't recognise the value of it. Down dog. It's a fabulous pose. So stimulating stretches the whole body and the mind," she windmilled her arms expansively, "so freeing." She turned and faced her daughter, "that's what I want for you darling. To be free. To be free of the constraints this world places on our physical beings. To share everything."

"It doesn't work for me any more Mother. I'm in love."

"Ah, love. love, love, love..." she paused and frowned at her daughter, "but you must let your love be free. Don't restrict it to just one person... or it will bring you pain." Donna turned away and watched her group of disciples again as they moved to child pose. "It only ever bought me pain to do that. And besides, you know that Rachel only *thinks* she's in love right now, don't you? Or have you forgotten that it's down to the gin your father so cleverly developed?"

"Father is an asshole. It has to be more than the serum. The way this feels. She loves me. I know it." Lisa was defiant.

"Your Father was *my* asshole," said Donna reflectively as the group moved in unison to cow face pose, "and you're deluded if you thinks this is real."

"Whatever. Father screwed you up and screwed you over."

Donna's face belied the effort she was making to stay calm, "regardless. You'll get screwed over too,"

"No, I won't. This is different."

Donna spun round, "it's always different. Except it isn't." She moved toward Lisa, finally showing her exasperation, "listen to me. You were given a task, to convert Rachel. She's capitulated and now all you have to do is hand her over. Theresa has lost her patience with you and so have I." She stepped back and regarded Lisa again, "maybe I should do it myself."

"No!" Lisa lunged towards Donna, who gracefully side stepped and rang the service bell. "Peters!" she shouted loudly as she simultaneously spun Lisa's arm behind her with the deftness of a seasoned yoga practitioner and placed her lips close to Lisa's ear, speaking gently, but menacingly, "there's too much to lose. You have to understand darling that this village has a tradition, a reputation, a route to wealth that it can't lose." She eased the pressure on Lisa's arm a little and softened her tone, "darling you know I don't want it to be this way, but we have to protect ourselves, to protect your future and *our* future." She smiled as Peters entered the room behind her, "Peters, Lisa needs some Quiet Time."

Lisa bit her lip in anguish. She remembered Quiet Time. She remembered the isolation and silence.

Peters nodded at Donna. "Quiet time, yes let's take you for some Quiet Time." She gently unlocked Donna's grip and held Lisa's hand, "come with me, now, lovely." She led the now obedient Lisa from the room as Donna smiled and sighed deeply, turning her attention back to the disciples on the lawn.

"Ah cockerel..." she hummed quietly as she watched the group, "such exquisite balance."

"You haven't written very much."

Frankie had her back to her as she entered the room and spoke as if she had been waiting to say the words for some time. Rachel stopped in her tracks, regarding Frankie as she sat at her desk, gently and slightly swiveling the chair and staring out of the window, straight ahead. Rachel's mind raced.

"No. I haven't." She noticed the overnight bag by the side of the desk, "it's a different environment, I haven't got my concentration right yet."

Frankie nodded, her back still to her.

"I'm going back to London."

They both let the heavy silence fill the air.

"Why?" Rachel's voice was small.

Frankie turned fully round in the chair to face her. "I should have planned it better. I don't think I'm in the mood for a holiday," she looked down at her hands on her lap, "I'm struggling with some things."

Rachel closed her eyes to steel herself and knelt before her, holding Frankie's hands in hers. "What is it, Frankie?" She brushed a few stray strands of hair over Frankie's ear, she had hardly dared ask, but she needed to know.

"I need to think." Frankie looked away, "it's..." she shook her head, "I have to go." She stood up abruptly and picked up her bag, then headed for the door, "I can't stand to be in this place right now." She ran down the stairs quickly. Alarmed, Rachel ran after her.

"Frankie!" she pleaded as she raced down the stairs too, "Frankie!" But the front door had shut. "Frankie..." she said more quietly this time—and then burst into tears and fell to her knees.

Lisa lay compliantly on the bed and stared up at Peters, who was a contrast in blue shirt and trousers against the starkly white room. White walls, white sheets, white furniture. The bright white light of a childhood that she remembered only with darkness. Peters looked back into her eyes gently as she folded the manacle round Lisa's left wrist. As she did so, she carefully raised her index finger to her lips, indicating that Lisa should stay quiet. Peters then pointed back at her chest and flicked her eyes backwards. Lisa got it. Peters was indicating that what she was doing was to avoid the camera that had whirred into motion, repositioning and refocusing on Peters and Lisa. Donna was watching. Peters held the manacle up and flicked at the buckle to show Lisa that it was unsecured. She then busied herself with the other manacles at the four corners of the bed, each time ostensibly fixed the restraints round Lisa's other wrist and ankles, but flicking the buckle each time to show it was actually unsecured. She leaned across and over Lisa, her head very close to her ear as she fiddled with the pillow to get her comfortable.

"I'll be back soon, be ready to get out quickly," she whispered urgently. Lisa gave an almost imperceptible nod, Peters straightened up and regarded her, "now Lisa, you know the rules," she said loudly, "keep still. Don't fight it. I'll come back with supper in a few hours and we'll talk." Peters faced Lisa directly again and winked before turning and leaving the room. Lisa closed her eyes and started to count the seconds, tears seeping from under her eyelids and rolling down her cheeks as she thanked heavens for the mercy of Peters.

The trading room was typical of its kind in the city. Rows of fast talking people, eyes glued to their screens, ears glued to their headsets, hustling for deals with similarly buzzing, hyperactive trading rooms across the globe. The huddled nature of the various trading desks ensured the constant competitive pressure of colleagues sapping each others bonuses with bigger and better deals. One up. Always one up. Frankie sat at her station and watched the green numbers dance by on her own monitor, fluctuating, undulating. She closed her eyes and pressed her fingertips into her temples, trying to relieve the pressure in her head.

"Jones! Jones!!" She snapped out of her reverie. She turned round to see her manager calling for her.

"My office!" He hoiked his thumb over his shoulder towards his door.

"Shit!" she said under her breath, rising slowly from her chair. It was never a good sign to be called into his office. Praise was an open affair shouted across the trading room to make sure everyone knew they had something else to beat. Punishment was another matter. She headed towards his door, intensely aware that the eyes that followed her would know she was in for a blasting.

"Shut the door." He leaned back in his luxurious leather chair, hands behind his head.

"Sit." He commanded as he indicated the much smaller, harder, plastic chair in front of his desk. So chosen to make its occupier feel tiny and worthless. She sat.

"What's going on? You pre-menstrual or something?" He barked at her. Typical trading room aggression and sexism.

"Nope."

"So why is it all tits up right now?" He leaned forward and threw his head in the air, in an angry, dismissive gesture that she knew was meant for the audience on the other side of his glass office wall. She knew the drill. She wasn't giving anything.

"Missed a couple of swap options."

"Too fucking right you did!"

He put his hands behind his head again. Leaning back, legs spread, swiveling his chair, a mean look on his face. She waited for it.

"If you didn't have the track record you have, you'd be fucking history right now!"

She gave a single nod. "I'm back on it." She stared him down.

He contemplated her. She could see him weighing up his options.

"Bonus time in 2 weeks. Not looking good for you right now, is it?"

"Nope."

"Better see some fucking improvement then, right?"

He stared hard at her. She resisted the urge to breathe a sigh of relief. She gave another single nod and he responded with one of his own. He flicked his hand dismissively towards the door.

"Get out."

She stood and left his office, closing the door behind her just as a bloke dressed as a yellow canary walked into the room. She silently thanked the Universe for his presence, which took the spotlight off her dressing down. His was a far more entertaining plight for the rest of the trading floor to enjoy, and there were whoops and hysterical laughter from the mainly male sales team. The canary trudged across towards its desk and she patted it on the shoulder as it passed by.

"It gets better," she said kindly.

The canary nodded, rubbing at its muddy yellow legs.

"We all had to do initiation. Where did they put you?"

The canary pulled up its beak to reveal the hot, flushed face of a man who couldn't have been more than eighteen years old, soft stubble giving away his youth.

"Tower Bridge. Tied me to the railings."

She nodded sympathetically. "That's a favourite. You ok?"

He humphed, "you try getting a stranger to let you loose when you're dressed like this."

"Actually I was dressed as a prisoner." She said smiling at his dejectedness, "that is much worse. At some point fairly quickly, someone will take pity on a giant canary. On the other hand, people are scared witless of a convict." She winked at him, "and honestly, this is a tough environment, you have to have balls, you have to know when to take things seriously and when to laugh at yourself—and you have to get yourself out of some tough situations sometimes. It's not for the fainthearted. This is your first test."

He stared at her, blinking. She thought he looked like he might cry.

"Bolly on the trolly!!" someone yelled out from across the office.

She held her hand out to the canary, "I'm Frankie—and it's getting better already, see? There's Bollinger champagne on the tea trolley today. Means the floor hit target for the week."

He took her hand in his big yellow glove. "I'm James. And thanks."

"Come on Birdy Boy, get your fucking chops round this!" someone called out from across the floor, holding up a sack of birdseed. Someone else wolf whistled. "You look sweet in yellow. You a bender bird or something?" More laughter.

169

Frankie looked at James as he reddened at the comments, not knowing what to say. He looked really innocent. They would soon beat that out of him. Within no time at all he would be joining in the lewd banter, giving as good as he got and indulging in the ritual humiliation of some other poor bastard on their first day. She patted his shoulder again, "you can pretty much give up on today, they'll make you stay in that get up until the markets close. Take it all on the chin. Tomorrow they will leave you alone. Tomorrow you will be a winner."

Frankie made her way back to her desk and put on her earphones to shut out the noise. Her mind returned to the thoughts that were the cause of her distraction from the job and she thought about the revelation that Theresa had made. Christ, after all these years. Talk about a head fuck. Why had they moved to that village? She breathed out and looked at her phone. Missed calls from Rachel. She knew she needed to talk to her, but sorting it out in her own head had to come first. She grabbed her phone and dialed quickly.

"Mum? Hey. Quick call, are you in tonight? Around six?" She nodded as she got the reply, "ok, I'll see you then. Put the kettle on. Bye." She looked back at the screen, knowing she had to blot it all out and concentrate on what she was doing right now. She needed to make some 'fucking improvement', she was fully aware there was always another canary waiting to take her place. She stared at the monitor, her eyes suddenly in sharp focus. She created the figure she had in mind for a bonus as an image in her minds eye, it was her usual trick to manifest what she wanted. See it, make it happen. She crystalised it, animated it. Then she blinked. Her mind did what it was not supposed to at this point; it let the external world in. She pictured Rachel and then a thought popped into her head that she hadn't expected. Was Rachel the cost of her determination to make money? She looked back at the screen. The green figures still flashed passed, but now they were a blur. She shook her head and smiled. They were meaningless. Meaningless numbers. She heard herself laugh. She had been missing the point. What the hell use was the money if she lost Rachel? Why was she here sitting at this desk, calling the shots on meaningless trades when what she really valued was her home, her family. Rachel. She opened her email and typed furiously on the keyboard, then read through her words and allowed her index figure to hover over the send button. She bit down on her lip and grinned, nodding as she firmly tapped the key. Feeling elated, she rose and grabbed her jacket from the back of her chair. She caught sight of her manager as he stood up from behind his desk, making determined strides towards his door, eyes fixed on her. She picked up her brief case and headed towards the exit, placing her hand on James shoulder and leaning down to his ear, all the while steadfastly holding the glare of her manager. "Enjoy the bolly, birdy boy."

He glanced at her over his shoulder, bemused.

"Jones!" her manager barked at her.

She stood tall right in front of his face.

"Fuck you, Stan. I quit."

His lip curled. "You can't you're fucking fired." He jabbed his finger at her. She grinned, "too late Stanny boy, you'll find the email in your inbox. Not. Your. Decision."

"Bitch! Get out!"

She started walkeding backwards away from him, still smiling, "Missing you already!" she waved and then turned back to the door, sighing at the huge wave of satisfied relief that washed through her and marveling at the stunned silence that filled the room so powerfully that she could actually hear it. Euphoric, she laughed out loud as she let the door close behind her.

Chapter 23

Peters stood behind Donna in the security den, the contrasting light of the multi-screen dashboard the only brightness in the otherwise dark and stuffy room. Donna regarded her daughter, her head tilted to one side, as though examining her. She sighed deeply, "I'm disappointed in her, Peters."

"I know. But she thinks she's in love. It's a phase, it will pass. Everything will get back to normal then."

"We need to deal with Rachel," Donna swiveled round to look at Peters, "I'll be having a little dinner party on Saturday. She'll be our special guest." Donna smiled thinly at Peters and stood up, "we'll need to have Lisa disciplined and back under control by then. We'll discuss that tomorrow morning. We'll leave her overnight to contemplate things. For now, keep an eye on her Peters, I don't want her to hurt herself like she has before." Donna looked at her watch, "I have to go. I have a hot yoga class."

Peters nodded and watched as Donna left the room, waiting silently for a few minutes to pass before turning on the intercom, "Lisa, don't look like you are responding to me, but make it look like you are going to sleep." She watched as Lisa turned her head to one side and closed her eyes. Peters froze the screen on the monitor and then quickly left the den. Silently she opened the door to Lisa's room and moved over to the bed, gently touching Lisa's arm. She opened her eyes, startled. Peters placed her forefinger to her lips and then motioned Lisa to follow her. The two of them released the loosened manacles and then Lisa tip toed behind Peters out through the door and across the hall to the kitchen.

"You need to be back here by around seven in the morning. I froze the image on the monitors in the security den." Peters tenderly smoothed Lisa's furrowed brow with her thumb, "it looks like you're sleeping." Peters smiled briefly and then became serious again. She looked into Lisa's eyes. "I'm sorry you're going through this." She paused, "I'm sorry for all of it. All these years." She drew Lisa into her arms and hugged her tight, "you deserve to find happiness, but it's going to be tough for you, you know?" Lisa nodded, biting her lip and drawing her fingers across her eyes to wipe away the tears, she sobbed.

"If you want to be with Rachel—in fact, if you want to be with anyone—you know you're going to have to leave, right?"

Lisa nodded.

"Your Mother's going to deal with this her way now, so you don't have long. You're going to have to explain to Rachel what's going on and either get out of here right now or come up with a plan that means you can deal with what's going on without either of you coming to any harm until you do find a way to leave. Lisa, I don't want to be negative, but you do also know that this might not be what Rachel really wants?"

Lisa nodded again as her head fell, "it would break me."

"No. No, it wouldn't. You're way stronger than that. I'll help in whatever way I can. Take the next few hours to decide what you want to do and then be back here by seven. We can talk then. I'll keep your Mother off the scent."

Peters cupped Lisa's chin in her hand and lifted her face up to look in her eyes again, "listen to me. Whatever happens between you two. Even if it's nothing... and it might be nothing," Peters looked searchingly into Lisa's eyes as she said it. Lisa responded by squeezing her eyes shut as if to keep the words out, "you have to face that possibility. So you need to be strong for *yourself.* And for Rachel."

Lisa hugged Peters. "It can't be nothing. But thank you." She drew herself up and breathed in deeply, "I won't let you down. I'll be back." She squeezed Peters hand and headed towards the back door of the pantry, slipping through it and into the back yard as Peters sighed behind her. She already knew it would be nothing.

In the security den, Donna flipped open the lid to her secret monitor and watched the screen intently. She nodded slowly to herself. As Peters locked the door behind Lisa, Donna tapped the monitor. "Peters," she said to herself quietly and a touch sadly, "I never thought it would come to this."

173

In Grace's small front room, a circle of people sat on chairs, most of them regarding their hands a little uncomfortably. Satisfied that everyone was now present, she drew the floral curtains in order to keep out prying eyes. She sat down in her seat next to Roy and cleared her throat.

"So, who wants to begin?"

Several hands went up instantly, which took her back a little, the enthusiasm to speak out was greater than she'd thought. She motioned to a heavy set man sitting directly across from her to indicate he should start.

"Hello my name's Matt and I'm um... I'm a Swinger's partner. Umm... actually, can I just check, is this the way I do it? Is this a twelve step programme?" He glanced at a few of the others. They all shrugged and looked at Roy. Roy then looked at Grace, who stared blankly back.

"Like Al-anon?" continued Matt.

Roy cleared his throat, "we'll try and make it a few less?" he ventured helpfully.

Matt screwed his face up. "Is there actually a programme?"

"We're working on it," replied Roy, "taking steps. I'm researching how best to go about it."

"Well, why don't you just do Twelve Steps, same principle, it's all addiction, right?" said Matt warming to his subject, "isn't this really about sex addiction?"

"Right, right." Roy decided to stand to address the group, feeling it would make him more authoritative, "but we also want to address whether the club should be under investigation to see if we can make it less invasive. I feel that's an important part of dealing with the issues we are all feeling as a result of this... addiction." He sat down again and motioned at Matt to continue.

"Oh. Fine, sounds like a good idea, but that's not really what I'm here for. I want the therapy side. To share and all that?" Matt glanced round at the group for approval. Seeing a couple of nods, he carried on, "can I kick off by talking a bit about Marjory's threesome's? It's kind of got me at the end of my tether. I feel really left out. I gave her a rollicking about it last week and I know it only makes things worse."

"Well, maybe we should talk about how the club should change its rules..." Roy started.

"I had the same problem with Graham, my husband," interrupted a woman in her late twenties, wearing a Gingham dress and a pair of old army boots. She was clutching a Bible and rocking backwards and forwards on her chair, "I'm Bella by the way."

"Well, the club..." Roy tried again, but his Swing Anonners were in full voice now.

"I'm fucked off about threesomes too!" a bearded man sitting next to Matt piped up, angrily, waving his hand across Roy's face to shut him up, "I'm Geoffrey. My Gemma's been out all hours these last weeks and it's more than an occasional thing now, I can't stand it!" Geoffrey's voice rose and he thumped his tightened fist down on his thigh.

"Shhhh now..." Bella reached over and grasped his fist gently, "let's talk about it and see if we can calm things down." She indicated that Matt should continue.

Roy sat back in his chair and folded his arms.

"Ok." Matt sat forward, clasping his hands together and resting his chin on his thumbs, "thing is, when she first started it was ok, you know? She told me about this fantasy she had to have a threesome and she described what she wanted. Sort of spiced things up for us a bit, you know?" He looked up and received the reassuring nods he needed, "so then things moved on and she said she really wanted to do it like. In the club. And that when she did it, she'd come back and tell me about it, spice things up a bit more." He paused and shrugged his shoulders, "maybe I was a bit too quick to say yes, you know? Maybe I encouraged it too much, maybe I shouldn't have, maybe it's all my fault... but, well, it kind of titillated me, you know?" He looked up again. The nods were harder, more encouraging, "so anyway," Matt rested his elbows on his knees and gestured openly with his hands, "one night she comes home with an um..." he cleared his throat and his voice dropped, "new outfit from that Annie Summers place," he sat up and crossed his legs and the group all simultaneously leaned in to hear better, with the exception of Roy, who sat still, looking exasperated, "it was leather. The bodice. And she had some fishnets and sussies." He sighed with the memory, "man,

I thought it was for me." He licked his lips and shook his head. You could hear a pin drop in the room. "So she puts on the gear and sort of parades in front of me, like a fashion show kind of thing." He blew out hard and shook his head again. Geoff was nodding like the Churchill dog and grinning inanely as Matt continued, "so anyways, I reached out to touch the fish nets and she grabbed my hand quick as you like to stop me. 'Eh, don't rip me tights', she said and shook me off!" He folded his tongue into his chin and shook his head harder, "couldn't believe it!" His voice rose and filled with emotion, "I was shocked like. Couldn't barely move and before I know it she's out the door!" he paused and looked up.

Geoff was frowning hard, fists in tight white bunches and his mouth screwed up into a contorted sphincter.

Matt went on, "just picked up her fucking handbag and flounced out the door. Not even a goodbye kiss!" Matt sighed and Geoff put up his hand to speak. "Yes mate?" said Matt.

"Man and woman or two men?" he asked aggressively.

"What?" Matt frowned.

"Or something else?" Geoff was quizzical.

"What do you mean?"

"I can't visualise it unless I know whether she was going with a man and woman or two men. Or something else?"

"You're not supposed to fucking visualise it, mate," retorted Matt angrily, "this is my wife we're talking about. I'm not here to create your fantasies for you!" He started to rise from his chair.

"Woah!" Bella grabbed one of Geoff's fists and put her hand out towards Matt, "steady on guys. Matt, I think Geoff was just trying to sympathise, you know?" she glanced at Geoff and nodded at him pleadingly, rubbing his fist as she did so.

Geoff glared at her, his tension palpable. The room fell silent waiting for his reaction. His body softened a little as he relaxed, "yeah. Yeah mate, just trying to sympathise. Didn't mean to, you know," he waggled his head side to side on his thick neck, "get off on it or anything." He jutted his chin forward, "just err, trying to, err work out what's going on like. Like Bella says. No need to get fired up." He sat back in his chair and crossed his arms across his chest.

"Look maybe we should stop here and think about the club a

bit more," Roy leaned forward.

"I haven't finished!" Matt was riled and terse.

Roy put both his hands up in a surrendering gesture and sat back again. He glanced at Grace and tapped his watch, shaking his head. She smiled thinly and then turned her attention back to Matt, clearly engrossed by his story. Roy glared at the back of her head. "What the fuck!" he whispered under his breath and let his head loll backwards, "give me strength."

Peters stared out of the pantry window, deep in thought, a half-peeled potato in one hand, the peeler motionless in the other. She hoped she'd done the right thing. She thought of Lisa, poor woman, poor girl, all those years of punishment. She sighed and prayed silently that she would make it back before seven. As she was about to start peeling again, she heard a noise behind her and glanced back. She turned, full round.

"Peters..." Donna stood with her arms crossed, next to her was the towering figure of Arthur the gardener. Donna shook her head and Peters instantly knew she had finally been caught out. She slowly put the potato and the peeler down on the draining board and crossed her arms too.

"Yes?"

"Why?

"Because she deserves a better life."

"This is her life. She has everything she needs."

Peters shook her head.

"Where is she?"

Peters shook her head again, calmly defiantly.

"Arthur, we'll take Peters to her room."

"Yes, ma'am." He knew what that meant.

Arthur walked over to Peters and took her arm. She shrugged him off, "you don't need to man handle me Arty, I'll come willingly."

Arthur nodded, feeling sorry for her. He let go and stood behind her ushering her forward. They followed Donna, who led the way to Peters bedroom. As they entered, Arthur sat her in an upright chair by her small desk and headed for a small cupboard, hidden away behind a

177

bedside table. He took out some rope and started back towards Peters.

"Use the restraints, Arthur."

Arthur looked apologetically at Peters. She nodded at him smiling, letting him know she didn't hold it against him and he returned to fetch the handcuffs.

Donna watched him closely to make sure he was properly securing her. She knew they had a deep mutual respect for each other and she didn't want a repeat of the trick Peters had played with her daughter.

"You can go now." She dismissed him and regarded Peters ruefully. Aside from her anger at her disloyalty, she was also peeved that she managed to look so relaxed given that she was manacled to a chair. Donna put her face up close to Peters. She didn't even flinch.

"Do you think I'm afraid to punish you, Peters?" She stared with steely eyes and felt her anger rise at the humorous glint she saw in return. She stood back. "Don't you have any loyalty for all the years I've given you? Supported you?"

Peter's laughed out loud. Donna frowned, she couldn't remember Peters ever having laughed in her presence, "you fucking ingrate," she shouted angrily. But Peters just smiled. Well, of course she. Donna knew she'd just made her lose her self-control.

"Where is she?" she demanded.

"She's sorting out her life," said Peters quietly.

Donna felt her anger and jealousy rise further. So quietly self-contained, so dominant in her gentleness, how did this servant of hers always manage to make *her* feel inferior?

"I'm a Countess! Answer me!" Donna closed her eyes and cursed her lack of self-discipline. She looked at the serene face of Peters and shook her head. She sat down heavily in the chair next to her. She felt a rush of shame. The weight on her shoulders felt huge. "Scusami, mi dispiace. I'm sorry."

Peters looked at her, recognizing that the barriers had dropped for a short while, so she took the opportunity to get the message through. "She's your daughter Donna. And she's so like you. Spirited, fiery, passionate... but also gentle and loving. You chose your way, but it's not hers. Let her go."

"I can't." Donna was adamant.

"You can. And you must. If you love her."

Donna looked at Peters for a long time, the internal battle raging as that soft core momentarily enjoyed the freedom to push at her heart and find some space to be heard.

Peter's continued, "you got broken. It's not your fault. It changed you. He changed you. Lisa's broken too, but she has a chance to make things better. You can give that to her. Why wouldn't you want that for your daughter?"

"Because she will leave me. And she will never come back and she will hate me forever."

Peters took her hand, "no. She won't. Her freedom will make her realise that you were trapped, that the walls you built around you were necessary—and she will love you for the strength you had to let her go."

"What have I done to her?"

Peters felt the breakthrough, "it's ok. You can make it better."

Donna stood and Peters watched as her eyes turned back to steel.

"No."

Donna stood and walked casually and deliberately towards the door, "I won't be needing you any more Peters." And without even a glance back, she left the room.

Rachel looked at her phone in exasperation. She'd tried Frankie six times in the last couple of hours, but still no reply. That had never happened before. Even when things were difficult between them, they'd communicate. Even if it was angrily, or tersely dismissive, they would keep the dialogue going to make sure they kept their connection. Frankie had never ignored her before. It was excruciating. She threw her hands up in the air, it was clearly no use to carry on trying right now, Frankie would know she was trying to get hold of her, she would just have to let go and either let her come back to her or try again later. She decided to see if she could track down Lisa.

Rachel entered the shop just before closing time. Disoriented by the dark, she lifted her glasses and glanced underneath to see her way to the counter. Ian frowned.

"Why you wearing sunglasses?"

"I, um, went running. It's to… they keep the bugs out."

Ian nodded knowingly, "I get it."

Rachel fiddled blindly with the packets of gum on the counter display.

"Have you seen Lisa today by any chance?" Her attempt at sounding casual made her voice come out in a thin whine. She picked up an unknown flavor of gum.

"No. And I'm closing up now me duck, so less you want something…"

Rachel put the gum on the counter.

"You been cryin' entcha?" he said quietly as he rang up the sale.

Rachel clenched her lips together and swallowed hard. She went to say something but only a sob came out and she nodded weakly, tears flowing down beneath her shades. The thought fleetingly passed through her head that she couldn't understand her emotions. She felt like she was watching them from afar like they were coursing through her but that they weren't quite hers.

Ian put his hand in his pocket and took out his handkerchief. "Here. It is clean. Just has a few holes in it." He nodded at her kindly and held his hand out towards her. She took the checkered hanky and lifted the shades to dab at her eyes. Ian tilted his head and scratched his patchy number one as he contemplated her. He glanced up at the CCTV camera that nestled into the corner coving above his head. He placed the gum in a paper bag and picked up a pen, scribbling quickly on the it before and pushing it towards her.

"That's seventy-five pence."

She glanced down at the bag, reaching in her jeans pockets as she did so with one hand and lifting her sunglasses with the other. She read the note. GIVE ME A MINUTE, I NEEDS TO SORT OUT THE CAMERA. IT'S BEHIND ME. DON'T LOOK UP AND DON'T WATCH WHERE I GO. GIVE ME MORE MONEY THAN

I NEEDS.

She looked up at him and handed over a five-pound note. Ian rang up the purchase. "Oh, darn it. Got no change me love, let me get some." Ian made to head out of the shop through a door behind the counter and then flattened his back against the cigarette shelves and inched sideways to the left. Surprisingly nimble, he levered himself up on a shelf below the cigarettes and straightened himself up, now just to the left of the camera and at the same height. He took a roll of tape from his pocket and stretched a length out, biting it off with his teeth. Carefully he placed it over just the microphone by the camera.

Rachel smiled as he jumped down and then walked towards her as if he had just come back through the door, thinking the wiley old fox must have done that before to have been so adept at it.

"There you go me duck." He gave her the change and then pointed back towards the gum section, "make it look like you're reconsidering the flavour you want and I'll tell you what I can to help you. The camera can only see the back of my head so can't tell what I'm saying."

Rachel took the bag of gum and reached in to take the pack out, "can I change this?" she mouthed the words carefully as she did so.

"Of course!" Ian pointed at the gum counter. "If you need to speak to me, turn around and face away from me," he continued, "then they can't lip read you." Rachel stood scanning the shelf, her brain partly questioning who might be lip reading her and partly concerned with how to make sure she got all the information she could from Ian.

"Walk over to the chocolate if we need more time," said Ian quickly, "there's a key swap at Effing Fred's tonight."

Rachel turned to look at the chocolate counter behind her.

"Effing Fred? Is he not very nice?"

"No... yes, he a great bloke. They call him Effing Fred because he effs and blinds all the time. And he stutters. He's got a dog called Fanny."

Rachel snorted, she couldn't help herself, "Effing Fred and Fanny?" she could barely say it for laughing.

"Yes. Well, he used to be called John. But he changed his name to Fred." Ian remained ernest.

181

"Why?" she chuckled harder and headed over to the chocolate counter.

"He used the village therapist. She couldn't get rid of his stammer, so she told him to embrace it. His worst stammering letter is F, so he changed his name to Fred and got a dog and called it Fanny. Anyway, point is, he's got a key party tonight, Lisa might be there."

Rachel nodded, smiling and shaking her head, bemused as usual by her conversation with Ian, which was hilarious and slightly mad to her, but completely normal to Ian. She collected herself, remembering the camera.

"What's a Key Party? Is it what I think it is?"

"Yes, almost certainly. It's with the club. A Key Party. A Club Key Party."

Rachel threw her hands in the air in exasperation at the mention of this mysterious club again.

"Don't do that!" Ian jabbed his finger up at the camera. "Make it look like you can't decide which chocolate bar you want now, so it ties in. I don't want no-one getting suspicious." He scratched his patchy scalp again.

Rachel picked up one chocolate bar after another. "When are you going to tell me what all this club crap is about?" she asked testily.

"Oh for fanny's sake," he said equally testily, "it's doing my nuts in this. You should've been sorted by now. Look, I can't tell you about the club. Go to Effing Fred's tonight at midnight and hang around outside, you might catch Lisa. I'll write the address down on a bag for you when you bring over your flamin' chocolate. That's as much as I can do." He beckoned towards her, "get on with it now, I gotta cash up and sort this mic back out. I said more than I should already."

Rachel picked up a Lion Bar and came back over, to the counter. She looked into Ian's eyes, recognising that he had really put himself out to help her, "thank you. Very much."

He nodded and scribbled on her bag as he placed the chocolate inside, "be off with you now." He waved her away irritatedly, but with a wink.

She took her change and headed out the door. "Thanks me duck." She walked out feeling at least a little more hopeful.

Chapter 24

The Swing Anon meeting had finished. The box of tissues that had been provided was all but gone and there were several teary dejected faces. As the group filed out, Roy stood by, hands in pockets, tapping his feet. He watched Grace as she smiled and shook hands with them all, finally holding the door open for Geoff, who was wiping his eyes with a man size hanky and mumbling his gratitude in shaky tones. She finally closed it behind him and turned to Roy with a sigh.

"Well, that was a disaster!" he said angrily.

She was taken aback. "I thought it went really well! There was a lot of release there, it's clearly a needed service. I think it was great for a first meeting. I mean I know we haven't thought through the programme and steps thing and we need to..."

"Oh fuck the programme! And the steps," he exploded disdainfully, "that's not what I did it for. I need to get some support up to challenge the club."

Grace looked shocked. "I thought you wanted to help these people!"

He glowered at her under angry eyebrows, "oh come on Grace. You can't be that gullible."

She was hurt. "Roy I knew you wanted to deal with club issues, but I thought it was part of helping deal with these people's pain."

"Oh, Jesus..." He rubbed his forhead, "I don't believe it... and on the subject of Jesus, what's happening with the church?"

She contemplated him for a few moments, "Roy, you did tell Theresa about that didn't you?" She looked worried, "you know that I'm only doing it to make amends... not to stir up more trouble?"

He shuffled his feet. "Roy, you did tell Theresa, right?" Grace let out an exasperated sigh. "The trouble I got into for defying the club was not worth it—I shamed my family. And it was a mistake. I was angry at Taylor, but it wasn't the right way to deal with it, I know that now. I want to put it right, do something for the village. And I might not want to get back actively with the club, but I don't want to be an enemy." She stared at him patiently waiting for him to respond. He stared back, blankly, "you didn't tell her did you?" she rubbed her chin contemplatively.

"I did tell her," he said finally, "just took my time about it." He regarded her and recognised he couldn't afford to lose her support right now. "Sorry," he took a hand from his pocket and patted her shoulder, "I'm tired. Things have been stressful, I didn't mean to worry you. About Theresa. She does know that you're well intentioned. Nobody wants you to carry on paying for the Taylor incident and when the club has a handle on our new residents, all the anger will go away. It will be forgotten."

She looked at him ruefully, "well, it can't be forgotten because of the branding. And personally, I don't think I'll ever get over the nipple clamps."

"Hmmm, bloody painful those things, not my cup of tea."

"But it's not about forgetting, it's about forgiving," she said seriously, "I just want to be forgiven. And I thought if we set this group up and people could let out their grievances, there'd be less animosity from the abstainers."

"I know. I know you mean well Grace. And it's a brilliant idea. It won't go unnoticed I promise. Just might take a little time."

"Maybe I should talk to Theresa myself?" she ventured meekly.

"No. No, believe me, now is not the time." He held her hand and patted it reassuringly, suddenly aware he needed to reel his neck back in, "you know how powerful the club is, I think the retribution showed you that right? You have to take things slowly and in the right order, otherwise, you risk even greater isolation—and believe me if Theresa thought for one second you were involved with any more anti-club activities she'd be at your door before you knew it. You'd be regarding those nipple clamps like pin pricks compared to what she'd do to you."

Grace held her breasts tenderly, a memory of pain passing across her face, "you're right, I should be patient. I don't think my breasts could handle any more from Theresa right now."

Roy nodded sagely and patted her on the shoulder again, "wise decision Gracie, wise decision."

There was silence in the room as they all gazed sullenly at the art deco bowl perched in front of them on the antique pine coffee table.

The Floosy picked absently at a hair protruding from a mole on her thigh, just above the edge of her leather chaps. Resting her teeth on her lower lip as she tried unsuccessfully to pluck it out.

Theresa leant forward and drummed her fingers on the table. She looked at her watch. "Right. Midnight. Looks like this is it for tonight." She shook her head and flicked a piece of crisp off her lace bodice, "can't believe there's only eight of us. Never had a worse turnout for a Key Party. The twiglets have hardly been touched." She elbowed the Master as his spurs dug into her ankle. "Move over," she said, pointing at the scratch he had made on her skin. He withdrew his leg.

"Not like you to complain about a bit of physical pain." He said it under his breath.

Theresa, ignoring him, picked up the bowl from the table and swirled the keys around inside.

"Ok. Normal rules. Pick your own, they go back in and you pick again," she glanced around and then held the bowl out as each of them selected a set of keys. As was usual, pairings were secret, none of the participants were aware of the partnerings other than their own. When the draw was complete, Theresa drew in a deep and resigned breath. "Ok. If you have a blue key, you are hosts. Go now and prepare. Your designated partners will be with you in half an hour."

Four of the guests stood and took their leave. Remaining were Floosy, Trevor, the Master and Theresa, who sat head in hands.

"What's up T?" asked Floosy.

Theresa sighed, "I got Effing Fred."

Floosy laughed raucously. "Well, at least he's well hung. I got Pete. Petite."

"Yeah but it takes him so f-f-f-f-fucking long to tell me what he's going to f-f-f-f-fucking do to me that by the time he f-f-f-f-fucking does it, I'm half f-f-f-f-fucking asleep."

The Master snorted, "I'm more f-f-f-f-fucking concerned about the turnout tonight. We need to get things sorted Theresa. What the fuck is going on?"

"Fear." Theresa sighed, "we're closing in on Rachel. When she's in, we'll be fine."

The Master laughed and shook his head, "Lisa's lost it. You

185

know it as well as I do."

Theresa glanced at Floosy and flicked her head at her, indicating she should leave. She stood and pulled her leather waistcoat down over her protruding belly. "Pete's waiting. He may be small, but he's always raring to go. I will talk to you anon." She flicked her cape dramatically over her shoulders and strutted from the room.

Theresa turned to the Master and stared coldly into his eyes, "you're on the wrong track with Roy. He's double dealing, maybe triple. There's the Swing Anon club with Grace—and more than that, he's caught up with Taylor. And she's plotting too. This is more than you can handle *Adrian*." She all but spat his name at him, "I'm serious now. Don't fuck with me." She jabbed her forefinger at him. He raised an eyebrow.

"Bit late for that love," he said sarcastically.

"I know more about what's going on in this village than you can possibly imagine. If you think you can get one over on me, then you're sadly mistaken. I'll swing before I'll let you take over."

He nodded and stood to his full height. "You're swinging alright. I've had enough of your games and your threats," he said as he strode from the room.

"F-f-f-f-f-fuck!" Theresa stood with her hands on her hips for a moment, then quickly grabbed her keys and headed out to her place, where she would be hosting Effing Fred.

Rachel rubbed her hands and hopped from foot to foot, trying to stay back in the shadows of the tree as she watched them leave one by one. Six people had so far exited Effing Fred's house variously clad in leather, thongs, chaps, trousers, bodices, metal spurs and various chains... and even a mask; or was it a balaclava? She thought one of the women had been the Floosy, but other than that they were difficult to recognise. As each of them left, she became more and more alarmed about Lisa's activities and had begun practicing the questions she would ask when she finally emerged. But as she recognised Theresa coming out having switched all the lights off, the words faded and she was overtaken by disappointment, knowing she wasn't to get the chance to ask even one question. Disheartened, she withdrew further under the weeping willow as Theresa passed by clearly agitated and repeatedly saying the f word, with what sounded like a stutter. She wandered vaguely if Effing Fred's stammer was contagious, but she couldn't find her thought funny. Feeling exasperated and desperate, she closed her eyes and sighed, tears pricking beneath her eyelids as she tried to assess her rapidly dimishing options.

"Aaagh... what the fff..." Rachel felt her heart leap into her throat and panic fill her body as a hand clenched tightly over her mouth and tug her back into the darkness, toppling her off balance and forcing her to lean heavily against her assailant to stay on her feet. She momentarily wondered if one of the people from the party had doubled back having spotted her in her shadowy hiding place and she felt a rush of fear.

"Shhhhhh... keep quiet!"

Rachel closed her eyes and felt the thump of blood pumping through her chest as both anger and relief rushed through her veins. As Lisa gently released her hand away from Rachel's mouth and used her other arm to steady her, she spun round to face her

"Where the fuck..."

"Shut up! Don't say anything." Lisa placed her finger on Rachel's lips, "I'll answer all your questions, I promise, but we have to get out of here. Follow me."

Lisa grabbed Rachel's hand before she could object and pulled her further back under the tree and out the other side where a dark alley led away from Effing Fred's house and back towards the centre of the village. As they entered the pitch-black lane, Lisa stopped and wrapped her arms tightly round Rachel, squeezing her as if she might never hold her again. Rigid with her arms straight down by her sides, Rachel was determined not to respond. Lisa placed her lips against her ear and spoke quietly, gently.

"I'm sorry. You have to trust me. I know this is all weird beyond belief, but I can explain everything. We have to go somewhere private. Is Frankie home? Can I come back to your place?" Rachel sighed, unable to maintain the tension. She relaxed her arms and tentatively folded them around Lisa's back, feeling hot tears run down her cheeks. She sniffed, embarrassed by the fluid emotion that started streaming from her. She released herself a little from Lisa's grip and grappled for a tissue from her pocket. Wiping her nose above Lisa's head, she struggled for composure.

"No, Frankie's not home, but I don't think it's a good idea..."

"Please? Please, Rachel? I wouldn't ask if I didn't have to, it's the only place we can be safe."

Rachel shook her head. "I don't understand..." it was almost a wail of frustration and despair.

"I know, I know, but you will I promise." Lisa looked up into her eyes, "please?"

Rachel relented. "Ok." She rubbed her brow, weighing up whether she could commit to her response, "ok." She nodded and looked back into Lisa's eyes, "but I swear, you better be honest with me about what's going on, I've had enough of all this secrecy and..." she struggled for words, "the weird... shit that's going on around here."

"I will I promise. I'll explain it all. All the weird shit." Lisa managed a small smile. "It *is* weird. I know." Lisa glanced behind them, "one of the weird things is the cameras. I'll tell you later, but they are everywhere in the village. We're being monitored." Lisa raised her hand as she saw the look of confusion and saw a question rise on Rachel's lips, "don't ask, not right now. But we have to get back to your place without being caught, so you'll have to follow me. It will be a circuitous route and we will need to get through some strange places to avoid all the lenses. Best if we stay silent and you just follow. Just follow wherever and whatever I need you to do. Ok?"

Rachel shrugged her shoulders and threw her hands up in the air, "more weird shit." She sighed, "ok, I'm ready."

Lisa ran the edge of her thumb down Rachel's tear soaked cheek, "you can trust me." She grabbed Rachel's hand and pulled her further into the alley, walking quickly into the enveloping darkness.

Chapter 25

Rachel scrambled in the dark under the plant pot to find the spare back door key, cursing as her fingers scoured the ground and came up with nothing.

"It's not here!" she hissed, exasperated and befuddled—she couldn't remember having had to use it at any other point, "can't we go round the front?"

Lisa chewed her lip. "You can, but you'll have to go via Wintery Lane to make it look like you're coming back from the shops."

"Oh for fuck's sake. This is ridiculous, what kind of weird shit place am I living in that I can't just... just... oh I give up! Tell me what route to take." Rachel hung her head, feeling exhausted.

Lisa took her hand, "I'm sorry. You didn't ask for any of this. It's my fault. I will explain I promise, but I can't go round the front with you, we'll be caught on camera."

Rachel nodded wearily, "ok so tell me the quickest route."

Lisa gave her directions, a circuitous route through narrow lanes; she repeated it twice to make sure Rachel had it mapped out properly. Rachel nodded and headed silently out through the back gate to make her way round to the front of the house. She turned right down a gravel path and cursed as the uneven ground gave way beneath her left foot and her ankle objected with a burst of pain. "God dammit!" She rubbed her foot and hobbled a little before it settled down. "Walk it off!" She said to herself, flexing her foot as she carried on towards a narrow lane that passed the park and lead out into the main street. Suddenly she stopped in her tracks. It was as if the pain in her foot had flicked a switch and she felt that now familiar flood of confusion about why on earth she had been so desperate to see Lisa again. She deliberately checked in with her senses—and her heart. Still Frankie. She let out a long sigh and continued on, grateful for the breakthrough. Coming out into the road, she looked up at the street lamp and noticed the camera, whirring into motion and turning in her direction. She felt like acknowledging it but resisted the impulse to give a two-fingered salute. Instead, she made her way along to the house, checking both ways along the street for any unwelcome company before opening her front door, feeling exasperated, confused and vulnerable all at the same time—and wondering just what the hell she had got herself into. Satisfied there was no one in sight, she turned the key in the lock and opened the door. She automatically went to turn on the lights, but her hand wavered over the switch as she hesitated about putting them on. No, maybe not. She shook her head. Why? She tutted at her fear and headed straight through to the kitchen to let Lisa in through the back door. Lisa smiled at her through the glass pane, hopping from one foot to the other agitatedly. Rachel pulled the door open and Lisa burst through, throwing her arms around her and leaning in for a kiss. Rachel pulled her head back and Lisa's face fell.

"No. Stop!" She was gentle but firm as she removed Lisa's arms from her and stepped back, "we need to talk. I need to know what's going on here."

Lisa stepped back reluctantly and Rachel drew out two stools from under the breakfast bar, indicating that Lisa should sit.

"Ok. I know. It's complicated, I don't know where to start...it's hard to even begin to explain..." she was hesitant. Rachel could hear the fear in her voice but wasn't having any of it.

"Try." She looked hard into Lisa's eyes to let her know she wasn't taking any excuses.

Lisa nodded, took a deep breath and began.

"Have you looked at any of it?"

Nathan shook his head, "only just got hold of it. You know that place, don't need to tell you that it's tough to get in there without anyone noticing." Nathan looked at his watch, "my Elsie's gonna wonder what's goin' on, tis nearly one in the morning, best get this done."

"Yes, I know, well done. Ok, so is this the only copy?"

"Yup." He stood with his hands in his pockets.

"Good. Thanks, Nathan, you did a good job." Nathan nodded and rocked on his heels. Waiting.

"You can go now, get back to your Elsie." She looked him steadily in the eye. He drew his head into his neck and frowned. He had expected to view the material. She stood and opened the door for him.

"Right." He withdrew his hands from his pockets.

She decided she needed to explain, "there are patients on this footage. I need to respect confidentiality. I can't let you see the material on here Nathan, medical examination and revealing intimate details."

He looked confused, "ain't that the point?"

"It's private medical information. We don't need to know anything beyond what is relevant to the club," she admonished him.

"Oh. Yes. Course."

"I'm looking for something specific that is essential for the club, everything else on here will be immediately erased, ok?"

He nodded, "I gets it. Yeah, absolutely. Private innit?"

"That's also why it's important that there are no other copies?" She made it a question just to double check.

"Nope. No other copies, like I said."

"Great. I've sorted out something for you by way of a thank you. I know you pushed the boat out on this one for me and I'm grateful for your trust. You can collect it from the Post Office on Wednesday."

"Much appreciated, that. Thank you. Shall look forward to finding out what it is." He patted her on the shoulder, "You am a good sort. You always be safe with me."

"I know Nathan. Likewise. And thanks again."

He gave a final nod and left. She shook her head; useful though he was, dealing with the likes of Nathan was so beneath her. Placing the disc in the hard drive, she hit the forward button and increased the speed just enough that she could rapidly view a succession of examinations and diagnoses of familiar village residents. Then she sat back and smiled, slowing it down and thinking that actually there was no need to hurry, she had plenty of time and why not enjoy what she was viewing? "Doctor Taylor..." she said it slowly, deliciously, "Doctor... mmmm." She loved saying that word, it had so many connotations for her. Apart from the splendour of its authority, the power it contained, the control, the supremacy. There was also that rush, that buzz, those hands, the ability to change the course of people's lives through those fingers, that towering intellect being used to heal - or not. She watched, smiling, reveling in what she was seeing. God, she had to admit she was amazing. Really amazing. So assured, so deft in her handling of

191

the patients, so absolutely perfect in her assessment; and look how she moved. She let out a sigh. Even in work mode, she was gorgeous, lithe, sexy. She chuckled. Look at that skirt, I love leather, she thought to herself. She found it amusing that as a Doctor she had the audacity to turn up in such tight fitting, almost revealing clothes. Hmmm, she found herself getting turned on and bit down on her bottom lip. She watched on, seeing her hands probe gently, such long elegant fingers. So gentle... she placed her forefinger on her lip and let it slip into her mouth as she carried on viewing, she groaned and placed her hand on her inner thigh, throwing her head back as she caught a view of the back of her legs as she walked back round to the chair behind her desk, calf muscles taught, slender ankles above black stiletto heels. "Oh, you really are hot." She breathed deeply, sensually, "hmmm," she let her hand fall closer to her panties as she watched herself put on her glasses and look at her computer screen. "Oh my god, you look so fucking sexy in those spectacles!" Her fingers edged under her silk underwear. She bit down on her lip and let her fingers move further...

"Bingo!" She put her hand on her mouse. Sitting up abruptly, she recognised what she had been looking for. She slowed the video and watched as Roy carefully placed coins round that self same mouse, marking its position on her desk. "You're a clever bastard aren't you?" She watched as he started to examine the files on her monitor, "but you've never been quite clever enough for me." As he accessed the patient records, she understood. "Of course. You needed to know didn't you?" she said as she read the name of the file.

"Ok." she nodded to herself. "Ok," her mind working on the implications of what she was seeing. She carried on with the footage, frowning as he rifled through the drawers. Then she saw the vials.

"Ohhhhh. Right." She paused the footage as he took the photograph. She tapped her lip contemplatively. "Right. Well, this all brings things to a head doesn't it Roy?" She rotated her chair and looked down admiringly at her outstretched tanned legs. She crossed them slowly, running her hand down her toned thigh muscle, looking at it lovingly, "gorgeous…" she let out the word with nonchalance, a subconscious reflex, her active mind rolling through her possible options, her next move. She swiveled back round, staring at the paused image of

Roy with his hands on her vials, "time to get on with things." Dr Taylor ran her fingers through her glorious hair. She thought through her plan and smiled as she caught sight of herself in the mirror. "Two of me," she said lightly as she enjoyed her reflection. She opened a drawer and took out a hand mirror, angling it so the reflection bounced off the wall mirror, "four of me..." she giggled, "who wouldn't want more stunning genii like us in the world?" she asked her reflections, "and so it shall be." She swiveled her chair and repeated to herself even more assertively, "and so it shall be."

Lisa had gathered the determination to fully explain what was happening. It felt imperative that if she was to have any chance of recapturing Rachel's trust, she would have to come completely clean on everything from the past—and the circumstances of the present. She started setting the scene.

"Like I told you before, when Father bought the manor and the brewery, they were ramshackle. The brewery hadn't been in action for years and the manor house was uninhabitable. He spent millions restoring them. He wanted to get the brewery back in business again. Anyway, one morning he was at the brewery, assessing the place to decide what he wanted to produce there, when he found a tunnel that went under the building that he hadn't been aware of before. He went into it and found it led down to a spring, you know, like a water spring?"

Rachel nodded, "yeah, I heard that there's a spring under there."

"No, not the spring everyone knows about, this is a secret one. The water is very pure and it has a distinctive, sweet taste. I don't think he thought too much of it at the time other than it being an interesting find. Then a couple of weeks later, he was clearing out the old brewery offices when he came across a recipe book. Mostly it was beer and the brewery has been producing that ever since, award winning, some of the best bitter in Europe. But he also found a recipe for a type of gin—and when he read it, he recognised that it was dependent on this water from the spring. And it had some other ingredients that gave it a special, well, let's call it a kick. He was fascinated," Lisa looked rueful, "Father was... well he wasn't exactly the most faithful of husbands, he test ran a lot of leading ladies. And not so leading ladies for that matter. And he tried a lot of substances. He was compelled by the idea of this gin. Sex and stimulants were his thing."

Rachel was fixated, her mind grasping the possible implications already.

"Anyway, he made up a small batch of this recipe—and test ran that too. And what he found, was that it had some special side effects. Like a sense of euphoria, a huge boost in sexual desire and a loss of inhibition. Like no sexual boundaries. It also effects memory in a weird way."

Rachel felt rising emotions starting to kick in. Anger, fear, relief, her thoughts raced.

"So... it's an aphrodisiac?"

"And some..." Lisa paused.

Rachel sought more clarification, "does it make you think you feel things for someone, but confused about it at the same time?"

"Yeah. Kind of attracted but you can't define why?"

"Cos that's the kind of way I feel about you. So... it's because of the gin?" She shook her head unsure whether to allow horror or relief to take the dominant position within her.

Lisa didn't like hearing Rachel say it that bluntly. She knew it wasn't the reason she felt the way she did about Rachel. It stung for her to listen to such cold analysis.

"Well, it's possible that..."

"No, but hang on, I didn't have any gin till last week... so how come I felt like that before?"

"Well it's not just the gin, I think, I mean I feel, I don't drink it any more and I..." Lisa tried to bring her own feelings to Rachel's attention, but she wasn't listening.

"What happened at that Love Honey party?" She could feel her anger rising and any feelings she might or might not have had for Lisa were at this point completely wiped out.

Lisa hung her head, not wanting to answer.

"Tell me what happened at the party... Lisa, tell me."

"Look why don't you let me tell you the whole story..."

"Fuck the story! Tell me what happened at the party!"

194

"If I give you the background..."

"Just tell me!"

Rachel's frustration started to boil over, she was suddenly desperate just to be able to understand why she was being tortured, why she was facing the ruin of her relationship with Frankie... for what?

Lisa contemplated her and seeing her distress, cut to the chase. "Dr Taylor injected you with a serum that is a distilled version of the gin."

"What?" She looked at Lisa in horror. "Why?"

Lisa chewed the inside of her mouth.

Rachel closed her eyes and saw the image of Frankie, back against the wall of the post office sobbing. She felt sick to her stomach.

"What the fuck! Why?" She grabbed Lisa's arms and shook her, frustration, shock and confusion were getting the better of her.

"Don't!" Lisa threw both her arms up violently to push Rachel's hands off, "never do that!" Lisa's face was contorted in fury.

"Ok. Ok." Rachel backed up and put her hands in the air, "I won't touch you again, I promise." She breathed deeply to calm herself, she really needed to get to the bottom of this, she recognised alienating or shutting Lisa down was a distinct possibility if she didn't back off.

"Please. Sit down," she said it gently and indicated the stool. Lisa regarded her suspiciously, "please. I'm sure you understand that I need you to tell me why?"

Lisa sat back down on the stool.

Rachel shook her head again, disbelief settling in, she took a deep breath in through her nose and blew out through her mouth. She spoke calmly.

"So, first of all, why on earth would there be a serum? I mean a *serum*? Really? For what?"

Lisa stared at her, suddenly comprehending the madness, the complexity, the bizarre and almost entirely unbelievable nature of what she was trying to explain. She felt her mouth go dry, but she knew instinctively that addressing this now could possibly be the best thing that could happen for her. "Ok, you're going to have to stay calm if you want me to get through this." She stared into Rachel's eyes and groaned inwardly; she knew she was going to lose her. She probably already had.

Rachel nodded, "ok. I promise... I promise." She saw Frankie again in her head, this time running down the stairs two at a time to leave the house. She let out an involuntarily sob and closed her eyes. She had the most desperate urge to just run from the house herself and get to Frankie in London as quickly as she could. To put her arms round her. To say sorry. To beg her forgiveness. She felt tears on her cheeks.

Lisa looked at her, suddenly mortified, "I'm so sorry."

"I don't understand. I feel like my life just fell apart and I don't know why. You have to make some sense of this for me Lisa?" She looked pleadingly at her.

Lisa suddenly found some strength. She instantly felt herself take a step from the murky darkness into some light and understood this was her chance.

"I know." She took Rachel's hand firmly in hers, "I will. None of what has happened is your fault. I'll make it right, I promise."

"But you can't make it right. I think I've lost Frankie." Rachel let her head fall forward against Lisa's chest and sobbed uncontrollably. Lisa held her tight and closed her eyes. There was no way back. And she was glad. She looked at her watch, feeling anxious. She held Rachel until she felt her calming.

"It's going to be ok. You can fix things with Frankie. If that's what you want. It'll be ok."

Rachel nodded miserably, "I'm so confused."

"I know. I know."

She looked at her watch again. Calculating how much time she had, "look there's something else I have to tell you before we carry on." Rachel opened her mouth to protest, but something in Lisa's eyes made her stop. "I have to be back at the manor soon, my Mother thinks I'm strapped to my bed in the White Room."

Rachel's face screwed itself into a disbelieving frown.

"I know. I know, it's all too weird to even begin to comprehend now, but I need to explain this bit because I have to make a decision about heading back. So. For the very reason, I am here right now, to basically tell you what's going on in this village, my Mother and Peters restrained me and locked me away to keep me from talking to you."

"Peters?" Rachel was shocked.

"Yeah, well I know what you're going to say, but actually Peters is on my side, she set it up for me so that I could come out and talk to you. But if I'm not back soon my Mother will find out, so I have to make a decision whether I play the game, or stick it out here and make the break from the situation entirely."

"How could your Mother do that to you?" She was incredulous. Lisa sighed, "well that's really complicated too and I'm not even going to try to explain that right now, but, look, whatever you think and whatever comes out in the future about my Mother, I love her and what she does is more a factor of the damage she's been caused than anything else. In her warped way, she's trying to protect me."

"Well, what do you want to do?"

Lisa thought for a few seconds, "ok, I've got a couple of hours and I'm going to try and explain as much as I can about all this—but then I think I should go back. I don't want my relationship with my Mother to completely break down."

"But will you be in danger?"

"No. Well not physically, it's emotional agony to be locked up in a silent White Room, but I can handle it. I think if I don't more alarm bells will ring and that would be worse."

Rachel nodded. "Ok. If you think that's best?"

"Yup. That's best."

In the living room of Rachel's house, Donna sat in the dark and listened to her daughter speak. She felt tears well up in her eyes. She couldn't remember the last time that had happened. So many years. But hearing her daughter say she loved her despite everything opened up something in her very core. She rose silently from the sofa where she had positioned herself, planning to catch the two of them out and haul them back to the manor. How glad she was now that Rachel hadn't turned on the light when she came in through the door. She looked down at the key she had removed from its hiding place beneath the plant pot outside the back door and glanced around the living room. She crept carefully over to a dresser and tucked the key behind a vase, then crossed the room and opened the front door, passing through it without a sound and pulling it shut behind her.

Lisa stopped and cocked her head to one side, "did you hear something?"

"No. What did you think it was?" Rachel glanced towards the kitchen door.

"I don't know." Lisa got up and headed into the living room, peering into the gloom. She stopped and listened hard. Nothing. She came back into the kitchen, "probably just me. I don't want to switch the light on. You didn't hear anything?"

Rachel shook her head.

"Ok." Lisa sat back down and continued, "it started with a small group of them. Mainly up at the manor. They'd drink the gin and basically, indulge in these all weekend orgies. Mother didn't want to get involved, but he basically gave her no choice—unless of course she wanted to leave. Which she didn't. She was in love with him. He was the leading player, obviously. It started to become a bit of a cult as word spread round the village. The place started to attract residents based on the fact you could get involved in this club."

Rachel nodded. The club.

"It was basically the gin that made everyone want to experience free love. Well, I'm not sure that I should use the word love. There weren't feelings involved. It was just about sex. Gin and Sex. So they called it The Gin And It Club. Then Father started to realise he could be on to a money spinner. He couldn't openly market the gin, but if he quietly spread the word that it was available to those who wanted it, he could grow a business out of it. Then he came up with the idea of making it a sort of closed community. He had friends in high places, local government. He paid off some key people and he had all the sign posts taken down to the village, to cut it off so to speak, and started buying up properties. My family owns almost all the land and seventy percent of the property in the village. The rest of the property owners know that if they don't sell to the club when they want to move, or they sell outside the local market without approval, they better move out because otherwise they'll be shunned by pretty much the whole village.

And there's a list as long as your arm of swingers from all over the world who want to move here."

Rachel was stunned. She had so many questions in her head she barely knew where to start. Might as well go for the most burning one, "so how come we got to move here?"

"Grace was supposed to sell this place to Dr Taylor. But I know from her directly that Taylor was going to screw her over on price. Taylor was supplying Grace's Father with the serum illegally. Well, as in 'club illegally'." She made inverted commas with her fingers, "he was breeding super cocks. She had him over a barrel. Selling to outsiders was Grace's revenge after her Father died."

"What the fuck is a super cock?" Rachel remembered that Thomas had kept his cocks in her pantry.

"Well, he had this idea that if the cocks were bred with this serum as part of their DNA, they'd be prized for breeding hens that were great layers. He was obsessed with eggs."

"I don't know whether to laugh or cry."

"Yeah well, there are some interesting people here."

"You're telling me. Fuck. And I thought we had soooo landed on our feet when we found this place." Rachel shook her head again, "so is this place pretty much worthless to us now because it has to be sold within the village?"

Lisa shrugged, "might be the opposite. You might be able to leverage that. I don't know. Best not to think about it yet."

Rachel suddenly started laughing, sardonically "so we basically moved into a giant swingers club?"

"Something like that."

"Is it still a money-spinner?"

"Oh God. Huge. The Club takes a monthly fee off every resident. That alone is worth over £4million a year."

"What? Crikey. No wonder they want to keep it a secret."

"And the land and property? We're talking hundreds of millions."

"Wow. That blows my mind. So me and Frankie could be disturbing lives and wealth on a pretty grand scale right?"

The penny dropped.

Lisa nodde, "you got it. Theresa's in control pretty much these days—I'll come back to the whys and wherefores on that at some other point, but she knew she needed to get you guys on side. So they decided to try and get you in the club, so to speak. It's the easiest way to make sure you wouldn't let the cat out of the bag outside the village."

"Well with that kind of money at stake, that could be quite considerate. People get bumped off for less, things can get pretty ruthless where there's that kind of wealth involved."

"People here are generally good souls. They just want to carry on with their business without being disturbed or judged. It's all voluntary, no-one gets hurt. Well, I say that there are a few whose other halves don't get it. They're called Abstainers and they don't get involved in the swinging. Sometimes there's jealousy, but beyond that, it's all consenting adults just enjoying some unusual activity."

"No-one gets hurt? I think that's a stretch."

"Yeah. Ok. Maybe. Well anyway, I don't want to get into that. Father built up his empire, his cult and everything was hunky dory. Mother pretty much lived her own life. Then Daddy fell in love. With someone in the village. He just stopped all of his other activity, stopped the gin, stopped the orgies, the parties and got religion. He decided he didn't want any part of it any more."

"Who did he fall in love with?" Rachel was curious.

Lisa looked at her, she had tears in her eyes.

Rachel frowned, "sorry."

"No. It's ok. I only found that out very recently, I thought it was because of me... but, anyway it's not... important." She paused, "so, this woman didn't feel the same about him and he couldn't handle it. He was heartbroken. He left, disappeared for years, left Mother to pick up the pieces. She kind of unraveled for a while. A lot of stuff came out of the woodwork. One of the things she found out was that Dad hadn't always been as careful as he should have been." She paused again, "apparently he had other children." Lisa shook her head. "Theresa was Mother's rock at the time. Helped her get the place back in order and agreed to carry on the day to day running of the club." Lisa looked at her watch, "so that's why Theresa has been really active with you two." She paused, "and why I have been."

"What do you mean?"

Lisa chewed her lip. "I was supposed to convert you into the ways of the club." She looked up under her furrowed brow for Rachel's reaction.

Rachel's mouth dropped open and she blinked hard several times, letting it sink in. "It was all a setup?" The colour rose in her cheeks. Lisa tried to grab her hand, but Rachel tore it away, "don't touch me."

"It was just a set up to start with."

"You set me up? You reeled me in like a bloody fish so that you could get me in the club? Deliberately?"

"No, I... yes. But only to start with, it's my job... but I..."

"It's your job?" Rachel spat it out angrily, "it's your job to split me up from the woman I love?" Rachel stood up and paced across the kitchen floor, her hands fists of rage, "you bitch!"

"No, no I didn't mean to..."

"You cold-hearted bitch!"

"No... nooooo!" Lisa protested, "I fell in love with you!" Tears streamed down her face.

"Oh don't give me that shit!" She blew out hard, trying to control her anger, "love. What the hell would you know about love?"

"Rachel don't..." Lisa wiped the tears with the back of her hand, composing herself.

"Don't don't me! I can't believe it. Hook line and sinker. You must have been laughing... fuck!" She put her head in her hands, "fuuuuuuuuuuccck!!" she screamed with everything she had in her lungs.

Lisa leapt up and put her hand over Rachel's mouth, spinning her round quickly and holding her tightly from behind. She could feel her heart thumping in her chest.

"Shut up!" Lisa said urgently, Rachel struggled against her. "Stop it. Stop struggling. You have to stop shouting, someone might hear, I don't want anyone poking their nose in and finding us."

She felt Rachel's resistance subside and tentatively removed her hand from over her mouth.

"Why would anyone, *anyone*, do that to another human being? It's beyond me."

201

Lisa shook her head. "When it started I didn't know. I've been shut down for years. Buried my emotions behind layers of protection."

"Oh, please, I don't want to know." Rachel held up her hands.

"Please believe me. I didn't want to hurt you. I fell in love... I..."

"Don't say that!" Her voice started to rise again, "stop saying that!"

Lisa closed her eyes, exasperated. Desperately disappointed. She looked at her watch, "I have to go."

"Yes." Rachel was curt, "yes, you do."

"I can't leave it here though. And you need to protect yourself."

"I don't care about anything but Frankie right now."

"Maybe you should go to her. Stay away for a few days?" Lisa tried to be reasonable, though it was breaking her to do so.

"Whatever I do it's none of your business."

Lisa sighed again, running her hands through her hair, feeling bleak, "I care about what happens to you."

Rachel laughed, "oh yes. Of course you do." She shook her head, "just go, I'll be fine. Good luck with your Mother."

Lisa took a step towards her.

"Don't!" Rachel held both hands up defensively.

Lisa nodded and turned to leave. She stopped for a moment, "I'm sorry," she said it without looking back, "I really am sorry. Take care of yourself." And then she headed for the front door.

Rachel paced the living room, back and forth, her mind in turmoil. Then sat down heavily on the sofa. She felt sick. She leaned forward, trying to stop her head spinning. She closed her eyes and again saw Frankie's sobbing figure outside the post office. "Oh my God..." she groaned and rocked herself back and forward, holding her knees, "I'm so sorry..." it was a whisper. She looked at her watch. Frankie would be at her desk in a couple of hours, she could ring her then. She shook her head, running through the revelations from Lisa, it was literally like being in a nightmare. If only she could wake up and it all be gone. "Unbelievable..." she said it out loud, "I mean literally fucking unbelievable!" She thought through the possibilities about what Theresa might have told Frankie—

how much did she know? She ran back through the previous weeks… the Love Honey party. "Oh my god!" she groaned again, she still didn't know what had happened… but Theresa did. She stood up, suddenly almost incapable of waiting to speak to Frankie, she needed to know. Like now. She felt sick again. Maybe she should try and sleep for a couple of hours? She laughed at herself. Yeah right… like that might be possible. Nevertheless, she made her way wearily up to the bedroom and sat on the edge of the bed. She wished she could switch off her brain. The thoughts were each like separate torture weapons, piercing her mind and drip, drip, dripping into her heart, corroding what she valued most. Anger started to rise and she cursed every person they had met in the last few weeks, starting from that bastard estate agent and the asshole lawyer who had acted so fast to secure them the property, to that bitch Lisa. Lisa, she dwelled on her for a while. Well, actually she needed to pity her more than anything. She sighed. Damn your compassion, she said to herself as her anger gave way to something softer. What an awful life she's had. Oh man… she chewed at her lip, anger rising again as she thought about Theresa. She put her head back in hands, "oh my god, this is unbearable. Why can't I remember?" She scoured the corners of her brain searching for a clue about the party. "What did I do?" she looked heavenward. "Ha!" she laughed at herself again, "why am I looking up there for answers when I am down here in hell!" Then she jumped, startled by her phone ringing. She looked down, knowing who it was before she clocked the number. She picked it up.

"Hello?"

"Hey."

She felt a rush run through her. She hesitated, heart in her throat, blood pumping a thousand miles an hour, "it's early."

"I know." Frankie hesitated too, "sorry I missed your calls. And that I ran out like that."

"It's ok. I…" Rachel started.

"We need to talk," Frankie continued on, clearly wanting to control the conversation, "but I have to sort some things out here first."

"Ok." She said it weakly.

"But I'll come back tomorrow, we can deal with it then."

Rachel closed her eyes tight and tears squeezed their way out and ran down her cheeks, "can I at least explain?"

"Explain what? Look I can't talk now. Seriously, I'll be back tomorrow. Around nine o'clock."

Rachel was grateful at least that Frankie was so calm.

"Yes. Frankie I..." But the line had gone dead. Rachel lay back down and wept uncontrollably.

Donna watched her daughter as she crept back into the room and lay on the bed, carefully rearranging things to make it look like she had never been away. Donna's head tilted to one side as she regarded her, "I'm so proud of you my darling," she said quietly, "I don't know how you turned out so beautifully." She rested her chin on her hands and gazed at Lisa as she closed her eyes. She zoomed in and felt a pain in her chest as she saw the tears roll down Lisa's cheeks. She brushed the screen, "I told you didn't I hmmm? I told you love would cause you pain." She rolled the chair back and tapped the desk with her long elegant nails. She flipped a switch on the console and watched Peters as she slept, slumped uncomfortably in her chair. "And what am I going to do with you, Peters?" She tapped her nails again, "I know you did it for the right reasons, but... hmmm, I don't know if I can trust you again." She pressed a buzzer on the console.

"Yes, ma'am." It was the sleepy voice of Arthur.

"Arthur go and release Peters from the chair Make sure she has food and some water. Then make sure you lock her in."

"Yes, ma'am."

Donna turned back to her daughter and watched intently for a while, "I need to protect you my darling, my precious little angel, it's all going to be ok." She picked up the phone, "Theresa. It's Donna. Yes I know it's early. It's urgent. We need to speak."

Chapter 26

"Call to the Order of the Sloe." The Master let the gavel fall onto its wooden block somewhat lackadaisically and the room fell silent. "Salute all those that honour the club." The attendants all raised their middle fingers in despondent salute. Theresa rose to give the agenda.

"There are three main issues for discussion. Firstly, the occupants of St Valentines and a progress report on The Chase, secondly the status of Club Activities and the setting of party themes for Theme Week and thirdly in preparation for the Village Fete and Show, appointment of the Show Organising Committee." She folded the paper and took a seat at the table, "I call upon the Master, He Who Shall Be Obeyed."

The Master stood again. "The Chase," he said it testily and glared at Theresa, "the floor is yours."

Theresa felt seven pairs of eyes boring into her. "Huh hmm.." She cleared her throat, "thank you, Master. Well, as we all know our plans for converting Rachel of the newcomers have come across a number of difficulties. But I can assure you that the matter is now in hand." She glanced up as low-level muttering started between members of the group, "if you'll let me continue?" She raised her hand to quieten the group. "I know this issue has a bearing on Point Two and members reluctance to participate in events without feeling safe."

"Too f-f-f-f-fucking right!" piped up Effing Fred, "and it's f-f-f-fucking af-f-f-f-fecting perf-f-f-f-ormance t-t-t-too." He stared hard at Theresa.

"Yes well I don't think it's helpful to talk about specifics here Fred, but I take your point." Theresa moved on, "I can report that I have had a meeting at The Manor and we now have intervention at the highest level. And we have a backup plan involving the second of the two incomers, Frankie. This will be resolved favourably one way or the other and we will get back to normal club activities soon."

The room was silent, the air bristled. Finally, the Master spoke, "there wasn't a busting lot of details in that report," he waggled his head. Theresa waggled her head back sarcastically, "well, you're going to need to have a little trust and patience. Calling Donna into the mix is a serious move. I'm sure she'd be very disappointed in your disdain." She cocked her head to one side and looked at him.

He sighed deeply, acquiescing reluctantly to Donna's authority. "Moving on. Club activities. I don't think there's a great deal to say here. We all know turnout is down and generally very poor. I think we all accept that most of us feel uncomfortable about being, let's say, under the microscope by those who have yet to appreciate the finer points of living in this village and the various traditions that we freely enjoy. Clearly, until Theresa has resolved the situation with Rachel and or Frankie," he waved his hand disdainfully in her direction, "we will probably still experience the same problems with turnout. In view of that and despite some splendid weather that might otherwise encourage us to indulge in outdoor activities, we're going to focus on some more intimate indoor events. It's theme week too, so we've got a number of fun games for you to engage in and some role play. And we're going to have a gin promotion to help boost attendance. Spice things up so to speak." The Master took out a sheaf of papers with a flourish, "Ian's got some floggers under the counter at the shop, but limited quantities so if you fancy one, best get in there quick. And as an added bonus we've got some free toys and outfits from Love Honey to add a little special something to the mix. Take a few of these leaflets each and spread them round your groups. Let's see if we can't get a bit of enthusiasm back into things." Everyone took leaflets, but there was little response.

The Master looked at Theresa ruefully and threw his hands up. "You need to get things sorted out," he said sharply under his breath.

She looked at him, strangely detached. It was all she could do not to paint a very clear picture for him of just how sorted out things were going to be. Instead, she just smiled, "I know," she said calmly, "it's all in hand." She turned and left, leaving the Master feeling distinctly uncomfortable—she never reacted with such calm assertion in his presence. He felt a sinking feeling in his groin.

Lisa lay in the bed, knowing that something was seriously wrong. Though her mind was necessarily pre-occupied with thoughts of Rachel and the implications of her confession, she was also seriously concerned about Peters. She had expected her to be waiting when she had returned, but there was no sign of her anywhere—she'd rushed around as many places as possible before finally having to give in and return to the White Room before her Mother got up. She was aware that Donna would know something was not right too—because she wasn't in restraints. She lay wrestling with her tangled thoughts and wondered what the time was? It was one of the most disorienting things about being in here, losing track of time, even of days of the week, completely. It hadn't been long yet, but long enough for her to become agitated. She'd expected her Mother to have come in to see her, to at least give her the chance to plead for her release, for her to promise to be a good girl and give up on Rachel. That, after all, was the point of all this. How ironic that she no longer had a choice anyway. She closed her eyes and gazed at mental images of Rachel; laughing in the playground; looking deeply into her eyes in the Barn; throwing her head back in ecstasy as they made love. "But it wasn't real, was it Lisa?" her mind piped up. She sighed. "I don't know," said her heart in return. "Yes, you do!" Her mind was insistent. "You're fooling yourself. You messed up. You fell in love with her and instead of being honest, you strung her along. You weren't thinking, were you? You turned a blind eye to the circumstances because what? Because you thought it would all be ok in the end? That the magic fairy would come along and wave a wand over her head and sprinkle stardust into her heart to magically make you her one true love?" Her mind was disdainful and persistent, "maybe you thought the fairy dust would make her forgive you, leave the woman she actually does truly love and run away into the sunset?" Lisa shook her head miserably. Her mind was on a roll, "you *hurt* her." It paused for effect. "That's not love Lisa. That's not caring about someone you love, is it?" Lisa groaned at the truth's stinging words. "I'll put it right," said her heart, "I didn't want to hurt her." She looked at the restraints, recognizing that she had her freedom right now and that she was making the choice to stay under her Mother's control. But for what? To keep the peace? To avoid her Mother's wrath and sustain the meager crumbs of love or affection she occasionally handed out? Sensing a change, her mind piped in again, "How long are you going to carry on trying to make her love you, Lisa? Trying to make her happy?" She acknowledged the truth in that, so maybe she should risk making a break for it? "Your Mother's broken Lisa, you're never going to get what you need from her, she can't do it, even if she wants to. She doesn't know how to love the way you want her to love you. It's not her fault, it's just the way she is. You can't change that." She knew there was truth in that too, though her heart sank at the thought of letting go. "Dammit!" She rubbed her temple with her fingers. What should she do?. Not having Peters there to help her with her decisions was excruciating, facing the fact she would have to take responsibility for her own choices in this situation did not sit well with her. "You know what?" said her mind insistently, "maybe it's time for you to grow up... to take responsibility. And maybe it's time for you to be brave and stand up to your Mother properly. It's been pretty half-assed so far, don't you think? Recognise her for who she is, wish her love and detach enough to start living your own life. You don't owe her anything, Lisa. Ok?" Lisa nodded. Her mind continued a little more kindly, "and this thing with Rachel, how did it make you *feel* Lisa?' Her heart responded without hesitation, "amazing, just amazing, I've been so happy!" She smiled broadly. Her heart cashed in, "well, that's your lesson. If nothing else you now know you can feel that. You can love. So, knowing that, why would you want to carry on spending your life this way?" Lisa nodded harder and her mind, embracing the breakthrough, added encouragement. "It takes courage to leave any place that feels safe, comfortable. Even though you also know it's a place of pain, you have some level of certainty here, right?"

"Yes, yes I do, even though it hurts," said her heart. "Sometimes I get just enough love to keep me here, but now I know I can have so much more. And I deserve it."

Lisa's hand moved automatically over her chest and she felt her heart's soft beat as her mind got the point. "You know. I know you know. It's time for you to stand up on your own two feet and find out who you really are, and how much more you can be."

She nodded firmly. "Yeah, maybe it is." She said it out loud - and in that moment her decision came. She stood up from the bed and headed for the door.

Theresa stared at the headboard and tried to keep her patience. She hadn't really been in the mood tonight anyway and when she drew Doug as a partner, she'd almost bailed out. But that would have been against the principals of the club and though she was sorely tempted given the impending changes, she didn't want to raise suspicion. So here she was kneeling on the bed, exasperatedly waiting for him to get his act together.

"Put it on 7!" She was rapidly losing the will.

He sat back on his heels and yelped; he'd forgotten he was wearing spurs. He grimaced as the metal sank into his bum cheek. "Shit. That hurts!" He raised himself gingerly off the spike. "I just pierced my ass. Who the fuck decided on cowboys and Indians?" he grumbled. "What did you say to do with it?"

"Put it on level 7," she said, becoming exasperated.

Doug looked down at his hand, trying to work out what that meant. She turned her head round, peering behind her, the feathers on her head piece scratching the wooden headboard and bending across her eyes, obscuring her view.

"It's the second button down. You have to press it seven times."

She spat at the piece of feather that had just crept its way into her mouth. She still had her hands bracing the bedstead in readiness. He turned the vibrator round, but still couldn't see what she meant.

"Hang on I'll get my glasses."

She sighed and leant back on her feet, "you'll look even less like Clit Eastwood in those," she complained.

"Clint."

"What?"

"*Clint,*" he said crossly, "it's *Clint* Eastwood!"

She tutted, "it's a play on words. If you read the card, it says *Clit* Eastwood."

"Well, that makes no sense does it?" He scratched at his beard and peered through the top of his bifocals at the buttons on the lime green shaft.

"What do you mean?"

"Well, I'm a man. I haven't got a clit."

She rolled her eyes, "it's a *game*, it doesn't matter whether you're a man or a woman. When you draw the name out of the hat, you just play the character you get. They're all plays on words. Like Johnny Wayne."

"Don't tell me you're Johnny Wayne?" He looked disgusted, "I'll never be able to watch him and Clint again."

"Do I look like I'm dressed as Johnny Wayne?" she said irritatedly.

"No. Suppose you don't," he said glancing over the top of his glasses at her, "who are you then?" he adjusted his chaps to stop them rubbing on his thighs. He jabbed at the buttons on the vibrator again without success.

"Poke Her Hontas." She pointed at her headdress and the bag of arrows she was wearing on her back as if to indicate it was obvious.

"Well, that's stupid too. You're not going to be poking me."

"I can if you like?" she ventured, finally thinking she might get something worthwhile out of the evening.

"No!" He set his jaw, "you know I'm not into that stuff." He adjusted his glasses and turned the vibrator up on its end, examining the battery chamber, "you sure the batteries aren't out on this?"

"Yes!" she huffed impatiently, "just give it here!" She snapped her fingers at him, then turned round and grabbed it off him. She sighed again and sat on the edge of the bed, pressing the button and setting the rampant rabbit into throbbing motion, "see? She pushed the buzzing tool back towards him. He sighed and looked at it.

"Listen Theresa…"

"Poke Her!" she said loudly. Doug looked confused.

"At least try and stay in character! This is supposed to be fun!" she shouted at him.

"Oh, I'm getting on me horse," he said crossly, "it's not fun any more. It stopped being fun a long time ago."

Doug inched sideways across the bed, trying not to lean back on the sharp spikes of the wheels again, then turned and backed off the edge of the mattress with a loud clanking sound, kicking at the Toy Story duvet that had caught itself on his left spur.

"There's no need to kick Woody in the head!" she said smiling and trying to lighten the atmosphere a little as he walked over to the chair to grab his Stetson.

"Fuck Woody!" he spat back as the duvet ripped away from his foot.

Theresa sighed. "Oh come on Doug..." she pleaded as he marched towards the door.

"Clit!" he said, "it's Clit!" and slammed the door loudly behind him.

Doctor Taylor swiveled in her consulting room chair and regarded Roy with an air of complete superiority. She spoke quietly but commandingly. "I want the bank account details."

Roy laughed. He shook his head, smiling at her, calm.

"If you don't hand them over, I'm going straight to her with your dirty little secret." Taylor's lip curled as she said it.

"Do it!" he challenged, shrugging his shoulders.

She contemplated him, her brain whirring. She sat back and crossed her arms as she looked at him. She turned away and looked out of the window, watching the sun as it sank slowly over the fields. She turned back to him. She cocked her head. "How come?"

He shrugged again, picking up the vial she had placed before him on the table and looking at it, "it doesn't matter any more."

She frowned. "Does she know?"

He nodded, comfortable in his bluff, "couldn't really hide it any more, I've been too erratic. She'll see me through it. She's my wife, she'll stand by me while I dry out."

"And what about the rest? I know you know." She pointed at the camera in the corner of the room, "don't you want her to pay?"

"No." Roy tried hard not to react to his instant realization that she had caught him in the act in her office.

Taylor placed her index finger on her lower lip and drew it across slowly, wondering why he was so steady, "you don't look shocked. Why?"

"I knew they weren't mine." Another bluff. In for a pound, he thought to himself.

She cocked her head again.

"Doesn't matter whose they are. Though I'm glad to know. But I wanted to know not to punish her, but to take the power away from you." He leant forward regarding her. He was impressed that she didn't flinch.

"Of course." She matched his measurement and his calm.

"Huh. You don't have an ounce of emotion in you, do you? Look at you. Re-calculate. Abort. Abort. Re-calculate. You're an automaton"

She smiled thinly, "it's all a game, Roy. You just changed the rules. I need a new strategy. That's how it goes."

He regarded her coolly, "I think you're out of the game."

She tapped the desk with her fingernails, "don't you believe it."

He smiled, "you don't have anything over me now. But I have plenty on you."

She smiled back and upped the stakes, "you have no idea what else I have."

The two of them sat silently, reaching into each other's eyes for a moment, both drawing a blank.

"Then we'll have to see what happens, won't we?" He broke the heavy silence.

"Don't bite off more than you can chew Roy."

He stood to leave, "fine set of molars I've got here. And not afraid to masticate." He winked at her before turning to leave.

After the door had closed, she let the cool veneer drop. She snarled and kicked the table with the base of her foot, creating an evenly rounded dent with the heel of her stiletto. She hated it when someone else got the last word.

Theresa sat in her office and switched on her PC. Nathan waited patiently at her shoulder while the monitor flickered and fired up. He held a disc out and she took it from him.

"So she believed you?"

Nathan nodded firmly, "yep."

She swiveled in her chair to face him, watching his face carefully for signs that he might be lying.

"You're sure?"

"Uhuh. One hundred percent."

She smile,. "you're a star. I'm going to take a look though now.

And I want you to remove the camera."

He looked exasperated.

"I know, I know," she patted his shoulder, "it's a tough one getting in there, but I don't want Taylor having any kind of influence over anything that happens in this village anymore. Ok?"

He nodded, "I'm off now. I'll get it tonight."

"Thanks Nathan."

She turned back to the monitor and clicked the play button.

Donna sat back in her chair. There was a lot to reflect on. She had been fascinated watching her daughter this morning, clearly wrestling with her thoughts. She wondered for what seemed like the fiftieth time what 'Yeah maybe it is' had referred to. Clearly, she had made a decision, but Donna had no idea what that decision was. She'd watched as Lisa had made her way out, collecting a bag of clothes and some food and drink and then headed out through the grounds into the village. She had debated stopping her, but her conversation with Theresa had made up her mind to see what would happen next if she let her go. She needed to be as aware as possible before Saturday of all of the implications of what was happening. And besides, she could rely on Nathan to keep a track of her movements in case she decided to leave the village all together, which was a freedom Donna was not yet ready to grant her. She turned to Peters and peeled back the tape that covered her mouth.

Peters whinced. "I think you just took my moustache."

Donna laughed, "you're too cool Peters, trust you to find something funny in all this."

"What can I say?" Peters retorted, "you've always made me laugh."

Donna shook her head, "You must be the only person in the world who can make me feel small."

"Someone's got to keep you in check."

"Where do you think she's going?"

"Well knowing your daughter and that great big soft as candy heart she hides away, my guess would be that she has a plan to put things right for Rachel." Peters looked straight into Donna's eyes.

"Don't do that." Donna looked away. She hated it when Peters kind and searching eyes penetrated through her steely resolve and touched her deep inside.

"She's your daughter Donna, you need to crack that shell of yours and let some love come out."

"I stopped that years ago." Donna was blunt.

"Just because he hurt you doesn't mean everyone else is going to."

"It's all going to come out. You can stop lecturing me. I've decided. But that doesn't mean I'm going soft."

"Well, it's about time. I'm proud of you. And it's for the best."

Donna tapped her lip with her long fingernails and thought for a while. "You know it's ridiculous how much power and control is wielded in this village. And for what? It's pure greed."

Peters stayed silent, but raised her eyebrows. She was surprised that Donna was taking things that far.

"I've locked myself away up here at arms length from all of it. And now it's out of control. When it started it was about freedom—well not the kind of freedom I wanted—but the freedom for people to explore who they were, without boundaries. That's what Eddie was about."

Peters gave a disdainful look.

"Am I being naïve?" Donna huffed. "Don't answer that." She sighed. "I know I'm being naïve."

"You would have—and still will—do anything to make sense of him. And that's admirable," Peters said sympathetically, "your shut down is a factor of his inability to give you even the tiniest amount of the love you deserve. You've never been able to accept that because it means you have to face the reality that he didn't love you as much as you loved him—or at least not in a recognizable way. That's not a reflection of you Donna, it's a reflection of him."

Donna bit her lower lip, "I had a call from Taylor."

Peters gave a slow, deliberate nod. "It was bound to happen at some point."

Donna nodded in agreement. "She wants to talk. She's coming here at six on Saturday. I'm sure I know what her gambit will be. But we'll know for sure then. I want to be pre-emptive."

"Sensible." Peters affirmed, "I doubt she has more than we already know. I suspect the whole situation with Rachel may have lead to some of the lies unraveling. Lisa has no idea of the can of worms she's about to open."

Donna thought about her daughter, "she's so like him in so many ways." She shook her head sadly.

"Yes, in some ways. But you can't punish her for that."

Donna flicked her a sharp look, "goddammit Peters, when did you get to be so perceptive?"

She smiled, "when I was born."

"Ha! Yes, I can believe that. You've always been an old soul." Donna regarded her.

Peters continued, "and another thing you can't do is hold on to her any longer because you can't bare to lose the last piece of him that you have."

She watched as Donna's face clouded and tears glistened in her eyes. There was silence for what seemed like eons.

"Why haven't you ever said any of this before?"

Peters dropped her head, "well, I could say it's because this is the first time that you've shown signs of being able to take the truth. But *my* truth is, that it also means breaking up my life and maybe losing the people that *I* love. So you could say that I have been weak and selfish too."

"Oh, the irony!" Donna smiled, "I think the score just evened up a bit Peters."

"Damn my honesty," said Peters with a mock rueful look on her face.

"I hope Rachel gets through this relatively unscathed," Donna was softer now, "she seems lovely."

"She is—and she'll be fine. Thankfully you didn't get past square one there." Peters raised an eyebrow.

Donna raised an even more arched eyebrow back. "Yes. Well old habits..." she raised her palms upwards, "and she's cute."

Peters shook her head, "and old dogs and tricks..."

Donna tutted, "below the belt."

"Maybe..." conceded Peters.

"It's not as if I look my age and I certainly don't feel it," complained Donna, "I'm as fit as most women half my years and I've kept myself young at heart. And I'm very bendy."

"You're beautiful and you're a real catch for anyone... just maybe not your daughter's lover." Peters hesitated and stared hard at Donna, "plural."

Donna looked rueful and then something Peters didn't believe she'd witnessed before, it appeared to be suspiciously like a look of shame. She felt her eyebrows raise.

"I'll accept that. Actually, it's shameful."

Peters nodded slowly, "yes. It's all gone much too far."

They fell silent again for a while.

"Have you..." Donna hesitated, "have you met the other one?"

Peters regarded her, feeling a sudden twinge of sorrow, "Frankie. Her name's Frankie. Yes."

"What's she like?"

"Strong. Intelligent. Serious. And charismatic too."

Donna smiled wryly, "of course she is. What does she do?"

"She works in the city. Financial sector."

"Would I like her?"

"Oh I think so," Peters smiled, "she's one of those people that you instantly trust. She oozes integrity."

"It's almost beyond my comprehension that they ended up in the village."

"I know. Unbelievable circumstances."

"Well. I need to make a plan. How to best handle this. I want to be sure it all comes out the right way. If that's possible. Will you help me?"

Peters was touched that Donna had actually asked her, rather than mete out instructions.

"Of course!"

"It's time to let go. Of all of it."

"It is." Peters nodded her approval.

"But Peters," Donna added a little steel, "this period of weakness will not last. Make the most of it while you have the chance, but don't expect me to stay this way for long."

"It's not weakness. It's strength. And yes, I know the walls might go back up." She emphasised the word might.

Donna smiled, "let's make a plan."

Theresa and Roy sat across from each other and stared into each other's eyes, both of them searching, like they were trying to see beyond the knowledge they had about each other and reach back for something that could ease the pain. Something deeper. Something they had lost so long ago that they didn't know if it had ever really existed.

"I know you know." Theresa broke the silence.

He carried on staring at her evenly, hiding the mixture of anger, fear and shame that flooded through him at her words.

"Nathan told me Taylor had him put cameras in the surgery. I've seen the footage of you in there."

"No-one gets the better of you, do they? Or at least that's what you think."

Roy looked down to break her gaze, "yes, now I know. When we married I was happy to adopt him, he's my son, he'll always be my son. It doesn't matter who his Father is, but..." he shook his head.

"I'm sorry. You know I've always loved you though?"

He looked into her eyes again. He shook his head, "I don't see it there any more."

Now it was her turn to look down.

"Well, I do." She took a deep breath, it had been a secret for so long. Though she was aware of the pain he must be feeling, she couldn't help but feel a sense of relief that he knew the truth. She asked him the question they had both been waiting for.

"So now you know who the Father is?"

He nodded. "I want to hear it from you though."

She paused, "the Master. Adrian."

He looked at her. His heart leapt into his throat, but he kept his calm.

"Do you love him?"

She shifted uncomfortably. It might as well be the whole truth.

"Yes."

He closed his eyes.

"But that doesn't mean I love you any less."

"Does he know?"

"Yes."

"About both of them?"

She blinked several times as she looked at him, feeling her face flush and her heart beat rise. There should have been no record. He stared evenly at her. She licked her lips.

"No. Is that there in the records?"

He nodded, "does the girl know?"

"She knows I'm her birth Mother."

"Why didn't you keep her?"

"I couldn't manage both. And she had some health issues. I put her up for adoption. It broke my heart."

"Are you still in contact with her?"

She regarded him. He was so cold. She felt confused. And that familiar gut-wrenching shame was rushing through her like a burning fire.

"No." She said it gently but firmly.

As he watched her, his mind was racing. Why was she still lying?

"Has there been anyone else?"

"What do you mean?"

"I mean aside from the swinging thing, have you ever had anything else serious going on?"

"No." She was adamant, "absolutely not."

He tilted his head to one side and fell silent.

"Taylor's blackmailing you?" Theresa changed the subject.

"She has been. I've stopped it."

"The blackmailing or the drugs?"

"I'm trying with the drugs. I told her you knew everything. I think she believed it." He looked down at his hands and then continued, "but you don't."

"I don't what?"

"You don't know everything."

"What don't I know?"

He remained silent.

"Roy, what don't I know?" She leaned forward. He stayed silent. She changed tack, "what did you give her?"

"Money. The accounts."

"How much?"

He shrugged, "half a million? Probably that in the last eighteen months."

She stared at him and shook her head, "half a million?"

He stared right back at her, defiant. Or at least as defiant as it was possible for him to be.

"Fuck!" She diverted her eyes and stared beyond him, thinking, calculating, wondering how she had failed to notice it happening right under her nose. "Anything else?"

"The club records. She pretty much has all the club material and how it's all set up."

She huffed in exasperation, words forming on her lips but then dissolving into a long exhale as she recognised the futility of her anger.

"Does she have access to the bank?"

He shook his head, "but that's what she asked for last time."

"And you're sure she hasn't got anything else?"

Roy gnawed at his thumbnail for a minute and then spoke again. Now it was his turn to change tack.

"I can't do this anymore Theresa. I've let myself get caught up in all this... mess!" He said it angrily, "I'm playing stupid games and I don't even know why any more. It's a waste of energy. A waste of life. None of it matters. It used to be so simple. Before it became such 'Big Business.' I don't need it." He closed his eyes as the words poured out and he felt the relief that comes from confession and capitulation.

"And you're not very good at it," she said pointedly.

"I don't want to be very good at it. That's your job and..."

"What aren't you telling me?" she cut through his words.

"You're a liar Theresa. I'll never be able to trust you again."

He watched as her eyes flickered, a frown furrowed in her brow.

"Roy, I'm not lying. I kept information from you, but only for the best."

He leaned forward slowly. "I know the Master is not their

Father."

Shock and confusion flooded her face. Her jaw dropped and her brow furrowed even further, "what?"

"I know he's not their Father." He leaned further across the table and looked angrily into her eyes.

At first, his aggression made her sit back and then, she leaned forward too, until their noses were almost touching.

"He. Is."

Roy shook his head in astonishment, "why are you still lying to me? It's there in black and white!"

"Roy, I don't have any idea why you're saying that. You've seen it, old Dr Taylor had the tests done."

Roy shook his head in disbelief and stood up. He walked over to his study desk and opened the drawer, taking out a handful of photos. He flicked through until he found the right one. Theresa watched him. He came back over and threw the photo on the table in front of her. She looked down and as she read the name on the photo of the medical records, her eyes widened and she put her hand over her mouth. She swallowed hard.

"Oh my god... Oh. My. God!"

He watched her. Puzzled.

"You really didn't know did you?"

She looked up at him, her face full of horror.

"That can't be..." her mind traced back... but actually, maybe it could be. She squeezed her eyes tight closed and trawled through the specific period of time—and her eyes flew open, wide and round as she found that it was just about possible. But then why would old Dr Taylor have told her it was the Master? Unless... she put her face in her hands. She felt Roy's hand on her shoulder.

"I don't understand," she said thinly, tears in her voice. She shook her head trying to work it out.

"Maybe the records are false?"

"Looked like originals to me."

"The tests were done by her Father. He wrote to me, I had it in writing. Why would he have lied?"

"I can't answer any of these questions for you Theresa. I wasn't

220

involved."

She shook her head again.

"Maybe you should speak to Taylor," he said quietly, "and maybe you should tell me the truth now."

Chapter 27

Lisa stood across the road and watched as Rachel paced the living room, momentarily undecided about what to do. As she watched her, she felt as if her chest might burst, it felt like her heart was literally breaking. Letting go of this was going to be about the hardest thing she could possibly imagine doing. She bit down on her lip. The turmoil was unbearable. On the one hand, the searing guilt of knowing what she had done was deliberate—and remorse for the pain she was causing both Rachel and Frankie. And then there was the love. The almost physically sickening yearning she felt for Rachel that dominated her every waking moment. She started crying, standing in the shadows with huge sobs wracking her body. Crying like she could never remember having cried before. She wiped her face with her sleeve and then jumped at a quiet tapping noise behind her. It was Ben. He pointed to the front door. She nodded and crept along the front of the house, keeping an eye out that Rachel hadn't spotted her as she did so. He was already there with the door ajar as she reached the doorstep. She slid in and headed into the kitchen.

"Well, you look bloody awful."

She wiped her sleeve across her nose and nodded miserably as he grabbed a tissue box from the table and handed it to her.

"Thanks," she mumbled through streaming tears. He stepped forward and folded her in his arms.

"Sorry mate." She let herself relax into his comforting embrace.

"Don't make a mess of my new jumper with your snot." She managed a small smile, his voice was gentle and kind. She stood back and breathed deeply, trying to stop herself, but her face just creased again and she let out another wracking sob.

"Go and sit by the fire." He indicated the door to the lounge. "I'll get you a brandy."

She turned and headed down the little stone steps that led into the snug and perched herself on a chair right by the stove, the door of which was open to a roaring log fire. Ben came in a couple of minutes later carrying two brandy bowls. He handed her one and sat opposite her. The two of them stared at the flames together, the only sound the crackling of the logs and Lisa's now gentler crying. The silence was easy, Ben knew how to be peaceful. As the clock ticked in the corner and time passed, Lisa calmed and sat mesmerized by the flames. Finally, she spoke.

"I've made a mess of things Ben. And I've broken my heart. And maybe someone else's."

He nodded, but said nothing, leaving space for her.

"I need to talk. If I tell you will you promise to keep it between us?"

"Of course mate. There aren't many around here you can trust, but I don't have any agenda and you know I have no connection to the club. You can say what you want. I won't breathe a word."

"It's about your neighbour, Rachel."

He nodded and she began. Telling him everything that had happened over the previous weeks. He didn't speak as she let everything out, all the words, the emotions that came with them, the tears. He nodded encouragement, hugged her a couple of times to give her courage and refilled their brandy glasses as she let it pour.

"I fell in love with her Ben. And I know it wasn't right and I know I have to let her go, but it hurts so bad. And I want to make it right for her Ben, Because whatever else, I love her too much to hurt her this way. But I don't know how best to help her."

He let the silence fill the air for a few minutes.

"Well, you know, love isn't easy. But how we deal with love and loss is a measure of who we are." He leaned forward, "firstly, for you. Even though you now have this pain—and I can't pretend it won't last a while or that it won't get worse before it gets better. But at least you now know that you can love. That you've had love and all that it means—and that means you can have it again."

She bit her lip, "I can't get her back can I?" She asked weakly.

"No mate. You're going to hang on to that hope and wrestle with it for a while, but the final answer is no. You have to learn how to let it go. But the good news is, you've been brave to know that you have to let her sort it out with Frankie. You got courage."

She nodded, even as her mind battled with acceptance on the finality of that statement.

"Secondly, you can't decide for her how she deals with this with Frankie. But you can give her as much information and support as possible to make it easier. So let's make an assessment and see what comes out. So who else knows about you two?"

"Well, Mother knows all of it pretty much. That I am in love with her." She thought further, "anything else will be what's on camera. I mean the club board know I'm supposed to recruit her, but they don't necessarily know the details and they don't know about my feelings. I've been pretty careful about the cameras, I think."

"That it?"

She thought through it again.

"And Peters. Peters knows all of it. But I can trust her. She's on my side."

"Hm. So. I don't want to make this harder, but sometimes you have to face reality," he nodded at her reassuringly, "ok?"

She swallowed hard and nodded.

"They're solid, those two." He pointed his finger back across the road.

She bit her lip so hard she drew blood, "sorry," she dabbed at it with a tissue.

He so felt for her at that moment, but he wanted to be honest and lay it straight out on the line. Though he knew he couldn't extinguish her need to hang on to hope for a while, he wanted to do his best to give her the tools to deal with the denial she would obviously stand behind. The best way he could think of to do that was to be brutally honest.

"I'm sorry. But it's good in its way. They'll survive this. They have that kind of connection. They can get through anything."

Tears flowed again. He leant over and hugged her. He stared back at the fire. Contemplative. Thinking about his own unbreakable relationship. "You want to make it as easy as possible for them though, right?"

She nodded.

"That's good, that's honourable. So. Here's what I think. And this is just an opinion, you have to make your own mind up in the end, ok?"

She nodded again.

"And you know I say that because whatever advice I give you, you can't use it to blame me if it doesn't turn out right? It's your choice to decide whether what I say has value, ok?"

"Yes. I get it. Thank you. I really appreciate this Ben."

"At the end of the day, you have to trust what it tells you in here," he placed his hand on his heart, "I can only give you an outsiders view." He looked at her, waiting for to acknowledge what he'd said and then gave her the bottom line, "so I don't think you should see her. At least not on her own."

Lisa's face fell.

"I think you need to speak to the people who might reveal any of this and ask them not to. That's better for you and for her. Then write her a letter. Explain to her that you will protect any outside knowledge of what has happened as far as you can and that you will happily personally explain why all of this was not Rachel's fault and not of her own free will, to Frankie, if that's what she would like you to do."

Lisa breathed in deeply and let the air exhale slowly through pursed lips.

"I know that's hard. It's also brave. And right. In my opinion."

Tears rolled silently down her cheeks again. His heart melted as he watched her.

"Lisa, you will know love again. I promise."

She couldn't speak. She knew he was probably right, but for now, it was hard to believe because her heart felt like it had broken into a thousand pieces.

"We can do it now. We can write the letter now, ok?"

"Ok."

"Also, you've got a packed bag there. Where are you headed?"

She shook her head, "I don't know."

"Stay here tonight. We can talk some more. Tomorrow morning you can decide what you want to do. Your head will be a little clearer by then."

"Thanks Ben."

"You're a pain in the ass. I've got to go and make a bed up. Fuck knows where the clean sheets are."

She managed a laugh through the pouring tears and he winked

at her.

"Right, I'm going to get a pen and paper. We can't have more brandy until we've written it. So we better make it bloody quick."

Frankie stood at the end of the gravel drive and stared ahead of her at the winding road, lined by magnificent trees that had stood their ground for so many years. She thought about their roots and how solid they were and the fact they had steadfastly been growing and spreading for centuries, firm and strong. How different to her own sense of uprootedness right now. She started walking, filled suddenly with a sense of strength and determination as if the trees had wound their roots around her and pulled her into a new direction. She stopped momentarily as the manor house came into view. It was magnificent— and despite its period grandeur, strangely welcoming, oddly familiar. Perhaps it was the warmth of the Cotswold stone that made it seem so homely. As she approached the arched entrance, the door opened, pre-empting her arrival. Donna stepped forward.

"Frankie."

It was a quiet, calm and familar greeting and, for a moment, Frankie had a sense of disquiet that she couldn't quite fathom.

"I'm Donna."

Frankie extended her hand and felt a tingle as Donna took it in hers, not to shake, but to hold and fleetingly caress. Frankie blushed.

"Hey!" She heard her voice sound weak and cleared her throat to add power, "good to meet you."

"Please do come in." Donna let her hand fall and waived her through the door, "we'll have tea on the garden room." She ushered Frankie to the back of the hallway and out into the incredibly light and airy glass conservatory.

Frankie turned to face Donna and the two stared silently at each other for a few moments. Weighing each other up.

"Did my Mum explain?" Frankie was the first to break the silence. She decided to get straight to the point, "she said you had something you needed to tell me? Something personal?"

"Well, actually we have a lot to talk about." Donna indicated that Frankie should take a seat on the sofa, "please sit down Frankie."

Frankie perched herself on the corner and raised her palms. "Well, I'm ready." She felt irritated and impatient. She liked to be in control and she didn't feel like she was.

Donna rang the tea bell, "let's get comfortable first," she said as Peters entered the room, "what would you like to drink?"

"Hey! How are you?" Frankie acknowledged Peters from their meeting in the pub. She felt disconcerted about having her serve tea to her.

"I'm very well Frankie, thank you for asking. What can I get you?"

"How about a pint? No, I'm kidding. Tea. Would be great. Thank you." Frankie addressed Peters directly.

Donna watched the two of them interact curiously, "I'll have tea also Peters. No crumpet today."

"No crumpet ever again. Angel cake only from now on."

Donna smiled and waved her hand at Peters and turned back to Frankie.

"So. Firstly tell me what you know from Theresa." She looked squarely into Frankie's eyes.

Frankie frowned, "well presumably you know what I know from Theresa? Is it entirely necessary for me to repeat it?"

"Let's just say that there's a lot going on in this village. Under the surface. Sometimes village... politics..." Donna chose her words carefully, "get in the way of truth. It would be far easier for both of us if you tell me what you know already—and also what Irene... your Mum has told you. Then I can... fill in the gaps. Or at least some of them." She regarded Frankie thoughtfully, "I know this must have come as a great shock to you. And that you must be in turmoil, but I want to help. Please trust me."

Frankie crossed her arms and leaned back. She closed her eyes for a moment as if taking a look inside would help her to make a decision. She nodded and opened her eyes again, "ok, I'll tell you what I know."

Rachel read the letter through again. How many times now?

She'd lost count. The last twenty four hours had been unbearable as her mind told her a thousand stories about what Frankie might know and how many people in the village could be aware of what had gone on between her and Lisa. She'd locked herself away, kept the house in the dark eaten nothing and roamed from room to room contemplating her fate. The 'What If' engine had been running on turbo charge and the number of permutations she had managed to generate had thrown her into a frenzy of anxiety, guilt and shame. She looked at her watch. Less than three hours before Frankie would be there. She hadn't slept a wink in the last two days. She looked at herself in the mirror and ran her hand through her hair, she looked as disheveled as she felt. She had already run through what she was going to say to Frankie a thousand times, not once had she come up with something that felt like anything other than a losing explanation. It just didn't feel like she could ever justify what had happened, despite Lisa's assurances that none of it had been her fault, that it had all been subconscious impulses from the gin. "Oh My God," she groaned out loud at that thought again, how ridiculous did that sound? "For fuck's sake!" She threw the letter down on the table. The bottom line was it sounded like she got drunk and had an affair. What if she told Frankie and never got the chance to prove that it was based on this effing gin thing because Frankie just walks out or refuses to give her the chance to prove it? She stared out of the window blankly into the dark street. The light went on opposite and she saw Ben. He peered out of the window into the darkness and must have seen her shadow. He grinned and flicked the V's. She managed a thin smile to herself and flicked the V's back, in a half-hearted way. He pointed at himself and then over to her. She hesitated. Then she put the light on. She nodded. He held up a bottle of whisky and pointed at it. She nodded again and as he turned to head out, she quickly turned the light off and went to the front door to open it for him.

"Ay up gal!" He marched through with his whisky and two tumblers, "what are you doing hiding in the dark? Or shouldn't I ask?"

She burst into tears.

He put the bottle and glasses down and put his arms round her. She was shaking. He rubbed her back comfortingly and drew away, "let's have a drink."

"Sorry," she mumbled still tearful.

"It's alright. I'm used to you being a miserable cow." He poured and then held out her glass.

She sipped at the whisky, feeling the familiar burn as it slipped down. He waited, sipping at his own drink.

"Ben, I've been an idiot," she said miserably, putting her hand to her forehead.

"Tell me something I don't know!"

She managed a small laugh, "you're a bastard," she said teasingly.

"That's a filthy rumour."

She laughed again and then fell back to her serious place. "I cheated on Frankie." She burst into tears again.

"No you didn't," he said gently.

She looked at him questioningly.

"You mean Lisa right?" He asked.

Her heart leapt into her throat as her brain screamed at her that the whole village knew. She felt her mouth gape open.

"It's ok..." he said hurriedly, putting his hand on her arm, "Lisa told me. It's not widely known. I only know because she came to me for help on how to deal with it. I promise you, only a few people know about it. Like it says in the letter."

She shook her head bewildered again.

"I helped her write it. I wanted to help you too."

Rachel relaxed a little. If there was anyone is this godforsaken village she knew she could trust, it was Ben.

"Oh Ben, what have I done?" She looked at him imploringly.

"You got caught up in village affairs. It's not your fault. Look, you know I don't..."

"Yes, get involved..." she jumped in with a heavy sense of irony in her voice, "and now I know why."

He nodded, "right. It must feel like total madness. It's very difficult to comprehend. You must feel unbelievably confused. But. You're a good sort. Just so you know, even though I don't get involved, I do know a lot about what goes on here," he tapped his nose, "and just in case you need it, I can be here for you as a therapist. I'm very good at that. Particularly with fruit cakes like you."

She couldn't help but smile, "how do you do that?"

"What. Make all women fall in love with me?"

She slapped him gently on the arm, "make me smile when I feel as miserable as sin."

"What can I say? I'm a charmer. So brass tacks. How much is Frankie aware of?"

Rachel shook her head, suddenly despondent again. "I don't know. I saw her with Theresa before she left for London the last time."

Ben raised an eyebrow. She waited. But he said nothing, so she continued, "she was really upset. She doesn't know I saw her. But I know Theresa knows about me and Lisa, so I assumed..." She started to cry again.

Ben took her hand. "Don't assume *anything*," he said deliberately and clearly, looking her in the eyes, "you have no idea what that conversation was about—and frankly, Theresa's agendas are so complex and manipulative, you really can't make any assumptions at all."

Rachel felt a flicker of hope, but it didn't last long.

"Now that doesn't mean you're wrong," he warned, "but it could be any number of things." He rubbed his stubbly chin contemplatively, "when are you seeing her?"

Rachel looked at her watch, "in a couple of hours or so."

They were both quiet for a few minutes.

"You two are strong. I reckon you can get through anything." He smiled at her, "you can just tell when two people are made for each other and you two definitely are." He watched her as tears streamed down her face, "I reckon when she gets back, you've got to just listen. Ok?"

She nodded.

"However long it takes her to open up, just wait and listen."

She felt stronger already.

"You're nodding now, but sometimes that's harder than you think. Because you want to get it out there and try to make it better as quickly as you can. But you have to wait. Let her tell you what's going on with her and then you can make a better judgment about how to deal with it. Be patient. And don't be too reactive. Take time to think through whatever she has to say and measure your response. Ok?"

She breathed out heavily, already feeling calmer, "thanks, Ben. I don't know what I would have done without you."

"I know. Nobody does." He had that glint in his eye.

"No wonder everybody loves you."

"What?" he said, winking.

She managed a brighter smile, "nothing."

"Now, I've got to go. There's a pint with my name on it at The Mucky Duck." He downed the last of his whisky. "And you need to clean yourself up. You look a wreck."

She laughed, "bastard."

"Again! I told you, that's a filthy lie."

She stepped forward and gave him a hug.

He shook his head, "can't keep your hands off me can you?" He patted her on the arm, "down girl. There's a queue."

"Oh, I know." Rachel winked back at him.

He squinted at her, "you're going to have to give me names. Right, I'm off. Remember what I said."

She opened the door for him, "I will Ben. I will"

"Seven o'clock, I'll be there." Theresa tapped the phone to her lip and thought through the possible implications of the invitation to the manor. Donna deciding to throw an impromptu cocktail party was out of character. And it had come across less as an invite and more as a demand that she should attend. She sat back on the sofa, flicking her flowing black hair extensions back over her shoulder and stretching out her stockinged legs. She sipped at her gin and tonic and absently bit on her finger nail as she thought through Roy's revelations about Taylor's records. The shock had been huge, but a couple of hours of reflection had made her doubt the veracity of the information he had imparted. In theory, it was just about possible, but so highly unlikely. So that being the case, who was lying? Roy or Taylor? She shook her head. She hadn't reckoned for this complication. The level of Machiavellian behavior was becoming unmanageable. There were too many people getting power crazy now. She needed to deal with it. And soon. She was deep in thought when the doorbell rang, she looked at her watch, it was just about time for the party to start. She picked up her witches hat and placed it carefully on top of her voluminous wig, checking in the mirror above the fireplace to make sure it was on straight and that her leather bodice revealed just the right amount of cleavage. Satisfied, she headed for the door and opened it. She looked at The Floosy and Doug as they stood in the doorway. She let out a sigh.

"Alright. Why have you both got soft toys strapped to your heads?" she asked exasperatedly.

The two of them looked at each other and then back at Theresa.

"They're pigs," said The Floosy, "are you going to let us in?"

Theresa stood aside and ushered them through.

"Alright. Why have you both got toy pigs strapped to your heads?" she asked after them as she followed them through the hallway and into the lounge. As they entered the room, The Floosy looked at Doug and then back at Theresa.

"Because. It. Is. A. Hats. And. PIGS. Party!" She couldn't contain her agitation, "and being CLEVER, we came up with something that does both!" She grinned at Doug triumphantly. He nodded supportively at her and then glared at Theresa, thinking back to how she'd embarrassed him over Clit Eastwood. It felt good to get one up on her.

Theresa looked at them and smiled meanly.

"Hats. And. WIGS."

The Floosy flushed. She turned to Doug and whacked him on the arm, "you said hats and pigs, you idiot!"

He huffed, "well that's what *she* made it sound like." He jabbed his finger at Theresa then tore at the makeshift strapping he had under his chin, "I've 'ad enough!"

"Well, you made a pig's ear of that didn't you, Doug?" Theresa laughed and rubbed salt in.

"You did it deliberately!" He was shouting now, "why do you want to make me look stupid all the time?"

"Oh, as if I would be interested enough in you to even bother to do that." Theresa laughed again, more meanly, "and anyway, I really don't need to. You do it well enough all on your own."

"Right. That's enough!" The Floosy found her voice, "don't you dare talk to my husband like that!"

Doug looked at his wife in shock, a smile spreading across his face as she took up his cause.

"He deserves more respect and I'm certainly not going to stand here and let you treat either him or me in this way." She grabbed at the pig on her head and tried to release it, "I think we can safely say that we have had enough of you and the club." The Floosy looked at Doug for support. He hesitated, clearly a little conflicted, but nodded his support, "so we're leaving it."

Doug looked momentarily crestfallen, until he saw Theresa regarding him with disdain, smiling at the knowledge that his predilections would make that a huge sacrifice. The bristling sense of power she exuded served to steel his resolve and he stood a little taller in his specially built up cowboy boots.

"Yes," he took a step towards Theresa and looked up at her, "we're done!" He took his keys from his pocket and carefully started removing the club key fob from them.

"Oh for fuck's sake, grow up!" Theresa looked down at his fumbling fingers, "you know you'll be lost without the club." She tried to grab at his keys to stop him removing the emblem, but he slapped at her hand and carried on. He held the fob up before her eyes triumphantly and then threw it at her.

"Nope," he said, defiantly, "that's it. We're off. Aren't we my darling?" He took his wife's hand and looked into her eyes.

She looked at him, astonished, she couldn't remember him ever having called her darling, "yes my little ewok," she said back. He frowned. She grimaced and mouthed, "I'm sorry."

Doug lifted himself to his full height and pressed the soft toy pig into Theresa's hands, "I am grown up," he said assertively, "and that's why I'm taking my life—and my wife—back into my own hands." He nodded back at his Floosy, his eyes soft and filled with love. "Arrivederty Theresa," he said as she looked at them both and shook her head, "come on me duck." Doug reached his arm around his wife and drew her close, "let's have our own party."

Mesmerised, The Floosy bent down and leant her head on her husband's shoulder as she let him guide her manfully back towards the door, walking past the Master as he stood in his blonde wig and tiara on the doorstep, without saying a word.

The key turned in the lock and Rachel took a deep breath in. Her heart was literally in her throat. She thought she might choke. She stood up from the sofa as Frankie came through the door, dragging her small suitcase in behind her. For the first time ever in their relationship, Rachel did not know how to react—whether to go over and kiss and hug her as normal, or to stand back and give her space.

"Hey!" Frankie said coolly from the door. Rachel went towards her. They shared an awkward hug. Rachel put her hands in the back pockets of her jeans.

"Hey. I'm glad you're home."

Frankie gave a thin smile. "I'm just going to take this upstairs," she indicated the case, "maybe you could get us a couple of glasses of wine?"

"Sure." Rachel heard her own voice shaking.

"Let's sit by the fire. I'll just be a couple of minutes."

As she headed off upstairs, Rachel went into the kitchen. She grabbed a bottle of Rioja, Frankie's favourite, a couple of glasses and some olives from the fridge, the whole time breathing deeply and telling herself to stay calm. She went back into the living room and placed everything on the table, closed the curtains and sat on the sofa to wait. She couldn't ever remember having felt this anxious. She sat back and draped her arm on the sofa, feigning relaxation. She tutted at herself, this was anything but relaxed. She sat forward and lent her elbows on her knees. She could feel her heat rising as she heard Frankie coming down the stairs. She looked up at her as she brushed passed to the other side of the sofa, her face seemed expressionless. Frankie sat and poured the wine into the two glasses. She picked them up and handed one to Rachel. They both took a sip in silence. Frankie put her glass back down on the table and turned her attention to Rachel. She took her hand and held it in hers and looked into her eyes. Rachel couldn't help the frown that filled her brow, the tightness in her chest or the depth of her breathing. Frankie looked down at Rachel's hand as she rubbed it gently.

"Before I left the village last time I found out something." Rachel could hear that she was struggling to hold back tears. She felt like she was about to die. She remembered Ben's words and fought with herself to swallow the apology that was trying to leap out of her mouth. Which she managed to do, but she couldn't stop the tears escaping. Frankie continued.

"This is really difficult for me, it's been shocking." Rachel held her breath and readied herself for the next sentence, "I got a call from Theresa at the Post Office, she wanted to talk to me." Frankie shook her head, "I should have picked up the signals earlier." Rachel breathed out heavily, "or at least clocked the name."

Rachel bit her lip waited for her to say Lisa's name. She waited. Nothing, she turned to look at Frankie. Frankie looked back at her.

"Jones."

Rachel frowned, "Jones?"

"I know. It's a common name, it's not like you'd normally think about it twice, is it?"

Rachel looked at her, deeply puzzled, "your surname?" She started to add two and two, "... and Theresa's surname?"

Frankie nodded, "she's my birth Mother."

Rachel drew in a sharp breath. "Oh My God!" She held Frankie's hand tighter. She didn't know what the stronger feeling was, the rush of relief or the shock and sympathy for Frankie. "Oh My God... is it true?"

Frankie nodded.

"Are you sure?"

"Yes. I went to see Mum last night. She confirmed it." Frankie shook her head.

"Oh Frankie. I don't know what to say. What a shock. My poor baby." Rachel lifted her hand and kissed it.

"I don't quite know how to feel right now. I mean it doesn't affect the fact that... my Mum's my Mum. I'm just... it's weird to know that someone else is my real Mum. Well not my real Mum, my blood Mother. Oh, I don't know, I don't even know how to describe it." Frankie huffed.

"Oh My God Frankie, I've already got a hundred questions lined up, you must be exploding with them."

"Well, I have been. I've worked through some of them and Mum helped me out. And Donna at the Manor."

"Donna?" Rachel was bemused.

"Yeah. It's a long story. Mum was a chef at the manor in her early twenties. When Donna and Eddie first lived there. Mum told me to talk to her about my birth. Donna knows the whole story."

"The whole story?"

"Yeah. It's complicated."

"Yeah. It is." Rachel saw a tangled web in her head, threads running between Theresa, Donna, Lisa, Frankie... it looked like a mess. She told herself to calm down. Again.

"There's so much. It's hard to take it all in. Where do I start?" She shook her head, "I've got a brother. A twin."

Rachel's mouth hung open.

"His name's Gary. Gazz."

Rachel raised her eyebrows. Speechless.

"We were separated at birth. Theresa couldn't manage both of us. She chose to have me adopted. Donna persuaded Mum to take me on. She knew Mum couldn't have children naturally but that she'd wanted to. Donna paid for Mum to move to North London. She's financed my whole life."

"Donna?"

"Yes. Donna."

In her head, Rachel was thinking, so Lisa's Mother financed my girlfriend's life. It was too bizarre. She tried to shake the thought out and concentrate on what Frankie was saying.

"Mum's really distraught. Theresa swore her to keep it from me—she can't work out why Theresa decided to tell me."

"And Theresa? Did she say why?"

"She said she had to."

Rachel frowned "Why?"

"To protect me."

"Protect you from what?"

Frankie shrugged her shoulders and held her hands up, indicating that she did not know the answer.

"Did she tell you about Donna?"

"No. Mum did."

"I don't get it. It's too weird."

"I know. Tell me about it."

They sat in silence.

"What about your Father?"

"Well you know Mum's story was that he had left when I was a baby. That she didn't know where he was?"

Rachel nodded.

"Well, that's the next thing. It's not true. She does know who my Father is."

Rachel waited for Frankie to continue, but she didn't.

"Who? Who is it Frankie?" she asked gently.

"I can't tell you." Frankie sighed, "I want to and I will, but you have to trust me that I'll tell you when I can when it's right... for everyone. Ok?"

Rachel pulled Frankie into her arms, "ok."

"I'm sorry babe," Frankie said it quietly, "and I'm sorry I had to get away. I know it's not been fair on you, but I couldn't get my head round it all. And I needed to speak to Mum."

In the course of the discussion, Rachel had all but forgotten her own guilt, but Frankie's apology brought it flooding back. She squeezed her eyes tight shut and held Frankie close.

"It's ok. Please don't apologise. Please. Please. It will be ok."

"I know. There's more that needs to be talked through with Donna. She's invited us to a cocktail party tomorrow night."

Rachel froze for a moment.

"Is that ok?" Frankie looked up at her.

"Yeah. Yeah of course it is, babe. As long as it's ok with you? Can you handle that right now?" She hoped Frankie might reconsider.

"Yeah, it's ok, I'd rather get it all out in the open and get to know the people who have been in the background of my life for so long." Frankie managed her first real smile of the night, "I'm glad you know now. I didn't like keeping you completely in the dark." Frankie kissed her lightly on the lips, "I want to know what you've been up to. What else is going on in this weird place."

Rachel smiled at her, thinking through the conversation she'd had with Lisa and the whole club thing. She decided to wait.

"You know what? It can wait. I'm going to light some candles."

"How many?"

"Four!" she replied grinning.

"Four candles?"

"Yep, four candles."

They laughed together at their ritual based on an old joke.

"I love you." Frankie kissed Rachel's hand and held it to her heart.

"I know babe, I love you too." Rachel sighed, "and I'm going to light the fire and we're just going to sit here and relax and watch the flames. Maybe watch a movie? And see what unfolds?" She kissed Frankie on the top of the head, "sound good?"

"Mmmm sounds great to me babe." They sat silently for a moment, "I might fall asleep though…"

Rachel smiled, "that's ok with me. It's all ok with me."

Frankie nestled into her neck. Rachel sighed and pushed Lisa to the back of her mind, stroking Frankie's hair gently and just wishing everything back to normal.

Doctor Taylor rocked back in her chair, ran the lid of the pen along her bottom lip and stared dreamily into space.

"The Taylor Foundation." She liked the ring of it. But it wasn't personal enough to her, "The V E Taylor Foundation." She scowled, why had her father had to be a Black Beauty fan? She humphed. "The Velvet Elizabeth Foundation. No." She stood up and pushed out her breasts, making herself feel more important. She flicked her hair back over her shoulders and turned to regard herself in the full-length mirror, twisting sideways and placing her hands on her hips to appreciate the way her body curved so deliciously in her tight leather trousers and sculptured silk shirt. She tilted her head back to let her hair drape down her back. She looked herself in the eye, a soft pout on her lips. She drew a deep breath in. "The V Taylor Medical Foundation." She sighed and thought of all those scrumptious, adoring young interns following her around like little puppy dogs, hanging on to her every word, walking behind her in the shadow of her power, desperate for a crumb of her attention. Oh, how she ached to get away from this little village, a practice that was so beneath her. She thought how her father had been an inspiration and a curse. Encouraging her to become a Doctor had been the best thing the world could have hoped for—and her first class degree and a PHD had been proof of his perceptiveness, but then to saddle her with this practice... she sighed. It was worth a fortune, but the terms of ownership prevented her from selling it for another ten years. It was stifling. She couldn't wait that long. There were so few people who deserved to breathe in her rarified air and none of them here. She thought again about her meeting the following day and how she planned to make a final gambit. To finally set herself free to be what the world deserved her to be. To get her hands on what she truly was meant to have. The wealth she had been born to but had been denied her for so long. She smiled and ran her finger lovingly into the centre of her cleavage, lowering her eyes and regarding herself more intensely. "You will be the mistress of your own glorious destiny." She closed her eyes and breathed in deeply, feeling the rush of exquisite pleasure she always felt when she touched her own sensually divine inner being, "ohhhh Professor Taylor, how I love you."

Rachel watched the shafts of light as they crept round the blinds and stretched themselves across the room, relieved in a way that the darkness was being broken, but feeling bone weary and still longing for the respite that sleep would give her from the exhausting and interminable mental torture of guilt and shame. She felt Frankie stirring in her arms and gently kissed the top of her head. Even though her mind was occupied with the dilemma of confession, at this moment, she was also overflowing with love for her. She had never been more sure of the fact that Frankie was her soulmate, her true love, the being with whom she shared the most wondrous connection—and that whatever happened, even if they parted physically, that the connection would be eternal and unbreakable in spirit. She felt Frankie stir again and her lips brush her breast gently.

"Mmmm... you awake babe?" Frankie said sleepily, nuzzling against her.

"Uh huh."

Frankie raised her head slightly, squinting with one eye and opening the other just enough to see Rachel. She laughed.

"Close your eyes darling. It's early."

Frankie let her eyelid drop and laid her head on Rachel's chest, reaching across with her arm and resting her hand lightly on her shoulder, "I haven't slept that long for... forever." She had fallen asleep almost as soon as Rachel had lit the candles the evening before, waking only for Rachel to lead her gently and slowly upstairs to their bed, where she had laid her down and removed her clothes tenderly.

"Hmmmm... feels so good."

Rachel stroked her hair, "go back to sleep sweetheart."

"Mmmm... you hungry?"

Rachel smiled, "always..."

"Mmmmm me too." Frankie's head moved across her and she felt her draw her nipple into her mouth, sucking gently. She groaned... but she couldn't. She stroked Frankie's hair.

"I need to talk to you, Frankie."

"Mmmm in a while..." Frankie sucked a little harder.

Rachel cupped her chin with her hand and lifted her head to look into her eyes, "no, I need to talk to you, sweetheart."

Frankie pouted and brushed Rachel's cheek with her fingers, "ok babe." She laid her head back onto Rachel's chest, "you need to get something off here?" She tapped Rachel's chest lightly, "but not me ok?" she quipped quietly.

"Yeah. Yeah, I need to tell you something."

"Ok, I'm listening."

Rachel swallowed and closed her eyes, steeling herself and telling herself to be brave. She barely knew where to start.

"This is a really weird village," she said finally, sighing. She felt Frankie nod, "you know all the strange... *things* that seemed to be happening, that made me feel like there was something going on?"

"Yeah."

"Well, I found out a whole shed load of stuff in the last week that made sense of all that." She let out an ironic laugh, "well, sense is probably the wrong word." She looked down and brushed Frankie's hair off her forehead so that she could kiss it. Then she held her really tight. "So I'm going to tell you the whole story ok?" She felt Frankie nod again, "but promise me you will let me finish?"

240

Frankie shrugged. "Sure, babe. I'm listening."

"Ok. Well, so the first thing is, that I found out about the club..."

Donna, Peters and Eddie sat round the table. Eddie's glasses were perched on his nose, he read through the contract in front of him, flipping the pages over. Donna regarded him with what she felt was a surprisingly objective and distant stand point. She hardly recognised him now from the dynamic, charismatic man she had fallen in love with. It seemed to her that it wasn't just the reckless enthusiasm of youth he'd lost, it was as if he had buried his core being, disguising his true self for the sake of respectability—and what else? She stared at him, fascinated by the change, intrigued by the transformation. Perhaps the shame and guilt of his former life and the need to bury the past had made him decide to reinvent himself—but in doing so, he had lost the essence of who he was. As he finished reading he took the glasses off and looked straight into Donna's eyes and for a flicker of a moment she thought she saw her Eddie, but he disappeared in an instant—perhaps in the instant that Eddie felt her penetrating his disguise. He cleared his throat and looked away.

"It seems reasonable enough. If you're sure this is what you want?" He lifted the stack of paper and tapped it into an even pile before placing it back down and then looking back at her. This time implacable.

"I'm sure," she said, switching off her own engagement with him and becoming strictly matter of fact.

"And are you sure there will be no repercussions?"

Donna glanced at Peters and then back again to Eddie, "as sure as I can be. I think we've covered every eventuality. Everyone has an interest in the future and those who have posed a threat in the past have been pretty much rendered powerless."

He nodded, "well. There's little else to be said then." He perched his glasses back on his nose and flipped to the last page of the document. He signed and dated it. He placed the lid carefully back on his ink pen and laid it on the table. He nodded at Donna, "it's done." He picked up his glass of red wine and raised it to each of them, "to your futures." He drank and then stood, "did you organise the items I requested?" He tugged down the edges of his waistcoat and brushed at a speck on his cuff.

"Yes. It's all been packed for you. Arthur is loading it into your car."

Eddie looked at his watch. "I should be going."

Donna shook her head, "so that's it? You really don't care about any of it do you?" she asked, evenly.

"Donna, I don't know what else you want from me, but I've just agreed to everything you've proposed. It will cost me millions, but I accept that this is what you want and so it is a price I am prepared to pay."

"And your children? Don't you have any interest in seeing them?"

He sat down again and sighed, "it was all a long time ago. And frankly, no, I don't really know them. And I don't see the point in creating any kind of... emotional bond when I'm unable to maintain any level of contact. And my wife isn't going to start embracing them on any level. It would just cause unnecessary pain."

"You speak as if it wasn't part of your life at all, you have beautiful children."

Eddie stared off into the distance, quiet for a few moments in contemplation. "I was a different person. I'm not proud of it... it took me years to deal with my... issues. I know I have beautiful children. But it's done. I can't go back there and I don't want to be reminded. It's not who I am now."

"And what about the children you left... what about your Angel?"

"Stop!" he was firm. He stood and smoothed his tie. "I don't want to know any more about it. I've read it." He pointed down at the document, "this gives me as much as I need to be aware of, for which I thank you. And this takes care of everything," he tapped the contract, "...of everyone."

Donna stood and walked round to face him, to look into his eyes. "It hasn't touched you at all has it?" He stared at her implacably. She searched his eyes for that flicker she had seen earlier, but it wasn't there, he had closed it all out completely. She tried one last time to appeal to him. "So the money, the possessions, that takes care of everyone, does it, Eddie?"

He looked at her for another moment, then his eyes glazed and he looked through her. "Yes."

"Well you might have changed your ways, become respectable, left your cult and your divine madness behind, but what you have become is not better. In fact, it's worse, you've lost your heart."

He looked down at her, "yes, perhaps."

He stepped to one side and picked up his pen, then he nodded to Peters and turned and walked from the room.

Tears streamed down Rachel's face, "I don't know what got into me, I honestly, honestly was so confused, it was like I didn't know what I was doing..." she gripped Frankie, as she felt her tears flowing too, as she lay there with her head on her chest. "I'm so sorry, I'm just so sorry. I love you so much, so so much..." she let out a sob, "I don't want to lose you. Please don't let me lose you..."

She felt Frankie stir and was almost too frightened to look in her eyes. But Frankie placed her index finger on her lips and looked at her softly, "shhhhh..."

"I'm so..." Rachel tried to continue, but Frankie placed her finger on her lips again, "shhhh... it's ok. It's ok Rachel, I know. Ok? I know."

Rachel was confused. "You know?" her brow furrowed, "you know about Lisa? How do you know?"

"I know because Theresa told me."

"What? But... why didn't you say anything?"

"I had to go away and deal with it all. If I'd have responded there and then... well... I don't know what would have happened..." Frankie sighed, "and I can't pretend it's easy. But I do know it's not your fault. Theresa promised me she would keep you two apart while I went back to London to figure things out. She agreed to deal with it through Donna and I trusted her to do that. You haven't been together since I left right?"

"No. No. Absolutely not!" Rachel struggled with a momentary anger that Frankie had known but still allowed her to suffer in her guilt. But then that was ridiculous, that she should transfer any sense of resentment to Frankie was absurd.

Frankie nodded, "and the other thing is, I needed to hear it from you. I needed to know if you would be honest with me." Frankie looked deep into Rachel's eyes. Rachel bit her lip.

"... and if I hadn't told you?"

Frankie paused, "I think if you hadn't told me, I might... well, it's always hard to know until you're faced with the reality, but well..." her voice trailed off for a moment, "I don't know, maybe we shouldn't contemplate that now. The thing is, I have to accept that I had my own part to play in this. I shouldn't have left you here. I shouldn't have carried on working. Just for the sake of money. You're my family and I love you. That's all that really matters. What's another bonus compared to the possibility of losing you?"

Rachel swallowed hard and held Frankie's hand tightly, then brought it to her lips and kissed it. She felt humbled by Frankie's admission of responsibility, her generosity, it almost made it worse "I promise you..." she shut her eyelids tight, "I promise you with all my heart that it was purely down to what they gave me. And as soon as I knew, as soon as I found out why, it started to make sense to me and the confusion lifted. It was like I came out of some sort of spell..." Rachel felt the words rushing out, needing to explain, to say it all, to make Frankie understand how mortified she was, "and I don't want her Frankie. Honestly, when I think about it now, it's like madness. And I don't know how long it will take me to forgive myself, but I truly, truly love you and I never want to be apart from you and I'll do whatever it takes and I can't stand the thought that I've hurt you, it nearly kills me to know that..." Rachel suddenly felt overwhelmed by the mixture of emotions that flooded through her, relief and shame, happiness and regret and fear, so much fear. She sobbed, unable to get out any more of the tumbling torrent of words in her head.

"Hey!" Frankie was firm, "calm down, ok?. Calm down." Frankie sighed, "I know we need to talk some things through at some point, but not now, ok? And let me tell you something you might not know. Nothing happened at that party. They drugged you, but gave you too much serum. You passed out and were sick. Then they brought you

244

home. Alright?"

Rachel closed her eyes again and released a long slow breath, "Oh my god, thank you, thank you. I'm so sorry. And the thing with Lisa... I didn't... it was just, I managed somehow... it was only... Oh my God..." she put her head in her hands and wailed, "please forgive me, Frankie, please say you forgive me..."

Frankie lifted her chin, held her firmly and stared strongly into her eyes, "stop. Ok? I don't want to know any details. It doesn't matter. It's over and I know it wasn't you. And it's not about forgiving. The way I look at it.... the way I *have* to look at it is that there's nothing to forgive. I have to believe that this was all down to the mad, fucked up way they do things in this village and that you got caught up in it. That's it. That's all there is. Ok? And that wouldn't have happened if I had been here instead of chasing money in the city. So stop being sorry, stop asking for forgiveness, because that's the best way for me... for both of us... to get over this."

Frankie leaned forward and tenderly kissed Rachel on the lips, soft, gentle, loving. Rachel felt herself trembling and she swallowed back the tears.

"I love you, Frankie. I'll always love you."

Frankie drew Rachel into her arms and nestled her neck into hers, "we're the perfect fit, baby, we always were, we always will be. I love you too. I'll always love you too. Nothing will break us."

Theresa stood outside Adrian's house and raised her hand again to press the bell on the front door. And again she pulled away just before her finger pressed his buzzer. It was a feeling she knew well. "The story of my life," she thought as she chewed her lip. She took a few steps back into the shadows and tried to think it all through again, on fast forward, to make sure her decision was the right one. It had all become so confusing. Such a tangled web of secrets and lies. She found it almost impossible at this point to work out her best next move. It was like a nightmare game of chess, where she couldn't reach a game plan that would topple the King. Or even know if she wanted to. She understood the irony of her having been one of the original playing pieces in this gambit. What irked her most at this point, was that she had originally been a pawn in someone else's game. Now she found herself by default being a Queen of strategy in a seemingly unwinnable gambit—and one in which her King was as good as absent. "One square away from defeat," she whispered to herself as she saw Adrian's shadow pass his lighted window, "or perhaps one square from victory." The last thought steeled her determination and she took a step forward... only to stop herself quickly as she saw a figure approaching Adrian's house through the darkness. She stepped back again and watched whover it was, silhouetted by a street lamp as she approached Adrian's front door—and "she" was most definitely of the feminine form. Dressed in figure hugging clothes, walking with what looked to Theresa like sexual purpose, elegant, languid strides. As the figure drew closer, the silhouette revealed shapes that conjured more detailed information. Long, lithe legs in what appeared to be thigh length boots and the shortest of skirts. Exceptional in shape, a body that was well toned and in perfect proportion. The woman, tossed her head as she grew close, long, fluid hair that stroked the velvet darkness in an almost slow motion display or eroticism. Theresa felt her brow furrow and her inner most self diminish in strength. She felt the animal instinct of jealousy. Her skin prickled with competitive aggression as if she were being made ready to pounce on a predatory threat. When the figure moved out of the shadow and under the direct light of the street lamp, Theresa took a sharp intake of breath and felt herself boil in unrequitable instant rage, recognising the unmistakable features—and arrogance—of Doctor Velvet Elizabeth Taylor. She gulped, feeling immediately sick to her stomach. Fighting back a retch, she watched as Adrian opened the door, his own silhouette a disturbingly obvious vision of intent, his left elbow resting laconically against the door jamb, his right hand extended in welcome, the metal studs on his leather gloves glinting under the street lighting as he beckoned her in what Theresa recognised as his specially expanded 1979 Elvis Presley style full leather shirt and trousers, standing tall in his Cuban heels. It was an outfit she knew he only wore for the most intimate of personal situations. She pressed her hand to her mouth in horror as she saw Taylor move in for a passionate embrace. She turned away knowing it was the end. Knowing that she must finally break apart her own intricately woven web.

Ben stood in the kitchen and rubbed at the stubble on his face as he regarded a thoroughly miserable Lisa sitting at his kitchen table.

"You have to face it—and I reckon sooner rather than later is better."

She carried on weeping, dabbing at her nose with a saturated tissue. He passed her the box again and she took another one without answering.

"You did the right thing. And it wouldn't have made any difference to the outcome if you hadn't. You know that."

She nodded.

"You know the whole club thing is bollocks—and these women aren't in the pool of people who want to get involved in any of it. Doesn't matter how much bloody gin they drink, they're not going to stick with it. They love each other."

She sobbed even louder. He sighed.

"It's tough to face that, but it's true. Look..." he tried to hide his exasperation, "you have to recognise that although you've lost her, you've found you. Now you know what love feels like—and even though it's painful now because you've lost it, you will be able to love again and you know it's worth breaking free from all the... shit..." he waved his hand towards the window, "that goes on in this village, to find it somewhere else."

She nodded again.

"I dow," she said thickly through a nose that was so blocked she could hardly speak, "I dow, bud I just wand this pain do be over. Id hurds so baaaad," she wailed.

"I dow—I've beed there," he teased her, trying in his usual way to lighten the atmosphere, but also earnestly assuring her. She gave a thin smile as he continued, "go back home. Go and see your Mum and make it clear that you're moving on." He patted her on the back. "Come on gal, you can do it. And you should do it now!" He glanced at his watch, "it's nearly noon and I've got a pub to visit and a pint to drink, so I don't want to kick you out, but I'm kicking you out." He winked at her, "tough love. It's for the best."

247

"I dow. I'll do id dow."

"It's had to understand you through all that snot, but I think you just said 'I'll do it now'. So that's good. Good lass. You'll be alright."

She stood wearily, "ok. Thangs Ben." She wrapped her arms round him for a hug.

"Mind me shirt. I don't want boogers on it when I go down the pub. The girls will think I'm with someone. Someone boogery." He patted her back again and gently pushed her away, but holding her hunched shoulders and looking into her eyes, "be brave. No-one's gonna think badly of you by the time today's through, I'm willing to bet you."

"I hobe you're righd. Thangs agaid Ben. You've been sugg a good friend."

"I know. That's why everyone loves me," he grinned, "now, you better dry out and get rid of that boogery nose. You sound like a dick. So go upstairs and have a shower and chill out for a while. And then you need to fuck off so that I can have my pint."

Rachel sighed and shook her head. "I don't think I can do it." She said it weakly as dread flooded through her. She felt Frankie's arms tighten around her as they lay on the sofa.

"You can. And you will. Because you have to."

"But why?" The question hung on the air for a few moments, "can't we just draw a line and walk away? Maybe we should just leave, sell this place, get out of here." Rachel stared at the flickering flames in the fire and waited for Frankie to respond.

"There are... things you don't know."

Rachel turned her head as far back as she could to look at Frankie, who was spooning behind her.

"Like...?"

"You're going to have to trust me." Frankie was firm—and Rachel knew from the look in her eyes she would have to capitulate. Still, it was worth trying given the circumstances.

"I'm going to feel humiliated."

"You might. At least for a while, but by the end of the night, you can be sure that any humiliation you might experience will be far outweighed by... other feelings. More positive ones."

Rachel turned her gaze back to the soporific flames of the fire, feeling like Frankie's assurances couldn't possibly compensate for her dread.

"How so?" She felt Frankie shake her head behind her.

"Not going to say, but you'll see."

She felt Frankie's warm lips on the back of her neck and closed her eyes, "ok. What time do we have to be there?"

"Well, the party is at seven," Frankie kissed her neck again, "but we need to be there earlier." She hushed the question that she saw forming on Rachel's lips with her index finger, "please just trust me that we need to talk to Donna?" She cocked her head to one side and she felt Rachel relax. "Still plenty of time to prepare though," she whispered into Rachel's ear and kissed the tender skin below her earlobe, her hand moving slowly under her jumper and caressing her warm skin.

Rachel groaned softly, "yeah, let's prepare..." She closed her eyes and the questions melted away as she let herself give in to desire and allow anxiety to float away.

Chapter 28

Doctor Taylor stood before the manor gates and looked at her watch. She counted the seconds down to five to six and then pressed the buzzer, a satisfied smile on her face as she contemplated the meeting she had anticipated for so long. As the lock clicked and the gates began to slowly open, she tightened her grip reactively on the small leather document holder in her left hand and brushed down her skirt with her right. She stepped through onto the grandly welcoming driveway, relishing the feeling that she was about to start a new journey. She breathed deeply, taking in the evening air and feeling mildly euphoric. Such a long wait, now she would finally be able to capitalize on her exquisitely executed plan and realise her true potential. She glanced around her, lip curling at the injustice that all this wealth should be in the abundant possession of the Danforths when her Father had been the real architect of this empire. It was, after all, his development of the serum that had been the success behind the club. She huffed, "how could he have been so stupid?" She shook her head at her Father's pathetically negotiated deal, a few thousand pounds to create something that had been the foundation of a 'business' worth millions. She stopped for a moment and closed her eyes, breathing in deeply again and calling on herself to be calm. Now was her time, she needed to focus on the opportunity at hand, not on past tragedy. She strode forward again, purposefully, reaching the front door. She checked her watch. Exactly six. She pulled the bell chain and listened to its ring, smoothing her skirt one final time.

"Good evening Doctor Taylor," Peter's smiled and waved her through to the hallway. Taylor nodded in her direction as she passed by.

"Peters." She acknowledged her with a disdainful nod.

Peters smiled to herself behind Taylor's back, "Donna is in the drawing room. This way." She led her to the door and opened it for her, ushering her through. Donna stood at the drawing-room window, her back to them, gazing out.

"Doctor Taylor for you," announced Peters. Donna turned and smiled broadly at Taylor.

"Velvet! A pleasure to see you!" She extended her hand.

"Vee." Taylor corrected, "likewise." She took her hand firmly and shook it.

Donna directed her towards the drawing-room table, where a teacup had been set at either end, "please, do take a seat." She herself walked towards the opposite end, "Peters, please bring tea."

As Peters left the room. Donna sat and watched as Taylor settled into her chair and crossed her legs languidly. Donna rested her chin on her hand for a few moments and regarded her coolly.

"So... Vee... there are things you wish to discuss." Donna pressed her palms together and then spread her hands to open the platform for Taylor to speak, "please, do explain."

Taylor smiled as she placed her document wallet carefully on the table and withdrew her papers, "I do indeed, have things to discuss." She interlaced her fingers and placed them on top of the papers, leaning forward as she did so, "about the club. And Eddie"

Donna nodded calmly, "the floor is yours," she said graciously.

Dr Taylor drew in her breath and regarded Donna with a cocky smile. She pointed at the papers, "I know about Eddie. And his children."

Donna nodded and smiled, "yes, well that hardly comes as a surprise. Your Father, after all, was complicit."

Dr Taylor's cocky smile faltered just a little, she had imagined her directly confrontational delivery of an opening line so full of implication would have shocked Donna. She pressed on, "the thing is, Donna, I don't think my Father was appropriately... rewarded," she said the word carefully, "for his part in keeping it all under wraps." The two women sat in silence for a couple of minutes, regarding each other, testing each other's cool.

"I see," said Donna finally, "and I assume you are going to propose something a little more... rewarding..." she delivered the word with the same care, "... for yourself given that you have access to the information?"

"Indeed." Taylor smiled, "although what I am going to propose will have a benefit far wider than just my own gratification, it will have a social benefit... a *considerable* social benefit."

Donna gave a sage nod, "I see. Well, perhaps you should clarify for me what that would be. And at the same time explain how I could be sure that any such reward might maintain your silence and that you would not continue to blackm... excuse me," Donna corrected herself with a little smile, "that you would not to continue to seek further rewards in the future."

Dr Taylor lifted her clasped hands and rested her chin on her them, "I'm proposing that you fund a new foundation. A medical foundation. The V Taylor Medical Foundation."

"The V Taylor Medical Foundation," Donna repeated slowly. "That sounds... impressive. And what will the V Taylor Medical Foundation offer the world?" She regarded Taylor inquisitively.

Taylor's eyes narrowed, Donna was too relaxed, less reactive than she had anticipated. She decided to be forthright. This would test her reactions, "research and development of new techniques in human cloning."

"Cloning?" Donna couldn't stop herself raising her eyebrows, but did manage to halt the thought that the world could do without a V Taylor clone from turning into actual words from her mouth. "I see. And what is the cost of a V Taylor Medical Foundation in cloning."

"I see it as a long-term investment plan," Dr Taylor handed Donna a wad of papers, "I've drawn up a proposal. Rather than talk numbers right now, I'd like you to read through it. Understand where I am coming from before you consider the financial implications. I'm sure there is value not just in my... silence about Eddie—after all, the truth coming out would probably place a considerable burden on the estate—but also in the value such an institution could have on the future of humanity." Dr Taylor waved her hand grandly.

Donna reached forward and took the document, "well, it seems rather a bold leap from a small practice in Hetherington, don't you think?"

"Ha! I am destined for far greater things. Far greater." Dr Taylor, tossed her hair back and stared into the distance and spoke as if Donna were not even in the room, "these people," she was disdainful, "have had the benefit of my talents for far too long. Some of them... some of them aren't even fit to breathe my air." She sighed and suddenly pressed her fingers to her temples, "I don't think I can bear another year of bunions, boils and back ache. The only slight bit of interest has been in the further development of the serum..." she looked up suddenly aware of where she was.

Donna raised an eyebrow, "the serum?"

"It's... it's the foundation of the cloning principal. I've... I've made a discovery." Doctor Taylor became animated, "it's a miracle drug. I've already cloned artichokes and I was working with my Father on his cocks. Roy's entry at the Village Fair is a clone too—though he doesn't know it. It's a clone, but it's bigger and better than the original. Like cloning on steroids. Oh my god, it's the biggest cock I've ever seen!" She bit her lip and couldn't contain the grin that spread across her face, "so on that basis, we can take the best of humanity and make it even better. Just imagine a clone of me that's even better than me! It hardly bears thinking about..." she shook her head in wonder.

"Indeed it doesn't." Donna was implacable.

"Or you, for that matter." Dr Taylor collected herself, recognizing the need to sell the concept outside her own desires, "cloned to perfection. I mean even beyond the current level of perfection. If that were possible."

"Oh stop!" Donna raised a hand, she shook her head, "I really don't need that. And I'm not quite sure why you don't understand that I am aware of everything that goes on in this village. So of course I'm aware of the size of Roy's cock. Perhaps you have become so involved with yourself that you forget there are others that have some authority here." Donna regarded Dr Taylor and saw her eyes draw back into focus as she recollected her composure.

"Don't underestimate me, Donna. It would be a mistake," she said coolly.

Donna nodded. "I don't," she said equally coolly, "I estimate you with amazing accuracy. That is something you will learn."

The two women once again regarded each other across the table. Recalculating.

"I suggest you read the document, Donna. It's a revelation. It's... genius. Genius that can be cloned. It outreaches everything, intellectually, that I could ever have imagined."

"And what motivates you to pursue this project Vee? What it can do for humanity? Or what it can do for you?"

Dr Taylor remained silent for a few moments. "What is the difference Donna?" she enquired in a coldly measured tone.

Donna contemplated Taylor's words. She internally admitted confusion. It was either the ultimate statement of egotism or an expression of equanimity. She sighed. It was too complicated to second guess. And in any case, her instinctive reaction to cloning as a principal overrode her need to decide which.

"It's noble. It's unquestionably brilliant. I will read your document. But be clear..." she leaned forward and stared Taylor in the eye, "blackmail is not a reason for me to approve your scheme."

Taylor sat back. "Read it, Donna. It speaks for itself. But let me be clear with you. I will use whatever means necessary to get what I need. To make sure this happens."

Donna smiled. "I see. And I understand." Donna pushed her chair back and rose, "please excuse me for a short while. I wish to take some time to consider the nature of your proposal. I hope you understand?"

Dr Taylor cocked her head to one side. This was not a response she had anticipated. "I don't need a response right now... and I don't expect it. This is a complex proposal."

"I understand fully. I will be back shortly. Wait here." Donna asserted, giving her guest no choice, "use the bell to call Peters if you need anything." Donna walked purposefully from the room.

Taylor watched the door close behind her, a little bemused. She hadn't reckoned on her making such a snap judgement, it seemed hasty. But then it was a quite astounding scheme. Perhaps despite Donna's objection to her strong arming the funding, she actually got it. That it was simply too brilliant to deny. She pondered momentarily whether the lengths she had taken to gain persuasive leverage had been necessary at all. She frowned and drummed the table with her fingernails as she contemplated Donna's reaction. No. It couldn't be that simple. She sighed. Though it should be. It was of course such an unnecessary requirement that she should need to pitch her brilliance at all. It should be obvious to the world by now. And it would be if she hadn't been stuck in this backwater for years. If she had been in her rightful peer group, she wouldn't need to go cap in hand to anyone. This represented such unnecessary prevarication. She shook her head. And it was such a waste of her precious time.

Lisa sat head in hands, a low wail streaming from her mouth. Peters rubbed her back soothingly as Frankie looked anxiously at Donna.

"I know this is shocking," Donna nodded reassuringly at Frankie and Lisa, "it's going to take time. To adjust. But I'll make sure you get everything you need. I'm so sorry darling."

Frankie reached over the table and placed her hand on Lisa's. "It's ok. It's going to be ok." She hardly knew what to say.

"How can you even say that?" Lisa glanced up at her, "I'm mortified. Heartbroken, how can I even begin to make up for this."

"It's not your fault," Frankie was gentle.

"Ooooh noooo, stop being so kind. How can you be? After what I've done... and now, now I know you're my sister too. Oh my God..."

"Well, only half-sister..." Frankie offered as if it might halve Lisa's pain.

"Stop being so nice!" Lisa wailed again, "it makes it worse. I tried to steal your girlfriend for Christ's sake! Oh My God!" Lisa turned to Peters and nestled her head against her chest, "I can't stand myself!" she said in muffled tones, "how can any of you stand me?"

Peters held her tight and grimaced at Donna, "it's not your fault my Angel," she said it gently too, closing her eyes against the agony she felt for Lisa, "you fell in love. We can't help who we fall in love with. It just happens." She rubbed her back again, "and you've had such a shitty life." She glanced up at Donna ruefully.

Donna closed her eyes, the tears squeezing out and spilling down her cheeks. "I'll make it up to you darling, I promise." Donna placed her hand on her daughter's shoulder, "I can't change what's happened, though God knows now I wish I could, but we'll get you all the help you need. And from now on everything is going to be so much better. All of this nonsense stops now. And for good." Donna looked across at Frankie, who nodded in agreement, "and you and your sister can get to know each other."

"That's right Lisa," Frankie added her reassuring voice of support, "I know this is going to take time, but I promise you I don't hold any bad feelings. I know it's not your fault, ok?" Lisa didn't respond, her face still buried. Frankie persisted, "well I know it can't just be ok, there's so much for you to deal with, but I just want you to know that I don't have any bad feelings."

"But I tried to steal your girlfriend!" Lisa tried to bury her head deeper into Peters' arms. Frankie looked imploringly at Peters, not knowing how to help.

"Well, why wouldn't you?" she tried to quip, "she's gorgeous!"

"Ohhhhh!" Lisa wailed more and sobbed.

"Oh shit, I'm sorry!" Frankie looked imploringly at Peters, who shrugged her shoulders, unable to offer any advice. Frankie rose and went round to Lisa, putting her hand on her shoulder too, "you'll get over it, I promise. We're going to leave you here with Peters for a little while. Me and your Mum, we've got some stuff we have to sort out now. But really, I absolutely promise it's all going to be ok." She patted Lisa reassuringly, "we'll be back in a little while." Frankie looked over at Donna who nodded back.

"Yes, let's get this over with." She glanced at Peters, who winked at her, Donna drew a deep breath in and put her hand round Frankie's shoulder, "are you ready?"

Frankie nodded, "absolutely."

"Vee?" Donna poked her head round the door and broke Dr Taylor's self-contemplative reverie, "I know this will probably seem rather off, given we have only just started our discussions, but I have some people next door who are interested to hear about your scheme. Would you join us?"

Taylor hesitated momentarily, "people?"

"Yes. People." Donna was assertive, "let's just say I have been more aware of your progress than you know—and that I anticipated that you would have something... interesting to offer." Donna smiled at her, "shall we?" she pushed the door open further.

Taylor stood and smoothed down her skirt.

"You know you surprise me, Donna," she said as she walked slowly towards the door, "frankly I hadn't expected such erudite and rapid assessment. I'm impressed."

"How kind!" Donna smiled warmly back and held her hand out to indicate that Taylor should head down the hall with her, "I've always found it best to act quickly when faced with such precipitously ground breaking developments," she explained, "losing the opportunity to capitalize on such valuable information is folly, wouldn't you agree?"

"Oh quite!" Taylor threw her head back and strode down the hallway, feeling strong and confident, "are these business contacts of yours?"

Donna indicated a door to their left and placed her hand on the handle, "invested parties, so to speak." She smiled back at Taylor and pushed the door open, guiding her firmly with her hand on her back to push her through over the threshold and quickly walking in behind, shutting the door. She watched Taylor's jaw drop and blocked her attempt to turn back round. They both heard the key turn from the other side and Taylor's face drained as she realised there was no escape.

"I think you know everyone here?" Donna held her hand out towards the group gathered in the drawing room and Taylor, with an angry glance towards Donna, span round to face them. Donna beckoned to Rachel and Frankie, who then flanked her on either side as she faced the gathering. Taylor's face reddened as she spotted Adrian, his eyes focused carefully on the floor in front of him as he rocked anxiously on his heels. The Vicar, Floosy, Doug, Roy all stared implacably at her. And then there was Theresa, who smiled triumphantly. Even Grace, who Taylor would have expected to cower under her gaze, was objectionably defiant. She shook her hair and thrust out her chin, staring above all their minion like heads.

"Ladies and Gentleman, I have some announcements to make." Donna tapped her glass, "largely on the back of a very, *very*, interesting proposal that has just been made to me by Doctor Taylor here." Taylor dropped her gaze long enough to see Roy smirk.

"Donna I don't think this is..." Taylor tried to halt the proceedings.

"Oh please, Doctor Taylor, I know you have a humble approach to your scheme..." There was a loud cough from Grace and someone at the back of the room sniggered, "and you may be concerned that I might reveal certain information, but please be assured I would never reveal anything that might be regarded as... confidential." Taylor was forced to recognise the unfamiliar discomfort that came with lack of control. She stayed silent.

"Vee. You don't mind if we all call you Vee?" she asked politely. Taylor shook her head, her face contorted with anger.

"Good. We're all friends here." She was enjoying Taylor's squirming distress at being included collectively with the group that stood before her, "so Vee, as I said, has developed an interesting proposal that she has just put before me. And she made it almost impossibly compelling for me to support her scheme. Not just because of its sheer brilliance, but because, well, because she tried to blackmail me!" Donna grinned and all eyes flew towards Taylor, whose face had reddened despite her attempts at continued dignity. "Now I am sure that must come as a complete shock and surprise to most of you?" The group continued to stare at Taylor. "No? No surprise there?" Donna turned her attention back to Taylor, "no. No surprise there because you have been systematically blackmailing, defrauding and otherwise extorting money from most of these people for quite some time, haven't you Vee?"

Taylor appeared frozen.

"Vee?" Donna cocked her head to one side as she regarded her, "nothing to say?" Donna held her chin and offered a mock surprise look to her audience, who were clearly relishing the humiliation of Vee Taylor. "Are you sure Vee? Because we'd love to hear from you on this subject?"

Taylor swiveled stiffly on the spot and stared coldly at Donna. "I'm prepared to reveal everything."

"Oh, I have no doubt," Donna's eyes too turned stony, "like the fact that Frankie here is Eddie's daughter?" Taylor appeared to crumple just a little, "or that Theresa is her Mother? Or even that Gazz is her twin brother?" She beckoned to Gazz to step forward, who did so and readily hugged his newly refound sister with warmth. Taylor looked at the group before her and expected shock. She saw none. What she saw was a group of people staring at her with a mix of hatred, scorn and worse, much worse, pity. She clenched her jaw and turned back to Donna.

"This won't stop me," she drew herself up, "the plan is still brilliant. You were my shortcut, but it matters not. It will have its day. I will have my day." She pointed at herself and visibly preened.

Donna smiled implacably. "I think not." Donna left a silence that prickled between them, "you do not have any rights to the serum. Or to any developments you may or may not have made. And if you make even the slightest, *the slightest* attempt to do anything with your supposed discovery, I will personally pull apart your reputation and dispel any notion that what you have has any veracity. And added to that I will expose your heredity."

Taylor blinked. Her composure dropping, "my Father? What could you possibly have on a man who behaved impeccably and with devotion to your family his whole life?"

"Oh indeed, old Doctor Taylor was, for the most part exemplary," Donna smiled kindly, "but old Doctor Taylor was not your Father." Donna watched the colour drain from Taylors face and heard the collective gasp from the group.

"What?" it was a small voice, almost unrecognisable as Vee Taylor.

"He wasn't your Father. He was impotent. But he knew your Mother wanted a child. So he made the sacrifice, he allowed her to have a child through another man." She watched as Vee Taylor struggled with the information, "and it pains me, Vee, it really pains me to have to do this, but you left me no choice. Your Father is a sheep sheerer from New Zealand."

"What? You're a liar. You're a fucking liar!" Taylor's anger boiled.

"Vee! Really, such language!" Donna mocked her, "why that's as low as a... sheep sheerer!" The group suddenly laughed and clapped as Taylor spun around, desperate to find an escape, "not, of course that anyone else here would have a problem with having a hard working labourer as a Father, but we've all been made painfully aware of your self-opinionated superiority." Donna held up a key, "here..." she held it out to the now frantic Taylor, "you can let yourself out." Taylor grabbed towards the key—but Donna pulled it back, She looked hard into Vee's eyes, "don't ever darken this place again with your presence. Got it?" Vee seethed, but nodded agreement. "Oh and one more thing, the surgery is owned by the Estate, as is your home, your father had the presence of mind to turn it over before his death. I'll give you a week to leave." Donna held the key out again and Taylor swiped it from her hand, turning on her heel and tryig to bolt for the door, but suffering even further humiliation as her stiletto heel snapped. She let out a groan of anguish as she fumbled with the lock. The room fell silent as they watched her distress, with not an iota of sympathy for her plight. Except for one person. The Master stepped forward and gallantly picked up the broken heel of her shoe.

"Vee. Let me help," he said gently as Theresa felt her heart break.

Taylor turned to him and looked into his eyes. His gesture seemed to somehow give her renewed strength as she took the broken heel from his hand and he opened his palm to take her hand in his. Taylor leaned in close to his face, "oh do fuck off Adrian," she said with ice coldness as she threw the heel on the floor and sneered in his crestfallen face, "and the rest of you can fuck off too." She removed the second shoe and snapped the heel of that also. Replacing it on her foot, she turned and opened the door, walking through it with head held high on now flattened pumps.

The Master, his head hanging, took a shamed glance back at Theresa and closed his eyes momentarily. He took a deep breath in, "I know it's over," he said to Donna, "and she was all that I wanted, so I am over too." He nodded and turned to the door, opening it with the quiet resolve of a broken man. "Goodbye Theresa," he said quietly without looking back, as the door shut behind him.

The room fell silent and all eyes turned to Donna. She set down her glass and let out a sigh before addressing the room.

"When Eddie made his discovery about the gin and its special potency all those years ago, he started something that he thought would set us all free. To explore the excesses that we all wanted—or perhaps that he *thought* we all wanted. But in many ways, it took away our freedom. To choose. So it's time to make amends. As of now, the club is no more. And the village property will be released into the hands of its rightful owners. All of you will own your homes—and for any of you who have been damaged, in whatever way, including financially by the club or Dr Taylor, we will be making amends. Frankie here is going to take over the interests of the brewery and Gazz will be managing the Estate here at the manor. And my beautiful daughter, Lisa, is embarking on a trip around the World. When she comes back, it will be to a stable, healthy loving home."

Donna paused for a moment and allowed her eyes to drift to the back of the room, where Ben quietly stood. He raised his glass. Donna smiled, "no more secrets. No more lies. And if you want to drink gin, it's because you choose to—and though I'm sure there'll still be plenty of It, that will be your choice too. Now, let's put Hetherington and it's gin back on the map, shall we?"

The Final Chapter - 6 Months Later

"I see Roy's cock's been withdrawn then?" Old Nathan winked at Rachel as she sat behind the Judge's desk.

"Now now, Nathan, you know that's a sore subject. We're done with all that right? And anyway, he's entered a substitute."

"Never knew substitute cocks was allowed. Not for me to say out though. Anyway, no-one stands a chance against my Matilda, right?" He winked again.

"And you know I can't possibly comment on that either Nathan, though you do have a splendid bird."

"Tis true. And may the best bird win. Where's your better half?" he asked peering into the marquee behind her.

"She's judging the fancy tarts." It was Rachel's turn to wink exaggeratedly, "you'll find her in the cake tent." Rachel threw her thumb behind her and Nathan nodded.

"She's doing a grand job at the brewery that one."

Rachel smiled proudly, "I know! Gold Medal Gin is some going, though she did have a head start."

"Yeah, who needs serum eh? Far better without it, makes the best Gin & Tonic I ever 'ad." He raised his thumb in approval.

"Well there's a free drink for you at the bar Nathan, we're celebrating the medal win with a new cocktail and everyone gets a free try."

"Oh ah, well I'll be having me some of that then. I'll see you later to pick up me winners medal fer Matilda, eh?"

"We'll see Nathan, we'll see."

Rachel smiled to herself and looked down at her list of winners for Best of the Best Birds and tapped Matilda's Gold Medal Winning entry. She couldn't wait to see Nathan's face. She sighed contentedly.

"Hello!" She recognised the voice and looked up, surprised and momentarily blinded by the bright afternoon sunlight, slightly blocked by the dark silhouette before her. She jumped up and ran round the desk.

"Lisa! Oh my god, you made it!" The two hugged and Rachel

grinned at the slim, beautiful woman who stood behind her. She drew back. "Introductions please?"

Lisa beamed and hung her arm round the woman's neck. "Rachel meet Joanna." Rachel took her hand, "we've heard sooooo much about you. I'm so pleased you let Lisa drag you all the way over here."

"Oh it's great," said the woman with a strong Australian twang, "I've been dying to meet ya's all."

"How long are you staying?" Rachel squeezed Lisa's hand delightedly.

"We'll be here for a couple of weeks, then we're going to Hawaii before we head back to Oz."

"Wow. Check you two!"

"Yeah, Joanna's filming in Waikiki and then we're going to The Big Island to see the volcanoes and swim with dolphins."

"I'm jealous! Hot and explosive! I'm so happy for you, maybe..." Rachel stopped as a horn sounded loudly from across the field, they all turned round to see what the commotion was. A huge JCB was lumbering its way across the grass, with a lone horn player standing on the front of it.

"Is that calling the hounds?" asked Lisa.

Rachel laughed, "well one hound... it's Trevor coming to drop it off for Doug to get him to the church."

"Whaaaat? Doug's getting married again?"

"No, they're renewing their vows."

"Wow really? Who would've known he could be that romantic!"

Rachel laughed again, "he's a changed man. In more ways than one. He's behind you, look..." Rachel physically turned Lisa round to face a slim, very handsome, clean-shaven man behind her.

Lisa gasped, "nooooo. That's Doug? I don't believe you!"

"I know, right? Who knew there was such a stud muffin hiding underneath all that hair?"

"Oh My God! And where's Floosy?"

"She's in the tarts tent with Frankie."

"Oh, figures!" laughed Lisa.

"She doesn't know Doug has the JCB. He's going to take over at the wheel and go and pick her up and take her to the church with him."

"Oh perfect, let's go and watch?" Lisa grabbed Joanna's hand, "you coming?" she asked Rachel.

"Wouldn't miss it for the world." Rachel grabbed her paperwork and placed it neatly in the drawer, "ok, let's go. Oh, hang on." She grabbed a white rose that was sitting on the desk and marched over to Doug, pinning it on his lapel and then taking his cheeks in her hands, "have a wonderful new start in life together." She kissed him square on the lips.

"Steady on me duck. None of that funny business no more. I'm taken. Twice!"

She laughed, "you certainly are."

She dashed back to Lisa and they set off for the cake tent.

"Is Theresa here?" asked Lisa as they joined arms to walk across the grass.

"She is. She's judging the cows. With Roy."

"Oh, so they're back together?"

"Hmm, kind of. It's shaky, but they seem to be working it out. Roy's had a tough time accepting the Eddie situation. He brought Gazz up as his own and he's found it difficult to adjust now that Eddie wants his son and heir in his life again."

"Yeah. Figured that would be hard for him. Dad's not exactly the most diplomatic of people."

"Well, we'll see, Roy's a good man, I'm sure he'll get through it. And he loves Theresa, there's no doubt of that, just a lot of trust issues to deal with."

As they approached the marquee, the booming sound of Floosy's voice greeted them.

"... so he said to her, dahhhling, I wouldn't mind getting my face in your gravy!" There was raucous laughter as The Floosy delivered a punchline just as they walked through the entrance to the tent. Frankie, who was sitting behind a long table with her Judge's badge on, saw them come in and waved. The Floosy was sitting on one corner of the table, in a white leather bodice that pushed her voluptuous boobs out to eye-popping levels. Her lacy wedding skirt was hitched up so that she could dangle her feet over the edge of the table, revealing red patent leather thigh boots with silver stiletto heels and white leather lacing. Her headpiece was at an angle across her brow as she threw her head back and laughed, simultaneously cracking her black leather, diamante sequined whip for effect.

Lisa laughed as she caught sight of Joanna's awestruck face, "some things never change. Come and meet the Floosy," she said, grabbing Joanna's hand and running over.

"Lisaaaaaa!" The Floosy stood and threw her arms around her, "oh dahling, how gorgeous to see you!. I'm getting married!" She squealed delightedly.

"I know! To some total hunk."

"Oh yah," her eyes widened, "I've been hiding that away for yeeeaars dahling. Got to tie him down now he's shaved his hair orf before some other bird grabs him. Oh God, talking of hunks, who's this gorgeous creature," she jokingly shoved Lisa to one side and grabbed Joanna's hand, "dibs on this one!"

"You can't she's mine!" Lisa shoved her back a little too hard and The Floosy had to steady herself against the table. She shrieked with laughter, "steady on girl, I nearly ended up in the tarts!"

"Oi," Frankie called from across the table, "mind my cakes!"

A giggling Floosy waved a long white silk glove in her direction, "don't mind her, she's a cream puff!" She pushed up against Joanna playfully and cracked her whip again. Then they all fell quiet as the sound of the JCB approached and it's yellow arms pushed the shovel in through the opening of the marquee. Nestling in the base was a huge bouquet of white roses. The Floosy let out a huge squeal as Doug jumped down from the cab and strode towards her, "alright me darlin'," he bellowed, "come to make sure you get to that church on time." He marched manfully up to her and swooped her up in his arms, "not going to lose you now." He turned and laid her in the shovel, nestling her gloriously amongst the beautiful flowers. She laughed raucously, "hold on tight, darlin', we'll be there before you know it." Doug climbed back into the cab and maneuvered the arms to lift the shovel until all everyone could see was the floosy's red leather boots and stiletto heels dangling over the edge. The JCB backed out of the marquee and turned around, dragging behind it two huge furry dice, bobbing along bearing the names Doug and Floosy on them.

"Tally ho!" screamed Floosy as the JCB lumbered across the field and out towards the church.

As it drove out of sight, Rachel turned back to the marquee and sat down by Frankie. "Hey," she said, nudging her playfully.

"Hey," Frankie nudged her back.

"There seems to be love in the air," said Rachel

"Yeah," Frankie sighed, "they'll be next." She nodded across the marquee where Donna stood with Ben.

"You reckon?" said Rachel

"Yep, they've kept it quiet for a long time, but I reckon Ben might finally be ready to make a commitment."

"That's going to break a lot of hearts." Rachel turned to gaze at Frankie.

"This is too." Frankie took Rachel's hand and pushed a diamond ring onto her engagement finger. Rachel gasped.

"Oh, baby. Have I told you lately?"

Frankie shook her head

"No. Definitely not."

Rachel stroked her cheek, "well I do."

"Is that a yes?"

"That's a yes."

"You've always been It for me."

"I know. And one thing's for sure. I never needed any gin to know you are It for me too."

THANK YOU FOR READING!!

WANT MORE GIN AND IT?
Visit www.ginandit.tv for more on related developments and products, including the novella Fallen Angel, Lisa's story.

AND FOR MORE ABOUT THE AUTHOR
Visit elainesturgess.com to read some of her other work.

Acknowledgement and Thanks

This book is dedicated to the memory of my dear Maria.

Huge thanks to those members of my family and friends who have helped and supported me, I am so grateful for all your love and encouragement during the last few years, I could not have done it without you.

To Anna, thank you for the happiness you bring and the possibilities for the future. I love you.

I am also thankful for the support of MacMillan Cancer Care. Their compassionate help was a blessing for both of us.

Printed in Great Britain
by Amazon